The Ranger of Mearcholt

The Ranger of Mearcholt

Skaldi

WEGSCAEWR PRESS

To those who walk the wild

CONTENTS

The People of Mearcholt

Heortlea

rangers

Holdric, beginning ranger

Kenndric, master of Heortlea rangers, Holdric's grandfather

Wymud, Kenndric's second

Hwaetearn, the Thane's son

Aschbroc, Holdric's cousin, son of Eikhram and Claefry

Eahstann, Holdric's childhood friend

family

Holthund, Holdric's father (lost)

Hleolea, Holdric's mother

Maethbry, Holdric's sister

Eikhram, Holdric's uncle and warden

Claefry, Holdric's aunt, sister to Hleolea, wife of Eikhram

Segli, young daughter of Eikhram and Claefry

Rinna, wife to Holdric's cousin Aschbroc

others

Frithwyn (Frithi), Holdric's love and childhood friend

Haestearn, Thane of Heortlea, father to Hwaetearn

Hauccael, bondsman to the Thane, warden of the fyrdhall

Hegwyn, alewife

Sparri, bondswoman to the Thane

Greatwatch

mountain of the great beacon

Hyrtwis, head man of the watch

Aesculf, elder of the mountain

Graffort, leechman

Wulfhert, Heggort, rangers of the watch

Blaccram, ranger of the watch, messenger to Ealdwyrc Torr

Ealdwyrc Torr

the furthest stronghold of men

Stalmaht, head man of the tower

Wydthoc, shieldling boy

Caltbruk, master of the kitchens

Rammort, **Byarmin,** horsemen of the tower, friends to Aschbroc and Hwaetearn

Acramm, charcoal burner, dweller of the far wild

The Hyssestead

hidden home of rangers

Eomud, master of the hall

Byrcstod, elder ranger of the hall, distant kin to Uncle Eikhram

Ulfraeg, ranger of the hall

Reodhoc, young ranger of the hall, messenger to Earnsclyff Watch

Eikhund, ranger of the hall

Earnsclyff Watch

the lonesome outpost

Aemud, ranger of the far watch

Barsti, ranger of the far watch

Forric, ranger of the far watch

Wulfort, ranger of the far watch

THE HYTHE
EARNSCLYFF WATCH
EALDWYRC TORR
GREATWATCH
THE MEARCWATER
ETTENMEDES
HEORTLEA

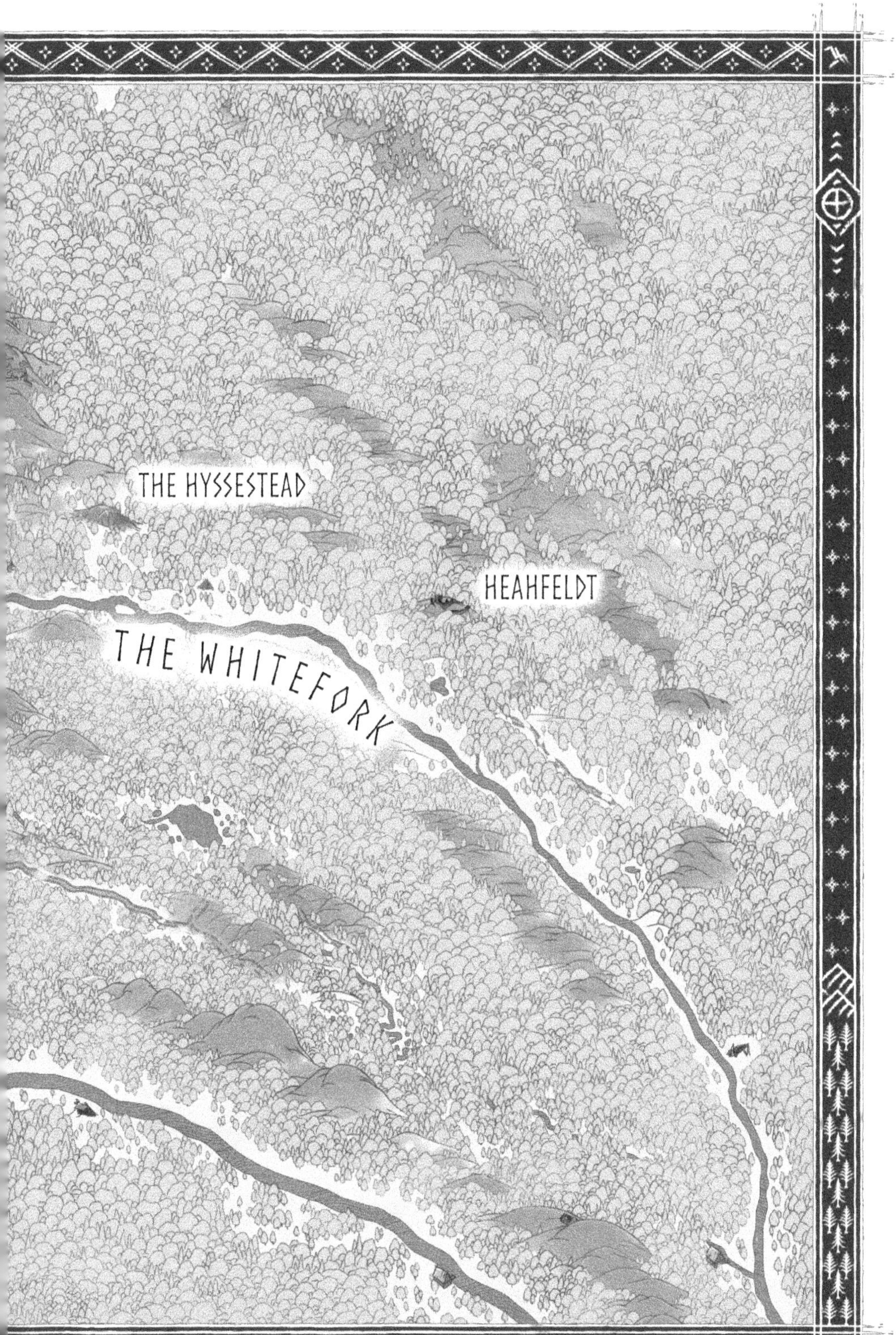

THE HYSSESTEAD
HEAHFELDT
THE WHITEFORK

CHAPTER ONE
The Last Day

The earth was still soft from last night's rain.

The line of the track was clean, the edge sharp. It had not been long since it was made—probably this morning. Holdric ran his finger along the pressed earth and felt at the edges of the sign. Cool wet soil met his touch, rough with sand and fine rock. The edge of the track fell in a smooth curve into the bed. Holdric grimaced.

Greotn's hoof was too long, the wall had folded over. The ram's forefoot badly needed a trim. Holdric peered through the wattle fence to where the old ram lay in wait… and there he was, sulking by a ragged blackthorn hedge. The ram ducked his heavy-horned head and stomped at the earth as he stared back through the fence.

Greotn looked angry. Greotn always looked angry.

Holdric sighed. There was no time left to catch him today. Uncle Eikhram would be in a high thunder when he saw the job left undone, but the old man would have to wait until Holdric returned before he could take it from his skin… if he returned.

He looked into the sky. Summer was wearing late, but it still had life yet. The long day had been warm, the sunlight hanging tired and faded in the air. The boughs of the great ash tree over the fyrd-hall were still. Farther up the hill, a small brown wren sang a merry tune in the apple trees. Holdric smiled. His Ollda had always said the little wren knew more than he let on. Given how much the bird sang, that was no small feat. From not far off came the laughing shriek of a small child—Brytta's youngest, probably.

Holdric stretched, drinking in the last of the full sun. If this was to be the last day he had been given to live in Heortlea, it had been at least a warm one, and happy enough. He'd known far worse.

He stood, his eyes drawn again to the distant rise of Greatwatch. The mountain rose high, far beyond the high palings of Heortlea's wall. Past the high strips of wheat and rye, over the open grass of the highfolds, far beyond leagues of woodland and over the wide Mearcwater.

Holdric had looked on that mountain all his life. He knew every slope, every dip of stone against the far sky. For long years it had seemed to him almost a friend, when every eye had turned hard and every tongue spoke cold. Once he'd even tried to reach it.

As a boy he'd dreamed of flying into the deep wild, of one day scaling those heights. He wanted to share the ready courage of the Greatwatch men, and to range past even them, deep into the Mearcholt beyond.

He had spent a lifetime longing for the ranger's cloak. Some days it was the honor of the cloak and horn he longed for. Other days he wanted only the simple peace of high trees and cool earth, to hear no voice but the wind in the high leaves. The evils of that far wood could at least do no more than kill. So at least he had told himself, until the summer grew late and his time grew near, and growing dread day by day overshadowed boyish wanderlust.

One more night.

Worry gnawed at him. But then something soft nuzzled his hand, and warmth came again to his heart. He did not have to look to know it was Dunwyn. Holdric smiled and knelt to scratch the nuzzling ewe. While the rest of the herd might be skittish or indifferent or pushy, she was always a sweet creature, straight from the day he pulled her slick and shaking from her cold mother on the highfolds. Uncle Eikhram had given her to him that day, and from her had come the small herd he now called his own.

He scratched absently at her head, and she waggled her tail like a nursing lamb. She nuzzled his tunic and from it he pulled a small handful of pilfered grain. She took it, eating fierce until she knocked the last of it from his fingers—then she looked up to him.

"No more today little one. The last gather isn't long, I'll save you some then." He leaned down and pulled at the lush grass just outside her reach. He held the grass out to her, and she grunted happily as she ate.

Idly Holdric ran his fingers through Dunwyn's wool. She'd be ready for shearing before the month was out, she and most of her brood by the look of it. Good, he could use the silver. He wasn't certain what he'd have to promise his sister for the spinning, but she'd doubtless be willing. He'd have to give her a share of course, and some also to his uncle for the infold graze, but still he would manage a few coins for himself.

With luck he was only a year from gaining the wreck of Old Barwud's cot. The thatch of the old place was half gone and some of the timbers soft, but it would be a hearth of his own. Add another year of work to make the cot more hall than barn, but after that…

He looked to the sky—the sun had just dropped to a hand above the far western hills. It was time.

"Be well, sweet thing. I've someone prettier than you to see."

Holdric tore off another handful of long summer grass and wedged it in the fence wattles for the chewing ewe. She gave him one more hopeful look, then turned back to the grass.

Two years, then. Two years would be a dozen rangings at least, more if the fyrd was called up. But if he lived, two years. His chances were good.

He knew the wild, his Ollda Kenndric had seen to that. Once it had taken the old ranger almost a season to catch him. And it had been almost two years since the ranging band had lost a man—Brythoc, elder brother to Eahstann. Holdric winced at the memory.

What was left of the ranging party had staggered through the walls in deepest night. The fyrdhall had been bright, brighter than he'd ever seen. Every lamp had been lit, little stars of fire under a broad-timbered roof. The fire in the hearth had been high, and mead had flowed like water. Everyone in Heortlea filled the hall that night. Everyone but Ollda Kenndric, headman of Heortlea's rangers.

The night had been hard. Eahstann was to say the words of parting for his brother, but could not, and so Master Uhlseid had said them in his stead. The slain ranger's cloak had been laid in haste by the hearth. Holdric remembered staring at it, the worn grey-green wool heavy-soaked with mud and worse. Holdric had hated himself that he had envied the dead man his cloak, and with it his honor. But still he had done so… and had done so since.

Holdric did not see his Ollda until the next morning. The old ranger had not spoken for almost a fortnight after. He had told Mum his silence was only lingering woldgast. But Holdric knew woldgast. Whatever had haunted Ollda Kenndric, it was not that.

What comes to them out there?

Holdric shook his head. It was better to use what time he had left on happier things. He made for the meeting place at a run.

Frithi was not there. Had he missed her? He looked about—a low stone wall followed the dusty path over a grassy hill, and a flash of color peeked from between the piled stones. He knelt to look closer and found a twisted knot of madder-red wool. She'd left him a token.

He grinned. The game was on! Frithi did love to tease him with a hunt, and in truth he enjoyed the game no less.

Which way then, sweet thing?

Just up the hill a spot of grass lay bent by a gentle step. He came closer and looked over the earth. Yes, there was the mark of her heel.

Baby-bird forgot her shoes again.

He knelt low and peered up through the green of bent grass, following her way with his eyes up towards the common hall, and to the woodshed behind. He leapt up from the grass with a grin and followed the path she'd made… but her way soon bent away from the shed. Grumbling he knelt again, seeking solid sign.

A shadow crossed his face. Something was off.

He got close to the grass and felt gently at the little tracks. Her footfalls were heavy in the front, the earth pillowed where the balls of her feet struck earth. Her stride had been even, but her pace brisk. He could see the shape of her walk as surely as if he'd seen her step with his own eyes.

She's upset.

Well, it was their last meeting, save muster tomorrow. He rose to his feet, pausing to stoop just enough to see the world at her height—he could just see Greatwatch through the trees. Yes, that must be it. He would have to put her at ease then. He sighed. It had been hard enough to keep his own fears in check. Well enough then, that was the way of things.

Her footfalls came again to the common paths of Heortlea. Few enough had passed since, and her pace was even. It was easy work. He followed her way with his eyes and a smile came again to his face. She had made for the south well.

It was the place of their first kiss, a cool well under branching cherry trees. She had always liked the morning sun from there. But as he strode over the little rise and made for the well, he saw it empty. At first he wondered… then he knew. The trees there were thick and green, but one more so than the others, the branches rich and full and close. He had her.

Ollda Kenndric had warned him against taking the brightest tree in the wood for his hiding place. Eye-sops, he called them. But Frithi had not learned at the old ranger's knee. That, or she wanted to be found.

Holdric walked to the well, keeping his back to the trees. He leaned against the cool stones with an easy smile.

"Building a nest, Baby-bird?"

He turned and saw her hiding in the branches. Her golden hair shone bright in the leaves, bright almost as her laughing eyes.

She smiled down at him. "You tracked me!"

He caught her gaze and smiled. "I knew where you'd be."

She watched him, waiting to see what else he might say. He kept her gaze, but spoke no words. His cousin Aschbroc always said a man could not go wrong with silence.

At last she broke, laughing. "Help me down?"

She held out her arms, and he reached up to take her slim waist in his hands. He lifted her from the branches, and if she came to earth faster than he had meant, still she laughed and threw her arms around his neck. She kissed his cheek and melted into him with a sigh.

He kissed her deeply as he lowered her to the ground. She leaned into his kiss, clinging tight to his shoulders… but then she pulled away. Her eyes were wet, her smile sad.

"It's only a fortnight," said Holdric. "I'll be back before you can blink."

Now it was Frithwyn's turn for silence, and the silence stretched far too long. Holdric held his tongue, dreading her next words. He had been right to dread.

"Father says no."

The words fell over him like winter ice. He clenched his jaw as she caught her breath.

"He says—"

"I know what he says."

Holdric punched the pail on the well-side and sent it clattering down into the depths. Frithi flinched as wood splintered on stone. Holdric turned away, running his hands through his hair. There had to be a way…

"We could go," he said at last.

She just watched as he paced before the well. "I won't make you do that Holdric."

"I've done it before," he said. "I can keep us safe out there. We…"

She only shook her head. "I won't do that."

Holdric's fists were clenched. He willed himself to say nothing, he willed himself to say nothing he could not call back. She stared at the earth, fumbling with her hands as he watched.

"I'm sorry… I can't… I have to… I have to go."

She pulled away and started for the lane to her father's hall.

"Frithi!" yelled Holdric. She froze, then turned to face him.

"At least watch for me tomorrow."

For a frozen moment she stood there, a cornered doe on the grass.

"I will."

And then she was gone.

In the branches above, a ruddock called sweetly into the sky. Holdric glared. "Save your songs, bird."

He struck the tree so hard the branches quivered. Water welled up in his eyes and he forced them shut. He clenched his jaw hard.

Not here.

Their one hope, gone. He—no, he could not dwell on this. Not here, not now. He clenched his fists tight as he stared into the fading sunlight. Then he shook his head and stormed from the well.

Uncle Eikhram had told him that nothing cleared the mind like work. Not that the old man ever rushed for the fields himself, perhaps his mind was clear enough as it was. Holdric spat a curse as he made for the wall.

His sister Maethbry had left her retting work on the south field to cure and had asked him to bring it into the weaving cot for her before sundown. Most days that task would fall to her, but she'd sworn this afternoon she hadn't time and begged his help. Smouldering he bent to the task, and when he reached for her sheaves of drying flax he heaved them up in great armfuls with a fury.

The load was a scratchy mess, but it wasn't heavy. He hauled the better part of it up to the weaving cot with a single trip. A second load served for last, and he cast the lot into Maethbry's bin with a grunt. He turned to leave, and saw in the dusty light a battered scutching post. On that post a scarred wooden knife hung from an old leather thong.

He took the thing in hand and a grim sad smile crossed his face. It felt smaller than once it had. The blade was scarce now the length of his forearm, no longer the great wooden warknife he had fought so many boyhood battles with.

The carved blade had not the water-flowing iron of his father's warknife, but still a graven hound had once run through graven trees along the blade, still a trail of graven stars once had marked the spine. This thing had been his, and he had loved it.

Now the wood was battered almost smooth, the carving-work worn to whispers. But it felt still nimble in his hand, and warm with old memory. He took a lazy swipe at the air.

How many fancied ghaestling had he slain on the high field? How many times had he rallied the desperate shield wall, bravely held the dike and saved all? Times beyond counting.

He had at last grown too old for such games, and too old for a boy's wooden blade. He had let Maethbry claim his little Brukthorn for her scutching work—though long after he would sneak out again when he felt not quite so old.

He ran the wooden tip against the scutching board, feeling for the crushed bruises in the post his games had left. How many times had it been? How many times had this… loss and hurt boiled up in him, and he brought the blade down hard upon the post. The haft cracked in his hand, and the splintered blade flew off into the shadows. He swallowed a curse and cast the broken handle to the ground. He turned to go, but a shadow blocked his way.

Widow Blóssig stood in the open door, her arms full of spun wool. Her eyes flicked to the shattered wooden knife, then up to Holdric. Her look was hard. A smirk crossed her aged face and she elbowed past him, crowding him out of the doorway.

"Mind your feet, boy." Her voice was cold. "… and pick up your sword."

Holdric's face burned. He snatched the shattered haft from the earth and stormed out the cot, sure that Widow Blóssig's eyes were burning into his back. At last he made it up the lane to his uncle's hall. Firelight glowed warm through timbered shutters, and merry voices sounded within. He stopped short of the door, took a deep breath to calm himself, then lifted the wooden latch and ducked inside.

The smell of warm bread and mutton washed over him. His tired heart leapt to see roasting meat on the spit, that a too-rare sight. For a moment he wondered the cause, then saw his cousin Aschbroc sharing some story with Uncle Eikhram in the far corner. Of course—guests had come. Aschbroc's wife Rinna was here also, at the hearth with the other women of the house. Aunt Claefry was there, and Holdric's mother and his sister Maethbry, and with them little Segli.

Maethbry looked up from playing with Segli and flashed Holdric a smile. He gave a weary wave and sat to pull off his boots.

There was a scrape of paws as their old hound Hunling rose creakily to her feet and trundled slowly towards him. He rose to meet her and knelt to scratch her ruff. She grunted and burrowed into his chest, then flopped again to the floor. Holdric gave her a squeeze and sat back in the warmth of the hall. Eight bodies in the little hall made for tight walls, but the place was home. Or home enough.

Uncle Eikhram's hall had been over-close for years. When Aschbroc had left to marry things freed up a bit, only for surprise child Segli to join them a year later.

"Ha Holdic!!" the little girl yelled, not looking up from her game.

"How's Frithi?" asked Maethbry.

"Well enough," answered Holdric. He kept his voice steady, but his mother caught the roughness in his throat. She looked up and tried to meet his eyes, but he only shook his head.

Aschbroc yelled to him from across the hall. "Cousin! Ready for tomorrow?"

Grateful to escape the unspoken question, Holdric moved to the table and sat across from his cousin. Hunling followed, then dropped heavy at his feet and lay her head upon his foot. Holdric reached down and scratched her old ears as he spoke.

"Fields are done, retting's in…" He took a deep breath, eyeing his uncle. "But Greotn needs a trim. I'll do it when I get back."

Uncle Eikhram's face darkened. "You know better! You can't let that beast…" The old man looked about to launch into another storm, then the words trailed off into a grunt. "Don't mind it. I'll do him in the morning. Just don't let him go so long again. We need that beast hale."

"Yah, Uncle. I will."

The old man grunted again. He was quiet but a moment, then began again. "So what's this about your girl? She find wisdom at the last?"

Before Holdric could find words to answer, the door opened with a knock. A man stepped through. tall and broad-shouldered, his face weatherworn and his white hair still streaked with ruddy gold. His tunic was the grey of the winter wood, and his cloak a muddy grey-green, clasped with a brooch of blackened bronze in the shape of a stag. He wore the tall leather boots of a ranger, and carried beneath his thinning cloak the fine-worked sword of the Huntslaed.

Hunling lifted her head and let out a halfhearted rolling bark.

"Hello to you, old girl" said the old ranger with a smile.

"Da!" Holdric's mother lit up. She half-ran to the old ranger and wrapped his shoulders in her arms. He gave her a squeeze, then moved to hang up cloak and blade.

"*Ollda! Ollda!*" cried Segli as she ran to him. He scooped the little girl up and held her to his side. She screamed in laughter as he bounced her upon his hip.

Aunt Claefry looked on smiling, then wiped her hands upon her apron. "Ever early, Da! Join the lads and we'll be eating."

Kenndric carried the laughing Segli by her hands, then with a grunt of effort lifted her to the bench. She squealed as he set her down.

"You're growing too fast, lambling."

He sat heavy at the table beside Holdric.

The board was heavy with roast lamb, with steaming greens, and butter and soft cheese, and warm loaves of true wheaten bread still crackling beneath the clean linen. Aschbroc had brought a small cask of honey ale, fresh from Alewife Hegwyn. They'd not had such a feast since midwinter. Holdric's mouth was already watering.

The table was cramped, but when Aunt Claefry moved Segli to her lap all could find room. Uncle Eikhram waved for silence and began the words. As he spoke the others followed:

> *By sun and earth, by wind and rain—*
> *The Light of Maesteald feed us.*

> *By Stag King's step, by Heron's flight—*
> *Song of Lihtenstil heal us.*

> *By kin-worn table, By heart-worn-hands—*
> *Bread shared bind us.*

> *And should the Wanderer find our table—*
> *let us not do him dishonor.*

> *Be it so.*

Holdric felt a bitter grunt rise in his throat at "heart-worn-hands," but held it behind his teeth. Cold as his uncle was, the old man had housed and fed Holdric and his kin for years, ever since the dread morning they reached his door wood-scratched and tear-stained and bloody.

Uncle Eikhram had spoken not a single word that long-ago morning. He had taken one look at Aunt Claefry and Mum crying in each other's arms and opened the door wide.

"There was no choice to make," he had said. Kin was kin. Not that kinship had stopped him from working Holdric bare and bent. Bondsmen had known easier days. Holdric could not say much love passed between them, but love or no, Eikhram's hall was home.

"Eat, boy."

The old man forked a chunk of mutton into Holdric's bowl. Holdric sat stunned. His uncle had never been so free with the meat.

"Thank—" he started. Eikhram grunted and reached for Aschbroc's bowl.

The meat passed, Maethbry grinned and lifted the linen from the loaves. She passed the first piece to Holdric, heavy with fresh-creamed butter. He grinned back at her and took a huge bite, cream dribbling down his chin. Maethbry laughed and reached up with her serving cloth to wipe it clean. He almost choked as he joined her laugh.

Aschbroc passed him a cup of watered honey ale, and the meal was well on.

"Drink your fill cousin, but remember I wake you before sunrise."

Rinna lifted an eyebrow. She looked at her young husband with narrowed eyes. "As if sunrise ever stopped your cups."

Aschbroc returned her gaze, staring hard into her eyes. He returned the cocked eyebrow and she burst into laughter. Holdric shook his head and knocked back his cup.

Kenndric broke in, "I am reminded Holdric, Eahstann has returned."

Holdric put down the cup, choking on the drink. "He's here?"

"At the fyrdhall. He arrived with Master Uhlseid just before dusk."

Holdric made to stand, but Kenndric laid a hand on his shoulder. "Ease lad, you'll see enough of your friend. He joins us tomorrow."

Now it was Maethbry who turned crestfallen. "He leaves so soon?"

"I know not the reason he came so late," answered Kenndric. "But he seemed most eager to see you all, should you come to see us off."

Maethbry looked to Uncle Eikhram, then to Mum. "May we?"

Mum smiled, looking to their uncle. He thought but a moment, then nodded. Maethbry beamed. Segli leaned in and whispered loudly to her, "Who Eys-tan?"

"You remember Eahstann, silly! The black-haired boy who played you a song?"

Segli thought, then nodded her head. "I like song boy."

"Song man, now," Kenndric said.

Uncle Eikhram turned to the old ranger. "Another old hand for you then. The usual run for your Hounds this time?"

Kenndric paused before he spoke. Long habit had left him cagey about his ways and roads, even to kin. "Usual enough," he allowed at last. "Stores for the Greatwatch men, then we see what may. Perhaps so far as Eomud's Hyssestead."

Aunt Claefry and Mum shared a glance. Eikhram caught the look.

"You'll be working the boy's legs hard."

Kenndric looked at Holdric and smiled. "I'll do my best to get him back to you in one piece, but he's still like to sleep a week when we're done with him."

Eikhram smiled, looked as if he were about to joke, then shook his head and took again to his meal.

Holdric grabbed for another piece of bread to sop up the last of his bowl. Then he looked to his Ollda. "Would I have a place at Eomud's if I offered my Oath?"

The table fell silent. Kenndric said nothing, but regarded him calmly. His mother nearly dropped her spoon. "Holdric! What about Frithi? What about the cot—"

"I'm only asking, Mum."

Kenndric's face was dark. "Think hard on that lad, before you ask such things. That Oath cannot be unmade."

Holdric shifted in his seat. "I have been thinking."

He forced himself to meet Kenndric's eyes, and the old ranger nodded, his face grim.

"Get the measure of Eomud first," he counseled, "and give him a chance to get the measure of you. If all be well, I will speak with him."

"Holdric, please—" started Mum.

Uncle held out a hand. "The boy's grown, he can give…"

"Holdic no go!" yelled Segli. "Holdic no go MudMud, Holdic no go *ever!"*

Aunt Claefry wrapped her arm over Segli's little shoulders and tried to calm her.

"I've got to go, lamb," Holdric said. "I'll be back soon, I promise." He looked to his Ollda, then back to Segli. "Nothing's told yet."

"No!"

Aunt Claefry eyed Segli sharply and the girl fell into a sulky silence. Then she tried another tack. "*Why* Holdic go?" she yelled.

The adults eyed each other, and Aschbroc held out his hand to hold hers. "Segli, remember when Greotn knocked you down, and Holdric scared him away from you?"

Her eyes got big, and she nodded.

"Well, he's got to go with me and Ollda Kenndric. We're going to go scare off some other things so you can be safe."

Aunt Claefry shot a warning look to Aschbroc. He returned the gaze, gentle but firm. "She's got to know, Mum."

"Mean old Geotns in forest to?" Segli asked Holdric, her eyes wide with horror.

Claefry looked to Holdric, her lips tight.

He swallowed. "Something like that."

"Why Holdic go? *You* go!" she yelled to Uncle Eikhram. For once, the old man had no words.

"That's enough, Segli" warned Aunt Claefry.

Segli pouted and looked ready to say more, but Kenndric gently held out his hand. She quieted.

"Your father's done enough little lamb. It's a younger man's turn now."

Uncle Eikhram shifted uncomfortably, feeling beneath the table at his twisted leg.

"Every man goes, honey," he answered. "He has to."

"No Maethy? Maethy no go?"

"I have my hands full with you, little lamb," Maethbry said.

Segli thought, still unhappy. Maethbry pulled her close.

"Let's get some honeycake and let your mumma have a break, all right?"

"Holdic get huncake?"

Maethbry winked up at Holdric, then gave Segli a hug. "Yah! He gets *lots* of honeycake."

"Then I have huncake too," Segli answered.

Maethbry lifted her from the bench and carried her off to the light by the hearth.

Mum hadn't stopped glaring at Holdric—and Kenndric.

"It's just a fortnight, Hleolea" said Kenndric gently.

She picked up her spoon and silently dropped her eyes to her bowl. Claefry reached over and took her hand. Aschbroc looked about the table, searching for other talk to make. "I walked up to the highcorn today, our strip fared well through the rain. Today's sun has been good."

Uncle Eikhram jumped in to follow his words. "Not much sun left. Maesteald willing, we'll have a good winter."

Talk flowed comfortably then if not happily, until bowls were sopped clean and greaselamps guttered low. At last Rinna yawned and leaned her head on Aschbroc's shoulder. Aschbroc smiled and gave her a squeeze.

"Sounds as if it's time to go."

He stood, helping Rinna to her feet.

"Na Na Na!" called Segli half-heartedly, before nodding off again into a doze. Aunt Claefry pulled her close and stroked her hair.

The others rose and walked Aschbroc and Rinna to the door. There, Aunt Claefry hugged her son hard and long.

"We'll watch for you tomorrow," she said, then took Rinna into her arms as well.

"Thanks Mum," Aschbroc said, kissing her head. "I'll see you tomorrow."

"And you!" Uncle Eikhram said, taking his son in arm. "Now go make me an Ollda also."

A shadow crossed Rinna's face, and she clung to Aschbroc. His smile came tight.

"We try, Da," answered Aschbroc. "Love to you all." He quickly embraced his father, then reached his arm out to Kenndric.

"Huntslaed, farewell…"

Kenndric laughed, took his arm, and brought him in for a slap on the shoulder. "Sleep well, Huntsman."

"And you," grinned Aschbroc. He then pointed to Holdric. "Especially you, cousin! Don't make me carry you from bed tomorrow!"

Holdric embraced him without a word, and then they were gone. No sooner had they left than Kenndric also reached for the pegs by the door, seeking out his blade and cloak. "My time as well, I think. There is much to make ready, and dawn comes too soon."

With another round of farewells, he was on his way. No sooner had the door closed but Holdric bent for his boots. His mother looked up, her face stricken.

"All's well, Mum. Only a moment."

He slipped outside before she could make answer. When he came out into the night he saw the old ranger had not gone far. He had been waiting.

"Huntslaed," Holdric said.

"Huntsman," Kenndric answered.

Holdric chewed on his words, he'd had no time to frame his speech. They stood long in silence. It was Kenndric who finally spoke. "Why the Hyssestead, Holdric? Why now?"

Holdric shifted on his feet. "The wild is more home to me than here. You know that better than any."

"Your young woman? Frithwyn?"

"No."

Kenndric sighed. He looked to the moon high in the sky, then back to Holdric. "A girl's heart can change."

"Not so easily a girl's father."

"Ah."

Kenndric leaned against the hall. "I met the same test, once. So did your father. And yet here you stand, Feorson."

Holdric stood his ground. "You know I can do this, Ollda."

"Of that I have no doubt."

"So then…"

"Tomorrow Holdric, I will be your Huntslaed. But tonight I am still your Ollda. I give you my word: though I wish you to remain with Heortlea's band, still I will speak with Eomud on your behalf, just as you ask. But mind me, offer not your Oath this ranging, for I will not yet vouch it. Do well, and things unseen may change. Your fate is yet unspoken. Will you mind me?"

Holdric set his jaw, but grudging he nodded. "I will mind you."

Kenndric nodded in silence, then clapped Holdric on the shoulder. "I must work, and then I must rest. Sleep well, Feorson."

"And you, Ollda."

Kenndric turned back for the fyrd hall, and with a last wave of farewell walked into the night. Holdric's eyes followed the old ranger, watching until at last the shadows swallowed him up.

Then he looked up to the waxing moon above. The air was cool on his skin, the rising stars of the summer swans sharp and cold. He let out a long weary sigh. This then had been his last night home. A distant thrush sang alone, far away in the dark. He took one last breath of night and passed again into the hall.

The air inside was hot and close. The sounds of feasting had given way again to the sounds of work. Mum and Maethbry were at the tub, washing up from the meal. Uncle Eikhram had moved to the hearthside to claim bits of bone from the ash for his handwork, and Aunt Claefry was whispering night-charms to little Segli, easing her into sleep.

His mother looked up as he came in, her face hard as stone. Holdric did not meet her eyes. He begged a small scrap from the meal for Hunling, tossed it her way, and made for his chest by the back wall. From there he pulled his worn goatskin pack, and with it the few things he'd not yet been able to stow away.

He moved with his things to the far side of the hearth, away from Uncle Eikhram. He tried not to look up, but the old man caught his arm as he went by. He spoke low, for only Holdric to hear— "I'll talk to your mum boy, fear not."

Holdric weakly smiled his thanks and went to his work.

He sat near the low flickering light of the hearth and unbuckled his pack. He pulled forth each thing and set it before his feet, feeling over each piece to make himself sure that all was in good order. He'd done this by hearthless fire so often he could manage now by touch.

Wooden cup and spoon, an old gift from Frithi. He scowled at that.

His extra fire stuff: char and grass, flakes of stone, balls of pitch, and a costly little candle, all rolled up in a well-greased bag of wildtan. Also a simple mending kit Maethbry had made him, and with it his nit-comb and his washing things and a little box of wound-salve.

Maethbry brought him food from the larder and left it beside him with a quiet kiss on his head. A small wildcloth sack held pottage meal with smoked mutton, and a smaller bag was filled with too little lard, an antler of salt, the promised honeycakes, and every extra sweetmeat Mum and Maethbry could stuff inside.

Next were a few spare boot soles, his woolens, and his spare linen, all rolled in the worn remains of his childhood bed tick. The old sack was short and stained, even the mended spots wearing through.

Still it would keep him off the cold earth if he stuffed it well enough. Most of him anyhow. That would go in his blanket come morning. He set the bundle in the fold of his goatskin pack. The rest was not his own to fill. At that he grumbled, and stuffed an extra pair of thick woolen socks in just the same.

He knotted his little knife tight and ranger-fashion to his belt, he emptied his pouch of things he would not need in the wild. His fingers brushed a charbox of hammered iron and a soft smile crossed his face. The little box was long-blackened from the coals of many fires, the metal graven with trees and stars. It was the one thing of his Da he held still for his own.

He fetched a new sharp flint from the wooden box by the hearth and nestled it away with his char. That done, he looked over his borrowed fyrdknife, sheathed and bound tight to a narrow belt of its own.

And that was all. He felt there should be more. Fourteen nights beyond the Mearcwater—he'd never gone so far, nor with so little. He fussed with his pack and pulled the buckled straps tight.

Uncle Eikhram looked across the fire, watching as Holdric managed his things.

"You'll do fine, boy. You'll be back before you know you're gone."

"I need a kettle."

"No you don't. Your band will have a common one."

"Ollda carries one, a small one. Aunt Claefry, could I take—"

"You're not your Ollda," his uncle said. "You need anything past what you have, they'll give it to you."

"It's not enough."

"You'll want to drop half what you carry already, mark my word."

Holdric wanted to ask how the old man might know, him scarcely a fyrdman. He wanted to ask what the old man had carried on the one march he ever made, and that a march cut short. But Holdric knew better, and he bit his tongue. He nodded in silence and moved to hang fyrdknife and pack by the door. There were no more words he wished to trade anyhow. A last round out the back and he was ready for bed.

He picked up his bed tick and blanket and made for a far corner of the hall. The tick was thin, the straw broken and flat. Maethbry had offered to fill it for him, but Uncle Eikhram had stopped her.

"Better Holdric sleep a little hard now," he had said. "It will make his time on cold ground so much the softer."

Always the old man talked as if he would know.

The little hall was still too hot for sleep. Holdric found a cool spot near an unchinked hole in the wall and settled in. He stared long into the roof timbers, at last alone with his mind. At least amid the clamour of family he couldn't worry. At least he could not dwell on Frithi.

He threw off his blanket. Not for the first time, he missed his old cot of brush out past the timberlands. It had been less almost than nothing, but it had at least been his. Now he had to start again. Two years for Old Barwud's cot, then he could...

He cursed. He had planned to surprise Frithi, he had planned so many things. But what were those plans worth now? Her father was not one to change his mind, no matter how gentle Ollda's words. Their way had been rough already. There would be no unmaking this, not now.

Still she burned in his mind. He thought on the curve of her waist, on the smell of her hair. He thought on the sound of her whispers and her hushed happy laugh. Then he thought on her sorrowed eyes at the well, on the terror in her face when his rage had risen hot—at that he winced. He'd frightened her. He didn't think that would mend... not that it mattered now.

No, there was no hope here. Not now, not anymore. What was an old mouldering cot but a pit to rot away in, watching as...

He rolled over and stared into the wall. If his face was wet, he made no sound. Hunling trundled over from the hearth and collapsed beside him. The old hound sighed as she laid her head on his tick, and Holdric absently reached down and scratched her ears.

It was long before sleep finally claimed him.

CHAPTER TWO
The Arrow and the Horn

They sat under apple trees bright and young. The boughs were soft and limber, bowed low with bright summer fruit. Little Maethbry ran under the trees, grasping at the sunny leaves as she squealed in delight.

Mum looked up and smiled. Da strode down from the stoneplace, and held his arms wide in joy as he saw them. Through the sweet orchards they walked, and over the spring, and past the brambleberries, and down to the outfolds.

The grass there was thick, and so high that Holdric could scarcely see. Mum and Da held Maethbry up by her hands, but he ran ahead, slashing at the high grass with his stick of a sword. He cried out for the delight of it, and they all laughed with him.

He startled the sheep from their happy chewing. Some came to their feet, and the young lambs bounded away, hopping and kicking. Holdric laughed all the harder, and Maethbry squealed to see them run. Over the dike and down the grass they walked, merry as they passed the giant beast-carved timbers and the bright-flowered aelfsthorn. Down they came from the heights, down past the broken stone and into the trees. The earth was cool under his bare feet as he ran.

Over the fish brook they went, and through the masting grounds, and deep into the quiet pines. Here they always came when the day was hot, down to where the trees were tall and the ground soft and thick with pine-smell.

He splashed in the water and he yelled with joy. Maethbry laughed and shrieked and tried to catch the ripples of sunlight in her hands. Holdric splashed water over the spiral-carved stone, and found it cool beneath his hand. More than cool, it was cold. Too cold for a shining summer day. It grew colder as he touched it. Chill seeped through him, the chill of long cold years… and something else beside.

Holdric woke.

He was cold. Hunling had nudged closer, pushing hard into his side until he had slipped from his thin tick onto the floor. Holdric moaned and rolled tighter into his blanket. Sleep took him again, sleep long and dreamless.

Long after, a hand shook his shoulder. Bleary he opened his eyes. Aschbroc knelt over his bed, a flickering greaselamp in his hand.

"It's time" he whispered.

Holdric groaned and pushed Aschbroc away. Aschbroc shook him harder.

"*Holdric.* Up. It's time."

Holdric nodded. He pushed Hunling aside and crawled from under his blanket. The old hound rose with a soft grunt, ambled creakily to Maethbry's tick, then fell heavy beside the girl.

Holdric moved half asleep. He quickly dressed, buckled on the large fyrdknife, and folded his blanket for the way. He slid his too-thin tick back under his mother's bed box. For a long moment, he looked down at her. In sleep she looked almost free of care, more than he'd seen in long weeks at the least. He had promised to wake her for a farewell before he left, but he found now that he had not the words… nor the heart. It was better that she sleep.

He looked around the small cot. His aunt and uncle were also deep in sleep, and little Segli too. Hunling pushed further onto Maethbry's tick, and his sister groaned in her sleep as she rolled away. Holdric smiled.

A fortnight, that was all.

He bound tight his boots, he pinned his cloak, and he took up his pack. Then he followed Aschbroc out into the night. He looked up as he passed through the door—the moon had long since set. The night was clear and dark, the stars of Slaugnwint high in the sky.

Holdric softly closed the door and placed his hand to sigils of sun and tree carved into the doorpost. "Watch over them, Hauwyr," he breathed, then he looked again to the sky, "and over us."

Aschbroc clapped his shoulder, and together they followed the swaying lamps to the fyrd hall. The earthen paths of Heortlea were never crowded, there were not souls enough inside the wall even for a market, but now the ways were near empty. Only rangers walked this early morning, those for the ranging and those coming to see them off. In ones and twos they walked, each in their own small islands of light up to the fyrdhall.

Aschbroc and Holdric walked together in quiet. Holdric fingered the haft of the fyrdknife strapped to his waist, and his stomach churned. He'd made this night walk dozens of times, for winter trainings in the hall, for muster walks under Wymud…but this time it was real. This time he'd cross the Mearcwater.

He swallowed hard, his throat dry. His fingers tightened on the strap of his pack. Part of him was eager, aching to race to the hall and be on his way. Part of him wondered what would happen if he ran for the gates, if he made for the wild, himself and himself alone. Still his feet walked only ever forward.

At the top of the hill the lights came together. Hard men milled before the hall in the warm glow of greaselight. Was that—

"Eahstann?"

A young man looked up. His once-pale face was now sunworn, his dark black hair grown to his shoulders. His woolens were dark, but the silver brooch at his shoulder gleamed bright in the flickering light. He stood baffled at first as he tried to make out who it was who had called his name. Then—

"Holdric!"

Aschbroc grinned and clapped Holdric's shoulder. "I'll see you inside, cousin."

Holdric waved after him, then ran to Eahstann. They embraced, laughing in a great back-slapping hug, then each stood back to take in the mark of time on the other.

Eahstann stood almost a head taller than Holdric remembered, taller almost than Ollda Kenndric, if not so broad. Harping-craft or no, the young man's arms had grown thick, his face stern.

Holdric felt some envy at that, but it seemed in Eahstann's eyes he had fared no worse. "My brother, when I left you were a grease-faced boy! And now you join us?"

Eahstann's voice was deeper, and different also. He had now a touch of the barding-speech to his words, clear if not so strong as that of Master Uhlseid. The shape of his words had little changed, but the roll of his voice now carried whispers of the long-rolling rhythm of ancient song.

"I join *you?"* Holdric asked. "You're the one who has come back to Heortlea! For how long?"

"Only until the Eorl's court. I range with the Heortlea men until he gives me leave for Ettenmede's fyrd."

"But… your bard-work?" Holdric asked.

Eahstann's face darkened. "Another time."

Holdric's face fell. He made to ask more, but Eahstann raised his hand. "I failed Holdric. There is no more to say." He forced a smile to his face. "But tell me of you! Your Ollda has told me yet little."

Holdric knew not where to start.

The heavy sound of footfalls neared them. Wymud, Kenndric's Second drew near. The dour man was short but stout, and his weatherworn face held no smile of greeting. He spared not a look for Holdric. "Eahstann, come. You are needed."

Eahstann turned to follow and raised a hand to Holdric. "Later, brother."

And so Holdric came alone to the wide door of the fyrdhall. The door was heavy oak, bound with well-wrought iron in the shape of the great trees of the old wood. The high lintel over the door was carved with twining beasts of ancient song, and above all stretched the wide antlers of a great stag.

Holdric swallowed. The door also bore carvings, winding branch and thorn beneath the trees of iron. Shapes seemed to move there in the flickering light, hinted forms of half-seen souls passing between the graven trees. Holdric felt almost he knew them, but he could not say how.

He gathered himself and laid his hand to the door. Then he lifted the latch and walked inside. Within the air danced with the light of dozens of flickering greaselamps, each a small star in the deep shadow of the hall.

Arrow-stuck, take your hunter,
Forest-kissed, guide his feet…

Holdric shuddered at the memory.

The hall smelled strong of sweat and woodsmoke. Shadow loomed in the high beams above, and in that shadow hung banners. One was stitched with the leaping stag Ealdorholt, arrow-struck under the great tree Maesteald. Another bore the brave hound Hauwyr. Here also hung the banners of the king's great bull, the Eorl's black bear, Heortlea's ancient stag and arrows, and more beside.

Long trestle tables had been raised over the training floor. Holdric had sat many long days at those tables, binding arrows and mending worn leather. Ranging men sat here now, and not only the few who would be going forth today. Some had come to aid in making ready, others only to sit with their cups and send off dear friends or share in memories of long-past days. Alewife Hegwyn was here also, helped by Sparri, bondswoman to the Thane. With them worked old Hauccael, the hobbling ward of the hall.

At each corner of the wide training floor was a raised hearth of stone. Most lay cold in the warm summer night, but over a far hearth a great camp iron had been raised. The iron held long hammered spits, heavy-forged to bear the whole of a slaughtered ox or long rows of kettles.

This morning the hearth hung only with a great kettle of morning pottage, and another of a waking brew boiled of wyrt and dark-roasted barley. Here also sat thick covered mugs of watered ale, warming in the ash where their owners had set them.

Above the fires at the high table sat Haestearn, Thane of Heortlea, and beside him was his last-living son Hwaetearn. Thane Haestearn was no ranger of the wild wood, but none knew armies nor horses nor men so well. Hwaetearn was broader even than Kenndric, his eyes keen as his father's. Kenndric sat with them, the three deep in talk, but Holdric could not hear their words. Still the Thane nodded his scarred head, listening hard as Kenndric spoke. His son followed close to every word.

Holdric turned away from the three lest he be caught watching. None seemed to mind him, each man was busy with his own task or his own friends. Holdric made for the back of the hall, to the place that had drawn him from the first time he'd been allowed into this place of ranging men.

He passed beneath the high banners and stole a glance to one side. There Eahstann and Wymud worked in a fenced arming stall between the timbers, looking over sheaves of arrows and pulling forth war gear from heavy chests.

Beyond, the walls were lined with raised benches and bed boxes. These were resting places for men visiting, or men healing. Save Eahstann's borrowed bench, all but old Hauccael's box lay empty.

Hauccael's place here was as much a kindness from the Thane for his lonely old bones as it was a duty. But still the hall was always clean, and still the stores well-kept. Holdric had never learned the measure of the old hall-ward. The old man rarely left the hall, and seemed often in his cups when he did. Still on the odd early morning Holdric would spy him tottering down the footpaths alone, quietly watching the sky turn grey over the far mountain.

Holdric came to the back wall. Here were the collected remembrances of the rangers of Heortlea. Graven upon the great beams were again the beasts of ancient legend, each acting out their stories between carved branch and thorn. Eyes glimmered with inlaid stone, each beast winding around a carved sun that glowed in the lamplight with peeling, thin-beaten gold.

From one great beam hung the sounding horns. Each was graven with name-runes and winding beasts. Each Holdric had learned to name. There hung Arncal, horn of Fyalstin and Bealdwulf after him. Beside it was Dunorbruk, relic of Heortlea's first days. Some of these horns came still to the wood, but many more were broken, hanging now in memory of those who once had carried them.

Above the horns were cloak brooches of the fallen. Some few of silver, most of bronze, many of simple antler or poor hammered iron. In life they had been blackened for the wild wood, now all were polished bright and gleamed in the lamplight like stars. Stags and hounds, trees and stars, bears and boars, each wrought for the man who wore it. Sigils of memory were carved into the wood around some, and love-knots of braided wool hung from many. Many of those knots bore beads, one for each child left behind.

One brooch however was not among them, a wayfinder's brooch of hound and star, of heron and turning gyre. That brooch would never hang here.

Holdric moved on. He found the brooch of Eahstann's brother, wrought bronze graven with a twisting fox and hare. This was the only of the hanging tokens he had seen on the breast of a living man. He had not known tall Brythoc well, but still he missed him. It seemed though that he should not think on such things now.

He moved farther down the wall to a place of hanging trophies and relics of older years. The finely carved spear shaft of Beragrun, he who first raised the wall of Heortlea. A splintered shield from the razing of those walls in Ollda's father's time. A well-wrought helm of iron from far-away Reodfel, the brow band covered in tales from those high mountains. Broken throwing spears of the ghaestling were here also, the long iron points barbed and wicked. But these were not what Holdric had come to see.

A ghaestling harness hung upon the wall, grim and terrible. The harness was a crudely fleshed jerkin of thick hide, tufts of black fur and ochre still poking out between nameless rib-bones bound down with sinew. Lashed between were bits of rusted mail, wild ram's horn, and black beaten copper. Crude sigils had been hacked into the bone, some still filled with ochre or long-dried blood.

The harness, and the creature that once had worn it, had been the part of too many childhood nightmares. Holdric stared at it in the dim lamplight, trying once again to make out what the sigils might mean. They made no more sense to him now than they ever had, but the broken lines left always an evil feeling in his heart.

Behind he heard Aschbroc's step. His cousin came near. The two stood in silence, looking at the relic.

"The bones aren't from a man, are they?" Holdric asked.

"No. Our fallen we bury, if we can. Those look to be boar, I think."

Holdric looked with doubt on the bleached rib bone. "Boar," he echoed. Was Aschbroc sheltering him, even now?

"Ghaestling always seemed like something from Ollna's stories," he said at last. "Not quite real."

"They're real." Aschbroc's answer was distant. His eyes also did not leave the bones.

"Uncle Eikhram said they brought this back from Heahfeldt."

"He told me that once, too," Aschbroc said. "I don't know. It looks older than that."

"You would know." Holdric's voice had taken a hard edge, harder than he had meant.

Aschbroc looked at him. "He's done his share."

Holdric's gaze didn't move from the bones.

Aschbroc's voice became curt, "You've not much time, Holdric. Best make yourself ready."

Holdric stiffened, then turned without word for the arming stall. Wymud had left, but Eahstann was still making ready. The harper was sitting upon a bench, rubbing silverblack into his brooch and eyeing it against the light.

Holdric edged past him to the stores. There under the watching eyes of the hall-ward Holdric rummaged through chests and racks of musty castoffs. Rope and boot irons, binding linens and healing herbs, each thing a mark against his name the old man would remember. Meager as the pickings were, Hauccael would work him dearly for anything he failed to carry home again. Still, until Holdric could earn his own he had to borrow.

He curled his nose as he drew forth a long-worn jack of linen, cast off from the Ettenmede fyrd by the look of it. It was cut down and dyed a ruddy pale brown, but the look of fyrd-work was plain upon it. Stink from the last wearer hung heavy in the quilted cloth, and despite the best labors of Hauccael a dull stain across the kidneys told a grim tale. For all that, the rent had been well patched, the stitches clean and ordered. More to the point, it fit.

This Holdric covered with a musty jerkin of oxhide, long since softened with hard wearing. Neither jack nor jerkin were what they once had been, but they would protect him from the weather well enough, and turn a careless blade or claw if luck was with him.

Over these Holdric pinned again the proud gift from his Ollda, his ranger's cloak of tight-woven wool, deep and grey-green as the shadowed wood. He borrowed next a leather-faced shield, and cast an envying eye to the heavy bows of yew hanging in their cases of wool and dubbined goatskin.

Holdric had failed the last testing, and ached in his shoulder for weeks after. It would be a year before he could try the bow again. Until then, the spear it was. Sighing, he pulled a short woodsman's spear from the rack. These were shorter than the tall spears of the fyrd, their dark-stained shafts of ash carved and stained in the deep colors of the forest. Holdric ran his finger over the battered carvings of the haft and gently pulled the leather cover from the head. The blade was long, and though the watered steel was long worn, old

Hauccael had stoned it smooth and keen. It would serve. Holdric eased the cover over the blade again and took up his shield.

He looked again to the hearth, eyeing how much time he had before the gathering of arms. The tables were not yet empty, but men were beginning to move. He would have to eat quickly.

He stowed his arms and made for the hearth. There he took a bowl from the common stock and came to Alewife Hegwyn and her breakfast kettle. She smiled wordlessly as she filled his bowl.

However hard the work, the people of Heortlea were as generous in feeding the fighting men as they could manage. The morning pottage was heavy with cheese, the cuts of sausage thick. Hegwyn graced each bowl with a snippet of fresh green. It seemed a silly thing, but her gentle herb cut clean and sweet against the heavy stew.

Holdric ate, wishing for more before he'd half finished his bowl. He was not alone in his hurry, already the tables were nearly empty. He felt a hand on his shoulder. He looked up to see Thane Haestearn looking down to him. Holdric choked and made to stand, but the Thane held out his hand, bidding him stay.

"Your first ranging." It was not a question.

Holdric swallowed hard. "Yah, Thane."

"Are you ready?"

Holdric faltered… then straightened his back and found strength for his voice. "Always ready, Thane."

"Hrmm." The Thane's smile was thin. "Just bear your load, son."

And then he was gone. The older men still at the table looked quietly at Holdric. He swallowed hard, feeling their eyes upon him. He returned to his food and ate in silence. When the order was called at last, it came not too soon. Holdric threw back a last gulp of the waking tea and made to take his place.

The men of the ranging band met beneath the broad antlers of the remembrance wall. Here broad tables had been set. Upon one table was their marching-food, a gift from the fyrd. Hard cakes of waybread were set in trays, bound in dusky bags of linen. A sprig of rowan had been set on each bag for good fate, and with them were carved boxes of bread lard and new-made waterskins.

The other table bore the pale calling horns taken from the wall, now dark in their shrouding wool. Fyrcal would be carried by Kenndric, and the Thane's Wyrgreot by Hwaetearn, and Eahstann would carry old Houlen. Holdric could not help but envy his friend, all the more because Eahstann was now an Ettenmede man. The horn belonged with Heortlea. But Eahstann had crossed the Mearcwater and he had not, so all was as it would be.

Master Uhlseid stood before them, and Thane Haestearn beside him. Each of the men laid his arms upon the table and Uhlseid spoke the words of blessing. Of the bread he bade Maesteald nourish their bodies, and of the water he bade the Lady Lihtenstil nourish their spirit. Horn and steel and bow he blessed to Hauwyr, that arms and man alike should not fail, but hold strong against the dark to come. Ealdorholt he asked to make sharp their sight, and that the great Stag should guide their steps through the dangers of the wood.

Holdric looked to Eahstann. The bardling's head was low, his lips silently following as the verses rolled on. Holdric kept low his own head until the blessing was done.

> *Though you walk in shadow, you walk not alone,*
> *though you bear pain, you suffer not alone.*

The old bard raised his hands and spoke the last words:

> *The light of Maesteald warm your heart,*
> *The water of Lihtenstil fill your spirit.*

The strength of Hauwyr give strength to your arm,
The sight of Ealdorholt keep well your way.
By sun and rain, by wind and earth, may all
watch over you, until we meet again.

Eahstann raised his head, and Holdric did also. *Until we meet again*, they answered.

Uhlseid stepped aside and Thane Haestearn took his place. He raised his arms and spoke.

By word and ring of King Eacandeor I send you into the fight. I promise you all aid in my power to give. I send you with the love of your kin, the honor of your band, and the trust of your king. Your forebears have held fast the way for you, and now you hold fast the way for your kin yet to come.

Men of Kenndric's Hounds, the life of your people is laid upon you. Ealdorholt keep well your way, until you come again to us your home.

He looked to them, and each man stood straight. As one they answered:

For kindred past, for kindred present, for kindred yet to come—we go.

It was done. They gathered their arms, they filled their packs, and they took their places. Holdric stood beside Eahstann as they made to leave the hall.

"Look sharp," whispered Eahstann. "They'll be watching."

Holdric scoffed, but still he stood a little straighter as they filed through the doors.

Outside the black of night had given way to earliest greylight. Few lamps still flickered. More folk were now gathered outside the hall, family and friends come to see off their loved ones. Holdric searched the gloom for his own kin. Maethbry spied him and waved. She had Segli with her, nodding and half asleep in her arms. Aschbroc's Rinna was with them, and Aunt Claefry, and Mum, also—but Frithi was not with them.

Holdric returned Maethbry's wave, and hoped he did not look so comforted as he felt at the sight of a friendly soul. He made his way to Eahstann.

The harper had his heavy bow in hand, thick-strung and over his own height. He wore a full quiver on his back, and the great horn Houlen also. He still looked almost an Ettenmede man in his worn tunic of pale dirty blue, but the ranger's cloak of grey-green about his shoulders told the stronger story.

Eahstann caught his look.

"Let's trade," Holdric said with a grin. "You know I'm better with a bow than you."

"Maybe with that bent twig of your uncle's you are," Eahstann said, cuffing Holdric's arm. "Next year, brother. Until then…"

He held out a second sheaf of arrows. Grumbling, Holdric slung the arrow bag over his pack. Eahstann grinned. Holdric grumbled again and looked back to the gathered folk of Heortlea. Where was Frithi?

He craned his head and peered in the gloom, but then had no more time to look, for Wymud passed through and gave the call to order. Each man stood and readied himself. Past Wymud was Aschbroc, and Hwaetearn beside him. The two were of an age, and like almost to brothers. Aschbroc bore also a tall bow and a heavy sheaf of arrows, while Hwaetearn carried shield and Fyalclef, famed sword of his line.

Ollda Kenndric, Wymud his Second, these three, and Holdric were all that would pass the gates this morning. *The fewer men, the fewer sign*, so Ollda had always said. It would be enough.

Wymud set aside his short cleaving-spear and stalked among them. He pulled on their baggage, grumbling under his breath. Without a word he reached over and yanked on Aschbroc's rolled blanket. Aschbroc staggered, but the binding held. Wymud moved on without a word, hunting each of them for fault.

He passed behind Holdric. Holdric's neck hairs bristled as the older man passed behind. He braced for the sharp tug he knew was coming… but nothing came, only a word.

"Feet."

Holdric lifted his feet in turn, showing his soles to Wymud. The old man grunted. "You have more soles?"

"Yah Second, two sets"

"Hrmm… Up"

Holdric jumped in place. His bundles joggled but little, there was none of metal's dread jangle, but the sound of sloshing water met his ears. He winced—he'd forgotten his waterskin.

Wymud scowled. "You sound like a rotting rainstorm. Fix it." Without another word, the Second passed on.

With a muttered curse, Holdric eased the air from the skin and set again the stopper in place.

A movement from the fyrdhall caught Holdric's eye. Hauccael ferried out several heavy strapped sacks from the fyrdhall, struggling under the weight. Holdric groaned. More to carry, feed and more for the Greatwatch men. At his turn, he heaved up his share of the load, a heavy sack of pottage grain that doubled almost his burden. He grimaced as he worked the strap over his shoulders and tried to find some place that wouldn't leave them raw and burning by noontime.

At last Kenndric came forth from the hall, deep in talk with the Thane. The elders of Heortlea followed with them, dark looks on their faces. One cast a quick look Holdric's way, and Kenndric nodded as another spoke quietly. Then the ranger readied his great bow and clasped arms with each of the old men.

Holdric's shoulders burned. The goodbyes had been too long, and still the old men talked. Finally Kenndric broke away, and walked among the men of the ranging to look them over himself. As he passed behind, Holdric felt a tug on the straps of his pack.

"Holdric, hold still."

Kenndric slipped a small bundle Holdric couldn't see into his pack, then pulled the straps tight again. The extra weight was nothing. Kenndric slapped his shoulder and moved on without a word.

Kenndric glanced at Wymud, and the Second gave him a wordless nod. All were here, all were ready, dawn was near. They'd be leaving any moment. Still Frithi was not in sight.

Holdric looked again to Maethbry. Surely Frithi would join her. Maethbry craned her head, searching the small crowd. Segli caught Holdric's eye and bounced.

"Bye Holdic! Bye-bye, beat mean Geotn!"

Holdric flushed as all eyes fell upon him. Grimacing inside, he waved back to her.

Hwaetearn raised his eyebrow and grinned.

"Save us Holdric!" laughed Aschbroc. Wymud scowled but said nothing.

And at last they moved on. Down the wide lane of Heortlea they passed. Many were awake now, gathered to watch the leaving of the band. Elders raised their hands in farewell as they passed. Two barefoot boys ran after, sticks for spears raised high.

Hauccael straightened as they passed and raised his hand in farewell, some ancient yearning on his face. Widow Blóssig watched too, and her eyes landed cold upon Holdric. In that she was not alone. Holdric told himself without believing that the whispers just past his hearing were not of him.

"… rotting castoff," he caught. There was worse he didn't. He kept his eyes on the gates and pretended not to hear.

At last they reached the paling-wall and the gates were opened. Beyond the first gold of morning washed over field and tree. The morning mist had fled the highfolds, and a first chorus of birdsong came floating on air still heavy with morning dew.

Thane Haestearn spoke heartening words of farewell to each as they passed through the gate. Hwaetearn went before him, straight and tall. Aschbroc next. Before Holdric had readied himself, he was before the Thane.

Haestearn clasped his arm, hand upon his shoulder. Holdric remembered just in time to grasp back, slapping the Thane's shoulder too hard in answer. Holdric's eyes widened as he caught his mistake, and for an instant it seemed a whisper of a smile crossed the Thane's face.

He heard not Master Uhlseid's last words of blessing, and the moment was over before he could think—then he was through the gate. He started to turn, but felt Eahstann's hand upon his shoulder.

"Don't look back," he said. "You're on the path now. Bad luck to look homeward."

Holdric forced his gaze to the far treeline until they rounded the lane and crossed over the stream. There he snuck a quick look back to the walls, and to Frithi's favorite hill above.

Her tree was empty.

CHAPTER THREE
Over the Water

The lane wound past grassy fields and under broad rolling hills. The air was thick and full of life, heavy with the smell of summer green and wet with morning dew.

The sun rose warm and the morning grew bright. Tattered leaves of oxfoot edged onto the earthen path. The near green was dotted with white tufts of meadowsheaf, and maslin-grass waved on the highcorn above, heads low with ripening grain. Were it not for the heavy weight on his back and the spear in his hand, Holdric would have felt it as any other day.

They reached the highfolds and one by one passed over the stile into pasture. Holdric looked over the fold with a shepherd's eye. The summer had been wet, and the highfolds lush. Now the season was faded and the forage grown thin. His gaze followed the old places of easy passing over the hillside, limbways now worn bare by the passing of many feet.

Sheep wandered high on the green above, still seeking to fill their bellies. The last week's rains had given the grass a last burst of life, but still the herd would need to be driven down soon, probably before the next moon was half gone. Uncle Eikhram would have to manage them himself this season. Holdric grinned. The old man could stand to do some of his own work for a change.

For long years now this fold had been Holdric's charge. His uncle had sat with him the first few nights, but soon left him to his own. He'd been terrified at first. He was sure the ewes would birth and he'd not know what to do, he had started at every hoot and cry in the far wood. More, he had been haunted by his Ollna's nightmare stories of ghaestling stealing away anyone foolish enough to spend the night outside Heortlea's timber walls.

Many long nights he'd spent up here since, alone with the quiet herd. While his family sang and laughed around the hearth, he'd slept here alone lest wolf or worse come near. He would lie on the grass outside the little bothy, watch the stars wheel overhead, and listen to distant owls haunting the treeline.

Sometimes his Ollda would join him, and they would tell stories to each other under the star-signs above. Most nights Holdric watched alone. At first he'd been lonely, but these last few years he'd been glad just to not be under Uncle Eikhram's roof. In truth his uncle had felt the same. Mum still worried for him, but then she always worried.

Holdric looked ahead, up to the far fold walls, and he could not help but smile. The long walls of earth and piled stone were to most of Heortlea only a place for penning up the herds. But for all Holdric's boyhood, they had been burgh wall and ship, high bridge and fearsome wyrm. Here he had fought a thousand battles.

Sometimes the running sheep of the highfolds were the frightened families of Heahfeldt, begging his help. Sometimes they were the creatures of nightmare circling the walls. Always Holdric had been the brave hero. He would fight beside Kenndric and Eomud and his Da and they would hold the dike against the horde. He would slay the last foe, and he would hold his wooden warknife high and shout his victory. The herds would scatter at his cry and the day would be his.

He smiled at the memory. There were less happy memories here also, childhood battles against flesh and blood that ended not so well. But still he had fought. He always fought.

At last they crested the highfolds and he saw again the slopes of far Greatwatch. His favorite climbing tree loomed not far ahead, a great wind-twisted ash. Like Maesteald of song, Holdric once had felt its roots must sink to the deepest earth, that its highest leaves whispered with the stars.

He would sit high in the branches and watch as rangers began their journey to the far wild. He would watch long after they passed out of sight down the grassy road, waiting eager for the day it would be his turn… and now his day had come. He looked up into the leaves, some part of his spirit almost thinking to see his younger self. He smiled and turned for a last look back to the walls of home.

How strange that this was for them just another day. Maethbry would now be with Segli among the hens. Mum would be deep into the cleaning from breakfast. And Uncle Eikhram, he would be doing Holdric's chores on top of his own. Again Holdric smiled.

He turned to follow his band. Well ahead of him now, his cousin was laughing with the Thane's son over some shared joke. The others had left the highfold and crossed over the old burying ground beyond, past cairns of stone where old folk mourned and young children played, past sweet knots of green under the trees.

Holdric ran to catch them and caught up in the last far orchards. Boughs drooped heavy with late summer fruit, staunchfeather and greensweet and lush clover thick at their roots. The air was thick with the sweet-sour smell of fallen apple, and bees danced over thick meadow flowers.

With a pang it came to Holdric that he would miss the cider-making. He remembered old men with their baskets, and mothers on low ladders, and children running over the grass laughing with fruit spilling from their mouths. He remembered better the sweet fruit of the last summer, and the sweeter things he had shared with Frithi… those things he pushed from his mind.

What was a cidermaking next to his first ranging? The sun was too bright to linger long on sorrow, so he told himself. He had looked to this day for far too long.

At the orchard they filled their forage bags and took up a happy march. Eahstann started the walking verse, and Hwaetearn sang, and Aschbroc joined with a tuneless shout:

> *I've living green beneath my feet,*
> *the gyre-road blue above—*
> *Ever on I go, I am Huntsman!*

Holdric laughed in the warm sun as he bit into a fresh apple, tart juice running down his chin. For a sweet summer moment, the ranging felt almost a frolic.

> *Though flood wash stone I follow still,*
> *the Windslaed whispers all—*
> *Ever on I go, I am Huntsman!*

Merry they passed between the tall bounding poles, and merry they passed through the warding groves of aelfsthorn.

> *I rest in walls of ash and yew,*
> *my roofboards rived of stars—*
> *Ever on I go, I am Huntsman!*

The road wound on, and one by one the traces of men fell away. Open hills covered with high winter's grass gave way to the coppicewood, and the coppicewood yielded to the groomed trees of the timberlands. The wild crept slow upon them, and before long they had left Heortlea well behind. High trees of beech and ash towered overhead, the low places choked with alder and elm and sharp blackthorn. The last signs of men were all but gone.

Grass grew thick along the road, and deer scat littered the packed ox-ruts. Holdric's eyes followed the easy limbways of the earth, and there he saw the push of deer against a young oak, acorns still high and green and waiting. All as he knew it would be. *Know your quarry, know his aim.* So had Ollda said.

The sun had just reached nooning when they neared the Old Holloway. A quick wave from those ahead caught Holdric's eye—Kenndric passing down the handsign for heron-march. Holdric's feet took him to his place without thought, so many times had they done this. Eahstann hung behind him as they moved to one side, looking out far ahead and into the woods along their right. On their far left Hwaetearn and Aschbroc did the same. Far ahead stalked Kenndric, spying out the ground ahead. Wymud carried the rear, watching behind lest any overtake them. So he said anyhow, it seemed often as not the Second walked tail only to catch Holdric's missteps.

Kenndric led them away from the old road, up onto a wooded ridge overlooking the way below. He melted quiet through the brush into the trees, and each man followed in his place. They shadowed the Holloway long into the morning, sometimes crossing over to search the road and the far side.

By now the way below had become more deer path than road, a narrow trail that wound long through the wild to the Mearcwater a day's walk away. Fallen deadwood littered the road, and new summer branches ducked low into the path. Each time they crossed over Holdric searched the earth for signs of passing. Here he found marks of passing deer, there the quiet steps of hares. Once even boar, but not a wagon rut nor an oxtread was to be seen.

Nor were there signs of ghaestling. Holdric had not thought for ghaestling so close to home, but still he had taken his Ollda's great unease with this place. Not only for the ever-seeming darkness or the forlorn emptiness, but for the tales told in whispers when none were meant to hear. *Whitemoon* was all the word they gave it, a winter's night when ghaestling fell on homebound rangers weary and eager for rest.

Too many had fallen that night. It had been the last great wound of Heortlea, and the making of Kenndric as Huntslaed. Once Holdric had pried the story from his Ollda, once only. The telling had been hard.

Holdric was eager for the tale, and one night his boyish questions had grown too much to bear. Kenndric had dragged him by moonlight here to the Holloway, and pointed to the place each man had fallen, and told how each met his end. Never had Ollda's voice been so hard, never even in his worst scoldings.

Not long after Ollda Kenndric had faded from their lives. His cot grew cold, and at last it fell empty. Ollda had been called away, so Mum had said. The new Huntslaed had ever to answer the call of the Eorl. Perhaps it was even true… still Holdric had never quite believed it.

The day wore on. In time Kenndric led them from the old road and bent their path west towards the mountain of Greatwatch. The woods grew deep, the trees untouched by man. They passed beneath thick boughs of elm and beech, through ancient groves of oak and holly, under giants of tall pine. All about them the wood was deep and silent.

Holdric looked into every shadow with purpose, seeking out each place where watching eyes might hide. He searched, but he did so with only half a will. He knew this wood. He knew these trees as no one else could, save perhaps Kenndric only. Here it was his Ollda had brought him in happy times. Here had been his lessons of root and branch, of stalk and sign. And here had been his harder lessons too, lonely lessons of cold and hunger and desperate fear.

He'd roamed this place from the far Kingswood to the hidden elder groves only he had seen. Every tree, every stone felt as home to him as the green-laced paths of Heortlea. More, truly. The wood was not safe, that he knew too well. But neither was it home to ghaestling, not in his time. Still he searched. His feet moved soft over thick beds of pine needles, his breath passed quiet in the cool forest air. Slowly and without his meaning it, woldgast took him.

Woldgast, ancient inheritance from the Fellaesc folk. Gift and greatest help to rangers from Reodfel to old Hauhlond, all the way back to the time of Aranmaede Wulfdotr's kin. All that was Holdric faded away. The voice of his mind, his knowing of days past and days to come, all fell from him as old clothes. Only his full-seeing sight remained. He knew only the smell of cool woodland air, only the sound of the wind in high-swaying leaves.

On the far wind sang a sparrow. On the earth below was sign of ants marching over a mouldered leaf, sign of fox seeking her den. A soft breeze bore the faint scent of mouldered birch. He knew them all.

Midday came and went. The air cooled and shadows grew deep under the trees. The others spoke, but their words passed over him. His legs grew warm with work, but he paid no heed. His burdens weighed heavy, but he did not feel them.

Slowly the ground rose beneath his feet. Beech gave way to poplar and aspen and then to beech again. Shadows lengthened. The sun sank towards the west and the long day waned. There would be a halt soon, a last meal this side of the Mearcwater. The time for work of hands was near, and the time for speech and the making of plans. Some part of him mourned that.

A good ranger had need of both minds, Ollda said. The woldgast of deep knowing was not enough. He needed also his shaping-mind, a mind that could prise meaning loose from simple knowing, a mind that could craft purpose through time. Holdric knew it true, but still he held to the quiet so long as he could. He had been weeks without leaving this quiet, once. He missed that above all things… almost all things.

Their path bent upward, a sidle-step that wound around a low hill. Holdric did not have to guess his Ollda's aim. The little rise ahead would hold good sighting ground over the way they had traveled—it was almost time to stop. Holdric struggled to gather again the shreds of his shaping-mind. Bit by bit he found again his words and bound them tight.

He was almost ready when Ollda signed for the stop. With a shake of his head Holdric took his place. The old ranger knelt at watch as they passed behind, then all searched the ground and watched in silence a time. At last content they had not been followed, each man put down his burdens and set to work.

Hwaetearn joined Kenndric at guard, and Wymud went for water. Aschbroc cut free a small patch of the forest floor and began to dig a narrow pit for their cookfire. Holdric sought the ground for dry deadfall, and Eahstann gathered the kettles and collected fodder from each man for the meal. Aschbroc scowled as Eahstann called for his last apple, but he handed it over, as did the rest.

The heat of late afternoon hung in the still day. Holdric stretched his back as he worked, muscles tired but well-warmed. It felt good. He brought boughs of deadwood whole to the firepit, then sat and quietly carved the boughs to length. The chips he saved for kindling, setting them where they could not be lost. As he worked, Eahstann took the cut wood and began building the cookfire.

They worked smoothly together, the fruit of long years moving side by side. Silence held still in Holdric's mind. Few words passed, but even those sounded strange and harsh on his ears. Eahstann held out his hand. Holdric wordlessly passed over his small iron charbox and turned back to his work as his friend worked spark to flame.

Holdric glanced again out into the wild. Through a cover of brush he could just see their empty backtrail. The place had been well chosen.

He felt a touch at his shoulder and turned—Eahstann passed back his charbox. Holdric took it, smiling as he passed his thumb over the graven trees and stars. He'd almost lost this thing once, on one of his teaching treks with Ollda. The old ranger had rousted him in dead of night, and Holdric had barely managed to get his boots in hand before he was sent running barefoot up a rocky creek.

The lesson had cost him a cup, one sock, and almost the charbox. The treasure had turned up two days later in his pack. Holdric had always wondered if he had left it there himself, or if Ollda taking pity had gone back by moonlight for it. Ever since he'd kept it close.

Careful he tucked it away again.

He looked about the little camp. Wymud had taken Hwaetearn's place on watch, talking quietly with Kenndric as they watched over the wild. Hwaetearn had joined Aschbroc, and the two faced each other across a small leather gaming mat spread over a stone.

Eahstann fed the young licking fire a lean fodder of thin dry deadfall and looked up into the stretching branches of hazel above. The fire was hot, and the smoke thin. It would not draw eyes in this late afternoon. Even were the fire seen, here there was little risk it would tell that a ranging party stalked these woods. Few ranged so far from the folksteads, but it was not unknown. Fyrdmen would sometimes roam so far, and more rarely swineherds seeking mast, or the odd hungry soul looking for root or wild green.

Fire licked iron, and the smell of cooking food began to fill the little camp. Slowly Holdric began to ease into the gathering. Hwae-tearn threw up his hands with a laugh and stood. When Holdric looked over, Aschbroc waved for him to take his place at the game.

Holdric rose.

"Don't hope," warned Eahstann as he nestled the last of the apples in amongst the coals. Holdric waved him off and sat across the stone as Aschbroc set again the pieces.

Holdric's little pack of dark wooden wolves aimed to catch Aschbroc's stag of bright carved antler. At first the game went well. After several moves Holdric had driven the stag into a corner of the board. He moved a wolf close, his trap almost shut. Aschbroc smiled—his play had worked. He leapt his stag out and over the trap, darting off to the far edge of the board. A master might catch him now, but from most he'd be safely to ground in but a few more moves.

Holdric gave a cursing laugh. "Ah! I had you!"

Aschbroc grinned back. "You played it too safe, cousin. The stag shoots the board if you pack too tight. Another go?"

"Nah nah. You've beaten me enough for one day. Tomorrow."

"Nah, next time you're the stag." laughed Aschbroc, pointing, "and *you* face the wolves." He grinned and drew the leather cord taught around the little board, drawing it to a pouch around the loose pieces.

"I warned you," Eahstann said. He then tapped Holdric's leg and held out an empty hand. Holdric bent to fetch his bowl and handed it over, then fastened again his pack.

Back his cup came, near to overflowing. Holdric took it carefully in hand and tried not to look at the carved birds joined in flight about the rim. He took the first taste. His stomach growled, angry with hunger after the long day. He closed his eyes and basked in the taste of the hot heavy broth.

"Enjoy it while it lasts," cautioned Aschbroc. "Once we're over the water the old man will be stingy with fire."

Wymud's voice came without care as he dozed. "Better you soft boys sleep a little cold than call ghaestling in to warm you."

Aschbroc shrugged, turning again to his food. He took another bite, and his face changed. "What's in this?" he asked, pointing at the bowl with his spoon.

"Meadow dock," Eahstann answered. "Wraenleoth learned it to me."

"Wraenleoth?" Aschbroc grinned wide, the meat still showing in his mouth. "Who's Wraenleoth?"

Eahstann grinned but would give no more. "Not for you to know, hound." Still he smiled as he worked.

Aschbroc would not take the answer. He bounded close to the fire. "Tell us, bardling!"

Holdric grinned as they tussled, then turned to look on the others.

Wymud had settled in to his meal, blind to the rest of the world. He stabbed his wooden spoon into the bowl for each bite, paying no heed to the flecks of stew upon his beard. Further up the rise, Hwaetearn and Kenndric leaned close as they eyed the surrounding wood. Hwaetearn shared a quiet story over his shoulder, and Kenndric laughed.

Closer, Aschbroc still ribbed Eahstann, shoving at him with a taunting grin and demanding the tale. Holdric shook his head and turned again to his food. The beef was rich, the herb was sharp. The smell of baking apples drifted through the hazels above. He looked up and breathed in the late afternoon air. All was well.

Too soon the meal was done. Holdric's bones might have wished to stay near the comfort of the fire, but Kenndric had taught him too well. Already he itched to leave behind the smell of cooked meat.

By wild hearth sleep, by wild foe wake.

Each man bent quiet to his work. Some cleaned the kettles, others ended the fire and buried the coals. Holdric was set to hiding their sign, scattering crushed leaves and rightening bent brush. In what seemed an eyeblink, no trace of their passing remained.

They walked another league. The trees thinned as they neared a last crest, then they crossed over and saw at last the great Mearcwater. The wide river cut through the land below them, shining a dull pale silver in the fading day. Beyond was only the Mearcholt, deep and lonely and green. On the far side loomed the great mountain.

Greatwatch rose gentle at first from the water, a broad rising ground of wood and stone. The mount gathered strength as it rose, until high overhead great stone crags broke from the trees into low wisps of cloud.

Kenndric turned them west and made upriver for the mountain. The river below was quiet, a long-ruined quay of stone the only sign of men's passing. Ever west they went. Ever the mountain grew in their sight.

"Ruhnleod it was called once," Eahstann whispered. "When only the Lonely Ones lived there, before the time of kings."

Holdric could only stare at the great high crag, wondering on the mountain and the men who peopled it.

They moved in silence as the sun sank low and the Mearcwater faded from silver to pale quiet gold. At last Kenndric judged them close enough. He led them down the slope onto a thick wooded rise that looked over the water. There they searched for sign of passing foes, and found none. Here was good sight of the whole of the slope, and here was good ground to fight or flee. The place was well chosen.

Holdric used the last of the light to make ready. This far from Heortlea he would not cut young boughs to make his bed, but still he could gather fallen litter for his tick. His eyes followed a dry creek bed up the ridge. He thought a moment, then shifted his bedding over a small rise. He bent to gently take two low-hanging branches of pine and bound them in place with a small cord. Eahstann looked to him in question.

Holdric grinned. "When the night chills, the wind on these hills will shift. A cold draught will cut right down that draw." He pointed uphill. "And so…"—he bent another branch and tied it into place—"I want a nest."

Eahstann looked about, then moved his own bedding. Holdric pointed him to a good spot, then carried on with his work. "Since they're not cut, they'll heal. No dead branches to make an eye-sop after we leave."

Eahstann finished with his bedding and looked again at the rude windbreak. "Huntslaed really is your Ollda, yah?"

"He taught me much." Holdric finished the task and lowered himself to his bed. "This I learned myself."

"Aschbroc told me. How long were you out here?"

"Half a year," answered Holdric. "Almost. Ollda found me towards the end of Wolfing Moon."

Eahstann almost choked. "That deep into winter? Alone?"

Holdric shrugged. "I didn't say all went well. I was half dead with fever when Ollda found me."

"It must have been welcome to see him again."

At that Holdric was silent.

Finally Eahstann asked, "Why?"

Holdric didn't look up. "Things changed."

Eahstann waited, but no more words came. He looked again at the bound branches, and reached to shift one more. Holdric shook his head and pointed. "No, that one. The cold will spill around that rise there."

"Thank you," Eahstann said. He readied his blanket and made the last of his bed. "Sleep, I'll take firstwatch."

Holdric did not look up. "I'll be up a while. But thank you."

Eahstann shrugged and pulled his blanket up over his shoulders.

Darkness gathered under the branches, and Holdric looked out into the gloom. He was almost ready. A quick round to the trees, a nibble of Maethbry's honeycake to warm his bones and a bare swig of water to wash it down, that was enough. He gave his tick one last fluff, wrapped himself up in blanket and cloak, and leaned back to watch the sky. With his roof of bent boughs, his back resting on the yielding sack of maslin-corn for Ealdwyrc Torr, he found himself more at ease than most nights under Uncle Eikhrams's roof.

The sky above darkened into night. High overhead the three jewels of the summer sky broke through the grey one by one. A diving-bird called out over the water, low and lonely.

Through the far trees Holdric could just see the shadow of Greatwatch, the great bulk of the mountain black against the coming stars. He had spent a lifetime staring on those slopes, a lifetime dreaming of the high beacon and what lay beyond… and now he was here.

Good night, Ruhnleod.

Water splashed on stone.

He reached out to touch it, to feel again the cool water on living rock. His fingers traced the ancient spirals, and something gentle met his spirit. For a fleeting moment, he felt them all. For a fleeting moment, he felt *her*… but then she was gone. They were all gone.

But he was not alone. And he was not safe.

He looked up into the broken green across the pool. A shadow was there, huddled between the stones. Something lurked in the gloom. Something watched. He tried to make sense of what he saw, but between the stones was only shadow. Da had said it was so, and so it must be. But still he felt a being there, something cold and cruel, heavy with an ancient hunger, dark and long past knowing.

Cold water bathed his ankles. He stepped from the pool, he felt the soft pillow of pine needles beneath his bare feet. The deep quiet of the ancient forest fell over his spirit. The night air grew thick. All was close and still.

And yet it watched him, somewhere close behind. The shadow was near. It lingered at the edge of memory, just past grasping. He searched in the night, but all fell away before him as smoke.

He found himself then in the gloom of early morning. He walked through the grey mist of dream down the hillside, stumbling on until at last the mist fell away and he came to the Mearcwater.

Here the river ran broad and deep, dark below the mountain. Water ran cold over the wet stone of the riverbank. Almost he thought he could see again the trace of strange-spiraled carving on the stone, almost he thought he could hear the working songs in a tongue he never knew.

He knelt to look close, to feel the cold water run over ancient stone… but all was not water, and all was not cold. Blood flowed over the stones, thick and hot. Then all melted into the river, carried away until all warmth was lost and the water ran clear again.

Rain spat upon the stones. Wind blew over the face of the river.

He looked into the sky and saw only the mountain, a great dark shadow over the water. Clouds wreathed the sky, and from far away came the dull rumble of far thunder, thunder so deep he could feel it in his bones. The air writhed with the itching crackle of coming storm. His breath came fast…

Something was coming.

The morning came cold.

Footsteps sounded on the leaves behind him. Too late he braced for the blow. A solid kick landed against his ribs.

"Get *up*, you lazy hunch-walking laggards!" hissed Wymud.

Holdric coughed. He threw off his blanket and rubbed his bruised back with a curse. Wymud's steps moved on uncaring. Holdric ran his hands through his hair and rubbed his face. It was still full dark, but morning mist clung cold to his skin.

He looked up. High above, thin clouds crossed the sky. The moon had long since set, bright Aeforliht and the stars of the Wael-stan shone high overhead—greylight would not be long in coming. Hurriedly he pulled off his night woolens and reached for his walking clothes. Another kick sounded in the dark, answered by Aschbroc's groan.

The camp came quietly to life. Holdric buckled fast his sturdy fyrdknife and made himself ready. He worked swiftly, his fingers moving blind in the dark. He emptied his tick and laid it upon his blanket. He brushed clean his night woolens, stowed them in the tick, and folded all together. Then he reached inside his pack and felt over each thing within to make sure all was in its proper place. Content, he buckled tick and blanket into the fold of his pack. Wymud had scarce finished his circle of the sleeping band before Holdric's last strap was tugged tight.

They would be moving soon. Ollda would not want to be on the water in daylight, not when ghaestling might see their passing. Around him the others moved as shadows against the stars. A rustle sounded in the near dark, the sound of tossed branches and kicked leaves—Wymud scuffling in the leaves as he cleared sign of their camp. Holdric rose to join him in the work, scattering the flattened leaf clutter and feeling for crushed growth.

He did not hear Kenndric's step nearby. Most likely their Hunt-slaed already circled their camp, searching for anything that might have crept close. Yes, there… Holdric could just hear him further up the ridge, softly moving through the brush.

Holdric unbound the branches of his little nest and guided each back to its proper place. As he worked, the first grey light of morning rose under the trees. He could just see a looming shadow against a nearby oak, watching over the wild as they worked… that would be Hwaetearn. Nearer moved two others, their shadows black against the trees as they leaned into their heavy bows. Aschbroc and Eahstann warming wood and muscle against the coming day.

From the darkness Aschbroc's voice came quiet, a half-whisper Holdric could just hear, "You good brother?"

The shadow that was Eahstann blew with effort, leaning into another draw. "Can't wait."

Holdric looked over his own war gear in the dim light, heat growing in his belly.

Kenndric returned. As he passed, he breathed a quiet word of safety and moved to speak with Wymud. Wordless the others made ready. Holdric cast a last look about the gloom—a trained hunter would find tell of their stay, but no sign was left to draw the eye from afar. It would be enough.

He shouldered his gear and moved to follow after the others. The shadows were thick with heavy mist, and through a break in the trees Greatwatch loomed dark against the northern sky, huge and close.

They made their way down the last slope to the riverbank. The broken rocky ground was thick with wet tangled green, the dew grew heavy on their cloaks. In the dim fore-morning gloom Holdric smelled the river before he saw it. The air was thick with the smell of mud and fish, and from not far away came the leaping splash of a hungry trout.

Holdric turned his eyes to the far shore, hunting the gloom for what lay beyond. Through shreds of mist he could just make out the shadows of high trees on the far bank, dull and grey beneath the towering bulk of Greatwatch.

Further down the slope Wymud made for a pile of brush. Aschbroc moved to join him, and together they lifted up a crude mat of willow, covered over in dirt and wind-blown leaves. Wymud snapped and pointed—Holdric came to his side and together with Aschbroc raised the mat high.

Beneath, two boats lay side by side in a low hollow. The craft were timber-built, a broad man wide and fair of line. Wymud took up a branch and braced it into the earth to hold all in place, then moved to the first of the boats and pointed to Eahstann.

The harper joined their work and soon both boats were turned upright and set into the water. Short carved oars were bound inside the boats, and with them were coils of tarred rope. The age-darkened wood had a few new mouse scars, the insides were dirty with old cobwebs and old mouldered leaves, but Wymud seemed pleased enough.

The old man backed into the water and moved the first boat into the current, watching as the river split clean around the bow. For a moment the hard-faced man almost smiled. Then he looked up, the unspoken order cold on his face.

Holdric took a deep breath and unlimbered his gear. He'd never taken well to water. Still he set his pack carefully in the boat and braced himself upon the sides as he'd been taught. With a grunt he heaved himself aboard. The boat sloshed wildly, the splash sounding across the waters as he landed hard, but he held his seat. Wymud kept the boat from pitching over and shot Holdric a disgusted scowl.

Eahstann came next. He moved with more grace than Holdric, if still not clean enough for Wymud. Wymud came last, vaulting into the boat quick and clean and taking up his oar without a missed breath. He dug the oar into the mud to anchor them against the current as they waited.

The others brought down the covering mat, hastily cleaned the site, and mounted the second boat. Soon all were ready and they began their journey upriver. The gloom of greylight fell away, and before long it seemed as if they skimmed through cloud. Only the thick smell of water and the whisper of oars told of the river beneath.

The trees of the far shore loomed dark and cold through the shrouding mist, the waters chill through the wet timbers. In time broad grey stones rose out of the mist before them. Behind, Holdric heard the crack of knuckles and turned. Eahstann's eyes were on the broad rock of the shore, his face grim. Holdric raised his eyes in question, but Eahstann shook his head. Holdric shrugged and looked again to the far shore.

For all the dread stories of the Mearcholt, from here the wood looked just the same. The trees were just as dark, the earth just as wet. Nothing sundered the two woods but mist and water, and yet the sundering felt no less real. From somewhere upriver came the splash of another leaping fish, and not long after the low call of a diving-bird.

Wymud pushed them hard, and Holdric leaned into his oar. The mist died quietly away as they raced against the morning, heaving against the river until at last Wymud pointed the bow towards shore.

There they pulled out of the current into a stony lee. Holdric pushed himself from the boat, drawing another scowl from Wymud as his feet splashed in the water. Eahstann was silent, his face stone as he crept from the swaying boat.

They had crossed over.

CHAPTER FOUR
Greatwatch

Kenndric and Aschbroc climbed the high bank. There they each set arrow to string and made watch while the others pulled the boats to shore. Holdric stood opposite the boat from Wymud and heaved on the boat's edge. The keel dragged a deep gash into the mud of the riverbank.

Wymud cursed him. "*Lift*, you worthless hollow-pate! We're not on a garden walk!"

Holdric burned, but knelt lower. He got beneath the timbers and heaved for all he was worth. His feet sank into cold grainy mud, the boat slick and heavy in his grasp. Heaving, he dragged the keel from the mud as Eahstann moved to his side. Together they lifted the boat up and onto dry ground. Wymud scowled. He jerked his head towards a low hollow just up the bank.

They lashed down the oars and water gear, quickly brushed off the boats, and settled them upturned into the hollow. Wymud led them in collecting dead brush and reeds to cover over the craft.

At last Wymud backed away to look over the work. He glanced at Holdric, then to the deep scars in the riverbank. His scowl needed no words. Holdric and Eahstann set to clearing their sign. They smoothed over the tear in the muddy bank and drew straight again the crushed river grass.

They worked fast against the swift-rising sun. Holdric was sticky with sweat before they were done, and his back ached from the work. Wymud at last gave a grudging nod. Holdric backed with care from the bank lest he be sent back to wipe away his own traces.

Wymud's grim eyes never left him. Then the old man's voice came gruff—"Marks?"

Holdric thought, looking through the thin morning mist to the far shore. "Near, those two large stones, by the twin-trunked pine. Far, that ash." He pointed higher up the far ridge. "… the tall one with the wind-broken crown."

Wymud bent his head to look. He gave a grudging grunt. "Good enough. Don't come running back alone."

Holdric bristled, but he held his tongue. "Yah, Second."

Kenndric turned from watching the heights above and passed down the sign for rest.

"Fill your skins quick, take a breath," said Wymud. "We leave before the sun tops the trees."

Eahstann and Holdric moved together to the water's edge and knelt beneath a great stone rising from the bank. Holdric watched first, looking out over the river as Eahstann filled his skin. Eahstann's face was dark as he worked.

The harper gazed unseeing into the mist, a whispered verse on his lips. With a last look downriver he stoppered his waterskin, slung it into place, and readied his bow. Holdric took his place at the water. The river flowed cold over his fingers, strangely clear.

Too soon they had to move again. The mist had burned away with the dawn, but still the air hung thick and wet over the bank. The day would be hot. Holdric shrugged at the sweat under his woolens and lifted his heavy burden to his shoulders.

They passed deeper into the trees, and before the first soft blue of morning they were well on their way. The ground was steep as they climbed away from the river. They moved over green-choked stones and around the thick elms of the near wood. The way was hard, but Holdric was well-used to the work. It felt good to feel his legs beneath him.

They crested the first slope and met a fleeting taste of cool air off the high mountain. Holdric could just see the peak of Greatwatch over the high branches, and his heart jumped at the sight. Whatever else was to come, he stood now among those men who'd crossed the Mearcwater. Uncle Eikhram could not say that. He turned to share a grin with Eahstann. Eahstann's answering smile was weak, but it came. Together they found their place on the wing and took up again their work.

Holdric hefted his short woodsman's spear. He felt the weight of the fyrdknife upon his hip, the heavy leather on his body and the shrouding cloak upon his shoulders. He felt himself a ranger true.

Woldgast would not come full upon him as they walked, but traces of it drifted through his mind. A single woodmouse perched on a fallen ash froze and watched as they passed by. Further out, a small finch left its branch in a tight flurry of wings.

Nothing else moved. The air under the trees was still. Far ahead, Holdric could just see his Ollda Kenndric through the trees. Some-times the Huntslaed was near, sometimes he would range out of sight far ahead, then wait for the band to catch up and sign back his will.

The dull sameness of it all sat odd in Holdric's belly. All his life Holdric had known that one day he would join these men. Some days he had ached for the wanting of it, others he couldn't sleep for the dread. But now that he was here, he found the ease of it strange. These woods were little different from the wilds past Heortlea. The ways and signs of the ranging were those his Ollda had taught him as a boy, far past even his first waking memory. He was with the rangers now, and even with his burdens he kept their pace, and he knew their work—his work now. It felt good.

Ahead was a tall green ash, leaves pale and faded in the late summer sun… it seemed familiar. Holdric looked back, looking again over the ground they had walked. Yes, they had been here earlier in the morning. Kenndric had looped them across their own trail. Already the Huntslaed was wary of a chase. The old ranger held them there long, peering back the way they had come.

As Eahstann watched the far trees, Holdric searched the ground for sign. There was his cousin Aschbroc's careful step, there the thaneling Hwaetearn's too-heavy tread. Looking farther Holdric found his own faint sign, and Eahstann's also. Kenndric's broad-footed stride he found only by seeking Wymud's step first.

There was no other sign to be found. For all Holdric could see they were alone. He looked up. The Huntslaed looked also content, and soon they moved on again. Their path wandered wide over the wild shore, and Kenndric crossed over their trail twice more over the morning. Holdric had thought they would reach the foot of Greatwatch by midmorning, but it was past noon before they began at last the climb.

The land rose slowly at first, Holdric scarcely noted the slope. Still it was not long before he was panting under the weight of his load. He knew he should not lean on his spear. Too often Wymud had cursed him for the deep scars in the earth he'd left on their muster walks, sign any child could follow. But even so, time and again Holdric caught himself just before taking his heavy weight on the ashen shaft, and time and again he cursed and heaved himself up on his burning legs.

As they climbed Holdric began to see sign of men. At first he saw only tracks. The footfalls were as well placed as his own, and showed care not to over-wear any one way. Often it looked that the men of the mountain took the harder path, the better to hide their steps from careful eyes. Still these men had no easier time on these slopes than Holdric himself. Here he saw a slide, there a deep gouge in the earth where a heavy-laden man had stopped a fall.

Holdric smiled to see the sign. So often had he made the same, stumbling up the wooded hills past the timberlands. As a boy he'd asked his Ollda teach him the art of sign-following. Kenndric had only laughed and told Holdric that the art was already his.

"Watch your own feet, Feorson," his Ollda had said. "Know your own feet and you know another's." The seeing had not always come so easily as the words, but it had come sure.

In time the signs became surer yet. There was bare ground where deadwood should be, and highbriar bare of foraged fruit. They drew near the common haunts of the Greatwatch men. Kenndric began to slow, and Holdric looked up just as his Ollda raised a hand. How long they waited he was not sure, it seemed an age… then a flash of moving shadow caught his eye.

Holdric forced himself to remain still. Another rush of grey moved quick through the trees, then was gone. His neck prickled under the watching eye. They waited long in silence.

At last a tall man walked out of the woods and strode to Kenndric. The two men looked much alike. The stranger wore a cloak the same grey-green as Kenndric's own, and he bore a very like greatbow of yew. A shrouded calling horn hung to one side, and a long warknife to the other.

He pulled back his hood and smiled through a thick black beard. "Kenndric my friend, your pack has grown!"

"The better to smell out your games Hyrtwis," Kenndric said.

They embraced, then the ranger of the mountain paused to look on their band. His gaze fell on Holdric, though Holdric could not say whether those keen eyes judged his mettle or only the weight of grain upon his back.

"Your Hounds grow younger," the ranger finally said.

"You grow older," Kenndric answered.

Hyrtwis laughed, and Kenndric laughed with him. Soon the man led them further up the mountain. Grey shadows moved still upon their flanks. How many they numbered Holdric could not say, for he could never quite lay eyes on them. Only the faint rustle of brush and the odd flash of grey told of their presence at all, and even that Holdric felt was meant to be seen. These men of Greatwatch knew their craft well.

At last the trees thinned and Holdric climbed out onto the open rocks. Their hidden guard remained behind in the treeline, and Kenndric's band followed Hyrtwis quietly in single order. Holdric watched the high stones above as they climbed, sure of other eyes he could not yet see.

He wondered how many dwelled here. All his days, Greatwatch had seemed almost more a dream than a real dwelling place of men. Now with the stone of the mountain under his feet, the nature of the forlorn place struck home.

As heavy as his burden of grain was upon his shoulders, he was sure that all his band carried up the mountain would be thin rations indeed for more than a handful of men, especially once winter winds brought winter cold. Could there be a dozen, at the most? Likely less. Ranging meat hunters or no, no great host could last long in this place. Nor could these men trust overmuch to stealth, their beacon lay where it lay. Holdric thought on the place as he climbed.

Their way was hard, and the path steep. Small white blooms of seolfrenblos nestled between the stones and wind howled in his ears. More than once he looked out over empty air to see falcons dance in the wind below. Time and again he had to gingerly pick his way along a narrow plank set over a deep gap, or mount up a steep ladder of timber.

That answered his question to a part. If ghaestling were seen, ladders would be pulled up, bridges kicked into empty air—but that would not be enough. Surely there were small fastnesses above where a good man with a strong bow could rain arrows on those below. Holdric thought he could make out a few of the little nests, and knew there must be more beyond his sight. But stones could be climbed, chasms bridged anew, arrows answered…then the knowing came. All these men could do was delay.

The thought struck him cold. There was no hope of holding this place, not if the men here be put to true test. Should ghaestling make it so far as Greatwatch unseen, all the arms of these high rangers were only to win enough time for their firekeeper to lay torch to timber. He did not wish to think overmuch on what must come after.

At last he neared the top. He heaved himself up a ledge of stone, and stood with trembling legs on the wide top of the mountain. A lifetime of wishing, and here he was.

The broad heights rose shallow for the better part of a corn-furrow's length, then broke hard again to the high peak. The ground here was mostly stone, though dry grass fought through the cracks of earth, and little knots of brush clung where they could. Cold wind bit sharp at his ears. He hurried to catch up as his band followed Hyrtwis up the last of the mountain.

The sky was so sharp, so aching-blue. He felt almost in the very branches of Maesteald the world-tree itself, and his heart leapt for the joy of it. He looked behind, and there the Mearcwater stretched silver through trees far past seeing. Shreds of cloud hung low over the wood beyond, each rolling hill fainter than the next until at last Holdric could not be sure whether he looked on mountain or cloud. Still he fancied he could just see the highfolds, and the wide green where once he'd sat dreaming of climbing to this very place. He smiled at the thought. Too soon, he turned to hurry after his band.

The wind was harsh on the high stone. He fought his way to the small rockhouse near the top, a low hall of rough-piled stone. The thin smell of woodsmoke promised fire within. Near the rockhouse were stacked cuts of timber, carefully laid beneath a shelter of stone. An old man worked there at splitting rough shakes from the wood. For a moment, they locked eyes—then a voice called to Holdric from within the rockhouse. He nodded to the old man and ducked through the low door.

Even in the high air, the little hall was heavy with the smell of sweat and festering flesh. Small windows gave little light, but there was enough to tell the tale: a man tossed weakly on a rough, low bunk. The man's leg was braced with splints of scavenged wood, his head was bound and his breath came ragged, his blue eyes cast about the little room unseeing. A second man bent over his wounds, reaching to pick free the crusted bandage at the man's head. The wounded man pushed him away, his voice weak and shallow.

"Get off!" He pushed feebly at the helping man's hands. "Get off me!"

Hyrtwis watched all. He raised his tired eyes from the wounded man as Holdric came inside.

"Welcome to the top of the world," the head ranger sighed.

Holdric fumbled for the words of greeting. "I… Life to your home, friend Watchlaed."

Hyrtwis' smile came, but it was grim now, and he did not answer. For a breath they stood in silence.

"How came he to be injured?" Holdric asked, fumbling for words.

Hyrtwis eyed Holdric as if he were simple. "He fell."

The leechman caring for the wounded man looked up. "Our men found him broken on the rocks. He and Heggort both."

Aschbroc looked up from the far corner of the hall, where he had been filling the watchmen's mealchest from his burden sack.

"Heggort also?" asked Aschbroc. "Where is he?"

"Heggort also," answered the leechman. "Dead."

Kenndric rose and reached for Holdric's burden sack and he passed it to Aschbroc without a word. He sat down at the hearth opposite the Watchlaed.

"You've had a hard time of it."

"Yah. That we have."

Hyrtwis reached for the hot kettle and passed them earthen mugs of a high mountain tea. Holdric bowed his head in thanks as he took his cup. The tea was sweet with some mountain herb he did not know. The brew was weak, but on this high peak even the hot water was a hard-bought gift.

The wounded man cried out as he rolled in his bunk.

Hyrtwis looked to Kenndric. "We were set by storms last week."

"I remember," Kenndric said. "I'd wondered how you fared."

"Well at first," answered Hyrtwis. "But when Wulfhert and Heggort came not back from watch, Dunnoc went after them. You see what he found."

"*Get away from him!*" screamed the wounded man. "*Get away!*"

Kenndric looked to Hyrtwis, eyebrows raised.

The ranger sighed. "He thinks he met his grudgeghaest on the rocks… or so we guess from his words."

Kenndric lowered his cup. "What?"

"I've had my men search that stretch of mountain, they've found no sign to vouch the tale. Still they look. Still we guard."

"You think the tale true?"

"I don't know," Hyrtwis said. "Wulfhert's word is good, and his eyes also. But his mind is gone, until he heals. If he heals."

"Get off! *Get away!*" the wounded man cried again. The leech-man eased back to let wounded man calm.

For long moments all were quiet, each lost in his own thoughts. It was Hyrtwis that broke the quiet. "Tell me happier news, Huntslaed" the ranger said. "How fare things in Heortlea?"

Kenndric thought a moment over his cup. "A cool summer, and a wet one. The hay is high, but the Thane fears the late rain will hurt the corn. A lean winter, he thinks, but we should have enough." At that he caught Hyrtwis' eye. "As will you. More than enough. Which reminds me…"

Kenndric bent to his bag and fished out a bag made of rough wildcloth. He tossed it across the narrow room. Hyrtwis caught it, then smelled deep of the herb within.

"I thank you, friend." He tossed the bag to his man, who tucked it carefully away with a clatter of pots.

"What of Brukli?" asked Hyrtwis at last. "Has her man finally given her that boy she wanted?"

"Fat and happy," answered Kenndric. "The babe looks not unlike yourself, come to think on it."

Hyrtwis smirked. "Not my doing, I've not crossed the Mearcwater this last year. Tell me of Acstan then, how fares he?"

"Still squabbling about that fool ditching. His water drowned half of Wydthram's green patch, and Wydthram is sure the dig was all for spite."

Hyrtwis shook his head. "Those two haven't had a day's peace in a crow's age."

"Nor are they likely to," said Kenndric with a sigh. "It's a wonder the Thane hasn't hanged them both."

Hwaetearn's laugh came across the little hall. "He's been tempted."

Hyrtwis laughed also, his weary face showing at last some peace.

Kenndric eyed him. "How fare you, Hyrtwis? Tell me true."

Hyrtwis sighed. "I lost a man, Kenndric. And worse. These men are hard, but they've faced much. Our stores are full again, thanks to you. Our leechman is good as any. But losing two men… we're spread thin. Last week's storm blew down the timbers over the old pyre, and wind has scattered what was left. We were fixing that when—well, as you see. I've another man sick on the east slope, and all those not at watch I have busy cutting and hauling timber.

"They're tired, Kenndric."

Kenndric nodded quietly. "How can we help?"

Hyrtwis held his peace a moment, weighing how much he could ask. His eyes moved over Kenndric's band.

"Can you spare men?"

Holdric's stomach dropped, but already his Ollda was shaking his head.

"Not for more than the day," Kenndric said. "I need them in the Mearcholt. But we make first for Ealdwyrc Torr. I'll have Stalmaht send you all he can spare. Can you stand the week?"

Hyrtwis cursed. "A man I've sent already to the Torr." Then he sighed, and ran his fingers through his beard. He looked to Kenndric, his face grim. "Forgive me brother, I should not have asked. My men have made it this long, they have another week in them."

The wounded man groaned again. The leechman wiped at the sweat on his brow.

Hwaetearn said, "When we come again to Heortlea I will ask the Thane my father to send who he can, and we will send word and aid to your man's kin. What more?"

"Tar," Hyrtwis answered quick. "We've had no chance to burn our own, and have used up our last. Nails and rope we need less, but I should like to have again what has been used. And each man with bread at least enough for himself, of course."

"You will have all," pledged Hwaetearn.

Kenndric held out his hand. "And you have us the afternoon. Put us to work, friend."

The talk was fast, and soon each man was tasked.

Holdric stepped from the low house into the biting wind. He pulled his cloak tight against the cold and followed the others onto broad open stone. Kenndric broke them into working bands, giving each to taskmasters amongst the Greatwatch men. Holdric he gave to Aesculf, old master of the mountain.

Aesculf looked over Holdric and seemed content. The old man bade him bear a great bundle of timber shakes, fresh-split and reeking of pine. Holdric shouldered the load as Aesculf took up his tools, then the old man started over the stones and bid Holdric follow.

The way was hard, a worn goat path that wound through the rocks below the mountain crest. They passed through a short stand of trees, scraggled spruce and fir that clung stubbornly to life through deep cracks in the grey rock. Far ahead Holdric saw the bright color of a single well-omened rowan tree, high up on an open slope.

Old Aesculf chattered the whole of the way over the mountain. The old man was glad for a new soul to talk with, and the words tumbled from his tongue. Once he had led the men of Greatwatch, but those days were now long past. Even when age had forced him to pass on the Watchlaed's ring, he could not bear to leave the mountain. So long had he lived here that he had no home below to return to.

"Besides," he had said, "I like the quiet."

Holdric looked out on the too-wide sky, to lands small and lost in the haze of distant cloud. Aesculf turned up another path, this one bending across the sharp crest of the mountain. The way was little used and narrow, in places storm-washed and crumbling. Holdric shifted the weight on his back and set his feet with care. Too easily could he see how poor Wulfhert had lost his footing.

Holdric looked down and shivered. Far below, broken scree covered the sharp slopes. Wulfhert was lucky still to live, if live he would. The wounded ranger had looked strong, but Holdric had seen wound-fever take strong men before.

The way at last opened out onto a narrow table of stone. As they climbed, the last scraggled trees fell away and Holdric could see again from sky to sky. Wind pulled at his cloak, and he measured his step with care as he climbed out onto the rocks. They had reached the beacon.

A pyre stood here—or rather, once it had. The piled stones of the beacon mound still stood, but the pyre itself had tumbled to earth, and with it the pyre's sheltering roof. Broken wood lay scattered, blown over the mountainside by the winds. Fresh beams had been raised to shelter a new pyre, but they were bare timber open to the sky.

At Aesculf's sign, Holdric clambered up the stones and pulled himself up onto the beams above. The fresh-cut frame swayed under his weight as he gained the top. He seized tight to the timber, his heart beating wild as the beams bent out over deep empty sky and shattering rocks below.

He held still, steadying himself on the frame. Aesculf looked up at him with an untroubled smile, then passed him an auger of iron and the first shake.

Holdric carefully braced himself with his feet and began to bore the holes for the first of the shakes. His stomach lurched as he felt the beams beneath him shift in their footings as he worked. His mind ached for anything to take his mind from the rocks below.

He looked to the old man. "Why a second pyre?"

Aesculf grinned. "Never hold only to a single chance, young man. Your foe will not."

He passed up fresh-cut pins and a mallet.

Holdric struck the first blow on the pin and the frame shivered beneath him. He hooked an ankle on the beam and drove the pin home. Another pin and—

One done.

"This pyre is an old one," Aesculf carried on. "We keep it still against the worst. If the other be lost, some hope will yet live. Like you men of the far wood, we also must be eyes in the darkness. Men cannot fight what they cannot see."

He passed up another shake. Holdric set it in place and began the next hole.

Men of the far wood… Holdric grinned. He had never thought his rangering would begin with the swing of a mallet. The wind stung his face as he worked. He looked again out into the distance, far to the north and east. Something there troubled him, but he could not say why. A too-familiar hump of land lay green and broad against the sky, hanging in his mind like a half-remembered dream.

The old man followed his gaze, his eyes also resting long on the far slope. "You're too young to know that place of ill-omen."

The sight held Holdric's spirit. He knew it somehow, a broad stretch of green, rising in the blue… "That's Heahfeldt?"

A troubled look crossed the man's face. "It is." He turned back to his tools and passed up another shake. "Or rather, it was."

The far-away fields did not look ill-omened in the late summer sun. It seemed to Holdric he could almost see the tall swaying grass, almost smell the broad summer folds. "Were you on watch that night?" he asked.

"I was. I knew not what I saw at first. It seemed a new star, or that sweet Aeforliht had lost her way…" Aesculf looked lost in memory as he told the tale. "When I came to myself, I knew I must be looking on their beacon, that they had seen far danger. Or so I thought it must be. But the fire grew, the whole hillside blazed, it seemed the sun rose in the north. I thought almost I could hear…"

He stopped. Holdric had not broken his gaze.

"Forgive me young Huntsman. Please have patience with an old man's stories. Have I troubled you?"

Holdric shook his head. "No! No, Elder. I only… I had kin there."

The old man stopped his work and turned to look closely at Holdric. His watery eyes grew keen, and he studied hard the shape of Holdric's face. A shadow seemed to cross over the old man, and for a moment his jaw set hard and his eyes turned cold. Then the old man seemed to choose something within, and whatever shadow had held his spirit passed over.

"Many of us did," he said. The words were not unkind, but they were the last he spoke.

The wind picked up again, sharp and chill as it raked over the stones. Holdric set the next shake in place and set again to his work.

When at last all was done, Holdric's band gathered again on the heights. Farewells were said, and as the day burned late they made their tired way back down the mountain. Holdric and Eahstann walked together, each quiet in his own thoughts.

They followed a narrow path through the rocks, the others just in sight ahead and behind. The light raked across the rocks as the sun sank low. Dusk would be upon them well before they reached the valley. They would be sleeping on the mountain.

Holdric eased himself around an outcrop, then looked down. They were still far above the trees. In the best of times the climb would be a hard one, but at least they had left their heavy burden sacks behind. A spray of kicked dust across a stone caught his eye. He spared a quick glance, but most of the sign had been lost in the passing of beast and man.

Eahstann saw him pause. "What see you?"

Holdric shrugged. "Mountain goat. Us. Them." He pointed to the spray of dust. "Aschbroc and Hwaetearn there, you can see the heel of his boot."

His gaze moved to the broken rocks above, searching for other paths that might have sight over them. Somewhere over the high slope was the beacon roof he had built, but even craning his head he could not see it from where they stood.

Eahstann followed his eyes. "What did they have you doing up there?"

Holdric shrugged. "Building again a beacon pyre with old Aesculf."

Eahstann shook his head. "I'm surprised every time I see the old man here. I thought he'd have been buried on the mountain years ago."

"He seemed spry enough to me," Holdric answered. He was quiet a moment, chewing on his words. "I think he saw my father in me," he said at last.

Eahstann thought. "Aesculf is kin to the Acstead-folk," the harper said, "and few of them are left. But I'd not worry, Watchlaed Hyrtwis weighs each man on his own. He has to. Oh!"—he fumbled in his forage bag and drew out a small handful of small red highberries— "I found these down on the rocks."

Holdric held out a hand for a share and popped them in his mouth. They burst sharp and sweet, then his tongue puckered with sour as the berries took hold. He screwed up his face and shook his head.

Eahstann laughed, then choked on the taste himself. "Remember the hedge past Buckstod's Hill?" he asked as he found his voice again. "How Frithwyn said she hated these?"

"Kept sneaking more though," laughed Holdric.

"Kept sneaking more of *yours*, you mean," Eahstann said with a grin. "How is she? Aschbroc said—"

"Doesn't matter," Holdric said, perhaps too quickly. "I've asked Ollda about giving Oath to Eomud."

Eahstann eyed him. "That's a hard road, brother."

"Maybe I like the quiet."

Eahstann held his silence. He seemed almost to answer, but Holdric spoke first. "Now tell me of Wraenleoth!"

Eahstann groaned. "You also?"

"Well?"

Eahstann sighed, and Holdric laughed. At last Eahstann gave in. "She is a fair thing of the Ettenmede," he answered. "And she is high of spirit and sweetly shaped."

"And?"

"And she sings fair in the moonlight. And she is better company than you."

"Only sings?"

Eahstann grinned. "Sometimes not," he allowed, "but tell not her father, nor her mother, nor her kin. They think still we wait for their word."

Holdric grinned. "You have my word, brother."

They came around a turn in the rock and the far valley beyond came into sight. The mountain fell away before them in a steep slope of bare stone, and beyond stretched only the wide Mearcholt. Holdric stood stunned at the sight of it.

He could just see the far crest where rose Ealdwyrc Torr. Between the high tower and where he stood, there were no things of living man. There were no cleared fields, no folds of tame beasts, only forest, deep and thick and dark, wood unbroken so far as he could see. And somewhere beyond even these empty woods lay the Hyssestead, of which he had only stories. Still he felt already he knew the land below. He could almost feel the soft earth beneath his feet, almost smell the thick scent of its wood. His hunter's blood rose hot and eager. He ached to be under those trees, to stalk the shadowed paths beneath. He smiled in the mountain breeze and he quickened his step.

The narrow path wound slowly down, broken stone giving way to thin soil and stubborn scrubby green. As the shadows grew long, they entered the high thin pine of the mountain highlands. The gold of late afternoon gave way to the grey of evening, the wind chill at their backs, and still they did not stop.

At last they passed through thick pines onto a wooded mountain spur. Before them lay a scramble of broken rock, and beyond that only empty air over the wood below.

"Take your places!" Wymud gave him a shove as he came up behind. They had reached the end of the spur. Just before the edge, a tumble of large stones surrounded a low shallow in the earth. This then would be their hide. They would go no farther today.

Holdric followed Eahstann to one edge of the broad shallow, and there they found their rest. Holdric shrugged loose his burdens and sat heavy against the stones. He rubbed his shoulders as he looked over his place. The stones would shelter them well enough from the wind, and better still from any watching eyes below.

Kenndric walked among them, looking over each man in his place and checking their sighting-lanes down the mountain. When he came to Holdric's side he pointed to a narrow goat trail high up the rocks above. Holdric quietly moved to gain a better sight of the path.

Kenndric nodded, then spoke low, "No fire, no light." He clapped Holdric's shoulder and moved on.

Holdric pulled free his cloak and blanket. Already the air was chill, and wind whistled high in the rocks above. The night would be cold.

He looked once more over his place, it was well suited for a hide. He paused… it seemed to him almost *too* well suited. There was no order he could see to the rocks, this was no well of graven sky stones. Still it seemed the great boulders were too well placed for this watching-place to have simply fallen into their beds. And yet a deep crust of rime told that if the stones had been moved, it must have been very long ago.

He puzzled, he could not be sure. The whole place seemed to whisper of subtle art. Were there more hides like this, sown like fox dens across the mountain? He had to think so. But not work of the Greatwatch men, they had not been here so long.

He shook his head of questions, there was little time left to him before night and he had one last task for what fading light was left. He felt over his place with his hands and looked over the ground below, knotting each fold of the ground to his memory while he could. *There* was where a foe might best creep upon the shallow hide. He bound the direction in his mind by the shape of the stone behind him. *There* was a narrow path of flight should the worst come, over scree to his left and down the slope until the heel-shaped rock. Before dark fell, he knew well his place.

Wymud walked a last circle around their hide in the deepening gloom. The air was clear and sharp, and high overhead cold wind whistled over the rocks. Holdric shivered at the sound.

He unbuckled his pack and sought for food to warm his bones before the hard chill fell. With a smile his fingers landed on one of Maethbry's bound little packets of honeycake. That would do. He drew his belt knife and sawed at the string that bound the packet closed.

A shadow fell over him. He looked up to see Wymud's shape looming above. The old man's eyes fell on Holdric's little knife.

"Give it to me," he said.

Warily Holdric handed up the blade.

Wymud tested the edge against his thumb and scowled in the dying light.

"I told you to sharpen it."

Holdric made to answer, but Wymud cut him off with a curse. He huffed and turned into the night, Holdric's knife in hand. Holdric looked to Eahstann as he left. Eahstann shrugged.

"It *is* sharp," Holdric cursed under his breath. "Just as Ollda showed me."

Eahstann's chuckle came out from the gathering dark. "Wymud doesn't think your Ollda wields a stone any better. Just wait."

Holdric grumbled and pulled at the strings of the cake. Eahstann dug in his own pack, and together they took their evening meal in silence. As they ate, the last of the light died away. Soon they were in full dark. Holdric looked up over his shoulder, up into the black where Ollda had pointed out the trail above.

"Did Wulfhert say anything of sense?" he asked at last.

Eahstann shifted in the dark. "Little that I heard… I was out fetching wyrt and flower for their leechman most of the day. What I did hear held little sense." The harper sighed.

"He spoke more of his grudgeghaest, or so he called it. A hooded shadow on the rocks, calling his name."

"Do you think it true?" asked Holdric.

Eahstann shrugged. "He was mad with fever. When he even saw I was there, he took me for his friend who tumbled."

"Huntslaed seems to take it as warning," Holdric said.

"Huntslaed is wary, he and Wymud both. Wulfhert would not be the first to miss his step on this rock, nor to see things in a fever."

Holdric stared into the night. "Perhaps."

"Have you seen sign?" asked Eahstann.

Holdric cursed. "None to speak of. But we moved too fast to do more than glance."

Eahstann shifted under his blanket.

"Moving fast or moving slow matters little," he said. "I have tended such wounds with Master Uhlseid. Wulfhert will walk with Ealdorholt, no matter the aid we fetch."

Holdric stared into the gloom. He had no answer.

Full dark settled over them, and the stars came alive one by one. They finished their eating in silence. A sinking chill worked its way up from the rocks and Holdric moved his pack beneath him. In time a quiet step came towards them over the rocks—cousin Aschbroc's step.

"Wymud sends you something," Aschbroc hissed. "Reach up."

Holdric reached blind into the dark. Aschbroc found his wrist by feel, then placed the familiar haft of Holdric's belt knife into his hand.

"Take care," warned Aschbroc. "Wymud leaves a wicked edge."

Holdric carefully tested the blade with his thumb, then cursed as the steel bit.

Aschbroc's laugh came from the darkness as he crept away. "I told you."

Holdric carefully sheathed the knife again, sucking his thumb and shaking it to clear the sting.

He pulled his blanket closer about his shoulders. Eahstann shivered beside him as they sat shoulder to shoulder against the cold. Holdric gazed up into the dark above, and out over the valley below. In time Eahstann's breath slowed into sleep.

The moon rose low behind the mountain, dim grey light washed over the rolling hills below. The trees seemed as silver waves on a forgotten sea. Above all shone bright Wegliht, homecoming star. Holdric's spirit stilled. He watched in long silence as the stars wheeled above, until at last his watch was done and he could let sleep take him.

The bush was full and darkest green, the small red berries thick under his hand. She laughed. He turned to look on her, and she smiled into his eyes.

Such a pretty little bird.

A teasing smile crossed her face as she leaned close. Hungry he reached for her. Quick she popped a berry into his mouth, sharp and sour. His tongue curdled and he shook his head. She laughed and backed away again. This time he caught her and pulled her near.

She laughed and she kissed his face, kisses soft and sweet and swift. He felt the spit of rain upon his neck. A shiver ran cold down his spine, he turned only away for a moment… then she was gone. The air was cold and empty where she had been.

Sharp wind came, and chill sleet followed. He looked to the earth. The dropped berries looked red upon the white snow, red as a spray of coughed blood. Yes, that was right, that was as he remembered. He was dying. The winter birds had sung, their mercy-mead had run sweet.

But that was not how it had been. He had died on a summer night, not on a winter day. In the winter, Ollda had come. Ollda had built him a fire, Ollda had built him a fire and carried him home… but now that warmth was gone. Gone to some place he did not know.

He looked up, out far into night, and there he saw the fire. High and far away it burned, fierce and bright against the night sky, a small far sun deep in a well of dark. But it was so far away, and it was so cold, and he could not reach it.

He shivered on the mountainside as he watched. Others watched with him, shadows sitting near beside him in the night. Silent whispered verses passed over the stones, verses of calm knowing. Then all the tongues were silent, and he was alone.

He stared into the quiet fire unspeaking. Something called to him from that far light. Something far away and sad and cold. Rain kissed his lips, rain and cold bitter ash. He stared without hope into the distant fire. True dark fell over him, daylight an ancient and fast-fading memory.

He knew there were screams on the air, far away, but he could not hear them. He knew the fire still burned high overhead, but he could not see it. He felt only the starlight, felt it clear through to his bones. The stars were strange, cold and too piercing-bright. He stared into them alone, without even his own being for comfort.

All was silent. All was cold.

Holdric woke to Eahstann's prod.

"Your watch." Eahstann's voice came, rote and weary.

"Watch is mine," answered Holdric.

The wind came chill off the mountain. He shifted against the rock and pulled his blanket higher about his shoulders. High above, the starfroth arced bright across the sky. Already Eahstann's breathing came soft and even in the dark.

Holdric looked across the valley below, every tree bathed in cold quiet silver. He sat in quiet and forced thoughts of warm hearths and warm sun from his mind. All was still. Not far away, Kenndric's shadow was black against the stars.

Holdric rose and made his way past sleeping men to where his Ollda kept his lonely watch. They needed no words. For a long time they sat, side by side in the night. The stars of Lihtenstil were high in the night sky, her heron-neck bent.

"The Lady's home." Holdric's voice was quiet.

Kenndric's eyes followed his to the sky. "You always liked her."

Holdric remembered long summer nights alone on the high-folds. He remembered a scared shepherd boy alone in the dark, and his ealdfather who came to visit. Of long talks in the night, and whispered lore of the wheeling sky.

He smiled. "I thought she looked like a duck."

"A duck? Her neck is long, why not a goose?"

"No, see"—Holdric pointed—"she's standing high. That one's her shoulder."

Kenndric craned his head. "Ah… I see."

The elder man's chuckle was quiet. Silence came again.

Holdric looked out over the dark valley beyond, to where the stars of Gyre and Hound and spilling Seolfrenblos circled over the far tower, lost now in the night. The far hills were black shadows under the sky.

He bent to look for the high stones of Heahfeldt. Whether by night or stone of the mountain, the place was now out of his sight. Kenndric grunted. The old ranger knew even in the dark where it was that Holdric looked. Still the Huntslaed kept his quiet.

"Have you been back there?" Holdric asked at last.

"I have."

"Are the whispers true? About the dead?"

For a moment Kenndric paused, but a moment only. "Yah."

"Did you find him?"

"No."

Kenndric was quiet now a long time, and Holdric also.

"Heahfeldt is in the past, Holdric," Kenndric said at last. "Young men should think on what is to come."

"I am thinking on what is to come."

Kenndric sighed. "Giving Oath is a long binding, and you are young."

"You know I can do it. You've seen."

Kenndric's voice came sad. "You're born to the wild Holdric. You're better in the wood even than I. But I fear out here you will lose your being."

"As you lost yours?" The words were out before he could stop them. They hung in the air, tight and cold. At first Kenndric did not answer.

"Sleep, Holdric," he said at last. "I have the watch." His voice left no doubt, the words were no offer.

Quietly Holdric rose, cursing himself. He turned to leave, but found his feet would not yet carry him away. "Ollda… I never thanked you for bringing me back."

The old ranger made no answer.

Holdric cursed his tongue. He made again to his nest in the rocks, and there he watched the sky. His eyes lighted on the broad bright-starred wings spanning the froth above.

Hifosidth do I know her, she-swan, singer of the sky.
Sweet-light she carries, foam-flecked feathers cross the flood.
Green grass-knots she brings, her maidens bright and laughing.
Sweet swan see me, and spark my summer-love.

The verse hung in his head, the verse and the sweet soft memories that came with it. Angry he pushed the memories away, burying them before they could bite deep. He watched the stars long, staring into the sky until at last sleep found him.

CHAPTER FIVE

Of Rain and Stone

Wymud's kick came hard. Holdric groaned, but did not yet stir. The old man had already passed him by. Holdric lay with eyes closed, holding onto one last measure of rest. The smell of coming rain was in the air, rain and woodsmoke.

He lifted his cloak from his head and looked about. The stones of the mountain were cold, slick with dew and dark in the early morning gloom. The clouds overhead were dark. With a groan he rose from his blanket and stretched his shoulders. Eahstann did not look over. The harper's eyes were fixed on the craggy rocks above.

"See anything?" Holdric asked.

"Just birds."

Holdric grunted, his hands moving from long habit as he packed away his bed. "I am *starved*."

"Hurry then," Eahstann said. "Huntslaed left to scout the circle not long back. We'll be off soon."

Holdric stood and cracked his back as he looked over the wide valley below. The forest there was dim, the trees overshadowed with low cloud. A cold wet breeze came off the mountain, and Holdric shivered.

He buckled tight his fyrdknife, stretched again, and glanced about for the cookfire. Aschbroc had started kettles of water. On seeing Holdric, his cousin waved him over. Holdric rummaged in his pack for his cup and made to join them.

The water was already roiling. Holdric scooped out a cupful and dropped in a measured hand of pottage meal. He sipped at the hot brew while Aschbroc and Hwaetearn argued over the growing foals of the Thane's herd this year.

Aschbroc swore the young greyling would be the surest. Hwaetearn held for a ruddy bay, swearing he'd seen the pace of her sire in her step. Holdric was about to back his cousin when something flashed on the rocks above.

Kenndric was almost in their midst before Holdric had sure sight of him. Their Huntslaed came near the fire and took an offered cup of tea from Aschbroc. At a wave, the band gathered aboout.

"None came near last night," he said.

Wymud grunted, eyeing the Huntslaed's face. "Not what you thought to see?"

Kenndric nursed his cup, deep in his own mind. "I'm not sure what I thought to see."

"So what be our road?" asked Wymud.

Kenndric drank, pondering the question as he looked over the ground below. Then he spoke, "The Torr, as we pledged. But by the Stoneway. I want to know Hyrtwis' man makes his way in safety. And I want to know who else has been on that road."

Wymud looked up into the gathering clouds. "The weather will be foul. And your friend Hyrtwis picked a good man, Blaccram knows that ground. Following him won't be easy."

Kenndric finished the tea and passed the cup back to Aschbroc. "It won't."

Wymud looked down into the endless forest, then once more to the dark morning sky. He nodded to himself and turned to the others. "You heard your Huntslaed! Eyes sharp boys, and step with care!"

Holdric hurried to wolf his scalding pottage as the others broke to their tasks. Aschbroc and Hwaetearn buried their fire and set each scorched stone back into place. Eahstann tended to the shifted stone and crushed grass, and Holdric rushed to join him.

Soon Wymud walked over their ground, looking for sign of their passing and finding none. Each man stood for his pulls and prods, and then they made their way down the mountain in the morning grey. The way was steep, a winding path through high dark pine. Their feet had just reached the deep loam of the forest floor when the first drop of rain hit Holdric's lip.

Soon the clouds opened and the dull drum of rain filled the world. They walked without stopping through the morning, the sky grey and dim and the high trees loud with water. The morning wore on, long and weary.

Holdric looked over the ground at his feet. Kenndric was not far ahead, but already the water had washed smooth what little trace he had left. By nightfall all sign of his passing would be gone. Holdric looked up through the trees ahead and sighed.

Eahstann followed his gaze. "Any sign of our wayrunner?" he asked.

"Nothing since he crossed that spring a league back," Holdric said. "The man knows his craft, but I can scarce see even your passing in this."

Eahstann smirked. "I thank you. I think."

Holdric grinned and picked his way forward. Not far ahead lay a low tumbled wall of piled stone. "We're crossing again."

Eahstann let out a tired sigh. "You first this time."

Holdric shrugged, then crept nearer while Eahstann watched over him. He made for a low broken place in the wall, a place mostly bare of green that made an easy way over the rock. He came closer and looked over the ground for sign, then he searched once more for watching eyes. Seeing none he passed into the road.

The fitted stones of the roadbed stretched far out of seeing before and behind. The way was ancient. Earth-heaves of many passing winters had long since broken up the way, mud and grass and even the odd tree had at last broken through the stone. Holdric looked on the cut rock beneath his feet. He still could not quite make himself believe such a thing could be made, not by men.

He looked to the wood on the far side. The ground there was long grown over in ash and oak, and the trees were not young. Still the earth there was flat and smooth. It had once been under the plough, of that he was sure.

He knelt and looked close over the stones. A trained man of Greatwatch would shun the road itself, but Ollda had bade him look, and so he looked. He searched the whole breadth of the road for long paces. Everywhere he found the faded broken caps of last year's acorns, the fruit long-stolen. Scat of deer also, and in the earthen places the deep ruts of boar. But he found sign of nothing on two feet save themselves. He leaned back on his heels, looking far up the puddled road as he thought.

Eahstann came close and followed his gaze up the road.

"Nothing," Holdric said, answering the unspoken question. "If any have walked this way, I cannot find their passing."

Eahstann gazed into the trees. Far ahead Aschbroc held up his hand in sign—they had found again the wayrunner's trail.

Eahstann sighed. "We fall behind. Best be off."

"Yah." Holdric stretched his shoulders as he stood. He grinned as he peered out through the rain. "I've decided what became of the Oncefolk," he said.

"Oh?" asked Eahstann. "Answer me this riddle that has bewildered all ages of bards."

"They spent all their days at cutting stone and starved."

Eahstann laughed. They crossed over another low stone wall into the wood beyond. "As good an answer as any I've heard."

They pushed deeper into the wild. Many times they crossed over again the ancient rain-washed road, and each time Holdric looked for sign of passing feet. What sign there was came scarce as the rain wore on, and then it came not at all.

The sun seemed a distant memory, the day dark under heavy cloud. Under the leaves the wood was thick with mist and grey with spitting wet, all still save for the unending drum of rain. They circled in search and they found nothing. It was if the man had been taken up by the mist.

Holdric felt cast out of time in the flat sunless gloom. From the rumble of his belly and the ache of his shoulders, he guessed it near midday. In time the Huntslaed bent their course again to meet the ancient road. As they drew near Eahstann brightened.

"You're going to like this."

At first Holdric could see nothing through the mist but the paler green of a distant clearing. Then he saw it, a craggy shape that loomed up in the grey, reaching broken from the earth like the dead trunk of a broken tree. But it could be no tree, it was too wide, too broken… too bright. Under the heavy mantle of forest green, the shape glistened the wet white of new milk.

Kenndric waved them to search the ground nearby. Holdric and Eahstann moved to the far side of the clearing, and there hunted though thick choked brush at the treeline. Holdric crept low through the brambles, searching for sign of anything that might have pushed through the green. Always the milk-white stone behind pulled at his eye.

There was more of the white stone under the mounded earth, that he had seen at a glance. Tumbled blocks of the cut stone lay half-buried under the green.

Holdric forced his eyes back to his work. He knelt over a young green acorn, lonely in the earth. "Your time already, is it?" he whispered.

He looked up, up to a broad ancient oak that towered high above. Its leaves were still in the thick green of high summer, but the acorn at his feet would not be long alone. Already the branches were thick with green mast. The rain was heavy with the smell of holywyrt and wet leaves.

Holdric's breath was quiet in his chest. "What is this place?"

"No one knows," answered Eahstann. "It was a holy place of the Oncefolk, Master Uhlseid has guessed from the telling. Though even he has not seen it with his own eyes."

At a low whistle Eahstann looked back, and Holdric followed his gaze. Wymud stood at one corner of the ruin, a scowl on his face as he waved them close. Holdric took a last look over the ground, then rose to follow his friend.

The earth was broad and flat in the center of the tangled clearing. Moss and grass pushed through a great earth-heaved floor of fitted stone. Broken trunks of white stone lay toppled in the brush, and in the middle of all was a rain-filled pool, moss-covered and green.

Kenndric waved them into a huddle. "What found you?" he asked.

Aschbroc answered first, "The rain has taken most of what might have been, but we saw sign of nothing on two legs."

"For us also," added Holdric. "I do not think Hyrtwis' man has been here."

Kenndric sighed. "Well enough." He peered into the wild, softly striking his fist upon the stone as he thought.

Wymud looked back the way they had come. "Back to the last sign then?" he asked.

Kenndric shook his head. "No. He's hiding his way now. We would have seen more by now otherwise. I'll not have us drawn into days of hunting, not with Greatwatch waiting for aid."

"We know where he means to be," said Wymud.

"That we do." Kenndric looked north. "He'll cross the Harewater in any case. We make north, then follow up the Harewater, see if we can find his sign again. That won't cost us more than half a day, and gets us closer to the Torr as we go."

Wymud nodded. He turned to the rest of them. "Wet beds tonight boys," he said. "Take some rest while you may."

He waved them free, and the two elders moved off to make their plans. The younger men sheltered under a great leaning stone, seeking at least some rest from the rain. Holdric shrugged off his pack and lowered himself to the earth.

Aschbroc cursed as he pulled forth a sodden honeycake from his bag. Hwaetearn laughed, and Aschbroc cursed him. Holdric dug in his pack, then tossed a cake of his own to his cousin. Aschbroc thanked him and leaned back to eat. Holdric leaned back against the stone, eyes closed. He sighed and looked up into the rain.

Above him on the milky stone were shadows of ancient carving. He stood to look close—the rock had been carved away to leave the image of a flowering vine. Long ages of rain had worn the work almost smooth, but still Holdric could find leaf and flower. He traced the faded carving with his finger… the shape of the leaves was strange.

He wondered if such a vine had once grown here, or if the Oncefolk had come from some far shore and made in stone a memory of a thing they once had known. He thought on what the living vine must have been like, and why the Oncefolk had loved it so.

Across the broken stone Hwaetearn and Aschbroc had fallen to chatter—horses again. Holdric let the talk spill over him. His gaze fell over the broad floor of broken stone that stretched beneath them. He knelt and brushed aside the earth for a better look.

Much was covered, much was broken, but still he could follow a winding pattern in the stone. Tiny pebbles of black and purple and green were set against the great white blocks. Once this place must have been a glory.

Eahstann watched as Holdric traced the pattern of the little stones with his finger.

"It looks almost like the sea," Holdric said.

Aschbroc laughed, his mouth full. "You've never seen the sea."

"As I imagine the sea to be," Holdric answered.

"There are places like this on the Blackstrand," Eahstann said. "My second season with Master Uhlseid we passed by them. They are broken worse even than this, but you can see what once was."

Holdric looked over the broken stone. "Ollda said the hall of the High King holds a floor like this, is that true?"

Eahstann smiled at the memory. "Far grander. But the stones were there already. The old king only raised his hall above what was." He sought his mind for the words:

Strange halls they settled, to star-thatched rooms
their froth-road ran. Restless their watch from wind-scraped wall, and bare
their grave-wrought bower. No warmth was found
for wave-born son,
wailing swaddle-squalled on stone-locked lays.

Aschbroc rolled his eyes. "Words. Why did you follow old Uhlseid anyhow?" he asked. "You're not a sightless wretch fit only for the hearth. You could always have had a life of your own."

Eahstann looked on him almost with shock. "Someone must," he said. "Our songs are no less a part of us than our blood. Without them, we're…" He paused, searching for words. Then he waved to the broken stones on which he sat, the tumbled wall behind. "We're this, broken and forgotten. Scattered bones lost in time, shorn of all meaning."

Aschbroc huffed. "Leave it to the hearth-sops then. While you play at words, you leak the stuff of your own life." He met Eahstann's eyes. "Live, and be content."

"Better it be Eahstann," Hwaetearn said, "than a hearth-sop who knows not life. Our brother has seen that of what he sings." He looked to Aschbroc. "And we do need the words. When shadow comes, when chairs stand empty, bread and ale are not enough to fill the night."

Holdric looked up—it was strange to hear the thaneling speak of anything but swords and horses.

Still Aschbroc only laughed. "That's when you hold close your wife and plough your field." He grinned and leaned upon the bow across his lap. "Or the other way around."

Eahstann snorted. "You half-live, friend."

The harper looked again on the mouldered stone. Words fell soft from his lips:

Breath to breath does memory pass,
Long lost the lives I carry,
Heavy-bought, heavy borne, my hoard of houseless hearts.

Aschbroc harumphed and looked to the far wood. "All of you, dream-sopped. You need a hump and a full belly."

Wymud's low whistle carried over the broken stone. Their rest was done. Holdric rose to his feet and bent to wring out his cloak.

"I'm not sure why you bother," said Eahstann with a weary smile.

"Neither am I," said Holdric. He spared a last glance over the long-faded carvings, then he gathered up his things and stepped out into the rain.

The rain grew heavier through the day. The sky dimmed almost to dark, and the clouds let fall a heavy pelting soak. Holdric's cloak hung wet and heavy about his body. Eahstann yielded at last to the rain, stowing away his bow and moving his sodden quiver beneath his cloak. He trusted now only to hatchet and knife.

Holdric shifted under the weight of his pack and peered deep into the grey mist ahead. All was an endless grey-green of rain and leaf. The wood was loud with clattering rain, their sight cut short by mist and shadow.

Long they walked through rain-drenched woods. Their way wound north and east, or so he guessed, for he could not find the sun. By the time Kenndric turned their path along a loud narrow creek, it seemed all the world was water.

The creek was swollen with rain, and with the rain any easy sign of crossing had been washed away. Still Holdric eyed the water, searching for scraped root or broken branch. In time their Hunts-laed bent their path away from the water—he had found the trail. On they went, casting back and forth across the wayrunner's path.

Sometimes it seemed Hyrtwis' man still made for the Torr, but the way now was tangled, so full of dodging feints they could not be sure. Fear haunted his steps, the man moved now as one hunted. But of his hunter they could find no sign.

Holdric grunted as he bent to look over the mud to search again for some sign of chase, and again he found nothing. Through the rain ahead, he could just see the Huntslaed bending their way again for another cut across their own path. He cursed.

Eahstann looked up, following Holdric's eye. Then he echoed the curse.

Holdric grumbled under his breath, "Nothing is *out* here."

"Those were not your words on the mountain," Eahstann said, his voice tired and sullen.

Holdric cursed again. "That was before we spent all the day drowning in an empty soup. I've seen nothing not furred, feathered, or creeping, and scarce any of that."

He pulled again at the weight on his back, freeing the skin of his shoulders from sodden clinging cloth, if only for a moment. Already his back chafed and his feet swam hot and itching in his boots. Weariness hung heavy upon him. He grimaced as his foot slipped from a root and tore a muddy scrape in the earth. He bent to smooth the track with a cursing grunt.

Eahstann looked up into the rain and groaned with weariness. "Even Huntslaed would not keep us going forever in this."

Holdric grumbled. "Yah he would."

The trail soon fell cold, the last steps swallowed up in a rush of water. They cast again across the sodden leaves for his path, but found nothing.

The afternoon grew late, and the rain fell cold. Holdric's eyes were on the dull earth when Eahstann nudged him. Kenndric had signed halt. Ahead the Huntslaed stood frozen still… then crept carefully on. The old ranger paused a moment more, then waved them in.

Holdric smelled the place before he saw it. The stink of death rose heavy, even in the rain. Eahstann cursed as they drew near. In a crush of broken green and shredded hide lay the wreck of a slovenly butchered doe.

Days had passed, and what remained had gone to rot. Still Holdric could see where the arrow had struck home, and still he could see the ragged tears where the most tender meat had been cut free. All the rest had been left to the wolves, and they had not been idle. Holdric cursed under his breath.

Wymud grunted. His voice was flat. "Ragfolk."

Kenndric sighed as he looked on the deer, he whispered quiet words. Then he looked up along the blundered trail.

"Think they found our man?" asked Aschbroc.

"It's been known to happen," Kenndric said as he looked over the sign. "Not often." He leaned back on his heels, eyeing the stumbling path through the wood. "Looks like this one is making towards Beorhtfel's March,"

"They used to keep a camp not far off the Whitefork," offered Wymud. "Flotsam from the Hythe mostly."

Kenndric did not move his eyes from the trail. "I think those have gone now," he said. He thought long as he peered into the wood. Then he stood. "It's worth the looking," he said at last. "We go so far as we may by light, then search up the March by morning."

"Eyes sharp boys," called Wymud.

Each man took his place, and they left the broken doe to the wood. They traveled until the light began to fade, the trees dark and shapeless in the mist. With each step it seemed the rain came heavier. At last they could go no further. Kenndric led them up a low bramble-covered mound, and each man found sighting ground over his own patch of wood.

Eahstann and Holdric tucked themselves into a hollow that looked out onto the way ahead. The bramble above kept off the worst of the weather, but still a steady flow of chill water came falling into their hide.

Holdric was cold. He was tired and he was hungry. Every part of him ached. With a grumble he pulled off his cloak and moved to stretch it over boughs of fallen deadwood into a rough shelter. A stream of water broke over one side. He shifted the boughs with a swallowed curse and pulled at the sodden wool. Rain streamed down his neck as he worked. At last he ducked under the cloak and tied off a corner with a short length of nettletwist.

"It's not going to work," Eahstann mumbled.

Holdric huffed as he stretched the last cord into place. "It is." He stretched as he reached up, tying off the knot. "It is… going… to…"

The taut wool slipped from his fingers and let a gout of water splash over his face. He cursed and grabbed again for the loose end.

Eahstann smirked, pulling his hood up tighter over his head. "Told you."

Holdric caught the last free corner and tied it into place. All was done. Water dribbled down the earth behind them, water streamed off the edges of the cloak past their feet, but from above came only the soft patter of rain on wool.

Holdric leaned back against the soaking earth. For the first time since the ruin, he felt no rain upon his head. "It's better than it was."

Eahstann sat in silence.

Holdric eyed him. "Say it."

Eahstann grumbled. "It's better than it was."

Holdric smiled.

He reached for his pack and pulled it close. As he dragged it over the mud, another stream of water spilled from the brambles above. Grimacing he hollowed out a narrow trench for the spilling water and shifted his rainskin beneath his haunches. Then he rubbed his hand clean upon his tunic and pulled at the buckles of his pack. He pulled forth the bag of pottage meal and poured a measure into his hand, then tossed the handful into his mouth and began to chew.

Eahstann shivered next to him. "By Maesteald I want fire."

Holdric grunted and settled his blanket about his shoulders. The inner part of the wool was still dry, or at least it had started so. Once over his body it steeped in the wet of his clothes, and soon it too clung damp and heavy about his shoulders. He closed his eyes against the cold and wet… they would be at the Torr in a day. He could last a day.

Eahstann nudged him, and Holdric looked over. Eahstann passed him a brick of waybread, clean and white. Holdric broke off a piece and popped it in his mouth. The bread was smooth, sweet and heavy. Holdric closed his eyes again as he let it soften in his mouth.

"Sieve-bread?" he asked at last. "They keep you well in Etten-mede."

"I miss Hegwyn's cakes," said Eahstann. "They're sweeter."

Holdric shrugged. "Sweeter or no, I've had nothing but. Here…" He rummaged in his pack, pulled forth what was left to him and counted out half. "Trade you."

"Done!"

They swapped, each packing away their treasure from the wet. Then they ate in silence, looking out into rain-soaked dark. Holdric took up again his bag of pottage meal, picking in it for more of the dried meat.

Eahstann looked over. "You'll going to rue that, when next moon's turn finds you with naught but molded barley."

"Hrmm." Holdric picked out another piece of meat, closing his eyes to savor salt and biting smoke.

Eahstann watched him. "Can I have some?"

Holdric smiled. He fished out a piece of meat and handed it over. Eahstann handed back a large crumb of dried cheese in trade. The cheese tasted of salt and herb, thick with the smoke of burnt alder-wood. Holdric sighed in simple pleasure. "No wonder you like it there."

Eahstann shrugged.

Holdric swallowed the last of the cheese. "Give me another."

Eahstann held out his hand. They made another swap.

Side by side they sat chewing in silence. A thin stream of water spilled again from the side of the cloak. Holdric leaned over and pushed at a wet branch—the water stopped. For a long time they sat together in quiet. Thoughts of home came to Holdric, but he pushed them away.

Instead he looked to Eahstann. The harper also stared quietly into the dark. "The verses you spoke today… at the stone-place."

Eahstann shifted in the mud. "They're mine."

Holdric smiled. "You're a lay-man now?"

"Master Uhlseid said I needed to craft words myself, that I might understand the masters."

He said no more, but Holdric smiled. "You've a gift for it. I never knew."

Eahstann grimaced as water ran beneath him. "I'll teach you the whole of it one day." He scooped out a small trench with his hand and sat back again, shifting where he sat. "You've the mind for it."

Holdric stared quiet out into the dark. Finally he spoke, his voice distant:

… long lost the lives I carry…

The words hung in the air. "It's about your brother, isn't it?"

Eahstann sighed and shifted again in the mud. "He should not be forgotten."

Holdric waited. Water sounded on the wool above them. Water spilled over the mud at their feet. At last Eahstann began to speak, low and quiet:

> *In shadow of branches we pass,*
> *Blood on the leaves as I carry you.*
> *Blood on bank, and blood on stone.*
>
> *Breath to breath your words meet wind,*
> *Washed as wounds in water.*
> *Blood on the wet stone seeping, Words in memory soaking.*
>
> *Breath to blood and breath again does the soul pass,*
> *While here behind only words remain.*
>
> *Breath to breath does memory pass.*
> *Long lost the lives I carry,*
> *Heavy bought, heavy borne, my hoard of houseless hearts.*
>
> *In shadow of branches we pass,*
> *Blood and breath on stream-soaked stone.*

Side by side they sat in long silence, looking out into the rain. Holdric asked for the verse again, and again Eahstann gave it. Twice more they spoke the words together. Holdric mouthed the words, turning each over in his mind.

At last he spoke, his voice low. "I'll remember."

Eahstann's answer came late. "I know."

Each took his watch in turn, and at last Holdric slept, long and deep.

He was alone in the water.

Once this water had been cool and gentle. Once loving hands had held him, soft on his back. Sun had flashed on the rippling waters of the pool, laughter had spilled over the water, his laugh and hers. They had all been here. But now they were gone.

He was alone.

He had said they would be here. he had said… something. Something he could no longer remember. All was in cool shadow. The forest was thick with green, flowers spilled over the old spiral-carved stone.

The blossoms were sweet-smelling and bright, a thousand tiny suns bursting in a sea of wet green. He bent to smell them, and they were sweet… they were too sweet. He knew this smell.

He looked across the water. He looked to the watching place, to the shadows where the bogey once hid. The smell was thick now. He stepped back from the pool and his gorge rose in his throat. He looked for what he knew he must find, but still could not see. Everything was thick with green. He could not see the earth beneath… but still he knew it near.

A white flash of bone gleamed wet in the green.

He looked back to the watching-place. Shadows grew there, dark and hungry. Above, the clouds rolled with sullen thunder. The sky was dark and heavy. The trees shook with blowing wind.

He heard her cry, far away up the hill.

She was scared. She was screaming, searching—searching for him. And another voice also he heard, faint on the distant wind… they were all so very far away.

A great raven's croak sounded in the trees, and he looked to see. Slaugnwint gloated there, wings black and wide. Slaugnwint, and something worse behind. Then the clouds closed and all turned to dark sullen night.

It was almost time.

A desperate cry sounded, far away and faint. Another followed, a panicked scream of pain and terror. Then another… and then many. A great fire rose up, high and far away. He stared into fire and smoke and could not make sense of what he saw. He felt himself pulled from the earth, felt himself held in desperate hands. Thorns scratched at his face, his hands were torn and bloody.

He cried out. His howls raged, small and fierce and full of terror. Cold wet hands tried to soothe him, and still he howled. All the world moved about him, but his legs hung in empty air. All around was dark and blood and thorns and cold. Mum tried to quiet him, a cool hand brushed his head. Maethbry was there too, a babe small and silent, her eyes so very wide.

He looked back, back far into the night where the great fire burned. Screams rose up from the smoke, and he had howled too.

Hush, babe, Mum had said. *Hush Holdi*, she had begged.

Still he had howled. Still they ran. All was blood and thorns and cold. His face was scarred, his hands were wet. Blood ran free and hot over his fingers, tears and blood and rain mingled in his mouth. Far away the fire burned. Sour ash fell over his face, distant screams lingered in his ears.

The fire guttered and finally died away. The rain fell uncaring.

All was still.

All was cold.

All was dead.

Holdric started awake, soaked and blinking in the predawn grey.

The rain still fell. One edge of his cloak had come loose overnight, and his careful trenching had long since flooded over. Water poured down the brambles about his knees and his woolen nest was sopping with water. He cursed and bound the cloak in place again.

Cold and wet as he was, at least it was morning. Soon they would be walking again. He leaned out into the rain and let it wash away the last shreds of dream. Then he grunted and moved from his puddle.

Eahstann looked over, then went back to his cup of steaming broth.

Holdric groaned. "You got a fire in this?"

"Huntslaed's fire."

Eahstann passed the cup to him. Holdric took it in his hands and breathed in the steam. He couldn't decide whether to be grateful for the warmth of it, or disgusted with yet more wet. He decided on the former and took a sip. Warmth flooded his bones.

He looked out into the trees. Morning rose slow, a dim blue-grey light floating through mist and drizzle. Nothing moved in the wild beyond. The birds and beasts had the right of it today, it was mad to travel in this. Still Wymud would soon walk among them, and soon they would be roused to their work.

Holdric took another sip as he watched rain dance on the puddles below. "Anything?"

"Quiet all night" answered Eahstann.

"Quiet all night" echoed Holdric. He took a last sip and passed back the cup.

For long moments they stared out into the rain in silence. Then from somewhere behind and across the hill, they heard the disgusted cry of Hwaetearn, followed by an angry splash. They looked at each other and grinned.

"Guess we're moving soon," said Eahstann.

Holdric looked up again into the rain. "Ready?"

Eahstann tossed the last of his broth aside and pulled up his hood. "Ready."

Holdric stood creakily, then ducked out from under their little shelter and pulled loose the knots of his stretched cloak. While Eahstann cleared signs of their passing, Holdric wrung the water from his sodden blanket and folded it away as best he could.

Kenndric came back to them from walking the circle, his face already weary. He signed that none had come near during the night, but did not speak. Before long all had gathered on the little hilltop. They shared a short cold breakfast in silence, each watching his own stretch of woods. All their words were spent.

Soon they were back in heron-march, winding their way ever closer to the Torr. Still they found no sign of the messenger, or of his hunter—if hunter there was. Holdric looked up to where the sun should have been, and he dreamed of warmth.

They reached Beorhtfel's March by midday. The road lived now only in name. A line of younger growth through the ancient trees told in places where once the way had lain, but any path had long ago grown over. Still Holdric spied here a scraped tree, there an over-worn root. In places he saw even foot-worn earth. Enough men had used this way the last few seasons to leave some trace, but of new passings he could find no sign.

Long into the day they searched. How long Holdric could not guess, all the sky was cloud and rain. He was soaked through to his skin. His cloak hung heavy about his legs, his feet stung cold in the sopping mess of his boots. The feel of dry skin was a forgotten memory.

He listened for stalking foes, but heard only the roar of rain. His eyes sought the ground for sign, but found only mud and leaves. A shiver ran down his back and he cursed beneath his breath.

Eahstann stopped at his side. Holdric looked to his friend—then followed his gaze. Through the thick green he could just see the grey of piled stone. Even from where he stood, Holdric could see that all was not right, that stones were missing from a high-piled cairn. Still they watched their places, until finally Wymud waved them in and they could draw near.

Again rose the sick-sweet smell of death. Holdric drew his wet midgescarf over his face as he came close. Even from the edge of the clearing he could see the place was a midden of broken crocks, torn cloth, and tossed bones.

The cairn was a wreck. Once the piled stone of the cairn might have looked mighty, holy even. But now the rune-cut naming stones had been pulled down, the winding carvings of stag and heron and hound and tree broken up and cast about the clearing.

A rude windbreak of brush was laid against the stones, and beneath it a hearth had been made from the stolen stone. A full side of the cairn was stained black with grease and smoke. On the far side of the wreck, Hwaetearn stood staring at the earth. Here a corner of the cairn had been pulled down entirely, the rocks used to half cover the bloated body of a man lying on the ground. A fragment of rune-stone was placed near the body's head in crude mockery of the burial rite.

Holdric drew the cloth tighter over his face. What lay beneath the rock had been too-long dead. No one needed to say this had not been their man. The dead man had been too sickly, too starved for a ranger of Greatwatch.

"Ragman," spat Hwaetearn with a curse.

The thane's son trembled with anger. He kicked at the deadwood of the shelter and began to pull apart the makeshift hearth, heaving each stone back again into place. Kenndric quietly waved for Aschbroc to help with the stones. Holdric and Eahstann he set to look about the clearing, while he and Wymud stood watch.

Holdric looked over the wreckage as he circled the camp. Low hovels of branch and bark slumped about the clearing. He had heard of ragfolk of course, had even seen a band of them once. Thieves and outlaws and broken men fled to the wild, and there they were joined by the mad and the kinless. Most haunted the dark woods between the folksteads. Only the most desperate crossed over the Mearcwater.

Rarely did any last the depth of winter. Holdric looked over the crude shambles that passed for their shelter. These men would not have seen spring, he was sure of that. Whatever had ended the half-buried ragman might have been a mercy.

Holdric crawled into a hovel and covered his nose against the stench. The piled brush of the roof was more hope than shelter, and vermin-chewed fragments of cast-off wool mouldered in the back corner. The other shelters were no better. Holdric pawed through each to see what remained within and found little else but rags. He backed out again and looked over the clearing.

The only care taken in the place had been the burning out of mash-bowls from open stumps. Rain filled them now, but even after many days they were thick with the sour smell of wildbrew, a drunken rotted mash of anything the broken men could find. It had been their one happiness, and their one labor.

Holdric backed away, taking in all the ground again. The limb-ways were worn bare of grass, but the rain had long since washed them clean of sign. Shards of rough clay bowls lay where they had broken, and a lone wind-shredded footrag clung to the branches where once it had been set to dry. But of step or fight or stumbling drunk, there was no new sign. The rains had taken all… or almost all.

A scrape of lichen on the trunk of an old and dying oak caught Holdric's eye. He came closer — something at a shoulder's height had scraped a patch clean, and not long since. Wary he crept deeper into the trees, and just missed stepping in what passed for the rag-men's night-midden. His lip curled. They'd lived like beasts, barely stumbling past the trees for their doings.

Still he searched the ground for sign. Rain and weather had worked long, but some marks still were left. Two puddles caught his eye, long shallow trenches a shoulder's width apart, the mark of heels dragged through earth. Between them deep sopping puddles told where heaving feet had dragged the weight.

He moved deeper into the wood, searching for the start of the trail. There he saw branches hanging broken in the rain, their leaves shriveled and limp. Deadwood on the forest floor was broken, moss was torn from stones. And a flattened spot where something—someone—long had lain, the green of the wood dark and dead beneath.

Beyond he found more broken wood and more scuffed bark. At first it seemed a trail, but the sign fell quickly away as Holdric followed the marks. Soon he came to nothing but rain-soaked leaves. If there was more yet to see, it was past his power to find.

Holdric came again to the cairn. Hwaetearn had finished stacking again the stones from the hearth and moved to the loose pile of rock over the half-covered ragman. He moved swiftly, his face half disgust and half rage. Aschbroc helped him, midgescarf bound tight over his face.

Kenndric looked to Holdric. "What did you find?"

Holdric started to speak, but as Aschbroc moved the next heavy stone found he could not make the words. His eyes would not leave the body. As the stone had been lifted away, the belly of the man spilled open. Aschbroc had turned his head away in disgust, but Holdric's eyes were frozen. The wound was not work of wolf or raven, even now Holdric could see where skin fell cleanly cut. The dead man's belly gaped, an unnatural hollow in his flesh dark and purple where the blade had bitten deep.

Worse was the face. Holdric had seen the dead on biers, or laid out on covered tables dressed for vigil, or shrouded and set with care into the earth, but this… his mind struggled to grasp that he looked on the remains of a man, no matter how broken and lowly he had been.

Holdric looked up to see his Ollda staring at him, patiently waiting for him to come again to his senses. He shook his head and tried to clear his mind. This time he met the elder man's eyes.

"Forgive me, Ol—Forgive me, Huntslaed," he began, "I found, I think, where this was done. Just past the clearing, in the trees. I found not why he was so far from his fire, but it was not a way any walked often."

"Searching for something?" asked Kenndric.

"Perhaps," Holdric answered. "Though his way looked fair-straight… until the place he fell." Holdric pointed. "There he lay some time—I guess days—then he was dragged here. By only one, so far as I can tell.

"In the camp, I found sign of at least two, but I think more. No more than six. By the paths they've worn and the castings they've left, they've been here most of the season. The rains make it hard to say—but none I think have been here for days."

"I'd say not," grunted Wymud, casting a look to the body. Aschbroc snorted, choking back a grim laugh. Holdric flushed.

"Anything else?" Kenndric asked.

"Past the killing ground there's a fresh trail, two or three days if I guess the leaves right. I followed it a short way, but there's no sense to it I can find."

The old ranger's eyes moved around the clearing as Holdric told his tale. He waited for Holdric to finish, then crouched to look upon the dead man once more.

"Not sure which way our knifeman went then?"

"Not after this long, Huntslaed, not in this."

Wymud grunted. "Hardly the first time ragmen have fallen on each other, and one run off in a fit."

"They're no better than ghaestling." Hwaetearn spat. "They fight even each other like mad wolves."

Kenndric sighed. "They do."

Wymud looked to him. "After the knifeman?"

Kenndric shook his head. "No. Greatwatch needs her men, and we have no more time to spare. If Hyrtwis' man has made the Torr, so much the better. If not, the more reason to get word to them quickly."

"Someone's made dire mischief already," said Wymud.

"And that man must wait," answered Kenndric, "for Greatwatch cannot. If Torrlaed Stalmaht has not yet sent his workmen, we will ask they come down by the March. Perhaps they will find what we have not."

He looked to the others. "We leave as soon as we may. Aschbroc, take another look at that trail for me. See if fresh eyes see something new, and mark the killing-place for the Torr men. Holdric, Eahstann, dig out a resting-hole for this man."

Hwaetearn looked to their Huntslaed, his face dark. "He's honor-shorn."

"So he is. But whatever he has done, death has settled his trespass. He is still your father's man. Will you be the kind of Thane who leaves even his lowest as food for beasts?"

Hwaetearn scowled, but he did not say more.

Kenndric glanced at Holdric. Work called, and the sooner started, the sooner finished. Holdric took a short spade from Aschbroc's pack and moved to a flat spot not far from the foot of the cairn. He gestured to the spot and looked to Kenndric, and Kenndric turned to Hwaetearn. Hwaetearn paused his work to look to where Holdric stood. At last he gave a grudging nod, and Kenndric waved his assent.

Holdric drove the spade into the earth. The grave filled with rainwater nearly as fast as he pulled forth earth. Soon he and Eahstann were covered in mud and sweat. Holdric pulled a heavy spade of mud from the bottom, grimacing as the side of the grave began to cave in. With a curse he pulled it out again.

Once only he paused from his work. He looked to where Hwaetearn still worked to set right the cairn.

"Who lies there?" he asked Eahstann in a whisper.

Eahstann looked over his shoulder, watching a moment as Hwaetearn worked. "Eorl Earnhaedth, called Ironeye. Hwaetearn's father's father's father."

Holdric stared at Hwaetearn, shocked. "Hwaetearn's kin was an Eorl?"

"Until his king lost."

"Ah." Holdric closed his eyes, searching his memory:

> *King he came by broken branch,*
> *Bright his claim-hoard counted.*

Kin-shorn crown he brother-bought,
Broken his kin-wife's cradle.

Houseless hearth he grudging-gained,
Grim-found mead in handless horn.

"You have caught it," Eahstann said.

They worked in silence, and soon enough the grave was dug. It would be a shallow rest, but still the broken ragman would lie in a better bed than many past the Mearcwater. Kenndric looked over the grave and judged it dug well enough.

"Let's get him moved." Kenndric's voice came weary, but he bent to the labor with the rest of them.

Holdric helped carry what was left of the ragman to the hole. He turned his face from the smell, and tried to force his mind to anything but the slick mess beneath his fingers that once had been flesh. There was little enough of that at the least, in life the man had already been half bones.

The rangers covered him over with earth and river stone. When the last stone was set, Kenndric drove a sapling-pole of ash into the earth near where the man's head had been laid. Upon the pole he shaved one flat face, and there carved quick the mark of Maesteald, and over it the sun-mark. It was a rude enough grave pole, but it would show the place to the man's friends—if any still lived.

Kenndric whispered the death song over the grave. Hwaetearn scowled, but he said the words with the rest of them.

The branch is broken and cannot be mended.
The leaves are flown and cannot be gathered again…

The words rolled on, and when they were through Kenndric gave a last look about the clearing, his face care-worn and tired. He nodded to Wymud, and with a grunt the Second set them in order.

"Wash yourselves boys, and let's be off."

The words came not soon enough for Holdric's liking. Even in the rain, his hands itched from the greasy stink of the work. He made quickly for the bank. There he scrubbed river sand over and over his hands almost until they bled before he could bear even to fetch the soap from his pack.

As he scrubbed, he looked up into the rain. Beside him Eahstann shook the water from his hands and stood. Holdric gave his own hands one last scrub, then weary he rose, heaved up pack and spear and shield, and took his place beside Eahstann. Together they trudged again into the wild. They would be at Ealdwyrc Torr by dusk.

Never had he been so grateful for the rain.

CHAPTER SIX
Ealdwyrc Torr

Rain filled the wood with a heavy, mind-dulling roar. Holdric placed one sodden boot in front of the other and forced his mind from the wet misery of his skin. He looked up into the clouds to rest his eyes from the dark wood. Heavy rain cast all in dim shadow, but true dark was not yet on them.

Aschbroc walked far ahead, just short of the crest of the next hill. He waved to Holdric, signing him to hurry, and Holdric pushed hard against the muddy ground to catch up. A few more steps and he reached the overlook—and lost his breath at the sight of what lay beyond.

Before them stretched a wide green valley thick with forest. A narrow river snaked through the rocks far below, and beyond the trees high ridges of stone marched into the far distance. From the nearer ridge a spur of stone reached down to overlook the river. On that spur stood Ealdwyrc Torr.

Holdric tried to guess the tower's size from the trees below and boggled. The Torr stood high as the tallest trees he'd known, as wide almost as his fyrdhall. And yet from where he stood it seemed a tiny thing, lost against the stone of the high ridge.

The foot of the Torr was hidden by a high paling-wall of timber. Watchfires held there against the rainy gloom, and Holdric's skin itched as he thought of warmth.

"It will be good to be in a place of men again," said Hwaetearn. "Even a place so other-homed as that."

Eahstann spoke low as he looked on the far tower:

Salmon-speckled, my stone greets sun,
Where sky scrapes stone, and winds shape wyrd..

Kenndric followed with:

Twice was my riving, and twice my rising,
I stood time, stood horde, stood man.

Eahstann turned a raised eye to Kenndric. "I had not thought Master Uhlseid spoke his own crafting in Heortlea."

"You are not the only one who listened at his knee." Kenndric said. "He's been turning those words over in his mouth for years. I think rather he should have let them be ages ago. He has long since polished the song from the steel, to my ears."

Wymud huffed, wringing the water from his cloak. "If any of you babbling geese walked half so much as you talk, we'd have already fire at our feet and food in our bellies. Move on, and keep your watch!"

Holdric spared a last glance to the far tower and headed down into the trees. The slope was steep and broken, the way thick with soaking green. He stepped carefully around a patch of wet mud and just caught himself from slipping on a rain-slick root.

He righted himself and breathed a tired curse. The ache in his limbs had long since given way to a deep weariness. His eyes were heavy, and he fought to keep his mind upon his work.

Further down the slope their Huntslaed moved with quiet care, pausing often to peer deep into the rain-grey wood. Always the old ranger grew wary as he neared a place of rest, always the hard-bought lesson of the Whitemoon weighed heavy upon his shoulders. Holdric tried to follow his Huntslaed's care, turning his eyes to the trees and holding sharp his sight.

Beside him Eahstann slipped with a hissed curse. Holdric bent quick and caught his friend's elbow before he could hit the earth. Eahstann grunted his thanks, and together the two crept on through mud and slick wet leaves.

In time the Torr came at last again into sight through a break in the trees. They were not yet near, but already it seemed to Holdric that he could just smell the waiting watchfires. Through the rain came now the distant *tink* of a smith's hammer on iron, the sound strange now after so long in the wild.

Soon he could see more of the tower. A long narrow road curved down from the tower heights, flanked on both sides by thick earthen dikes and a paling-wall of sharpened timber. They were almost there.

At last they neared the bottom, and just beyond the trees opened to the rippling shallows of the Whitefork. Holdric stared glumly at the wide water and sighed. It was not as if he could get more wet.

Before him Wymud knelt in the cover of trees at the riverbank. The old man's fingertips dipped in the current as he gazed upstream. The ford was swift and swollen, but still the water was wide, and shallow despite the heavy rain. The crossing would be safe enough.

On the near shore the waters rushed over an ancient bridge footing, now long-drowned and covered over with green and muck. Across the river the sister footing had been built out into a small rude dock of timber, and not far away a jumble of rude sheds stood at the foot of the muddy Torr road. Nearest the dock was a work cot, woodsmoke curling from a hole under the roof. A half-naked man sat there, sheltering from the rain in the cover of an upturned boat.

The man looked up as Holdric's band broke through the trees and quietly watched them as they waded into the ford. As they passed into the open water a sounding horn blew, long and loud. Only Holdric looked to the sound, and to the Torr looming tall and lonely high above. The others only trudged on through the water.

The old man followed them with his eyes as they came near. A jumble of wicker fish traps sat in a tarred skin currock at his feet, and he busied himself with another in his lap. His hands worked idly over his trap, long practice making up for the loss of two fingers from his left hand. White scars streaked over the old knotted muscle of his forearms. Holdric could not help but look on the fisherman as he passed. The old man met his eyes for a brief and doubting glance, then returned to his work without a word.

Holdric looked away, and as he gained the far bank his eyes turned by long habit to the earth. It was open ground here, all mud and scrubby grass, and days of rain had not been enough to hide the long-worn passing of ways.

Still this was a lonely place. Lush oxfoot pushed into the path not far from the trees, and though a narrow horse trace followed alongside the river, the upstream way was narrow and overgrown, and the downstream way less traveled yet.

Above and to each side of the steep road to the Torr rose high dikes and paling-walls, but here at the river's edge the workings were little more than halfhearted withy fences around tired thin gardens.

The road itself was old and long-used. The steeper parts of the way were timbered against the long passing of many feet, and deep ruts from heavy-laden carts had been worn into the wood. All was covered over with the crossing sign of man, goat, and horse. After so many days with only the tracks of the wild and his own way-brothers, the riot of passing ways was almost too much for Holdric's sight.

Kenndric looked over his men and led them up the last long trudge to the tower. As they passed along the paling-wall, Holdric saw more than a few timbers leaned loose in their footing, soft and grey-green with age. He kept his eyes on the earth as the climb wore on, shoulders weary under his heavy load.

Still his mind could not help but puzzle out each passing of man and beast. The passing of a tired cart horse with one tender leg caught his eye, and the stumbling place where the poor beast had struggled against a steep rise in the earth.

The road bent as it climbed, and the way grew steeper yet. The paling-timbers came newer and stronger as they neared the heights, black with fire and tar where they rose from the thick walls of raised earth. As they drew nearer their ears filled with the alarmed bark of a hound and the screams of geese. Holdric looked once more over the far deep wild of the distant valley… it felt strange to hear such sounds here, so far from farm and field.

Their way rounded under the paling-wall, and piled earth gave way to a wall of stone. The wall had the look of scavenge-work, horse-sized blocks of stone lain together as best they might fit, the gaps filled with river stone. One odd stone, covered over in ancient carving work, was set on its side. Holdric turned his head and tried to make sense of the weatherworn figures of mounted men riding sidle-ways up the wall. Eahstann nudged him and they walked on through the rain.

Above the mounded earth and fitted stone, hulking high over the sharpened paling-wall, there rose Ealdwyrc Torr, cobble-colored as a summer trout.

Twice was my riving, and twice my rising…

Cold water poured over the ancient stones. The smell of wood-smoke grew heavy, and Holdric's bones ached for warmth. Their way ended at heavy iron-bound gates of oak, high and broad enough for three mounted men to pass abreast, set into a thick wall of cut stone and mounded earth.

Above the gates was stretched a broad walking-way of strong thick timber. Banners hung there, sad and heavy in the endless rain. One banner bore King Eacandeor's bull, upon another was stitched a rearing horse and spears—that sign Holdric had never seen before.

Grim men looked down upon them from the height. Beyond the wall came still the angry bark of the hound within, and one of the guards turned to shout for quiet.

A man came to the walking-way. His face was weathered and his golden hair was giving way to grey, but his face grew bright with a broad smile when he looked upon them. "Kenndric my friend! You and your drowned Hounds come to us from the far wood!"

"Hounds in need of fire and meat, friend Stalmaht!" answered Kenndric. "Life to your home! May we enter?"

"Hale be my guests, friend Farstride!" answered the man, echoing the ancient words. The man laughed and waved an arm to his men below.

The massive gates opened with a heavy creak. Kenndric led the way within, and as Holdric passed beneath the great timbers the rain upon his hood fell silent. The sudden quiet after so long under the weather sent a shiver up his spine. He turned for a last lingering look out to the trees behind... then he too walked within.

They passed through a short tunnel under the burgh wall. The air beneath the earth felt thick and still, but soon they were out again in the rain-washed gloom of open air. Here inside the wall, paltry watchman-fires burned on broad raised shelves of stone, and the rangers hung close to drink the warmth into their bones.

Above them the tower loomed high. It was taller even than Holdric had guessed, taller than all the trees he knew. The tower door itself was well off the ground, reached only by an open stair that snaked up one side.

The scream of geese on the far side of the tower yard took his ear. He looked across the grounds… even in the steady rain the work went on. Against the far wall were sturdy bays framed in timber and roofed in thatch or split shakes, and within the bays stables and small rough worksheds. There a handful of men worked at their crafts and tended to stabled horses. Hens sheltered under a low roof near a goat pen, and fat grey geese strutted across the muddy yard. The place seemed almost a small village in the wild, were a village peopled only by fighting men.

The men of the tower were not like the rangers, nor even the people of Heortlea. Their speech was loud and their steps were heavy, and everywhere Holdric saw long warknives under sodden woolen cloaks, and spears easy to hand, and more armor of mail rings than he'd seen in his life. Even when the Eorl passed through Heortlea, never had so many been at arms. Here it seemed most every man was wearing iron. They bore the weight easy, carrying about their work as though their metal coats were nothing more than summer tunics. Still there were fewer of them than Holdric had guessed there might be. Parts of the wall lay unwatched, and much of the work in the yard looked hurried.

The geese screamed again, louder still than the hammer of the smith or the bleat of the goats. Holdric flinched at the noise. After so long in the quiet of the wood, the bustling tower yard battered at his ears. Here he could not see beyond the thick walls of earth and stone, he could not hear over the din of man and beast. For all the comfort of the high walls, to be so deaf and so blind left him unsettled. Some part of him longed already for the deep trees.

A heavy tread on the boards above caught his ear, and he turned to see the master of the tower and two guards make their way down thick timber stairs to greet the newcomers. A great wolfen hound ran before them, thick-coated in his pelt of grey and brown, broad of chest and bright of eye. The creature let out a growling whine as it ran and bounded for them as an excited pup.

"Wyrling! Down!" shouted one of the guards, but it did no good. Wyrling leapt among them, smelling and squirming and whining in greeting. Kenndric laughed as the great beast came near, and Holdric went to one knee and reached to scratch the great hound's shaggy ruff. Wyrling bore his head hard against Holdric's chest, shoving and whining and madly wagging his tail.

"Wyrling?" asked Eahstann asked as the men drew close. "A well-fated name."

"Not all have the Beast of Aranmaede watching over us, friend Huntsman." returned the guard with a grin. "We must make do with our mortal beast-friends."

"Kenndric!"

The man who had greeted them at the gate came striding across the tower yard, holding his arms wide. His cloak was rich, his coat of rings well-kept even in the hard rain. A fine-worked sword hung at his side.

Kenndric embraced him as a dear friend, and the two slapped arms.

"What have your Hounds dug up, friend?" asked the great man.

"Have you not then word from Greatwatch?" Kenndric asked, his face grave.

The light fell from their host's face. "No. Not in the last moon. What troubles them?"

"Hyrtwis has lost two men, and a beacon pyre beside—to storm or mischief he knows not. His wayrunner should have reached you before us."

The man looked grave. "Then his man is not the first to be missed." He looked about the gathered band, their cloaks hanging cold and wet. "We will speak of this within, but first we must get your men out of this accursed rain." He then turned and shouted towards the tower, "Wydthoc! Attend!"

Turning back to rangers, he looked then to Holdric. "Your newest, I take it?"

"He is," answered Kenndric. "Holdric of Heortlea. Trained by myself. Holdric, Torrlaed Stalmaht, master of this place."

Stalmaht took Holdric's hand without pause, clasping it strongly. "Welcome to Ealdwyrc Torr, Holdric of Heortlea. Any man of Kenndric is welcome at my table."

A youth ran to them and stopped just short of the Torrlaed to wait for word. The shieldling was more boy than man, gold of hair and still slender. He was too small yet to fill his jack of linen, and his heavy warknife hung awkward at his side. He looked on the weather-stained rangers before him with open awe.

"This… this way, my… my… Spearmen," he stammered.

"Huntsmen" Stalmaht corrected.

"This way, Huntsmen," the boy said, grateful. He turned and led them to the inner gates.

Kenndric and Stalmaht moved away, making for the Torrlaed's guardhouse. Wymud looked to the rest.

"Get dry, get warm, make no trouble." He grunted, then turned to cross the yard towards the crafter's shacks against the far wall. Hwaetearn and Aschbroc backed away from the knot as well, Aschbroc craning his head as he looked over the tower yard.

"We go first to see Byarmin," said Hwaetearn.

"Wait—I shall join you!" called Eahstann. He looked to Holdric, the question on his face. Holdric looked between the three and the young shieldling, who now shifted his weight from one foot to the other as he watched each of his charges desert him in turn. Holdric groaned within. He had little taste for more talk with his band, but still less with the shieldling boy. Still he wished to see more of the strange Torr.

"I shall stow our things first, and join you later," he answered.

Eahstann shrugged off his pack and passed it to him, then followed after the others. The boy calmed though as he saw some portion of his charge still with him.

Holdric looked to him. "Lead on, Shieldling Wydthoc."

Eager now, the boy led Holdric to the high tower, leaping up the great stone steps two at a time. Holdric picked his weary way with care. The stair was worn smooth and hollowed by the passing of many feet, and a shallow stream of rainwater fell from each step to the next. To his left the way was open to the tower yard, and soon Holdric looked down on roof thatch and muddy walks from a bird's height. He set a hand on the stones of the tower to steady himself, pausing to look close on the cobbled jumble of the tower wall. Cut white blocks bearing the faintest whispers of long-ago carving sat jammed in place alongside common river stone.

Above him Wydthoc reached the gate and threw it wide. "I'll show you the whole thing!" the boy called. "There's nothing like Old Ealdwyrc between here and Kingshall!"

Holdric followed him through the door, the walls thick almost as the whole of an ox. Within it felt strange. The air was still like the den of a beast, but the room was high and open almost as his own fyrdhall. Beneath his sodden boots the stone gave way to a thick oaken floor. What little light passed through the narrow windows was aided by greaselamps, but neither could banish whole the dim gloom within. Holdric doubted even a bright sunlit day would add much cheer to the open hall. Was this what the strange white stones in the wood behind had once been like? Somehow he could not think it so.

Wydthoc walked before him, waving his arms at the broad hearths of stone and the wide tables of the common hall, naming each place of honor. Here was the Torrlaed's seat, there the high table of his guard. Long tables filled the room, and past them lay the kitchens. Below were great stores and cisterns that could last the whole of the tower long seasons.

Then the boy waved for Holdric to follow and charged up a narrow stair. "You'll be up here!"

The walls felt close and cold about him. For all the grandness of this place, Holdric found he missed the warm-timbered halls of home. Wydthoc was nearly hopping as the stair opened onto the barracks floor. Stacked bunks of dark-worn timber lined the length of the walls, save a few places where narrow ports looked out onto the grounds below. In the center of the cramped room were worn bench-chests of wood, each carved with the mark of its owner, and near them stood stands of arms, shields and bright-polished spears ready for war.

Most of the ports in the wall had been shuttered. Two left open let a gentle wisp of fresh, wet air flow through the room. A small fire smouldered in a tiny hearth in one wall, and it was there Holdric moved to lay out the gear of his band.

He worked with long practiced hands, wringing their soaked woolens into a stone basin. Then he brushed them clean and hung all to dry near the fire. Wydthoc watched in silence as he worked, awed to see the strange gear of the rangers hung out before him.

"What's it like?" the boy finally asked.

Holdric looked up from his work. "What?"

"Being… out there all the time. What's it like?"

It was not a question Holdric had thought on. He'd as soon answer what it was to watch the sun rise. "It… just is."

Wydthoc stood awkwardly, searching for some way to stretch out the talk. As Holdric finished his work, the boy offered, "Do you want to see the top?"

Tired as he was, Holdric couldn't stop a smile at that. "It is overclose in here."

Wydthoc nodded and wiped his brow. "Yah, you're right. Overclose! Follow me! I know just where you want!"

They made their way up turn after turn of narrow stairs. Holdric caught teasing glimpses of the far wild through the narrow ports in the wall, but had to run to keep up with Wydthoc. Soon they squeezed through a small tight door onto a narrow walk, open on one side to the sky.

Night's dark was coming fast. A wind-blown rain brushed at Holdric's lips as he looked out onto the far valley. Shreds of mist hung in the trees below, and for a moment he felt himself on an island in the clouds, looking down as a falcon over the earth below.

"I come up here to think sometimes," said Wydthoc. "When it's clear, you can see the Himlgartn."

Holdric sought the far clouds, but could see nothing. "When I was young," he said, "I'd climb the highest tree in Heortlea to look for them."

Wydthoc was entranced. "You can see the mountains where you come from?"

Holdric smiled. "Once, I thought I did." He peered deeper into the northern gloom, trying to tease out the shape of far high mountains from the heavy clouds. "But I think now I must have been wrong."

Holdric followed the walk around to the valley side—that suited better. No ringing hammers, no stuffy rooms, only the open air. He sat back against the wall and let his eyes rest on the far wood below. His mind wandered over each fold of ground, thinking on how the earth must feel underfoot there, how the wind must smell…

Wydthoc still hovered near. Holdric cast his mind for the right words to send the boy away, but more talk came.

"Are you scared out there?"

Holdric wasn't sure how to answer. "I suppose. Sometimes."

Still the boy did not leave. Just when the silence seemed to last, Wydthoc spoke again. "I saw a ghaestling once."

A chill ran down Holdric's spine. He turned to look at the boy. By the look on the shieldling's face, it was no idle boast.

"What did you see?" Holdric asked.

Wydthoc fumbled with his sleeves as he searched for his words. "It was walking-in time, yah? And I was coming in with the boats, and, and… and our horseguard followed us on the shore. And night was coming, and we thought we could make it all the way in, but we couldn't, and then we heard them, and they… they did what they do. I didn't see it all, didn't see most of it. Just… lots of yelling, and the horses…"

It was now too dark to tell for sure, but by his voice the boy was fighting tears.

"Master Haukr, he made me hide, didn't want me to look, but I did look. I looked through the boxes on the boat, and one of them, one of them came out to the edge of the water, and it looked at the boat. It looked at me."

Holdric kept silent, waiting for more of the tale, but no more came.

"I'm cold," Wydthoc said, "and it's dark. I'm going down. Do you want to come?"

Holdric thought. "No," he answered. "I'll be down later. I need the air."

"As you will," Wydthoc said. As the boy reached the narrow door, Holdric could just hear him huff to himself in disbelief, "… Huntsmen."

Holdric smiled and turned his eyes back to the darkening wild. As his eyes wandered over the rolling shadows of the wood below, his hand idly brushed the stone beneath him—then stopped as his fingers moved over an odd pattern of timeworn scratches.

He looked down, shifting to let what little light was left hit them fully. Marks had been graven here, strange sigils cut across a stone of the floor. Holdric had not the art of the ancient runes, but he knew them well enough to know this was something else. Another trace of the Oncefolk then, their meaning lost in the deep of time.

All these long ages, and still their words stood locked in stone like the ice-bound trail of a long-dead deer. What might it be like, to be able to follow their words as easily as one followed wildsign? To know the thoughts of men long dead, men who passed from the earth long before ever he had lived? It was a strange thought. And yet now even their memory was gone. No breath filled their ancient words, no living blood walked still upon the earth. All were lost past knowing.

Holdric looked again to the far empty valley. He had heard it said that the Oncefolk had in ages past held all the far wood, that traces of their living had been found so far as men had yet been able to walk and still return.

The thought came unbidden… *"they were stronger that we…but now they are gone."*

For a long time Holdric looked on the dark forest below, brooding until the very last of the light fell away.

At last he rose and made his way below. Shreds of woldgast clung still about his spirit, the clamour of the tower men below rough and jarring to his ears. Still he made his way down the steps and forced his mind into the spirit of fellowship.

The air grew close and hot with the press of bodies as he neared the tower's hall. Harp and song echoed up the stair, half-drowned by the roar of loud talk.

He turned into the hall. The men of the Torr might have been few, but it seemed every one of them had packed into these walls this night. Before the room had seemed vast, but with so many about the tables it was now cramped as Uncle Eikhram's hearth.

Food and drink, song and laughter put Holdric in mind of feast times in the Thane's great hall, when all would gather for company and the passing of winter mead in the Thane's great gilded horn. But here no lady of the hall bore the great cup, nor did wives and daughters sit upon the benches with their men. No elders sat by the hearth, no children elbowed through the press of bodies. This hall had more the air of a fyrd meet, all gone to merry-making after the war talk was done. Holdric found he missed the high laughter of Maethbry, the babble of little Segli. He missed other things also, sweet memories of whispered touch in shadowed corners, but those he pushed from his mind.

He looked further. A wide hearth smouldered against the far wall, the fire low and little needed. Above the hearth was mounted the great skull of a mountain bear, wide almost as a horse's chest. Upon the skull perched a broken leaf-crown of gold, fine-worked with some strange ancient craft, the hammered leaves casting the flickering light of greaselamps into little stars of light against the stone wall.

Men sat singing at a near table, one bearing the tune with the strum of his battered harp. Their song was old and long-worn, a verse of mighty Hearoch. The men shouted as much as they sang and their laughter filled the hall. Holdric could not help but smile along with them.

He felt a jostle from behind and turned as a grizzled man in war gear limped past. The old warrior gave Holdric a companionable nod and carried on his way through the crowd to the cooking hearth. On seeing the food, Holdric's stomach clenched in hunger.

He followed the old warrior and took up a place behind him in the line before the hearth. A waft of meat and thick warm ale filled his nose as he came close. He took up a bowl and earthen cup from a common pile, and in his turn stood before the cook of the Torr.

The cook was past his best years, but still his eyes were bright and his face bore a smile. He ladled a full helping into Holdric's bowl—then his gaze fell on Holdric's weather-soaked boots. He studied Holdric's face. "I've not seen you before… Huntsman? Just in?"

"Yah," Holdric answered. "Kenndric Farstride's band. Just before dusk."

The old man gave a grunt, then ladled a second helping into Holdric's bowl. "Good band."

Holdric started to make his thanks, but another jostled in behind him, a wet weary-looking man still in his iron shirt. "Make way, Huntsman" the man grumbled. "We're all hungry."

Holdric stepped off and smelled deep of his bowl. He couldn't wait, he took a deep sip of the rich broth. The heat burned his tongue but he didn't care. Warmth flooded deep into his bones.

Bread he found also, and more than his share of thick cheese. That and a mug of rich ale and he was happy. The fare seemed food of the holy tree after the long days of rain and cold. He blew again across his bowl, taking another sip of broth as he looked for an open spot at the benches.

Hwaetearn had claimed the corner of a long table and held it merrily with Aschbroc and Eahstann. With them were two men of Hwaetearn's age, hard of face and clothed in the worn blue of the tower men. Aschbroc spied Holdric across the room and called him over with a wide smile and a wave.

"Holdric! These are Byarmin and Rammort, men of…"

The two men paid no mind. The one called Byarmin was deep in story—

"… so Broccort, he slips, yah? Ass-first, right into this *Great. Big. Pile.*" The man cried with laughter as his hands grew wider with each beat. "And he sees the thaneling coming, yah, and he jumps back on his feet, and tries to make hisself look busy. So when Arnsien gets there, and dumb Broccort is just standing there, keeping his ass to the back of the stalls, and his hands behind—back like this, just like this—"

Byarmin was up now, acting out the scene. His friend Rammort just saved a full cup as Byarmin threw his arms wide.

"Now here—here the thaneling comes, and sees this halfwit lookin' like he's hidin' somethin' yah? So he sees what Broccort's doin, but he's some dumb thane's son—no offense—and goes to see. Thaneling then just starts leaaaanin' around, tryin' to see what's behind. And Broccort, he's not thinkin' either, he starts jess sidlin' round, keepin' 'is britches hid—and these two just start circlin' round each other, makin' this merry little dance, and then Torrlaed Stalmaht, *he* sees this, he comes up, and…"

Byarmin was nearly doubled over in laughter. All were laughing with him, and Holdric struggled to keep the ale in his mouth.

"By the Stag, I miss old Broccort. Never will we see his like."

"To Broccort," answered Aschbroc, raising his cup in salute.

"To Broccort!" laughed Byarmin, meeting cup with cup.

"When did he fall?" asked Holdric.

"Fall? Pish," answered Byarmin. "The wild ended that blunder-pate. Said he'd a day free and made to walk down the Trace to trade with the boatmen at fish camp. We looked for him a week, found him not a league from the Torr, drowned in the fens. Like he tried to walk through the night, fell in some hole or another, and drowned his fool self."

A serious look came over his face. "Ghaestling or no, folk shouldn't go into the wild alone. You Huntsmen are mad."

"The wild's not so dire if you know the way of it," Holdric said. "I've done seasons out there on my own."

"Seasons?" Byarmin's eyebrows went up. Then a grin came over his face and he looked to the rest of Holdric's band. "I didn't know your Huntslaed took little ragboys under his wing!"

Holdric burned under the laughter. "I'm not ragfolk," he snarled.

"Outlaw then?" the man grinned, still prodding.

Holdric felt the eyes of the table on him. How had the boast gone so sour? His mind raced for an answer… then Aschbroc broke in with his ready smile.

"My cousin was too eager to show up his Ollda."

Byarmin paused only a breath—then he laughed.

"Hah! Mine was the same! I had this one wild cousin, and once the rascal…"

Their talk was overcome by a cheer passed down the table, and by the harp that followed on its heels. It had come time for the next man to play for the hall. Eahstann reached eagerly for the songboard, set it upon his knee, and felt out the strings.

"No old laments tonight, brother," said Aschbroc.

"Never!" answered Eahstann with a laugh. He tightened one sour string and set to work. His tune was sprightly and quick, an old laughing-song of an enraged ploughman hunting a wild hare. Soon enough the words faded to a simple tune and a shouted chant, and all stamped their feet in time.

Talk moved then to hunting, and Aschbroc launched into a tale of a clever stag that had stalked the spring highcorn with his does, churning up the earth and laying waste to the planting. Uncle Eikhram had been beside himself. Holdric smiled at the tale, remembering the wily creature and the hunt that had followed.

Eahstann listened also, his fingers drifting idly over an old half-forgotten tune as he listened. First Aschbroc fell silent, then Byarmin and Hwaetearn. Soon all in hearing had turned to Eahstann. With a shrug and a smile, the harper began to sing. He sang of love and dreams and dark hopeless nights under the trees. He sang of the huntsman's ache for hearth and home, of the call of the wild wood on a young man's heart. He sang of the joy of brothers, of triumph and joy and loss and despair. He sang of Ealdorholt life-warden, of the Night Forest and the empty sky, of the fading memory of an empty hearth behind.

His words at last died away, the last echoes of his harp hung over all the table. None wished to break the spell of fading strings. All were still.

It was Hwaetearn who finally spoke. "I knew you to be a harper, brother. I did not know… did not know of this."

Byarmin found next his voice. "Why are you not a bard, friend Huntsman? You have the gift for it."

Eahstann's hand faltered only for a moment before returning to the strings.

"I've not the memory," he answered with a too-quick smile. "Play me a tune, it's mine forever. But to hold all the histories in mind… for that, I've not the knack. Ask Holdric, he always won our Huntslaed's remembering games."

"But I've not your voice," Holdric said. "Put those strings in my hands, and you'll all be begging your Wyrling to howl for you instead."

"The two of us then—" Eahstann reached for his cup, and he raised it high. "Between us, we'd make the best bard in all the land."

He drank deep, then set his fingers quick again to the strings, his eyes careful to meet no other.

Byarmin raised his cup. "To the ragman and the bard!"

Aschbroc answered him. "To the Hounds and the Horsemen!"

"Hearoch Was a Hero!" demanded the table behind them, and a roar and banging of cups followed. Eahstann laughed and bent to the tune. Soon the whole of the hall was in song.

"Hearoch was a hero!" shouted Eahstann.

"Hearoch mighty hero!" came the answering call.

"Hearoch's sword sun-fang!"

"Sharp! Sword! Sun-fang!"

The song was ancient, the song was simple, and the song was loved. Mugs clattered and ale flowed freer still than words.

Safe behind strong walls, warm and full-bellied, they made merry late into the night. Cup followed cup, song followed song, and Holdric felt not his feet when Aschbroc helped him up the stone stairs to find his bunk again. All was dark, and if some still sang below, Holdric did not hear them.

He shot awake. It was deep night. The room swam about him, the air was hot and close. His stomach roiled. For a moment, he knew not where he was. Heavy snores came from above… he was in the barracks-room. He sought his memory but could find only a dim sense of laughter and ale. At the thought of ale, a foul wave swept through him.

Pain speared behind his eyes and his stomach heaved. He squeezed his eyes tight and tried to keep all within. Gorge rose hot and biting in his throat, he scrambled from the bunk and toppled to the floor in a tangle of linen and sweat-stained blanket. Again he forced the gorge down, but it was a losing battle and he knew it.

His hands sought madly in the dark, they closed on a chamber pot beneath the bunks, he took it in hand and choked out his innards into the putrid bowl. Bile burned his throat as sour ale overflowed the bowl into a puddle about his knees. He couldn't care. More came, and the smell from the pot drew forth more heaves still.

At last he was emptied. He fell back spent against the floor and looked up into the dark. All the world was swimming, the air was too hot, too close. His empty belly clenched once more, but nothing was left within.

He needed air.

He dragged himself to hands and knees and steadied himself against the floor, he tried to find his feet as he half-crawled, half-staggered for the far wall. On hands and knees he started, then found his feet as he reached the winding stair. Up, up he went, until he came again to the narrow door. He squeezed out onto the narrow open walk and found his place again by the ancient sigil-carved stone. There he laid upon the cold ledge, and there he found rest in the open wind.

The rain had passed. Stars shone bright—too bright—through shreds of cloud high above. He closed his eyes. For a long time he could only breathe in the night air, feel the cool stone beneath him, and wait for the world to still. He dozed under the chill naked sky for he knew not how long.

High bright moonlight speared through his eyes and dragged him back to waking. He groaned under the light and threw his arm across his face and listened to his breath. The air had grown cold. A shiver ran through his body.

Willing himself to wake, he rose and looked about. The sky had cleared. The far valley below was bathed now in clear bright moonlight. The silver light shone bright on the countless pools under the far trees, floating strange through the low-hanging mist.

The valley stretched far to the north and east, rising at last to a broad stony ridge that carried on northerly past seeing. And there in the farthest distance, shining silver and small, a wall of snow-white mountains held back the sky. His heart broke for the aching beauty of it. All was so clear. So open, so empty… so lonely.

He leaned against the wall and watched the ice-sparkle of the stars above. The salmon Aeringif was high, his mother Hifosidth in the starfroth beside him.

> *… she-swan, singer of the sky.*
> *Sweet-light she carries…*

He wiped at his face and hauled himself up. His eyes came to rest on the far stone ridge across the valley. As his eyes followed each moon-shrouded shadow, a deep crashing wave of loss and loneliness finally claimed him.

> *…Sweet swan see me, and spark my summer-love*

He would not weep… he would not. He had not dwelt on Frithi in long days.

Good.

His eyes fell to the dark wood below. He had sought solace in the wild before, and there he had found it. Cold comfort and hard, but comfort nonetheless. He knew the craft of the deep wood and he knew it well. He thought of Wydthoc's awed stare and smiled grimly to himself.

Here they called him Huntsman. And Huntsman he was, born and bred for the wild. He was made for it like no other. He let his eyes roam over the valley, and the wood beyond… his wood. This was his ground, soon to roam. The pools of the fens below shone silver in the moonlight, and far beyond them, somewhere in the unending forest beyond, lay the Hyssestead.

He bent, following the silver moonlit course of the Whitefork until he lost it in the night. Somewhere far down that water-road lay the place where the thread of his life began.

Heahfeldt.

He told himself he could almost see that cursed high hill, black against the far dark night. Perhaps even he could.

What might have been?

Not for the first time, he dwelled on the thought. What if the ghaestling had never come? What if….

No. No, he could spare no thought on paths untaken. That way lay madness, so had Ollda said. A man must think on what was. But what was that? He had no home of his own. No home and no name, he the landless son of a coward. A half step from ragfolk, dragged back like a tantruming child by the ears.

He cursed and he looked again over the dark land below, seeking out where the Hyssestead might lay. There he would find again his honor. There he would find again a home. He was a ranger, and he would be the best they'd ever known.

Long he mulled on the shadowed wood below, until at last weariness fell over him and he lay back against the stone. He watched as stars wheeled high and cold above him, and it was long before sleep found him.

But find him it did.

He looked over the broad wood below. The sky overhead was strange, the stars were of high summer… and yet the air was cold, too cold to stay outside. He passed into the tower, but still he could not find warmth.

All about he heard the passing of many feet, the speech of tongues both familiar and strange. The dark filled with hushed words that held no sense. He sought the voices, he passed through chill rooms of white stone. The words came louder, hushed and hurried, and then full of wrath.

He rounded the corner and saw two brothers of ancient house. Somehow he knew them kin. Rage and grief flowed through him, though he knew not why. The two brothers fought, a knife sank deep, blood flowed thick and bright and red over the stones. The growing pool held his gaze.

Another man walked past unseeing. This man was strangely dressed, a leaf-crown of gold upon his head. The man knew something, and so he followed. Soon they were again on the tower top, side by side on the wall, and together they looked out over the deep valley below.

Down in the tower yard bands of armed men moved in strange order. Boys held the reins of horses, and men in iron mounted high. Their blue cloaks… no, their cloaks were red, a red clear and bright as summer flowers. They were clad in bright sunlight, and their bronze shone like summer.

Through the gates the men rode, and down the road, and out in the far grassy fields. These men—*his* men—were riding to… something. War? No…not war. Knowing came to him, though he knew not how.

His men were leaving. His men would leave, and he would here remain. He was to be the last. He looked out over the broad valley—his valley now. Here he would dwell always, apart from them all, until the very end. But it would be well. A strange gentle creature waited for him, far off in the wild. So she had pledged.

But where was she? His eyes passed over the trees of the broad valley below, the stones of the ridge beyond... then grief twice over shot through him like a spear of ice. He heard the rush of water, he heard the screams of many men.

He looked down to the valley below. The grass there was bathed in red summer flowers, dark in the moonlight. Then he knew he saw not flowers, but blood. Blood that pooled in the drowned wood below, dark and foul. Blood that seeped over the stones at his feet.

Behind him came the cry of men slaughtering each other, begging brother to brother as a laughing hunger seeped over the wreck. The hunger grew, a hunger that waited as a coming storm, a cold and gloating dark that shrouded all before him.

He looked up to the stars above and all else burned away. The stars were cold now, cold and hard. Before they had always seemed a cool comfort, but now they drew too close. Their light was fearsome, they stabbed at his heart, his eyes hurt to look upon them. And still the sky drew closer. All was bright... too bright. The time was coming.

He felt eyes upon him. He looked. The strange captain in the gold crown was looking at him—the strange captain *saw* him. The stranger's mouth moved without sound.

Someone called his name. No, not his name. Some strange barbarian name. Holtus? Holt... Holt...

CHAPTER SEVEN
Greenflood

"Holdric!"

A rough hand shook him awake. Holdric groaned. Gorge rose in this throat and pain speared through his head. Bleary he put out a hand to stop the shaking and raised himself with a grunt. The stone was ice beneath his body. He rubbed at his face and worked the sleep from his eyes.

The stars of deep night hung above. Beneath him was cold stone, and beyond only wind. Where was he? Tatters of dream haunted his mind. Below the land was dark, the moonlight chill on the trees… he'd lost something. A formless guilt hung over the stone, but he could not say why. Dull he stared out into the night.

"Holdric!"

Eahstann stood above him, shielding a greaselamp from the cold mountain wind. "What in the castoff depths are you doing out here?"

Holdric's voice came in a croak, "Needed… air."

Eahstann bristled, his words were cold. "I saw. I cleaned your spew. Don't make me do it again."

Holdric started to nod, then clutched his head as pain again took him. Eahstann cursed him. "Huntslaed calls. We leave before dawn. Get up."

Holdric looked to the sky—the stars of Hifosidth and Aeringif were sinking to earth, and with them sank the near-full moon. Greylight was not far off. But still the trees of the far valley pulled at his eyes, and still shreds of dream pulled whisper-quiet at his mind.

"I… dreamed."

Eahstann had already turned back towards the stair. "You know we don't talk about dreams out here. Tell me when we get home."

"Heortlea is home now?"

Eahstann cursed again and ducked back inside the tower. Holdric was alone.

He looked out again into the night. Mist hung thick over the black trees below. Some part of him clawed for the fleeting remnants of dream… all was gone.

A last look to the high stars, then he cursed the chill and rose to his feet. He felt his way within, steadying himself against the stone, smooth and cold under his hand. Shadows pooled black on the stair below.

The greaselamps had guttered low, some already starved to darkness. By the sound of snoring he found the barracks. Too many bodies filled the close-set bunks, the air was thick with the smell of sweat and puke. A wet slick on the floor shone in the dim flicker of greaselight. Shame and anger warred within him, and he tried his best to push them aside.

He made for where his things hung against the now-cold hearth and felt for his cloak… it had been moved. He cursed and found it by feel, still damp and cold from the day before. He cursed again and fumbled tired and bleary for the rest of his things.

Damp and cold, all of it. He looked one last time about the stuffy dark of the room. Lonely as the wild was, it was better far than this. He slung his shield and felt for his spear, and then he made his way below.

He came soon to the common hall. A few of the tower men already milled around the tables. One looked his way and smirked. Deeper in, Hwaetearn and Aschbroc held a table near the hearth, laughing with the old cook. Holdric joined them, and as he came near the fire bathed him in soothing warmth.

The hot smell of food though turned his belly, and Aschbroc's laugh crashed in his skull. Wyrling lay near the hearth, and as Holdric came near the hound pulled himself up and thumped his heavy tail.

"Shhhhhh…" Holdric answered as he set his hand out for peace. He dropped heavy onto the bench beside Aschbroc and cradled his head in his hands. The cook placed a bowl of the last night's pottage before him. Holdric groaned and pushed it away.

Aschbroc laughed. "Caltbruk, he favors not your craft this morning."

Holdric peered through his fingers and saw a smirk on Hwaetearn's face as well.

Caltbruk cocked an eyebrow. "Don't think I don't remember you two after Ostliht's Night, lad."

Wyrling came to Holdric's side, nudging his thigh and wagging his tail. Numbly, Holdric took the bowl and lowered it to the floor for him.

Caltbruk turned back to the hearth, pulled down a heavy earthen jug and a handful of dried herbs, and set again to work. Wyrling lapped at the bowl, tail wagging. Holdric closed his eyes and wished for quiet. A spoon clanked against the jug and he winced.

"You lads said you were making for Eomud's?" Caltbruk asked.

"Yah," said Aschbroc. "After that, Huntslaed has not said."

"Kenndric Farstride and Eomud Blackboar under one roof. That should be a night."

Holdric raised his head from his hands. "I thought they were friends. Ol—Huntslaed said they fought at Heahfeldt together."

"They're not foes," Caltbruk said, turning from the hearth with a mug in hand. "But not all folk from Heahfeldt get on."

He set the mug before Holdric. Holdric grunted as he shoved the mug away.

Caltbruk shoved it back. "Drink."

Holdric grimaced. He took the mug in both hands and warily lifted it to his nose. The brew was heavy with the smell of broth, sour with vinegar and thick with herbs. He sipped and scowled at the taste, rough and bitter.

"Trust me lad," Caltbruk said. "You're not the first young ram to lose his head his first night cut from Mum's apron strings."

Too tired to fight, Holdric took another sip. The brew did ease his belly, and if his head still felt trod by oxen, at least his bones took well to the warmth. He drained the rest of the bitter drink in gulps.

Aschbroc clapped his back, and Holdric cursed him.

Wyrling's head was upon his thigh, and the hound let out a short pleading whine. Holdric reached down to idly scratch the dog's ruff, resting again his head upon the table as Aschbroc and Hwaetearn carried on their banter. Horse talk again.

"Shhhhhhh…" he hissed. Aschbroc laughed all the harder.

Holdric felt more than saw a shadow across the hall—he looked up. Wymud stood there, armed and ready. The Second's look was dark.

"Move, you fat-assed pigs! Greylight is coming!"

The others quickly stood, and Hwaetearn clapped Holdric's shoulder as he passed by. Holdric groaned. He looked again into his mug to see if a last taste remained, and finding none he rose from the table. Caltbruk watched him rise.

"I thank you," said Holdric.

"Get going, lad. They're waiting on you."

Holdric took up his burdens and passed through the heavy door into the open air. Deep night held the tower yard, the stars shone crystal-hard in the sharp air, the moon low behind the far hills. All was shrouded in hanging cloud.

Wind came cold off the heights. In the dim light of low-burning watchfires, Holdric could just make out the shadows of his band making ready under the gates. He braced against the wind and made for them, his blood sharp and alive against the chill.

He felt little heat as he drew near. Above a pair of grim tower men kept their tired watch. The others of his band worked in dull rote, tightening straps and readying gear. Holdric wordlessly fell in beside them and set to make himself in order.

He pulled on again his jack, grimacing at the damp that still held the heavy cloth. No amount of wringing and hanging could dry the thing in a single night, even had it stayed near the fire. As it was the thing all but splashed as he shrugged it on. His cloak too was cold and heavy, and the smell of damp wool and stale woodsmoke filled his nose as he pulled it on about his shoulders.

Wymud was cold as he looked them each over.

He came to Holdric. "You took too long."

He began to work Holdric over, muttering as he went, "I thought you wanted to be a Huntsman, not a dawdling hearth-sop."

Holdric bit his tongue as Wymud pulled at his straps and dragged him in place. Once the Second's rude shoves and tugs had been a terror. Now they came only as a passing bother. Finding nothing to curse Holdric over, the old man moved on, and his words for Aschbroc were no better. Holdric smiled to himself. It was long past time someone else felt Wymud's tongue.

He let the words flow past him and looked about the tower yard. By greaselight he could just see a single horse dozing against the door of the far stable. The geese were silent at last, huddled sleeping in some far corner of the yard. A lone guard prowled the far wall.

Overhead the first stars began to fade. Greylight was near, and still their Huntslaed was not among them. Holdric itched to be moving. His gaze fell on the watchfire and he rested his gaze in the dull orange light.

At last came the creak of the tower door. Holdric looked up and saw at once the shadow of the watchfire dancing green in his sight. He cursed his clumsiness, and then cursed again to see two kitchen boys behind the swimming fire-shadow, each struggling under the weight of heavy burden sacks.

"You get the boar's share" Aschbroc said to Holdric.

"Pup always gets the weight," answered Hwaetearn with a grin.

Behind the boys came Caltbruk, the great hound Wyrling bounding ahead past the boys and their burdens. Holdric eyed the load that would be his as the sacks hit the earth, and already his shoulders ached.

While the rangers worked at binding their burden sacks, Calt-bruk passed among them, one of the kitchen boys at his side. From a large basket the cook passed out hearth-warm oatcakes to each man. Holdric held one of the cakes to his nose. It was still warm from the second baking, rich with the smell of ash and oats and the sharp scent of highberry. The kitchen boy carried with him a pot of rich goosefat sweetened with honey, and Holdric hurried to get his little bodger-box ready for a share.

Eahstann straight away went to eating most all of his in a stretch, smearing each bite with the sweetened grease. Holdric yearned to do the same, but the road would be long. He ate half of one cake and tucked the rest away.

Wyrling watched each move as Holdric stowed away his food, and Holdric eyed him back with a smile. Finally he gave in, and knelt to share a single dab of the sweetened fat. Wyrling licked his fingers, wagging his tail wildly.

Soon all was packed away, and still they waited. More high stars faded. Grey seeped across the sky. Holdric's feet began to itch, he ached to be going. He was scratching Wyrling when he heard at last Aschbroc's sigh of relief.

"He took long enough."

Holdric looked to see Kenndric and Stalmaht come from the tower, both deep in talk. He could just hear the Torrlaed's words as they drew near.

"… and my thanks for looking in on Acramm. He's no kin left. I worry."

"We'll see what's to be seen," Kenndric answered, his voice hurried. The two clapped shoulders, and Stalmaht smiled. Then he clapped his hands and looked at the waiting rangers. Wymud nodded to Kenndric. All were ready.

Stalmaht raised his arms, and spoke over them the words of journey. He began in simple friendly fashion, but the words carried rhythm of their own. Before the verse was done, a hint of bardspeech echoed in Stalmaht's voice.

"… *Men of Kenndric's Hounds, the life of your people lays upon you. Ealdorholt keep well your way, until you come again to us of Ealdwyrc Torr,*" he finished.

"*For kindred past, for kindred present, for kindred yet to come—we go,*" uttered the band in answer.

The gates were opened. Holdric peered into the gloom beyond, shielding his eyes now from the watchfires. Eahstann buckled his jack closed, grim resolve on his face.

They passed through the gates and under the quiet earth. Holdric idly ran a hand against the rough stones as he passed. His fingers brushed the old carvings, their shape long lost to rain and wind. The old walking song drifted through his mind:

Though flood wash stone I follow still…

Then again they were again in open air. The road between the palings was dark, the stars of Hernweart still in the southern sky before them. In the heights above, the last stars of Slaugnwint gave way to the rising Waelstan. Greylight loomed.

They were not long between the paling-walls when their Hunt-slaed broke to one side. He led them through a gap between two loose palings, and passing through the wall they came out onto the rocks high over the far valley.

Holdric thought he could just see a glimmer of grey on the Whitefork in the gloom below, but they made not for the river. In-stead they followed Kenndric's shadow as he pushed down the rocks towards the fens. The Huntslaed waved them apart, bidding each man to pick his way over the rocks in the predawn gloom. They raced against the rising greylight, making ever for the shrouding mist of the fens.

They had left too late. Even in what light grew, Holdric felt na-ked on the stones. A scratch of gorse in the shadowed rock brought a curse to his lips, but he did not slow. Not far off Aschbroc echoed his curse, though whether from thorn or stone Holdric knew not.

They were moving faster now, Kenndric hurried them down the rocks. The slope grew shallow and the rocks thin. Holdric moved through shreds of mist, the air hanging heavy as a half-remembered dream, and in time the ground grew soft and wet beneath his feet. Some nameless dread seemed to grow in the cold clinging mist, though he could not say why.

Soon the bare branches of a drowned elm stretched out before him. He moved around a deep puddle onto drier ground and picked his way through thick branches of young alder and drooping sallow. In the growing light of morning, he could just see Eahstann moving off to one side, grim and silent as a shade.

Kenndric waved them together. The look on his face was troubled. He waited for all to draw near into a close huddle, then spoke low: "It seems the wood has swallowed up more folk than we knew. Stalmaht also misses a man, and asked we seek him."

He looked then to Wymud, "Old Acramm."

Wymud scoffed and looked to the sky with a curse.

Kenndric sighed and looked to the others. "Acramm burns charwood for the Torr, and had pledged a load now days past, by the last quarter moon. The Torrlaed wishes to know of Acramm's fate—and of the char he promised."

"What of Greatwatch?" asked Hwaetearn.

At this Kenndric's look darkened.

"Stalmaht has said he can spare no men for the mountain, and so sends word upriver to the Hythe. From there one will make for the folksteads and raise men for a work crew."

Wymud scowled. "That's many lost days."

Kenndric looked no happier. "It is all he will do."

"And Hyrtwis' wayrunner?" asked Eahstann.

Kenndric sighed. "The horsemen will search, he has pledged. He would not say when."

Aschbroc cursed.

"Their man Wulfhert will not live," Hwaetearn said.

"He was not going to," answered Eahstann, quiet in the shadows.

Aschbroc looked about to protest, but Kenndric waved him quiet. "Eahstann is right. Wulfhert is like already under a cairn, no matter what is done. We have gained what we can from the Torr for the others, and that with cost."

Hwaetearn's eyes narrowed. "The cost being Old Acramm?"

Kenndric's smile was sour. "You know the Torrlaed's mind, Thane's son."

Hwaetearn cursed under his breath.

"We've burden for Eomud," Aschbroc said. "What of that?"

"We make still for the Hyssestead," answered Kenndric. "But by the Drownedway. That will take us near enough to Acramm's field."

None were pleased, and Kenndric looked hard to each man. "This must be done, and it is we who must do it. It is dark chance indeed for the wood to eat up so many, all in the span of a moon. We must be wary. Keep sharp your sight. If you see anything, man, horse, ragfolk, *anything*, call halt."

Wymud grunted.

Kenndric kept on, "If we are broken before the Greenflood, make for the Torr. After, to the Hyssestead. If you know not that road"—at this he looked to Holdric—"make back here for the Torr and wait our return."

Holdric set his jaw, but he said nothing. Quietly each man found his place and soon they were on their way. The mist burned away as they trekked through the damp scraggly wood, and dawn gave way to the pale gold of morning.

They had not walked far before their boots were soaked again. The smell of the fens grew thick, and soon the midge clouds found them. They wound their heads in their midgescarves and moved on in glum silence. Each man forced his cursing mind back time and again from the whining bites.

It was almost midmorning before they made the Drownedway. They took to a low wooded rise overlooking the wreck of the ancient road, and on that high ground they stalked in silence. Even on the heights the earth was soft and wet, and below the road was utterly broken. Many swift brooks cut over the ancient stones, streams rushed through deep-carved ruts and pooled deep in the low places.

The water flowed swift and brown, swollen with the last rain, but Holdric could see this was no passing flood. Alder and sallow choked what had once been road, and water-bracken filled every hollow. The Drownedway had come well by its name.

Holdric looked further along the way they traveled. A small flat press of earth not far ahead caught his eye and he moved close to look. The mark had been there some time, green already crept over the smear of earth. As he let his fingers trace the ground, he found sure sign of a horse's shod hoof.

Seeing him, Eahstann waved a halt, and all spread out to search the ground. There was no doubt that men from Ealdwyrc Torr had passed here. It had been some weeks though, the horse-sign was much worn, the way well overgrown with thick summer grass.

Kenndric watched over the way ahead as they worked. The old ranger's face showed no feeling as he peered into the far shadows, but Holdric knew his look. It was not long before they were moving again.

The sun rose higher and the day grew hot. Holdric's jack grew sticky with sweat, his cloak scratched about his throat. He itched to be rid of them. With a muttered curse he pulled at the heavy straps about his shoulders. Already he missed the high clear air of Ealdwyrc Torr.

Sometimes their way wound high, and he caught the scent of holywyrt on the air. He learned quick to search the ground at the smell, for soon he would spy the tumbled stones of a ruined hall under the weeds. Sometimes the stones were tumbled over with the blue flowers of bee-blossom or gold mayweed, others they sulked low in bracken or were buried over with fallen deadwood, but almost always they were there if he hunted.

There was other ancient sign also, long mounds of earth raised surely by the men's hands, and woodland so broad and flat that it fair shouted of the plough. Once there had been halls and fields and folds here. Holdric could almost see the high maslin-corn growing, the broad hills of high grass along a winding road of stone.

Dream tugged at the edges of his sense, and for a moment it seemed he could just hear the ancient whispers, just see the red-cloaked horsemen riding tall through a riot of summer flowers. He shivered in the heat of the day.

He looked to Eahstann. Eahstann spared him but a glance, then looked again deep into the surrounding woods. A few times more they found sign of Torr men, but the signs came fewer as the day wore on, and soon the last traces of the horsemen fell away altogether.

It was near noon when he heard the fast-rushing water—they neared the Greenflood. Ahead Kenndric signed warning, and careful they came upon the water. Wymud walked through them to join their Huntslaed, then gave them leave to rest.

Holdric unlimbered his pack with a groan. He sat on the heavy grain of his burden sack as Kenndric and Wymud judged the river. The rains had swollen the waters to overflowing, and water ran high and swift well up the thick trunks of trees on the far side.

Holdric looked to Eahstann. "Is there a better place to cross?"

Eahstann shook his head. "This *is* the good place to cross, unless we go back almost to the Torr. Upstream all is drowning fens, and down from here to the Whitefork all will be swifter still."

Kenndric was lost in thought, brooding over the far bank. *Find one way worn, fear one way watched*, so he had always warned. The words held him still. Holdric followed his eyes, searching the shadowed green across the water.

Finally the old ranger stood—he had made his choice. High water or no, here they would cross. He signed to Wymud, and the Second moved among them and pointed, signing each man to his task. Kenndric and Hwaetearn would go first. They readied a rope and stripped off their burdens. As they worked, Aschbroc and Eahstann readied their bows and took their places to watch over the crossing. Wymud pointed Holdric back the way they had come, bidding him watch their rear.

Holdric grumbled under his breath, but found a hide and settled in to his task. The sounds of the crossing came quiet, hushed words and splashing water followed by a hanging quiet that seemed to last a season. Holdric ached to turn and look, but knew Wymud's wrath would catch him.

A great splash and a curse was too much. Holdric stole quick a glimpse and saw Kenndric dragging Hwaetearn back to his feet in high-rushing water. Holdric watched until they made the far bank, then turned again to his watch.

For too long there was only the sound of the rushing river. Then came another splash, and grunts of effort as another man made his way into the water. At last a snapping of fingers caught Holdric's ear. He turned as Wymud pointed with a scowl—his turn had come.

Aschbroc was over the water now, holding watch back over the way they had come. Near him a rope was stretched across the river, bound fast to the drowned trees at each bank. On the near side only Holdric himself, Eahstann, and Wymud remained.

Holdric backed from his hide and hurried to make himself ready. His baggage he pulled high, his shield he buckled tight, he checked again the guard on his spear. The river ran loud and fast.

He swallowed and took a deep breath to steady himself. Then he took rope in hand and stepped into the fast-rushing river. The current was strong and cold about his feet, and then his knees. Already the flood pushed hard against him. Holdric wrapped his arm about the rope and clutched it tight and crossed into deeper water.

The river reached his thigh and he fought to keep his footing. The stones beneath his feet were slick with river slime, the earth beneath them soft and yielding. His spear sank deep into grainy mud as he braced himself against the bed. He he cold and pushed deeper into the water.

He passed the halfway point. Hwaetearn had slipped somewhere near this place.

Water shoved hard against his chest. The current tugged at his straps and the cold pulled the air from his lungs. He clamped down hard on the rope. His breath came fast. Across the water Hwaetearn caught his eye, he was almost there. Step by step he made his way forward. His fingers grew numb, his teeth began to chatter. Another step, and another… then the rock turned beneath his foot.

He braced, but knew as he tumbled it was not enough. His feet slipped out beneath him in a tumble of light and water, straps dragged at his throat as water rolled over his head. He leaned hard on the rope and kicked for the river bottom. With rising panic he flailed against the water. He choked and reached, he felt his arm pinned against his side, his spear wrenched from his hand. He kicked again, unthinking—

"Stop! *Stop!*" Hwaetearn shouted in his ear. A fist landed against his head. He was in the air, then hit the rocks of the riverbank hard as a landed trout. He pulled himself up onto crumbled stone, coughing out the river. Hwaetearn threw himself on a nearby stone, soaked and panting.

Holdric heaved himself to his knees and looked about. Aschbroc came from the water, his face dark, Holdric's spear in his hand. He reached down a hand.

"You hurt?"

Holdric cursed and waved him off as he tried to stand. He looked to Hwaetearn, but the Thane's son was already back on watch, his hand on the hilt of his sword. The others also looked now to their places, all but Wymud, who stood over Holdric arms crossed.

Holdric wrung out his gear alone while the others kept watch. He moved swiftly as he could, but still he felt the burn of watching eyes as he worked. Every straightened strap, every shed drop of water seemed to take an age. Finally he gained again his feet and took up his burdens.

Wymud looked up from coiling the rope and waved Holdric into place with a scowl. Just as the others moved off, he called to Eahstann, "Don't let our water rat freeze."

Holdric ground his teeth. Eahstann handed over his spear. "Don't worry on it. We've all been pulled out one time or another."

Holdric took the spear with a curse and made for the trees. Eahstann made no answer. They walked together in quiet, the only sound the sop of Holdric's socks with each step.

He barely noticed as at last the ground grew steep and firm beneath his feet.

CHAPTER EIGHT
The Missing Man

The ground rose steadily and soon they were again in high dark forest. Drowned alder and rustling poplar gave way to long-broken rows of ancient elm and slumping groves of wild apple. The earth grew thick and mouldering beneath their feet, and as the sun rose high they came again under wide branches of ancient beech.

They had left the road well behind when the trees began to thin. Not far ahead blue sky shone through high branches— they neared a clearing. Kenndric paused well back from open ground and waved them to guardwatch just inside the treeline. Holdric crept with Eahstann to their place, and there they looked over the ground ahead.

The clearing was wide, easily a furrow's length in each direction. Piles of cut slash littered the high summer grass, and already spiny thickets of gorse and eager young birch were growing up into the open space.

Near the center of the clearing was the collier's burning ground. A half-dozen earth-covered charring mounds had been raised there, each the size of a large ox. Some paces past the mounds slumped a ragged-built woodsman's cot, and past the dwelling lay a handful of rough-hewn sheds. The smell of old woodsmoke hung damp in the air, sour and faded. They had reached the collier's home.

There was a rustle to one side, Aschbroc knelt near the Huntslaed and his Second. The three watched the clearing as Kenndric spoke in a low voice Holdric could not hear. Aschbroc nodded understanding and Kenndric clapped him on the shoulder.

Aschbroc made his way towards Holdric and Eahstann. As he moved, Kenndric shrugged off his quiver and passed it with his heavy bow to Wymud. In trade he took the Second's short cleaving-spear and bared the blade. Wymud set arrow to string and craned his head for better sight over the open ground.

Aschbroc came near and signed Holdric and Eahstann into a huddle. "Huntslaed expects no trouble, but we take the place at a bound just the same. He and Hwaetearn make for the burning ground, you two have the cot. Wymud and I hold arrow-guard over you. Move when you see Huntslaed take the grass. Yah?"

"Yah," breathed Holdric, and Eahstann signed his knowing. Aschbroc returned Eahstann's sign, then passed again through the leaves. Eahstann readied his arrow and looked grimly over the open ground beyond.

Holdric unlimbered his shield and bared his spear. He looked under the far trees, searching for watching eyes, and saw nothing but shadow. All before them was quiet, the little cotstead lost in a great sea of green. Save for one scratching field mouse, nothing moved.

Eahstann shook his head as they waited. "That kinless wretch is mad living out here alone," he breathed.

Holdric tensed. "He must have his reasons."

Eahstann seemed about to say something more, but held his tongue.

A moving shadow caught Holdric's eye—Kenndric was in the open. The Huntslaed moved low and swift through the high grass, cleaving-spear in hand. Hwaetearn moved with him, shield up and ready. Holdric nudged Eahstann and broke cover. He strode fast, shield and spear in hand. He felt more than heard Eahstann behind him at his heel.

After so long under the cover of trees he felt naked in the open air. His steps came swift and sure, his breath came fast. They were halfway to the cot yard. Aschbroc and Wymud would be moving by now. Holdric did not look, all his mind was on what was before him.

Still nothing moved.

He strained his ears and listened for any call of alarm as they came close. All he heard were his own steps, and those of Eahstann behind him.

Kenndric and Hwaetearn reached the burning ground and passed behind the mounds. The piled earth was slumped and scorched, that Holdric saw. He took no time to mull on the meaning of it.

They were almost there. Holdric paused in the shelter of an old goat cart, Eahstann close behind his shoulder. The cot stood not far before them.

A lone hen scratched at the earth before the door. All else was still. Holdric looked to Eahstann, he tensed to move… then Eahstann pointed to the cot yard ahead.

Holdric craned his head around the cart to gain better sight. A sagging hip-high wattle fence stretched from one wall of the cot to close in a small sideyard. Movement flashed through the withies, then all was still again. He looked to Eahstann. Eahstann nodded, arrow ready on the string.

Holdric bounded for the fence, spear at the ready. He moved low and steady, then covered the last few paces at a run. As he neared the wattles he rose high—

BAAAAAAAAAA!

A bony old he-goat bellowed back at him. Holdric grinned. The goat glared back.

Holdric looked over the rest of the pen. But for the he-goat, it was empty. And not just empty, but picked clean. The water trough held a small foul puddle from yesterday's rain, but not a scrap of fodder remained inside the walls. Even the withy poles bore the marks of the creature's hunger.

BAAAAAAAAAA!

The old goat butted at Holdric through the fence, kicking at the earth in anger.

Holdric smiled. "Settle, boy. We'll get you looked after."

Eahstann came up behind, just as a faint scratch came from inside the cot. The two looked to each other, then edged towards the open doorway. Holdric peeked within.

Inside a half dozen birds clucked and scratched, roaming over and around an old rough-hewn table near the low stone hearth. A kicked over corn chest lay by the hearthstones, and what was left of the collier's meagre stores had spilled over the hard earthen floor.

Holdric came close and the hens scattered before him in a panic. The cock rose up on the table and clucked his warning, but made no other move.

Holdric eyed the bird's wicked spurs as he came close. He spotted then a small splash of blood across one corner of the toppled chest. He grinned to himself at sign of the little battle. The story told itself: some poor field mouse had tried to sneak a share of the spilled corn, and soon become himself a part of the birds' ill-gotten feast. The cock eyed Holdric warily.

"There, on the floor." Eahstann pointed to the back corner of the cot.

On the floor behind a toppled chair lay a woodsman's axe, the blade still bound in its guard of bone and leather. Holdric cast about for where it had come from… his eyes landed on an empty peg on the wall nearby. Near that empty peg hung also a tattered cloak, a nobbly short hunting bow of yew, and a weatherworn quiver. Wherever Old Acramm had gone, he'd left his home hunting neither man nor beast.

They went back to searching the little cot. The hearth was cold, the coals long dead. The lone iron kettle over the hearth bore the blackened remnants of a sparse pottage, long since boiled dry. Eahstann poked at the old man's pack basket standing empty in a corner.

"He didn't mean to be gone long, wherever he went." He looked to Holdric. "How long has it been, do you think?"

Holdric looked again over the tiny cot, his eyes resting on the hens as they scratched the dirt floor for any missed grain. "Not more than a few days."

Eahstann thought. "Acramm is not young. My wager is the others find him by his burn mounds."

"Alive?" asked Holdric. His voice carried doubt.

"Maybe." Eahstann's face showed no more hope than Holdric's own.

Holdric looked again about the cot. "That doesn't answer for the axe."

"Could be the birds knocked it down," offered Eahstann.

Holdric looked over the hard-packed earthen floor. What little sign it might have once held was long covered over by the scratching hens. He shrugged and left all as it lay. They left the cot to the birds and passed again outside.

The he-goat bellowed at them as they came out again into the sunlight. Holdric opened the pen and shooed the beast out. It bounded for the cot yard and the overgrown clearing beyond and began to gorge on the ragged brush. It paused to cast a scornful glare to the two rangers, then turned again to its eating.

"That pile of bones isn't going to live past the first wolf pack that finds him out here," Eahstann said.

"If Acramm lives, he'll catch him back again," answered Holdric. "If not, better to chance the wolves than starve in his pen."

Eahstann shrugged.

Holdric looked on the rest of Acramm's cot yard. The scattered worksheds had been little better than bark-bound branch and thatch in their best days, and had been kept up poorly since. Hunting through the nearest, Holdric found a last brooding hen—she screeched in rage as Holdric pulled open the shed. He smiled and let her be.

Years of passing man and beast had worn the paths bare, even the thick summer grass had given up on the hard-packed dirt. Foot-worn paths bound cot, beast pen, and garden together before following a gentle slope down into the dark woods. But that was not what caught Holdric's eye.

There had been another passing also, a torn scrape in the earth not far from the cot door. Holdric came near and squatted to his knees, taking the dried roots of torn grass in his fingers as he looked over each rain-smoothed pock and divot. His eyes were drawn down the hard-packed trail to the treeline.

"Found your bogey."

Eahstann's voice broke his thoughts, and Holdric looked up. Eahstann was standing over him, a scarred piece of wood in his hand. Holdric held out his hand and Eahstann passed him the wood—a broken withy pole.

Holdric looked over the thing. The wood was a weathered dull grey, but still it bore scars pale and fresh. He looked to Eahstann, who pointed to the far side of the cot yard. There lay a pile of broken and scattered timber.

"Lead on," Holdric said.

Eahstann led him to what had once been the collier's smoke shed. Some few poles of the rough walls still leaned crazily in the earth, most had been pulled down and trampled into the dirt. The smell of smoke and meat still clung to cold remains of fire, but only a few gnawed scraps of bone were left on the ground.

Holdric knelt, idly tracing the rain-smoothed mark of a large hind foot pressed into the earth. He had no need to look close, a child could read the sign—bear, and a large one. The collier's smoke shed had made a feast for Old Browncloak then. But where was the collier himself?

Holdric stood and looked again over the packed earth. The way was worn by long years, but there had been no move made by man to gather up again the ruins of the shed. He backed away to see more of the ground. Rain had taken most of the sign, but he was sure… the only marks since the bear had been made by Eahstann and his own feet.

He looked up. Kenndric and Hwaetearn still searched the earth about the burn mounds. Some distance beyond, Aschbroc and Wymud knelt in the tall grass watching over them, just inside sure reach of their arrows. Holdric let his eyes pass over the men, turning as though he had not spied them in the grass. He raised a hand to sign all was well.

"Where now?" he asked.

Eahstann looked again about the broken down cotstead.

"What's left? Where does he get water?"

A pit sank in Holdric's stomach. "I think I know."

They crossed the cot yard and peered down the little path into the trees. The way into the wood loomed dark before them.

"Likely his wellspring is through there," Holdric said. "He goes that way often enough."

Eahstann warily eyed the shadowed path, then checked the set of his arrow on the string. "Well enough. You first."

Holdric snorted, then hiked up his spear and ducked into the trees. In the still quiet under the branches he could just hear the gentle burble of water, the spring could not be far ahead. He picked his steps to one side of the path and bent low as he searched for sign. The trees above had shielded the path from the worst of the weather, but rain-flood had wrecked whatever story had once been made.

He sought the telling-places where the earth might still hold sign, he brushed mouldered leaves aside with care and looked under overhanging grass. Still he found nothing worth the telling. And still his heart raced. He forced himself not to dwell on the size of the bear sign they had found. The hind paw had been long as a man's foot… the creature had to be huge. He flicked his eyes up, stealing a quick cautious look at the surrounding forest. Eahstann caught his worry.

"I'm watching." Eahstann said. His voice was curt.

Holdric cursed under his breath and went back to his work.

"See anything?" Eahstann asked.

"No." snapped Holdric. "…Wait."

There it was, the tell-tale flat earth of passing feet. The mark was covered with clutter, half wiped away by weather, but it had been pressed deep when it was made. Holdric traced with his finger inside the curve of what had once been a footfall… the footfall of a man.

There were still traces of a steep-raised ridge to the outside of the foot, a smear to the inside—the man's step had slid upon the earth. Holdric picked at where the step should have pushed away from the earth, trying to find packed ground under the drowning silt.

The track seemed to tell of a rolling, loping, running step, but so little was left that Holdric would be hard pressed to prove it even to his Ollda. He flattened himself near to the earth, looking up the path for another sign.

There! Maybe? A faint flat spot ahead seemed too far from the sign he'd found, though perhaps at a run…

"How tall was Acramm?" Holdric asked.

Eahstann thought. "I only met him once, at the Torr. About Wymud's height. But scrawny. It's bare living out here."

Holdric shook his head. The pace was too long for such a man, even at a run—and far too heavy. Maybe it was from the bear after all? That would explain the strange loping roll… but no, not with strides so long. Nothing made sense.

Holdric crept forward, trying to find anything sure in the rain-washed mud. Ahead in the undergrowth flashed the pale gray of piled stone, and thoughts of the far-away tumbled cairn haunted his mind. For a moment it seemed almost he could smell the rot that had lingered under those stones. Here under the trees the smell would linger…

No. The smell was only in his mind, it had to be. Still his neck grew cold. He squeezed his spear and crept forward. The sound of running water grew clearer as Holdric drew close, and at each step his stomach grew more sick with dread. Some part of him knew he was no longer looking for a living man.

He broke through the last of the green and found only water, earth, and stone. The forest floor fell sharp away into a swift rain-gorged creek, so high the water spilled over a low bridge of piled stone. On the far side of the water the earth rose steeply away again in a jumble of overgrown brush. Whatever rough road the little bridge had once served, it had long ago been swallowed up by the wild.

Holdric came to the water and looked now more carefully over what was left. Part of the bridge footing had long ago been picked apart, carefully built anew to hold a small clear pool of swift-flowing water. This then was Old Acramm's wellspring, though by the look of it not his alone. The mud nearby was thick with sign of deer, badger, and other dwellers of the nearby wood.

He stood back from the spring and quietly watched as water spilled over the stones. In another time and place, the soft murmur of the spring might have stilled his spirit. But not here. Not now. A chill pall hung over the place.

Holdric knelt and ran his hands over the stones, cold and slick with the running water. Unbidden memories came as he touched them, memories of wet stones on far-away walls slick with rain, memories of shame and old-chewed rage…

"Nothing?" Eahstann's voice broke the air.

Holdric started, then cursed. "Nothing," he said at last. Still the air of the place was sour.

He shook his head and went back to his work, feeling over each of the stones about the pool. Some did feel just out of place in the little spring, but that could have happened in a thousand ways, short days or long years ago. Wait… no.

No, some of the stones stood loose in the mud, something had shifted them not many days since. He looked again across the creek, thinking on the look of wild places where a beast had finally cornered its kill. High water or no, there would be no missing something like that, not with prey the size of a man. No broken branches told of panicked flight, no well-worn trails led further into the wood. If the old collier had stumbled away from this spot, he'd left no easy sign.

A deep grunting huff came from the thick cover beyond.

Holdric's stomach dropped.

Eahstann's voice came low and quiet. "Holdric, come here. Come here slowly."

Holdric knew the sound too well. His spine ran chill.

"Holdric… move *now*," Eahstann hissed.

Holdric tried to move, but his feet would not heed him. His breath came fast, his spear strangely light in his hand. Dull came the sound of Eahstann's horn, dim as if from far away. Strange came its echo, from farther still.

The great bear rose up through the brush, a great wall of fur and muscle. Holdric strained to move but his legs were rooted to the earth. The bear stalked towards him, grunting with each step. Holdric raised his spear with shaking grasp… and it fell through his fingers. He looked unbelieving into the beast's eyes over his empty hands. Someone yelled, far away.

The beast charged. Holdric was driven down to earth, lost to all thought. A storm of shouts and shoves sounded in his ears, hot breath covered his face. He kicked in a panic, his screams joining with the shouts above and a great unending roar. Something hit him hard, and for a moment he lost all sight.

The clamor grew louder, steel flashed in sunlight—then the hot salt of blood poured down over him. Something fell heavy. There was blue sky, and blood-flecked fletching, and the dour faces of men above him. Hwaetearn was there, panting and blooded, his bright sword red in his hand. Aschbroc stood near, worry upon his face.

A clean spearhead shone above Holdric in the light… his spear. Wymud held it against the sunlight, a look of disgust upon his face. He let the spear fall beside Holdric and turned away.

Holdric looked to Eahstann. Eahstann looked back, his face blank. Holdric cursed and reached for his spear. Wymud looked first at Holdric then at the heaving, dying body of the bear.

"Bring the meat," Wymud said coolly. "All you can carry." Then he looked to Eahstann. "Don't help."

Wymud walked away without another word. Kenndric came near and held out a hand to help Holdric up.

"Ollda, there was sign—" Holdric began.

The Huntslaed's eyes looked over the bloody mud, then back to the clearing. Hwaetearn was limping, and Aschbroc tended a hurt upon his arm. Wymud muttered darkly as he wiped clean his blade.

Kenndric leaned close to Holdric. "Not now, Feorson. Attend to your Second's word."

Then the Huntslaed took Eahstann by the shoulder, and together they left Holdric alone in the mud. Holdric watched them go and cursed beneath his breath.

He set to the bloody work. While the others carried on with the search, Holdric fought in the mud with the heavy, sticky mess. No sooner had his knife cut skin but he turned his head from the smell. Swallowing his gorge, Holdric carried on. The work was hard and hot, and the work was foul. Blood and worse covered his hands, and the heavy scent of spilled offal filled his nose. Whatever Old Browncloak had been dining on, his was no sweet flesh of summer berries.

Holdric turned his head and spat. He spared a look to the clearing where Wymud no longer stood, and the truth came to him: the Second had no interest in the meat. This task was meant only to drive the scolding home.

He cursed and took up again his knife. He heaved on one thick leg to shift the carcass… then paused in his work. He held a great forepaw in his hands. He looked on the long claws, then to the great lower paws of the beast. There was no way upon the earth that this creature had made the sign he had seen.

Quickly he let the clawed foot fall. Watching eyes would think him hunting for some unearned trophy, and that would not be a shame to easily die. He took a last look at the great paws, then shifted the carcass and set again to cutting out the loins. His gorge rose again at the smell, but he only wiped his blade upon the shaggy pelt and carried on.

None of this was just. Eahstann had distracted him, Holdric had not his bow. If he had been given a proper weapon, if Eahstann hadn't gotten in his way, if…

He hacked at the meat with a snarl, then cursed again. He knew already what Wymud would say to a sloppy butchering. He cut again, cleaner this time. At last he'd worked free as much as he could carry, and wrapping all in a scrap of the bear's hide, he bound it to his burdens.

He washed the blood from his hands and rose. Though he staggered under the weight, he was sure the old Second would say he'd left too much behind. Still he set the load to rights as best he could and made after the others. He had no sooner reached the clearing to join them than they rose from their rest.

The sun was already low, and long leagues lay ahead. Holdric groaned beneath his burden and followed after. His shoulders went from painful fire to a deep numb ache. His burdens had been heavy enough at the start of the morning, and with the wrapped meat added to his load he was bent almost to breaking. Time and again he caught himself staring at the earth like a broken beast, and time and again he tore his sight back to the wild.

The sweet scent and piled stone of long-ruined farmsteads grew sparse, the land grew rough and still more lonely. Now and again the thin trace of a beast-trail wound near their way, but even these grew scarce as the drowned bottomland dropped further behind.

Still the bright sun shone through dappled leaves, and still the birds sang sweet. The day was too bright for Holdric's dark mood. Far over the Mearcwater he'd come, and here he was less ranger than packhorse. But at last the shadows grew long, and in evening gloom they came to rest in the ruins of an ancient farmstead.

He pondered the place as Kenndric sidled them up and over their path to good sighting ground. At the crest of a low hill lay a jumble of overgrown stone. There Kenndric and Wymud would make their camp, the better to watch the way ahead. Aschbroc and Hwaetearn were set over the way they had come, and Holdric and Eahstann were given the broad southern slope below. Long-feral grapevines tangled over the hillside, spilling over broken tumbled stone. Holdric followed Eahstann to a dip in the earth, and under the vines they found shelter.

Holdric dropped his heavy burdens beside a pile of stone. He groaned as he carefully lowered himself to the earth. Eahstann flopped down beside him, less broken if just as weary. For long moments Holdric could do nothing but breathe, his head against the stones. At last he gathered enough strength to roll up and pull off his boots. He rubbed at his sore feet, and he ached for night and the release of sleep.

He looked up into the clear sky, a deep blue that was fast fading to night. He could not smell rain. At least the night would be dry. Still the chill that gnawed at his bones would grow no warmer. He reached to unbuckle his blanket when he felt a shadow cross over him in the gloom.

"No fire." Wymud stood above him, his face grim. "No light."

Holdric nodded and signed his understanding as he raised himself from the earth. He couldn't help a short groan of pain. For a moment, it seemed Wymud smiled.

"Holdric, double watch. Keep sharp."

Holdric had not the strength left even to scowl. "Yah." His voice was a weak groan.

Wymud stopped. The old Second turned and waited.

"Yah, Second. Double watch," Holdric said again.

Wymud scowled and passed on. Once he was gone, Holdric slumped again and rested his head upon his knees.

"I'll take it," Eahstann offered.

"No," answered Holdric. "I said I'd do it. I'll do it."

Eahstann shrugged. "As you will."

Holdric sighed, then leaned back against the earth and reached under the tangled vines above. He picked a grape from low beneath the leaves where none could see, popped it into his mouth, and grimaced at the sour taste. The vines had long ago grown wild, most of their old sweetness long gone. But fruit was fruit, and so he took another.

Their meal was cheerless and cold. His hoarded oatcakes from Caltbruk were more wet crumb now than bread. He tried a taste nonetheless, scooping out a finger of the sweet mess from his clammy food sack. A single taste and he spat it back out, all was dank with river water. His waybread from Heortlea was in scarcely better shape.

He hunted for a last bit of meat in his sodden pottage-sack, but there was none left to be had. He settled for a handful of barley, soft and musty with the river. He leaned back and groaned, losing himself in the sky above. From the darkness beside him came the soft crunch of Eahstann finishing the last of his share of the oatcakes. Holdric felt a fleeting wish for a share, then shame for the wishing of it. He kept his quiet.

Long after the sound of eating stopped, Holdric let his gaze pass back to Eahstann. His friend sat quiet, eyes cold as he stared out into the gathering gloom, his hands upon his blades. Whatever stirred in Eahstann's heart, he was in no mood to share it. Holdric looked back to the far trees.

Wymud had been right, and in his heart Holdric knew it. He had failed at the spring. His faltering might have doomed Eahstann. His friend was right to be cold.

Holdric cursed under his breath. Maybe he did take after his father. Maybe he was a useless castoff coward. Maybe he would earn a life like old Hauccael, a scorned bondsman of the fyrdhall kept more from pity than need. His heart roiled in anger at the thought. Better the shame of a ragman than that!

He snarled, his hand closed about a rock. For a moment he meant in his rage to hurl it into the darkness… then he willed his hand to open again. He would not be the one to break the quiet. He swallowed his curses and lost himself in the sky, looking on as the first stars of night kindled in the gloom.

Ruhnliht, jewel of bards and fishing-men.

Wegliht, light of homecoming.

The many other tiny lights followed, and he watched them as they came to life, one by one. He closed his eyes and set his mind upon his breath.

In he breathed, and out again.

And again.

And again.

The moon rose as night came. Slowly he opened his eyes. He watched the far wood as gloom gave way to night. First far pockets of shadow hardened into black, then the trees, and at last night drowned all in dark.

Holdric tried to let his mind fade with the light, moving his sense from eyes to ears as the world faded before him. Slowly the song of birds fell silent, until only a lone far-away thrush held out against the night. Then even that fell to quiet.

Woldgast took hold. Holdric's mind at last fell away, and with it his pain. All about him was dim and distant moon-shadow, above him only the silent stars. He knew not how long he sat in darkness, how long he sat in peace, but when at last the moon rose high and full, the bathing light found him still and quiet.

There in the light of the wanderer's moon, Holdric came grudgingly back to himself. He lay his head against the cold stones and watched Wegliht drop towards the far trees, Ruhnliht lagging slow behind. The moon's silver light seeped over the ground, rising like mist to embrace rock, grass, and tree.

He looked again to where Eahstann lay. The harper was still awake, looking out on the wilds as his hands worked absently at silent strings. Their eyes met.

"Sleep," mouthed Holdric.

Eahstann shook his head, short and curt. Holdric shrugged and went back to his watch. The Lady Lihtenstil rose high in the sky, and deep night came. Eahstann fell finally to sleep.

Holdric's head nodded and he jerked himself back to waking. He shook his head, angry at his flesh as it tried to drag him down into sleep. He had failed at enough for one day, he would not fail at this. Heavy, his eyelids closed to slits. He bit down hard on the inside of his cheek.

He had known more than one night from dusk to dawn. Most wretched, a few happy, but this was hardly the first. He could do it again. He looked again to the stars, telling himself again the story of each one.

His thoughts were broken by the whisper of a footstep. The step was guarded, and the step was quiet, but it was sure. Slow and quiet, Holdric's hand went to his knife. His fingers closed on the hilt. Another step…another…

Holdric's grip relaxed. It was Wymud.

Moments passed, and the black of the Second's shadow blocked the moonlight. Holdric looked up, fixing his gaze to where the old man's eyes must be. Wymud grunted once, then passed on. Holdric was once more alone in the night.

The stars of the Lady rolled now full into the heights of the sky. The cold of night set in hard, and Holdric pulled his too-thin blanket tight about his shoulders. Even in the cold, he ached for sleep. He craved sleep. He shook his head, biting again at his mouth to stay awake. He looked again to the far sky, pleading with the moon to sink low, for his doubled watch finally to end.

From his side came a whimper. Eahstann shifted in his sleep, lost in dream. The dream was hard. Pain crossed Eahstann's face, and as Holdric watched he flinched, groaning as he moved. Holdric laid a hand on his friend's shoulder. Eahstann started a moment, then lay quiet.

Eahstann did not belong here. He belonged back in Ettenmede, or wandering the Blackstrand with Master Uhlseid. As glad as Holdric was to have his friend alongside, Eahstann belonged no more with the Heortlea men. Holdric worked at his aching shoulders and looked out again into the night.

Many things were that shouldn't be.

He kept his eyes to the far woods, and watched as the moonlight grew dim. At last the stars of Rammlouf passed beneath the far hills, only his seeing-jewel Seahnliht still in the sky. The moon was low at last, only a fading glow left now upon the earth.

Holdric wanted to wait longer for Eahstann's sake, but could hold back sleep no more. He reached back to give his friend an uneager shake. Eahstann started at his touch. In the dim moonlight Holdric saw the glint of the harper's small axe, then again all was shadow. Eahstann grunted in the darkness.

"I have the watch." His words came hoarse and quiet.

"You have it."

Holdric was asleep almost before he closed his eyes.

But he dreamed.

Sour vines spilled onto the earth, thick and overgrown. The air was thick with the sweet stink of rotting fruit. He edged deeper into the shadow beneath the vines. Across the meadow someone shouted… the old man was cursing him now.

It had been a hard road, and a brutal one. He remembered all he had seen, but knew not how he remembered. Muddy red cloaks had covered unmoving men. Soldiers had lain broken beside their ruined horses, and not soldiers only. Boys. Old men. Wives and daughters and babes in arm. Even the beasts lay broken and still.

He had passed through never-ending rain and flood. He had crossed water stained black, reeking of sour rot. He had… fought? That seemed not right, and yet still he bore the pains of it.

He looked through the vines to the hill behind, back to where the master's hall at least still stood. He had not gone inside. He had seen at the door that there was no need to.

Below the old man shouted again, calling him coward… perhaps coward he was. He had not wished to come here. And he did not wish to go on.

The wheat-corn below was dull and grey, broken stalks bowed heavy with mouldering heads. The field promised little now worth the eating, but still there would be something, there must be something. All their bread was gone now, even the seed corn eaten. At home they had begged him, they had cried with hunger, and at last he had come. Even though he knew it would not matter, he had come. And so he was here. But he was not alone.

He walked into the grass, scythe in hand. He made his first cut, but the stalks of grain held like iron and the blade slipped from his hands. He bent to take it up again, but his fingers would not close upon the wooden haft. The old man would shout, the old man would curse him for his weakness…but no shouts came.

The meadow was silent. All was still. He willed his fingers to close upon the tool, but still they would not. He tried again, and again and again until finally his grasp held. He passed deeper into the wheat-corn, but even as he walked he knew all hope was past. Every grain and every stalk lay trampled and rotting in the mud. There was no more to be had. He had waited too long, he had come too late. He had failed. Worse still, his blade was clean… he had scarcely tried.

Wind came, and with it the night. Leaves rustled in the shrouding dark. There came a mocking laugh, and soon another followed. The things were near again. They had seen him in the field. Now he would die a coward and a failure both. He held fast to his little weapon, but with it he held no hope.

Smoke filled the night. A far light caught his eye.

Far past the meadow, far away on distant fields, funeral pyres burned high. The fires poured bright golden sparks into the night, strange distant pyres for a strange distant people. Then the sparks faded one by one, eaten up by the night until all was dark.

Above stretched a great hunger, a hunger that settled gloating over the heat of the pyres and drank them dry. As it fed, chill gloom fell over the earth. All grew dark. All grew cold. He watched and knew he was at last alone. Alone but for the stars above, and the killing beasts in the dark. Only the stars would see him die. Only the stars would know.

Let it be, then.

He looked to the sky. Hopelessly far away, the stars glistened with cold piercing light. He stared into their light, stared until it seemed their light was close enough to touch. He reached his hand out… and something moved within.

A cold silver light rose behind the pyres. He tried to hide his eyes, but the light was too chill, too cold. Still the light held him. He looked into the night where the dead had burned, where the nameless hunger had once settled to earth, now cast far away. Something else walked there now, soft as moonlight on snow. Before even his eyes could tell, he knew what he would see.

There in the far trees the great stag stood, white and moonlight-bright.

Ealdorholt.

All the loneliness of the dark empty wood fell over him, a loneliness and a deep longing he could not name. His heart ached. Shadows melted in the night.

Ealdorholt moved among the far pyres, nose in the grass. The stag smelled at each with the innocence of a child.

He watched as the creature moved through the far trees, and dread rose up within him. His breath came fast, and he knew not why. He needed to flee, he needed to run. At some silent sound the stag raised his great head. The silver creature listened, searching… and then looked his way.

Holdric started.

He looked about, then up. The stars of the Waelstan were high and fading, dim in the first hint of greylight. He groaned, still weary from too-short sleep. His clothes were damp with chill dew, his head a dull ache where yesterday Old Browncloak's giant paw had come down hard.

He choked down a bit of dried meat and raised his waterskin—it was empty. Eahstann offered his, and Holdric took it with a grunt of thanks.

The smell of grass and leaf was heavy on the morning dew. Beneath both was the lingering scent of too-ripe fruit. The far trees were already thick with the calls of ruddock and thrush, and in the vines just above a merry wren sang to greet the morning.

Eahstann followed the flitting bird with his finger, smiling as he spoke,

> *Wing, wing my little wren, dancing in the dew…*
> *laugh, laugh my morning-love, sleepy in the sun…*

Holdric's stomach rumbled, and he reached up for more of the sour fruit. His arm spooked the little bird, and it flew off into the early morning gloom. Eahstann watched it go, quiet and sad.

Behind them came the sound of thrown blankets and Wymud's muffled cough. They would be moving soon. Holdric closed his eyes, resting in the gentle birdsong. He felt almost at home here. Idly, he reached back for another grape—then spat it out as the taste of mold filled his mouth.

Eahstann grinned as Holdric spat again into the earth. Holdric glowered and reached again for the waterskin. Eahstann handed it over with a quiet laugh. From the far side of the vines came Wymud's steps.

Holdric handed back the skin and rushed to fold away his blanket. The wool was still damp from dew, but the dawn looked clear and there was no more water to cross. Likely he'd be dry at least part of the day. As he rose he pulled his burden sack close, and winced as he felt the wet from the grain inside.

"Eomud is going to call down a storm," he said.

Eahstann shrugged it off. "Like as not half of that was going to end in his brew stump anyhow. Don't worry on it."

Holdric leaned on the bag, trying to force out some of the water. Eahstann grimaced to see the froth against the weave.

"What is the tale with Eomud and my Ollda?" asked Holdric. "Caltbruk said they were not foe, but not friend."

Eahstann shrugged. "Huntslaed talks little of those days, and Eomud less. Eomud had a brother at Heahfeldt, that much I know—"

"You say had, he died there?"

"He died there."

Holdric set his jaw and looked up the path ahead. The Hyssestead would make a harder road than he had guessed.

Eahstann saw his mood. "Eomud takes not well to any at the first. Mind your tongue, walk strong, you'll find his better side in time."

Holdric gave a grim smile, then leaned on his pack to tighten the straps. The sound of coming footsteps sounded above them—Wymud's step.

Holdric looked up. He had all in order. He smiled.

Try to find fault, sourbeard.

Wymud looked him over for long moments, then quietly nodded and passed on his way. All were walking again before the first true glow of dawn.

CHAPTER NINE
The Hyssestead

They spoke little through the morning. Their path took them up a gentle ridge, and soon the last of the old ruins were well behind them. The trees grew thick. Beneath them the air was hushed and cold. There was no birdsong here, no skitter of startled woodmouse. Above were only shadowed branches, the sun far off behind thick-layered green.

They crossed that ridge, and then another. Each valley was higher than the last. Earth pillowed beneath their feet, and hulks of ancient trees moldered to earth around them. The cloak of beech gave way to ancient and twisting oak. An owl called alone in a crooked hornbeam tree.

How long they walked Holdric could not say, for the sun sulked behind sullen cloud. By his belly he guessed it not far past noon. Something gnawed at him, but he could not say what. Slowly he grasped it… he had not seen familiar ground for some time.

He looked back, checking over his marks again… yes, they were no longer crossing over their own path. Holdric watched his Ollda tighter now, trying to guess his mind. Soon Kenndric signed them into falcon-march, and Holdric grasped the aim—the old ranger feared wearing a scar into this ground.

Holdric spared a quick look over his trail behind. He smiled to see the soft earth carried only little sign of his passing. Eahstann crept more carefully now, and Holdric did the same. The afternoon wore on and the sun began to slip from its height.

Their course wound around a thick hedge of blackthorn. At first Holdric gave the bramble little thought, but soon began to feel uneasy. He looked deep into the surrounding wood, and his unease grew to wariness.

Something was wrong.

The thorns fell across the land in a rambling mess, broad as any deep-shaded bramble, all as thick and close as a farmer's hedge. The hair rose on Holdric's neck, but he could not say why. All the wood was empty, only leaf and tree, bramble and stone…

He dropped to one knee and peered beneath the thorny boughs. The growth here was thick, but pushing beneath the tangle of branches Holdric found the old scars of coppice work. Some boughs had been trimmed, others bent with such art as to drive each year's new growth to further fill in the living wall.

Holdric's brow furrowed. How long ago the spiny hedge had been tended he couldn't say—years, easily. The growth was thick, and the rootstock wide. He turned on his knee to look over the wood, carefully eyeing the pillowed earth. There were no signs of men here, these steep hills had never felt the plough. No flattened earth held the memory of a ruined cot, no herds had had worn their way through this earth… and yet someone had taken care to lay a thorned hedge, and to hide its purpose. A chill ran through him when he grasped the meaning, his fingers tightened on his spear. He was on a driving ground.

He craned his neck to look ahead, searching for his Ollda farther down the narrow draw. Dimly he saw the old ranger… then the Huntslaed pushed deeper past hedge and stone and was gone.

All around were countless folds of land that might hide an unseen foe. There were no guards on high palings here, no ancient stone towers or flowing banners. Still every part of this land whispered of hidden eyes. Stone and hedge forced their path as surely as a herding dog forced a flock.

No, this was more than a driving ground. This was a killing ground. He sought shadow and tree for the watchers he knew must be there, but found none. Holdric looked to Eahstann. Eahstann returned his look with a wry smile.

The harper's voice came in a whisper, "It took me a dozen visits to notice. You're quick." He held out a hand to lift Holdric to his feet. "We near the Hyssestead. Keep walking."

The afternoon grew warm, and the trees filled with a still-golden light. High above, Holdric could just see the clear blue of a late summer sky through tall ash and twisting oak. Beneath his feet the rolling ground was thick with soft-mounded turf and tumbled broken rock.

He worked his way over another cleft of stone, grimacing as he ducked around another dense knot of blackthorn onto a clear patch of rock—another murdering spot. He'd gained a feel for the place now. He picked his cloak free from the thorns and looked further up the ridge for the shadowed hunter's blind he knew must be there. He grinned as he found it, and smiled to the unseen watcher. No answering sign came from the dark hollow.

Content, he looked again to the earth. The sign of passing men was faint, and it was well hidden, but it was there. These men knew their craft, but too many had walked this path to hide their passing entirely. Holdric's band was drawing close.

At last the ripening berries of thick aelfsthorn caught his eye, and past that, just where he would expect to see bounding poles, there stood a gnarled ancient oak. Coming closer, he found carved into the living wood the sign of a boar wreathed in thorns. Holdric looked to Eahstann as they passed the bounds, and smiled to see the look of lifted cares on his friend's face.

Ahead the light of a clearing grew brighter, and soon the only thorns left were those of a tame fruiting briar that climbed young plantings of woodapple. Between these, in patches of afternoon sunlight, grew hand-sown patches of wild greens and lush untrampled oxfoot. Holdric's smile grew broader—even berry-thieving birds could not betray this hide of men.

He heard voices ahead and quickened his pace. A last rise and they entered the clearing of the Hyssestead. There stood the rest of his band, and there Kenndric spoke with a man Holdric had not met.

At first Holdric missed the hall itself… then his eyes made sense of what he saw. The hall was not hidden so much as it simply grew from the forest. It was not large, Holdric reckoned the hall not much bigger than his uncle's home. But the roof was of turf rather than thatch, the hall a faded green hillock covered over with late summer grass.

The turf of the hall spilled down both sides to melt into the rolling earth of the wood. The only timber Holdric saw was the doorway itself, a narrow way flanked by two carved posts so grey and weatherworn they seemed to melt into the forest beyond.

Only the faintest tinge of woodsmoke might pull in the unwary for a second look, and then only the pale flash of two fresh-dressed deer hides stretched against the turf might draw the eye. The place could not be better hidden. Holdric grinned at Eahstann and quickened his step.

Kenndric turned as they drew near, and waved Holdric over. "Byrcstod, my daughter's son Holdric. Holdric, Byrcstod of the Hyssestead."

The man held out his hand, and Holdric clasped his arm.

"Well met lad," Byrcstod said. "Your Ollda has spoken well of you."

"Thank you, elder," answered Holdric. It seemed to him that the greying Hyssestead man looked not unlike his Uncle Eikhram. Leaner, perhaps a knuckle taller and well-worn, but still something in his face looked familiar.

"Are you of Larkfell?" Holdric asked.

Byrcstod's eyes narrowed. "Not myself, though I've kin down past the spur."

Kenndric grinned. "He sees my girl's husband in you I think. Eikhram of Heortlea."

Byrcstod thought. "I know not the name. Is he of late Whitram's kin?"

Kenndric laughed now, and the two men set to working out the relation.

A shadow crossed the hall, and Holdric turned. Eomud Burn-bristle—for Eomud it must be—stood in the open door. One look at the man's stocky frame told the tale of his name. A shock of black hair and beard covered his head, greying strands flying free from coarse thick braids. His face was tanned and weather-creased, his pale blue eyes flat and stone-silent.

He wore a tunic of worn grey wool, grease-stained and ravelled, the sleeves pushed up over his thick forearms. Worn trousers of wildtan covered his legs, and boots of heavy leather shod his feet. From a dark belt of carved leather hung a palm-wide broadknife, sheathed in blood-red leather and bound in bog oak and beaten copper.

Eomud crossed his arms as he locked eyes with Kenndric. A faint nod passed between them. Holdric shifted uneasy in the thick silence. Kenndric turned to face Eomud, pausing a moment to collect himself. His voice was formal as he spoke the words of greeting:

Hale be Eomud Blackboar, Eomud Burnbristle, Laed-
man of Hyssestead—Life to your home! Kenndric Far-
stride comes, by ring of Eorl Ufthugh we beg shelter.

Eomud's expression did not change. His answer came tight:

Hale be the Farstride, roof and board I give you and your men.

Kenndric bowed his head, but Eomud had already turned back within. He sighed, then clasped arms with Byrcstod with a smile. "Be well, kinsman."

Kenndric clapped the Hyssestead man on the shoulder, then turned to strip Holdric of his extra burdens. The bear meat he passed to Byrcstod, and the heavy burden sack of sodden grain he took onto his own back. Then he led the way to the hall. Holdric followed behind, working his shoulders under his lightened load.

The Hyssestead was all he had dreamed. The wood of the doorway was weathered grey, the heavy timbers bore carvings simple but well-wrought. Between them was a door of ancient oak, heavy and thick as Holdric's own wrist.

He passed within. Carved pillars of wood flanked the long open middle of the hall. Arms hung there in good order, well-worn spears and thick sheaves of arrows. Dark leather-faced shields hung on the walls, and the wide benches beneath were covered in the way-things of many passing men. Eahstann took Holdric's spear from him, and hung it with his own bow upon the guest rack.

Holdric peered into the shadowed corners of the forest home, dreaming of his own place within.

"Who's the whelp?" Eomud's rough voice caught Holdric's ear. Kenndric drew Holdric close, and presented him to Eomud.

"I am Holdric, Steadlaed Eomud," Holdric said as he stretched out his arm.

Eomud took it, his grip like iron. "Holdric of?"

"Holdric, Holthund's son," said Kenndric.

Eomud's eyes barely changed, but change they did. He let go of Holdric's arm, but he did not break his gaze. Holdric stood his place and did not look away.

Eomud scowled and turned with a muttered curse. "Come then."

Holdric followed as they passed the long stone hearth. In the high rafters of the roof hung fresh game and wet new sausage, all wreathed in smoke from the smouldering hearth. Sunlight spilled through the eaves above, dancing in the woodsmoke. The smell of meat was thick on the air. Holdric's belly rumbled, and to his shame Eomud turned at the sound.

"Never fear Holthund's son, you'll see your belly full—if do your share at the stump."

Kenndric cast his eye to the fresh meat, a curious look upon his face. Eomud caught his look. "The deer are thick this season," he said. "We took two this morning."

Kenndric frowned. "They're early for this part of the valley, are they not?"

Eomud shrugged. "Ulfraeg said the same. It's been a chill year."

"Well enough," Kenndric answered. Still he gazed at the meat, unsure.

Eomud knelt at the wide-planked bench near the hearthstones, then shoved rough bedding aside and raised the boards beneath. Within were heavy jars of fired clay.

Kenndric passed the still-damp grain sack to Eomud. The black-haired man paused to weigh it in his hand, and with a doubting look gave the bag a sniff. He shrugged and dropped it beside the jars, then gestured for the next. Eahstann stepped in and offered up his own sack. Eomud nodded, then stood aside as Eahstann emptied it into a jar. Each of the band did the same, then moved to the far side of the hall to claim a space on the benches and unlimber their gear.

Kenndric caught Holdric's elbow as he moved to follow. The old ranger unbuckled Holdric's pack and fished within, then plucked out the wrapped bundle of oiled cloth and tossed it to Eomud. Eomud caught the bundle. Unwrapping the bound rags he pulled forth a darkened arrow point.

"Fresh from Calteag's smithy," Kenndric said, catching Eomud's eyes. "You said you needed steel."

Eomud's eyes narrowed. He eyed Holdric. "I did need good steel."

Kenndric held his gaze, his face stern. Eomud did not flinch. Then a shadow fell over the doorway. A man stood there, tall and flaxen-haired. He carried himself as a young man, but was made older by a craggy scar along the left side of face. The eye was gone, the lid tight across a muddy smear of flesh. Holdric was fixed, trying not to stare into the old wound.

If the newcomer felt the stare, he made no sign of it. "None follow them," he said. "Eikhund watches still."

Eomud grunted his approval, then gestured to Holdric. "Ulfraeg—Holdric, Holthund's son. Boy, Ulfraeg of Ternfrd"

The man merely nodded in greeting, then ducked out the doorway and was gone.

Eomud made his way to a battered cask. He filled a cup for himself and one for Kenndric. Then he sat. "Tell me your news Farstride, and I'll tell you mine."

Kenndric began the talk by speaking of the lost men of Great-watch, then of the tower captain's orders and the missing collier. Holdric kept an ear to the talk as he joined his brothers at the open benches. Eahstann moved aside, leaving him an empty space.

Holdric wriggled out of his pack and groaned, rubbing at his shoulders. Eahstann looked over with a tired smile. Holdric could only sigh. His hands moved by habit, grateful at least for a clean space to work. He emptied his leather pack, then brushed it clean and looked it over for wear.

Kenndric's tale reached the bear fight. Holdric winced as his own part was passed over in a breath, but Eomud asked no questions. Holdric bent stiff to his work, willing any sign of feeling from his face. He hung his pack to air, then began sorting through his things.

Kenndric's tale soon came mercifully to an end. "… but of the collier or what remained of him, we found nothing, not hide nor hair."

Eomud grunted. "Like as not he's a pile of bones under the brush now, left by Old Browncloak."

Kenndric shook his head. "My men know their craft. They'd have found those bones if they were near."

Eomud considered. "Perhaps he was taken farther afield, then. Acramm's cracked over the years. My men have found his sign all the way past the Bonemounds."

Kenndric's voice was quiet as he thought. "Stalmaht said nothing of that."

"Stalmaht wouldn't know," Eomud said. "You've seen how stretched for men they are on that rock. They hardly make it past the Greenflood at all these past years, and they stick to the Old Trace when they do. His horsemen cover upriver to the Hythe well enough, but he's half blind this side of the Torr."

Kenndric pushed the point. "Acramm was not journey-minded. His cot was standing open, an old cock crowing master of the house on his table, his pot full uneaten, his cloak unworn."

Eomud shrugged. "He'd not be the first old man to seek the Stag in the wild than wait for him abed."

Kenndric nodded quietly. "Perhaps."

Holdric walked to them, breaking the silence before Kenndric could stop him. "Huntslaed, the sign."

Eomud looked up at Holdric askance, but said nothing.

Holdric spoke on, "A man's tread, too large for Old Acramm. A running step I think, by the wellspring."

Eomud looked to Kenndric and raised an eyebrow.

"Sign lost in the fight, I fear," Kenndric answered.

Eomud harumphed. "You're not the first to take bear for man, boy. Though most whelps guess the other way."

Kenndric held out a hand to quiet Holdric before he could answer. "I believe Steadlaed Eomud has work for you, Holdric."

Holdric started to speak, but caught Kenndric's warning stare. He went quiet and turned to go, his ears burning as he made for the door. Behind him Eomud spoke on. "I'll send Ulfraeg to poke about the place if it will ease your mind. But before you go…"

Holdric walked stiff from the hall, silently clenching his fists until he was well clear of watching eyes.

The splitting pile was not hard to find. An oft-trod path of bare earth led around the hall, and there he found a low open-faced shed. Like the hall itself, the outbuilding was covered over with turf, all but melting into the rolling wood from which it had been raised. One side of the shed was filled with split firewood of oak and bright maple, the other held a low worktable, sundry tools hanging above.

Before the shed in the workyard was a well-scarred cutting stump, and struck into the stump was an old woodsman's axe. Nearby were piled rounds sawn from last season's deadwood. Grumbling, Holdric took up the axe and the first of the rounds and set to work.

Ollda should have let him finish. With a curse, he set the round upon the stump and brought down the axe.

CRACK.

It was foul enough that Eomud wouldn't give him the space to speak, but Ollda failing to back his word? The Huntslaed knew his skill. Holdric steadied the split round and readied the axe again.

CRACK.

The round split.

They had not been just!

CRACK.

The last of the pieces fell away.

He tossed down the axe and set another round, then pulled off tunic and shirt in the hot sun. He took up the axe again and brought it down hard.

CRACK.

Another split.

Holdric knew sign like none other. How many days at his Ollda's knee had he toiled? How many empty nights on the highfolds had he spent, how long alone in the wild with nothing but his wits?

CRACK.

He was better than any of them, in this one thing at least, and still they would not trust his word! He pictured Eomud's head as he readied another round.

CRACK.

Timber splintered. How was he going to overcome his name without even his own kin behind him?

CRACK.

The next round wore Wymud's face.

CRACK.

…Ollda.

CRACK.

Kindling flew as Holdric crashed the axe down hard with all his rage. They took him for nothing! His hard-won skill, learned in pain and loneliness… no matter how good he was, how hard he worked, it counted for nothing! With a howl he tore into the wood with the axe, striking the splintering wood again and again…

Until he missed.

Perhaps the blow went wide from the fury of his blows, perhaps from the stinging wet in his eyes. But still the axe hit wrong, the helve twisted in his hands and ripped free. The heavy iron head bounced back, and his leg went numb as iron cracked hard against bone.

Holdric swore as he jumped back, then fell back upon the earth in shock. He clasped his stricken limb to his body. He cursed, and cursed again.

Gingerly he felt at his leg…

It was dry. No blood met his fingers. He dared a look. The heavy iron had pummeled his shin, but luck or fate had spared him from the edge. Holdric cursed and stood, walking off the pain and dread.

He took up the axe again, he made to throw it in a rage against the earth—then his mind caught better of it. He ran his hand through the sweat in his hair and looked up into the high pines.

Let the bent iron cool… so Uncle Eikhram would chide him. Sometimes even that sour old man was right. Best to do something else and gain again his temper.

Holdric stuck the axe home again, and bent to gather up an arm-load of cut wood. Back and forth he went, gathering and stacking armload after armload into the shed. Before long he had finished, but the sun was still too high, the time for working not yet done.

He might as well rive kindling. He took the last armload of firewood and made for the working bench. He reached without thought for the riving blade—then stopped dumb.

Holdric stared at the peg upon the wall, and at the long iron knife that hung from it by a leather thong.

It couldn't be.

Gingerly he reached out. He took the blade in hand. Still his mind would not believe what he saw. Iron in hand, he slowly walked out into the sunlight to look on it more closely.

The spine of the blade was swollen from mallet-blows, the rowanwood of the haft had split and been bound tight again. A too-familiar hole had been bored through the wood to hang the thing upon the wall… but his hand knew this haft.

Stunned, he sat upon the woodsman's block, his thumb rubbing at the weather-darkened iron. He spat upon the metal, he wiped at the blade with his sleeve. Still his mind would not believe. Still he worked. Through the rust and grime, he began to see graving upon the blade—a running hound.

With spit and cloth, he worked to clean the water-flowing iron. With each mark he uncovered, the more sure he became. Here was the same hound, the same trees, the same trail of stars along the spine… it was true. It had to be.

He had not seen this blade since he was a child in arms. And yet he had known this blade all his life. He changed his grip and swiped at empty air. For a moment, he was once more a boy upon the highfold walls. For a moment, he set again the foe to flight.

He remembered fleeing sheep leaping in the sun. He remembered his yell of triumph. And he remembered other things. He remembered waiting at the highfold for his Ollda to return, not willing to believe his crying mum. He remembered the beatings he took on those highfold walls, and the taunts that came with them. He remembered every doubting, sour, scorn-filled look.

He looked again at the worn old knife. It was as he thought, this was Brukthorn. This was his father's blade.

He set again to polishing the heavy warknife clean, his mind spinning. Slow sank the sun, and slow faded the heat of the day. The sound of laughter caught his ear. He looked up, then turned to look on the hall behind him.

The faintest smear of smoke escaped the Hyssestead. The smell of meat was on the air, and within the others laughed. His friends ate without him. They shared meat with the Hyssestead men, men who used his bloodright as a common tool, a castoff for the woodshed.

Holdric's blood rose hot. The evening breeze was chill on the sweat of his skin.

He stood. If nothing else, he would have answers. If nothing else, he would have the truth. He strode to the door, naked blade in hand. He placed his hand upon the wood and breathed deep to steady his nerve. Some small part of his mind screamed its warning.

Let it rot.

He jerked open the door and charged inside. The air within was close and hot. At the head of the hall sat Eomud. Kenndric and Hwaetearn sat near him, the others not far away. A half dozen rangers of the hall filled the benches. Some Holdric had seen, and some were yet strangers. All were deep in talk.

Two men looked up as he entered, their faces unsure as they tried to read his meaning. Holdric stood shirtless, the battered warknife in his hands. Byrcstod saw him from the benches and came quickly to his side. The old man placed his body between Holdric and the hall, he leaned in to speak low. "What mean you here, Huntsman?"

Holdric clenched his hands against Brukthorn, bare edge sharp against his palms. "This blade is mine," Holdric said. "Mine by right. I mean to claim it." He felt his blood rise as he spoke. His face was hot.

Byrcstod looked back over his shoulder to the head of the table. Already some there looked on the two standing in the doorway. The older man leaned close. "Take it then, it will not be missed. Go now kinsman. Clean yourself and return."

Holdric bristled. "I'll not have Steadlaed Eomud call me a thief on top of a laggard."

Across the room, Eomud looked up. Kenndric's eyes followed Eomud's gaze, and his face fell.

All talk fell quiet. Feeling the eyes of all upon him, Holdric stepped past his kinsman. He drew himself tall as he could, holding Brukthorn low at his waist as he waited the Steadlaed's word. Eomud met Holdric's gaze, then the man's eyes went to the blade in Holdric's hands. The Steadlaed took Holdric's measure. He paused to weigh his words, then finally he spoke. "There is no kindling here, Holthund's son."

A nervous quiet laughter came from the benches. Holdric swallowed, but he did not shrink. Kenndric's eyes pleaded with him. The old ranger's face was guarded, his eyes showed… was it grief?

Let him grieve, then. Holdric could stand, even if his Ollda would not. Holdric looked square into Eomud's eyes, and spoke. "This is Brukthorn. I know its making. This blade belonged to Holthund my father. How came you by it, Steadlaed Eomud?"

His voice had not faltered. He had held his ground. Good.

Eomud held his gaze, then looked to the men of the hall. "Holthund's son is my guest," he declared. Then he fixed Holdric's gaze in his own. "He is welcome to whatever scrap of my workyard he feels worthy of his name."

Holdric burned. His jaw set, his hands clenched on the blade, he sought his next words… then he felt a hand at his elbow. Byrcstod leaned close as he took Holdric's arm in hand.

"Say your thanks, boy," he hissed. "Say them and go."

Eomud waited in silence, his face dark. Holdric met his gaze unblinking. His body burned to fight, to run, to howl. Dim in his memory sang his Ollda's words, *where pride leads, blood follows…* but Holdric minded not blood.

He looked to the Burnbristle, then to his Ollda. Kenndric's eyes flicked to Byrcstod. Subtly, he nodded towards the old man. Holdric chewed his lip, then met again Eomud's face.

Grimacing, he forced the rage from his voice. Grudging he bowed his head. "I… thank you, Steadlaed Eomud."

Eomud threw up his hand and turned back to his table. Byrcstod pulled Holdric back, walking him fast to the doorway and heaving open the heavy door.

"*Stay!*" he hissed, and shoved Holdric through.

The door closed with a heavy thud. Holdric staggered as he caught his balance, blood pounding in his ears. He made to shout, and only by pride and long practice did he keep the sound behind his teeth. He stalked hard to the woodpile, swiped the empty air with his blade, and struck it hard into the chopping stump. The warknife sank deep into the wood.

With a growl of frustration Holdric sank against the turf of the hall. Breath followed breath, and as his temper cooled he felt chill breeze on his naked shoulders. He reached for his tunic and shirt and pulled them on with a snarl. Then he lay back again against the hall, staring into the sky as he clenched his fists. Through the turf he could dimly feel muffled talk within.

Let them talk.

High above the three summer jewels gleamed against the dimming sky. He breathed deep and watched the sunlight fade.

Soft the door opened, then soft it shut again. Holdric closed his eyes, he listened for the step of whoever had been sent… Aschbroc. He could never mistake the sound of that walk. Loneliness and resentment rose within him, and Holdric clung tight to the hurt. Of course his Ollda would not come himself.

Soon he felt the weight of his cousin standing above him. He did not open his eyes.

"Why you?" he asked.

There was the soft whisper of grass as Aschbroc sat beside him.

"My kin, my care," he answered.

Holdric said nothing, and Aschbroc sighed. His voice came quiet, but it came stern. "I'm not your foe, Holdric. None of us are."

Holdric's jaw clenched. He sat up and looked out on the darkening trees.

"It's not just," he said at last. No sooner were the words out of his mouth than he winced, angry to hear the whine in his own voice. If Aschbroc heard, he said nothing. Together they watched dark gather in the far trees.

"No," said Aschbroc at last. "No, it is not just, but you will bear it just the same."

Holdric snorted. "Easy words from your tongue," he snapped.

"Perhaps."

Holdric would not answer. Aschbroc sighed and got to his feet. He walked to the chopping stump and looked down at the warknife sunk into the wood.

"Going to chide me now for wrecking the Steadlaed's stump?" asked Holdric.

Aschbroc's gaze lingered on the scarred face of the old wood. "Look at it, Holdric. You're the sign-follower. What do you see?"

Holdric looked—even in the gathering gloom he could see the wood was deeply battered, the old stump covered over in axe scars. Not only in the middle where work was done, but on every side. Cuts chipped the wood where no true axe-man would leave a bite. The scars were deep, many were old… some were days fresh.

Aschbroc looked to Holdric.

"You think Eomud has never done the same?"

He bent and carefully pried Brukthorn from the wood, then raised the blade against the dying light and sighted down the spine. He grunted with approval.

"You're not the only man to curse his fate, cousin." He passed the blade to Holdric. "Most men here do, for one cause or another."

Holdric took the blade, studying the edge without looking up. "They had a say in their fate."

Now Aschbroc scoffed. "Eomud called in the ghaestling to take his brother? Byrcstod begged his kin be flayed like beasts, or his children taken by fever? Ulfraeg prayed the Lady to take his eye?"

Holdric snarled. "It's not the same."

Aschbroc was unmoved. "Isn't it?"

Holdric shrugged and looked away. Aschbroc looked again to the sky, then back to the hall.

"Kettle's open. Coming?"

Holdric's stomach groaned, but pride held his tongue. Aschbroc waited a long moment, then shrugged.

"Your choosing."

Holdric did not watch as his cousin walked away. For a moment there was light upon the grass, then the door closed with a heavy thud. Holdric was again alone.

The moon rose high, silver light washed out the weaker stars. Laughter sounded dim within the hall. He paid no heed.

The evening grew chill. A cold breeze blew down from the high ridge above, and Holdric cared not. High above the cloudy starfroth stretched up from the southern trees. Through faint wisps of wood-smoke Holdric's eyes followed the starry path though the sky. There was Liefcradl, the twin boughs of the Rushes, and there the trickster stoat Cuiccandt. Brightest of all shone Hifosidth and her consort, carrying the jewels of summer with Aeringif their son.

Holdric smiled to remember again the long nights on the high-folds, learning with his Ollda the name of each… his Ollda who should have aided him.

His Ollda who should have stayed. Even he.

Holdric closed his eyes. His eyes were not wet, they did not burn with a cold breeze on wet cheeks. He refused the tears. Somewhere far off, a chattering chorus of wolfsong floated through the night. Eyes shut, he listened as the chatter broke into low mournful howls.

The sound lulled his spirit, and his mind faded at last into sleep.

He lay upon mounded earth and thick summer grass. Above him moonlight whispered through high swaying trees. All was so still.

Then sounded a midnight cry, far away. It hung on a cool gentle wind, a wind sweet with the smell of deep-layered pine, a wind too soft for such a dread sound. He could not sure he had even heard it… he listened for more, but nothing else came.

All was still.

He found himself in the trees. He followed a path through the chill summer night, picking his way over the forest floor. Sign was here… a running step, wide and limping. Bear? No, man. Which? There was too little light, and he could not see.

On he moved through the night, on until at last the moonlight spread under an opening in the trees. He had come to the laughing-pool. The strange running sign was here also. That sign, and something else. The air was still and close. He dared a whispered call, but no answer came.

He said they were here. He said…

The pool called to him, black beneath the empty sky. Fearful he searched the banks, there by the strange-carved stone where once the boy had loved to play.

Where are they?

Something moved in the far thorns, something dire.

Knowing fell upon him. Shadows closed dark under the branches, thorns pricked at his flesh. He felt the trickle of blood on his hands.

No! Not yet!

A gathering chill fell over his bones. Cold light seeped over the still black face of the pool. Mist crept over the water, writhing under the moonlight… no. Not moonlight. This light was too bright, too searing-silver.

There would be no more time. He wished to shield his eyes, and could not. He wished to hide his face, and could not. He clenched tight his fists and slowly he raised his gaze.

There on the far side of the pool stood the white stag. Clear as starlight he stood, pure as moonshine and cold as the barrow-grave. Ealdorholt passed through the shadows, picking his way through the dark thorns. Shadows fell away as silver light rose bright under the trees.

And then the great stag turned towards him.

He felt his heart fall away, he felt his blood run chill. His hands fell open and all the strength fled his body. Cold crept up his back-bone. He was naked, alone, frozen where he stood.

Their eyes locked, and he was not alone in his mind.

The white stag saw everything. He was bare as bone, locked alone in that cold all-seeing gaze. Fear caught shut his throat. The words formed in his mind, but he could not bring his mouth to shape them, could not find breath to speak. Still his question echoed in the space between them.

Are you here for me?

Ealdorholt beheld him unmoving. Silent.

It was too much. He tore his gaze away, he hid his face in his arms. His heart raced, his breath came fast. He wanted to follow, to follow forever. And he wanted to run, anything to hide from that soul-stripping gaze. His being tore, aching with yearning for he knew not what.

Still the light grew brighter.

He knew without looking that the stag drew close. Half in longing, half in dread he reached out his arm. His ice-shrouded spine rang like struck steel. Cold stretched into his limbs. He forced himself to open his eyes, to look at least upon the earth at his feet. The ground was stark and sharp in the hard silver light.

Too bright…

And then the stag passed him by, and the silver light faded.

He was left alone beneath the trees, grief and yearning at war within him. Slow he sank to the chill earth. Alone in the wood, he pulled his knees to his chest and stared unseeing into the black water.

All was empty.

❧

He was awake.

Clouds passed high above. The light of the waning moon was hard upon the earth, the stars of Lihtenstil the Lady high… the night was still deep. He stared he knew not how long into the sky, mulling on shreds of half-remembered dream. Cool wind bit sharp on wet cheeks.

Enough. He would go within. He rose quietly to his feet, gathered his things, and made for the door.

Within the hall was dark. The air was close and warm, the hearth glowed dull and red. Dimly he heard the sound of sleeping men. All were sleeping—all save Eomud. The master of the hall sat before the dull hearth, staring into the glowing coals. He did not look up.

Then he spoke, his voice dull and low. "Come to stab me in my sleep, Holthund's son?"

The sound of words shook him, and Holdric shook his head to search for his own. "Come for my blanket, Steadlaed Eomud."

Silence hung thick between them.

Then Eomud spoke. "Sit."

Holdric came closer, and took his place across the hearth from the dour man. A whisper of smoke curled up from the hearth as they each stared into the coals. Eomud did not look up when again he spoke.

"Ask your questions."

Holdric looked into his face, red by firelight. "What came of my father?"

Eomud did not break his gaze. "You won't like the answer."

Holdric swallowed, but did not look away. "Still I will have it."

Eomud smiled at that, breaking his gaze as he prodded the fire. Holdric waited long for the words. Just as he was about to stand, Eomud spoke.

"We made warding walk, down below the bounds. Your father held watch." Eomud bent forward, taking hold again of Holdric's gaze. "You're old enough to know what that means."

Holdric set his jaw. "Of course."

Eomud grunted. "The moon woke us, and we found Holthund gone. He'd left his watch, and us blind in the dark. Acramm was sure he'd gone down into the thornwood, so we followed."

"Old Acramm was with you?"

"We were all younger then, boy, if not so young as you. Even he. Shall I stop?"

Holdric shook his head, and Eomud spoke on.

"We had good moon, but it wasn't enough. We were half the night after him. It was almost morning when Kenndric saw the fire."

"Heahfeldt," said Holdric.

"Heahfeldt. So you have it," answered Eomud. "We weren't fast enough, of course. We were too far. The hayfield was burning before we made the rocks." Eomud stared lost into the coals. "We found some alive, folk sheltering down past the mastwood. We found them, and then ghaestling found us. We pushed those back, but they just found someone else." Eomud stabbed at the coals with his iron. "I don't know who."

He cursed and tossed the iron into the hearth. His strength had left him, and he stared long into the hearth. When his words came again, they were tired.

"We were weeks after that searching. Those we found alive we floated down the brook to the Whitefork. The rest…" He shrugged. "What's left of the rest is still up there."

Holdric sat silent, staring into the ash.

"And the blade?" he asked.

A hard shadow crossed over Eomud's face.

"I found it half a moon later, down under the south lookout. Their whole band had been cut down, dead before the fight even started." Eomud looked up. "By someone who knew where to find them."

Holdric shook his head, he set his jaw as he looked into the shadows. He started as Eomud took up the iron and stabbed again at the hearth, sending sparks floating towards the roof.

"So, Holthund's son," he said, "be you glad I named your father only coward. I nearly named him betrayer. I did you mercy."

Holdric ground his teeth, but made no answer.

"Look at me boy," ordered Eomud.

Holdric lifted his eyes.

"I do not have to like you, Holthund's son. And you do not have to like me. Prove you have not his bend, and the stain will fade. Your son's sons will have the honor your father lost. That will have to be enough."

Holdric stared into the coals, his spirit gone.

"Do you hear me?" Eomud's voice now was hard.

Holdric looked to him, jaw set. "I hear you."

Eomud looked back to the fire. "Take your bed then, boy. Your Huntslaed needs you on the morrow."

Holdric moved to where the others slept on the long benches. There he slept in dreamless quiet.

He woke to the sound of moving men.

The air was heavy with the first sharp chill of fall. He shivered beneath his blanket. For some breaths he lay still, weighing the light through closed eyelids… greylight threatened, but it was not yet morning.

There was the soft clank and rustle of hearth work, the scrape and pop of rekindled fire. Holdric wanted nothing more than to burrow deeper into his blanket and sleep until the sun was high. But he heard also the scratch of Wymud's whetstone. Better to rise on his own than give the old man's boot the pleasure.

Grudging he pulled himself up, blearily rubbing at his eyes. Byrcstod was at the fire, and for half a moment Holdric thought himself at home, staring up at his uncle from his tick by the hearth.

His kinsman saw Holdric stir. "The whelp awakes!" Byrcstod said with a grin.

The elder man ladled out a cup of waking tea from a steaming kettle and passed it over. Holdric sat up and took the cup in both hands, breathing in the warmth.

Holdric carefully sipped the tea as he looked about the early morning gloom. He was not the last to wake. Aschbroc still snored in a far corner, tangled in blanket and cloak, and even those awake had not yet broken their fast nor readied their gear. As Holdric looked on, one of the Hyssestead men rose yawning from the benches and ambled to the hearth. There he helped himself to tea and a sausage hot from the ashes.

Holdric's stomach growled loud, and he remembered with pain and hunger that he had not eaten. He too looked over to the hearth for food. Byrcstod grinned, and forked a whole sausage into a bowl of morning pottage and passed it over. Holdric hurriedly set down the tea and took the bowl with both hands, wolfing down his break-fast.

Byrcstod smiled. "My son ate like you."

Holdric tried to speak around the food. "You're more open-hand-ed with the meat fork than my uncle."

Byrcstod laughed. "You spoke with the Steadlaed last night."

Holdric swallowed and nodded, wary now. "I did."

"Did you learn what you wished?"

Holdric grimaced. "I learned. Not what I wished."

Byrcstod nodded, but did not say more. His eyes went to the blade lying beside Holdric. Holdric took Brukthorn in hand, mulling again on the patterns graven into the blade.

Byrcstod watched him. "A naked blade is a troublesome inheritance, kinsman."

Holdric shrugged. "Ollda says a man fights his battles with what he is given."

"It is so," answered the elder. He paused to drink of his brew. "Still, best not open your own skin."

He set down his cup and walked to a far bench. He rummaged there a moment, then returned with a thick grey pelt and heavy-braided leather lace.

Holdric's eyes furrowed. "Wolf?"

Byrcstod nodded. "They harry ghaestling no less than man, this far out we leave them be if we can. When we can't…" He shrugged.

Then he held out his hand for the knife, and taking it from Holdric's hand, he folded the pelt about the blade. Careful he bound the pelt tight with many knots, his fingers moving quick from long practice. "That looks to serve, until you can make better."

Holdric took the bound knife. He ran his fingers over the well-knotted binding. "This is no mean gift kinsman, I thank you."

Byrcstod waved him off. "It is my honor. Do your young folk better when your turn comes."

Holdric clasped hands with him, then with a smile stowed the blade in the fold of his pack, haft set where he could reach it at need.

A sharp, choking snore came from across the room as Aschbroc turned over in his blankets.

Byrcstod looked to Holdric. "Does he always snore so?"

Holdric grinned. "Only when he's under a roof."

Byrcstod raised an eyebrow and Holdric carried on, "Uncle Eikhram has threatened to send him out with the herds more than once."

The older man laughed and took up his cup again. It was a good morning.

From the far end of the hall the scratching of Wymud's blade on stone fell silent. It was time to be moving. Holdric wolfed down his sausage and threw back the last of his tea.

Aschbroc groaned as Wymud's kick landed.

Holdric sat up and reached to buckle on his knife belt. He pulled close his pack and rushed to gather his things as the hall filled with the sound of readying men. Soon all were at table, those slow to wake hurrying to fill their bellies. Kenndric stood over the table, tea in hand.

Hwaetearn looked to him. "Where now, Huntslaed?"

Kenndric regarded his tea. "Sounds like north—" He looked up to Eomud.

Eomud grunted as he rose from the hearth to join them. "North. Earnsclyff." He drank from his mug and spoke on, "I have a man running sack up that way, and he's two nights late. I'd thought to send Ulfraeg up after him, but your Huntslaed has told me of your missing men. If we've a knifeman out there, better a band does the hunting. My men I'll take out along the Whitefork, root up the latest hide-holes your ragman might have gotten into. We meet back here in… four days?"

"Five to the quarter," put in Wymud.

"Make it five then," answered Eomud.

Kenndric looked up from his tea. "Five days. We'll see you then."

He set down the cup, and with that the talking was done. Holdric rose with the rest as each fetched the last of their gear. He shouldered pack and shield, took up his spear from the guest rack, and strode out into the workyard.

The air was crisp and chill, the sky high and clear. Holdric shifted the weight on his shoulders and reached back to feel the haft of Brukthorn. It wore well there, hilt at the ready. Eahstann looked over and rolled his eyes. Holdric grinned.

Soon Wymud moved down their line. The Second gave Holdric's pack a doubtful eye, but carried down the line without a word. His turn over, Holdric breathed deep and glanced about the yard. As his gaze swept the hall, he by chance locked eyes with Eomud. The Steadlaed stood watching them from his door. Was that a nod? A quiet truce? Holdric could not be sure. Still he nodded back, the barest sign.

Eomud paid no mind. The big man laid aside his mug and came from the door of his hall to bid them farewell, speaking by rote the words of parting. Holdric's eyes closed as Eomud's words passed over them:

Men of Kenndric's Hounds, the life of your people lays upon you…

Holdric glanced up. The moon was low in the west, just sinking below the trees in the morning light.

… Ealdorholt keep well your way, until you come again to us.

Eahstann nudged him, and he spoke the answering words with the others.

For kindred past, for kindred present, for kindred yet to come—we go.

And then they walked out again into the wild. Holdric's feet seemed to move of their own will, so familiar had all become. They passed again the carved bounding-oak, they passed again the sharp-thorned hedge. Step followed step, league followed league, and Holdric's mind fell away, lost in the distant call of birds and the quiet smell of deep wood.

Ancient oak and beech gave way to high swaying pine and the rustle of poplar. The ground rose slowly beneath their feet, and on a high cold hill he saw the first color of fall, bright red-splashed leaves on a last lonely oak.

CHAPTER TEN

A Path Once Broken

Dawn gave way to full morning. It was good to walk again, good to be out in the open wood. Holdric breathed deep. The air was alive with the first fall chill, and with it the rise of his hunter's blood. Ahead his brothers crept quiet through the trees. He could just see Aschbroc and Hwaetearn far to his left, his Ollda just in sight ahead.

Eahstann stalked behind him, watching at his shoulder. This morning felt like one of their old muster walks in the timberlands, as if all the last year and more had never passed. The sky was clear and aching blue, the morning sun just warm enough to gentle the sharp breeze. Though wary, Holdric could not bring himself to feel grim. His limbs burned and he ached to run for the sheer joy of it.

Their way worked across the ridge and back again as they moved north. Ever they searched for sign of Eomud's wayrunner, but ever they found nothing. Holdric peered through the wild ahead and tried to guess the mood of their Huntslaed. The old ranger moved steadily on, his eyes moving from earth to shadow to tree. He stepped with wary care, more care even than was his custom.

The day wore on and sunlight grew bright beneath the leaves. In time Wymud's low whistle came low through the wood, calling all to halt. Holdric looked back to see the Second sign to them, then point them to their place.

Holdric found a sheltered fold of ground that looked down over their trail, and the two broke to rest.

"You first," offered Eahstann. The harper dropped his pack and stood to watch. Holdric signed his thanks, then shrugged off his own pack and sank to his feet. He took a quick swig of water and dug hastily for food.

Eahstann did not look down from the trees. "In your time."

Holdric mumbled another thanks and pulled forth a handful of crumbled waybread and Maethbry's rough bag of sweetmeats. He had also a few shreds of smoked boar, a last parting gift from his kinsman Byrcstod for some happy time. This bright nooning was good as any. One piece he ate straight away, another he passed up to Eahstann. Eahstann nodded in thanks, but kept his eyes on the wood as he worried the meat in his teeth.

Holdric closed his eyes in bliss at the sweet smoke of the meat. He stretched out his legs, drinking in the cool air as he rested in the sun. Their ranging was near half over if he reckoned the days right. He almost felt sorrow that soon they would turn home again.

For all the pains, it was good to be deep in the wild wood. He closed his eyes and breathed in the air of the forest. It smelled of cool and tired green, fading into fall. Somewhere far off he heard a raven's croak. It was a perfect day.

Too soon it was Eahstann's turn. Holdric rose to his watch and eyed the far trees as he took a last sip from his waterskin. His hand stung, a blister from yesterday's work at the woodstump. He took his eyes from the trees for a moment to fish in his pack for wound-salve. As he busied himself wrapping his hand in a scrap of linen, he heard Wymud's low whistle. Holdric looked up—this was not the Second's short chirp to return to the trail. Something was wrong.

Found came the call. *Come now.*

Eahstann cursed, hurriedly packing away his unfinished meal.

"You go first next time," offered Holdric.

"Rotting right," answered Eahstann as he shrugged back under the weight of his pack. Quickly they looked over their place of rest. Holdric stuffed all in the pouch at his waist, then plucked up a single crumb, the last sign of their passing. Together they hurried through the heavy green.

Wymud's low murmur was just ahead. When they ducked under the last branch, Holdric froze. The others stood near a lone boulder the height of his waist. On that boulder were three stones, each the size of a small nut. Two lay stacked, one atop the other, the third beside them.

The loreless eye would pass over the pebbles with little thought. To Holdric, the placing of the stones spoke louder than any graven mark of the Oncefolk. They held a single word of message: *Hunted.*

Just beyond, a broken branch showed the way like a banner. Below the trail led over soft ground, the wayrunner had not even tried to hide his sign. Kenndric knelt over the runner's trail and looked close. The old ranger's face was grim. At last Kenndric rose and looked back up the ridge, back to where the man had come from. He signed Wymud to his side, and the others into a wide falcon-march. Quietly each man fell into his place and they followed after the lost runner.

Kenndric led the hunt, his eyes on the earth. Wymud had taken up Kenndric's greatbow, and with it kept watch over the dark wood ahead. They moved quick. The wayrunner's path was not hard to find.

The trail ran down and across the ridge, and as they moved Holdric's path would sometimes cross over the sign left behind. He could not help but steal glances from his watch to see the tale at his feet.

The wayrunner's toes had dragged as he ran. There was a shallow punch in the earth where he had stumbled and caught his fall. The man had been tired, but not tired only. His steps were halting and unsure. A broken branch told where he had tripped upon the earth and reached to catch himself. Had he then moved at night then? There would have been but little moonlight here beneath the leaves, it could be so...

Holdric felt a nudge in his side, Eahstann pointed on to Kenndric. The Huntslaed signed back the message—*Ghaestling. Chased by one.*

A chill rolled down Holdric's back, but he forced his stride not to break. Their way wound down the side of the ridge. Again his path crossed over Reodhoc's sign, a crust of dried mud where the wayrunner had slipped in once-wet earth.

The chase had happened during the last big rain then, or soon after, when the ground was still soaked. Holdric counted over the days in his mind… it had been three mornings since the downpour. Yes, that matched Eomud's words.

Eahstann pulled their guard wide, the easier to watch Kenndric's flank as the old ranger followed the runner's flight further down the ridge. Ever their man had taken the downward path, the easy path. His feet had dragged, he had been too tired to sidle-step the hunters. He was no longer thinking. The story knotted itself together in Holdric's mind. Weary, alone in dark and rain…

Another flash of smeared ground caught Holdric's eye. He looked close, then froze. Cold knotted in his belly.

He had never seen ghaestling sign before. His Ollda had told him of it, had drawn it in the dirt for him, had given him no end of teaching. But Holdric had never seen the mark himself, not until now. This could be nothing else. The footstep was like a man's, but strangely wrong. The strides were too long, the foot stretched and oddly narrow. Still the things had moved not unlike men, and their steps were swift and sure. Holdric could almost see them as they stalked along the earth. He could not look away.

Eahstann stopped. He saw Holdric's gaze fixed to the earth, then he also saw the sign. "How many?"

Holdric shook his mind free. He looked over the ground… more than he could quickly count. He raised his hand and signed, *Ghaestling. Many.*

Wymud scowled, but passed the sign on to their Huntslaed.

The hunt moved faster now. A bright flash of bare wood caught Holdric's eye—a branch had been nearly lopped free of a leaning birch. More, the tree had been hacked with great shuddering blows. Eahstann's eyes went to the tree and his mouth drew tight, his eyes grave.

More sign joined the way as they worked their way down the ridge. The ghaestling were eager now. Broken branches came more often, sprays of earth were flung from their path where they jumped in glee, the ground was pushed and torn where they skipped as they ran. A feeling of frenzy hung over the path.

More broken green lay ahead. Kenndric moved faster, the trail was easy now. Holdric had followed enough wild hunts to know they were nearing the end. Then he saw it, and his words came unbidden. "Oh no."

The sign could not be missed. Ghaestling toes had dug deep into the earth. Ghaestling feet had sent dirt and leaf spattering behind in a furious run. Eahstann looked to Holdric, and Holdric whispered in answer, "They found him."

At that moment Kenndric's low whistle echoed through the trees. Eahstann's eyes closed in sad knowing, and both looked into the wall of forest ahead. There had been no great need in the low sound, no call to battle, no plea for help. Only a simple sad message: *Come. Found.*

Together they walked to where the Huntslaed waited. The way was straight, the ghaestling pace long and sure. As Holdric came near he saw again the wayrunner's sign. The man's pace was broken. The ground was torn and smeared where he had slid through mud. Every step screamed of panic, of raw unthinking fear.

Hwaetearn and Aschbroc stood not far ahead, and just beyond Kenndric and Wymud huddled at the foot of a great yew. Something dark lay crumpled at their feet. Holdric swallowed, his belly clenched tight as he walked. Even as he drew near he could see the grim color of open flesh.

The breeze was cool. Daylight shone sharp and gold. From far away came the sweet song of sparrows… but all felt wrong. Kenndric looked up as they came near.

Holdric had known what to expect. Still the sight hung crooked in his eye, bent with the queer air of the slaughter yard. What remained of Eomud's wayrunner lay upon the earth, no longer living man, not yet mere meat. Clots of burned pitch lay on the grass, blood clumped where rain had not washed it away. Holdric did not wish to bear the sight before him, but still he knew it would lurk forever in the shadows of his mind.

The runner's hair was the same ruddy gold as Holdric's own. More, they had been almost of an age. The young man's tunic bore the grey-knotted weave of the Dorbruk men, and though he wore like trousers of wildtan deer as his master Eomud, the leather was only little-worn. He could not have served at the Hyssestead long.

Wymud sighed. "It's Reodhoc. It's him."

The Second knelt beside what was left of the wayrunner. He plucked the brooch from the young man's cracked chest, then paused to wipe it clean of blood. He let it slip into his pouch, a new sad star for some distant wall.

"Take your rest, son."

Kenndric rose.

They spoke as one. The verses fell strange from their lips, the words too mournful for the bright open wood:

The branch is broken and cannot be mended.
The leaves are flown and cannot be gathered again.
The shadows gather cold.

The bended track is empty, cold breath hangs still.
Your voice has passed beyond all hearing.
The night-wind has blown.

I cry to wind for you, and my cries are lost.
I feel for your being, but stone-veil blocks my way.
Starlight fills the void.

Arrow-stuck, take your hunter,
Forest-kissed, guide his feet.

Reodhoc, Follow Ealdorholt, follow shaded-path
against the thorns of night.
Reodhoc, Follow Ealdorholt, follow to sun-kissed grass,
follow to the place prepared for you.

Follow to your kin before,
Go and wait us yet to come.

In summer's green, take your rest.
Beneath Maesteald's leaves, take your rest.

Until we meet again.
Until we meet again.

All fell to silence.

They needed no more words to make the little grave, nor to wrap the young man in his tattered cloak and lay him into his last bed. They covered him over with stone and soil of the wood. Kenndric carved the sigils of sun, star, and tree for him upon the old yew under which he lay. Then then they left the place to the wild.

The air blew sweet as they climbed away from the killing ground. Grim sights still clawed at Holdric's mind, but he pushed them away. He looked only out into the wood, and he thought only on what he must. Soon they had left the spot well behind.

Each man moved in dark and quiet watch, alone in his own thoughts. In time they came to a great tumble of rock beneath a fallen pine, and there the Huntslaed signed them to circle near for talk. Each man took his watching place. All were still. The old ranger looked to each of them, and when he spoke his voice came hard: "We will end them, fear not."

The cool afternoon bit at Holdric's skin. His limbs raged, full of fire. He was hungry for the fight.

Kenndric's look was dour. "We must be wise. I would hear your words."

Wymud spoke first. "Hunting ghaestling is our work. We hunt them."

Hwaetearn shook his head. "The man came from Earnsclyff. We know not how far the ghaestling followed, or what news he may have brought. Two should go on to the Watch for word. The rest of us give chase as Second says. We meet back at the Hyssestead, share what we know."

"They've numbers on us as it is," said Aschbroc, "and we know not how many others they may have. I say we are not enough to part company."

Kenndric nodded. "To that I agree."

"We are still near the Hyssestead," offered Eahstann. "Eomud's men can help us with this band. Hunt them together, then make for Earnsclyff."

Kenndric sat in silence, mulling their words. He looked to them for more, but none spoke again. Then he made his choice.

"Hwaetearn has grasped the iron, there is yet too much we do not know. Seeing how things lie at Earnsclyff must be our first aim—Eomud's men can best a hunting band of ghaestling if that is all we face. But the Earnsclyff men are on the very edge, and they are few. If they have seen more, we need to know. If they need aid, we are the nearest. We go there together, we see what is to be seen.

"Then—with or without Eomud's men—we hunt this band to ground." At this he looked to Wymud. "That is our work." He looked then to each of the others. "Questions?"

There were none.

"Then it is done and bound. Take your places, and keep your watch sharp!"

The Huntslaed rose and set his arrow to string. In scarce a breath all were again on their way. From his place on the wing, Holdric's heart raced. He looked into the wild and his hand clenched tight the shaft of his spear.

They pushed hard, and he relished the heat in his limbs as they climbed, the careful watch that pushed grim sights from his mind. Fall's chill turned cold, and shadow began to gather under the trees.

Eahstann walked ahead to join the Huntslaed for news, then paused to wait for Holdric to reach him.

"What's his word?" asked Holdric.

Eahstann looked up the ridge, his face grim. "We push late, to the Fellstones."

Holdric almost laughed. "That sounds a place of cheer."

Eahstann smiled, but his smile was tight. "So you have it. The place is an old fastness, or so Wymud reckons. Oncefolk-built. The workings are gone, but it is good ground. We will not be overseen, and at the worst can fly where we will."

Holdric looked up after Kenndric, just in sight before them. "How far?"

"Most rangings? Midmorning tomorrow. Huntslaed means to make it by evening."

Holdric grew wary. "Woe take us if ghaestling wait there, and we come blind and weary."

"He weighs it worth the daring. We can reach it by nightfall." Eahstann grinned. "At least the rest of us can."

Holdric cursed and hefted his pack. "Push much faster, you'll be begging me to carry you."

Eahstann laughed and quickened his step.

On they walked, though the way grew harder with each league. Now and again the trees would open over the valley below. The wood below was thick and green, but already traces of mist hung over the trees. Across the valley was a high ridge, and at the far southern foot of that ridge rose Ealdwyrc Torr, lonely against the sky. Holdric turned away lest he stare too long.

They moved fast. Rarely did they stop, and scarce for more than a few breaths when they did. Maple and beech and poplar gave way to thick tall pine and high mountain yew. The earth grew hard beneath their feet, and more than once Holdric stumbled cursing on the loose stone of the heights. Just as the light began to fade, Eahstann's weary pace quickened.

"Almost there," he breathed.

Ahead through thinning trees, the Huntslaed signed a stalk. Warily they neared the top, watching for hidden foes with each step. On the far wing Aschbroc and Hwaetearn drew near. Above the way grew steeper yet. They paused just short of the crest, and there Kenndric held them in quiet.

The Fellstones lay bare above them. Somehow Holdric had expected more, what rose above looked little more than a tumble of rock and earth. They waited and listened. After a long quiet Kenndric crept up alone, and finding nothing he waved them to the top.

The crest of the ridge was broad and flat, a great stretch of hard-packed earth and stone. Once many men might have made camp here. Even now the raking light of dusk told of what had once been old narrow roads. Dips and shallows crossed the crest in square order, all now long grown over with thin wind-ravaged pine. Rain had brought low the long-ago walls of earth, and if timber palings had once stood, the forest had claimed them long ago.

Holdric looked closely over the ground. Were the high trees about them brought down, he judged the place would have good sight over all the western valley, even to the Torr itself. He peered then through the trees to the east. That valley also would be in sight, perhaps all the way even to Heahfeldt. Whatever had come to the Oncefolk, they had placed their workings well.

Wymud set them to search in the fading light for signs of ghaestling. Holdric looked over the stretch of ground given him, Eahstann at his side. In a bit of soft earth he saw the fresh steps of his Ollda. They were heavy in the toe, and not so well-placed as was his way. Holdric grinned at the sight—even the mighty Huntslaed could weary on the high stones.

He looked up. His Ollda was not far off, eyes fixed on the near wood. Holdric looked again to the sign before him, and now his own brow furrowed. He knelt to look close on what the Huntslaed had seen… the ground was thick with deer sign. A small herd had passed over this ridge from the east, heading now down into the valley behind them. As Holdric followed the way of the beasts' passing with his eyes, Eahstann spared him a quick glance, a question on his face.

"Huntslaed's wary," Holdric said.

"He always is," said Eahstann, turning again his watch to the trees.

Holdric shook his head. "Not like this."

He let his eyes follow the way the deer had roamed.

"What do you see?" asked Eahstann.

"More deer than I would think for this place," Holdric answered.

"Seeking feed?"

Holdric looked up at the thin mountain pines, then over the earth.

"There's little mast here," he said at last. "I don't think so."

"But only deer?" asked Eahstann.

"Here at least, only deer."

In time their search was done. The others had found little, and none had found sign of ghaestling or of men. This Kenndric thought well enough, and bid them make their camp.

Eahstann laid claim to a low ditch that looked over the way they had come. Holdric dropped in beside him. He laid his arms near and pulled off his pack, then at last lay back his head to rest.

Both sat long in quiet. Eahstann passed him a piece of smoked cheese. Holdric had little left to trade but scraps of dried apple, but that proved enough. Together they ate in silence.

Holdric's eyes fell on the haft of Brukthorn in his pack. He reached over and pulled the great warknife close. His old fyrdknife he unknotted from its belt and moved to his pack. In its place he bound Brukthorn, setting the knots of its pelt that he might draw the longer blade at need. When he was finished, he pulled free the blade. Eahstann watched as Holdric began to absently work rust from the old knife, but said nothing.

As Holdric worked he pondered on the trees below. They were tall, and they were thick. Many long lifetimes must have passed if once they had been cleared enough to see the valley below. If ever a burgh wall had been risen here, now only broken stones remained, stones long since tumbled over the soft-worn earth and into the rocky ditch in which he now sat. Holdric shivered and turned his eyes back to the shadows beyond. Better to watch for what could be helped than to mull on things long dead.

Cold breeze bit at his neck and he raised his hood. As dusk fell the wind picked up, sharp and wet over the stones. Holdric ducked lower in his ditch, and there saw faint markings on the stones at his knee. These were not the aimless scratching of shifting rock and winter ice, he was sure. Something had made them.

He looked closer in the fading light, brushing away long ages of grime from the crude-scratched scene. There two twisted figures held what looked to be a man between them… or parts of a man. The things looked to be wrenching him to pieces.

The doomed man wore a strange great-maned helm, and a broken sword was scratched upon the ground beneath him. One of the wild things held high what looked to be an arm. Great sprays of what must have been blood were scraped into the stone with a wild glee. Holdric cursed and kicked at the scratches, then looked out again from the trench. It helped nothing to think on these things.

The ridge below was empty, empty as it had been all the day. No ghaestling stalked after his band, he was sure… or so he told himself. But still the things roamed out there, somewhere out in the gathering dark. He held Brukthorn close.

The chill bit sharp as evening gave way to night. For a time he braved the cold, eager to stay tight-bound and ready. But the cold ground on against his spirit and at last he gave in. He unbuckled his blanket from his pack and pulled the coarse wool about his body. Beneath the blanket he rubbed his aching shoulders and wished for fire.

Beside him Eahstann was already asleep, his mouth hanging open, his body slumped against the cold stone. Holdric smiled. He looked into the sky as he nibbled on his last crumbles of honeycake, and listened as the wind whistled on the rocks far below.

He looked up, high into the sharp-sparkling sky. The starfroth spread across the black deep of night, and the chill grew harder still. Wind licked above their trench. The stones sheltered them from the worst of the wind's bite, but still the cold earth drew away their warmth. He shouldered closer to Eahstann. The harper groaned, but did not wake.

In time the moon rose low over the rocks. Dim silver light whispered through the leaves, and Holdric searched the black shadows beneath. He almost wanted the ghaestling to come. Better a real fight than waiting without end. But still he saw only shadow, and still he heard only wind.

His mind taunted him, showing him over and again the picture of torn flesh and cracked bone that had once been living man. Dirty wool and shining white bone danced in Holdric's mind. He squeezed his eyes shut, willing away the sight away. He would think of happy things, of summer rain and wind-swayed golden rye. Frithi and her sweet smile, her laughter as she danced in the bright warm sun…

High overhead the stars of Hifosidth shone bright. He cursed under his breath to see those stars, and the too-warm memories they kindled in him. That hope was lost to him now. He could not, would not, dwell upon it.

He closed his eyes again, he forced his mind clear and stared up into the cool silver moon. Slowly his thoughts stilled. All passed away but the sharp cold stars above and the distant whisper of wind in the far trees.

He watched moonlight play in the high waving pines, he watched the shadows below for anything living. Ever he saw nothing but wind and air and stone. He knew not how long he watched, but his mind fell at last away and woldgast claimed him.

Hifosidth left the heights of the sky, and he heeded her not. The Rushes rose high behind her, and he did not mind them. The Lady came next as night slipped deep into the second watch. He did not move to wake Eahstann. There was no need.

Then came a distant scrape in the grass, a small faint scratch.

For a breath, he felt the night terror of a child, but only for a breath. His first nights on the highfolds he had quaked at every scratching field mouse. Every sound had seemed to him a hungry wolf, this was no different… but still the scratching went on. And still the sight of broken Reodhoc haunted his mind. Dread grew in his heart.

At last he gave in. He would seek this thing, and prove to himself his fear was foolish. He felt again for Brukthorn and lifted himself from the trench up onto open ground.

Cold wind bit sharp at his flesh. He shrugged it off as he worked up the dike on his belly. He moved over rough stone and dry scratching grass, he made scarcely a sound as he crawled towards the faint noise, searching over the moonlit earth… and saw a flash of faded bone.

The bone scraped soft against stone as small teeth worked upon it. For but a glimpse he caught the shine of moonlight in the eyes of a wary stoat. Then it turned, and was lost to the night. For long moments Holdric watched the quiet spot where the creature had been.

And then he heard the voice.

"… to send the boy back."

The words hung in the night. They were Wymud's words, quiet-spoken, just loud enough to hear. Holdric froze as he listened.

"… and Reodhoc makes three. That's too much for chance."

Soon Kenndric answered. "It was Holdric who found that sign, recall."

"And it was Holdric who stood dumb as a dew-eyed lamb when the bones rolled. He's weak like his father. Send him to Eomud come morning and slay two beasts at a blow."

After long silence, Kenndric's voice came again. "We have had words enough of Holthund. We will not have more now."

There came a gruff grunt from Wymud. Taut silence stretched long. At last Kenndric answered, "I will think on the rest."

Holdric's heart collapsed.

So Ollda doubted him also… and not without cause. He had faced his chance, and he had failed. Hope died away as he crept back to the trench, spirit too broken for words.

By the faint sound of breathing, he found where Eahstann still slept. Quietly Holdric dropped again into the hide. He looked to the sky—the Lady was in the heights, Slaugnwint at her heels. His watch was long past over. He elbowed Eahstann.

"Your watch."

Eahstann gently stirred, there was a faint rustle of wool as he moved against the stones. Holdric tried to shut his ears as Eahstann yawned himself awake.

"Where did you go?" Eahstann asked at last.

Holdric's eyes burned wet in the wind, the far stars dim and bleary in his sight.

"Nowhere."

He sat in dull stubborn silence until sleep claimed him.

He climbed up through looming shadow. Shadow of sharp palings, of fitted stone in a well-ordered wall. A last heave and he was inside.

He walked alone down the packed earth of the camp. He felt more that saw the press of many shelters, felt more than heard the dull murmur of sleeping men. He strained to see in the gathered night, but could not. No stars shone above. No moon hung in the sky.

All was still.

A lone howl cut through the air, then a chorus of shrieks. Dim and far away he remembered the chattering wolves of the timberwoods… but these were not wolves. The shrieking clamor pulled at his mind like iron on ice. He covered his ears, but still the sound would not stop.

Then came the shouts of men. Their words were strange, their voices faint as if from far away. Still they seemed near as breath. Shadows flowed over him as a river. He heard the bark of orders just past hearing, the shouts of raging men, the crash of battle. A great rushing wind broke upon the wall. Angry shouts filled the dark, then howls of sudden pain.

Then as if the wind had turned, all sound fell away.

The stones beneath his feet felt strange, they seemed to shift and cast him to the earth. There came a mortal cry, the howl of youth meeting too-soon death. The echo of a last scream hung broken in the empty summer night… and then all was still.

He was alone in the dark wood.

Starlight shone cold upon the ground. He blundered into the night, thorns caught at his clothes. He tried to pull free and blood flowed soft and slick over his fingers. Cold mist bathed the forest floor.

Come.

The words were gentle in his spirit, words without voice. He ached to push them away, though he knew he could not. He raised his eyes, begging not to see what he knew was there.

The stag's great antlers gleamed. His coat shone with starlight. An arrow wound shone now bright and seeping in his side. Heartsblood dripped upon the earth, black in the silver light. Holdric stared at the great stag, and into the dark thorned night beyond. Dim he heard the howls, faint shrieks far beyond the reach of the silver light.

The stag was unmoved. His eyes of deep starlight never strayed from Holdric's own, a gaze that drove into the deeps of his heart.

The thorns felt close about him. He pleaded without knowing why.

Please, not again. Not so soon.

Ealdorholt heard him, heard him with a gentle patience, but the stag was unmoved. Holdric heard the wordless voice in his head and in his heart. The voice came gentle as a spring breeze, cold and unyielding as the most ancient stone.

Come.

Holdric's heart raced. His breath came fast. He couldn't go there, not again. He couldn't bring himself to move, and he couldn't make the words. He backed away, he felt thorns close and sharp and thick.

Come.

Holdric's own voiceless words hung in the night.
I can't.
Still the stag waited. Silence stretched between them, vast as the great starry sea.
…I'm scared.
In a breath, or in a countless turning of seasons, Ealdorholt backed away. The silver light faded, and all was night.
"Wait!" Holdric cried. But the light was gone.
Long moments passed in stillness. The shadows of men and walls were gone, the rock beneath his feet scoured clean. The sky above was empty. The air was still.
He was alone.
He stared into the silence where once stars had gleamed, and then even the dream faded away. Holdric was alone in all-shrouding dark. Time yawned deep, and then there was nothing.

CHAPTER ELEVEN

The Farthest Watch

A drop of rain struck Holdric's cheek.

A familiar hand shoved at his shoulder and grudgingly he woke. The sky above was dim, the world shrouded in a wet clinging mist. Above him Eahstann's shape hung dark against the first dull light of coming morning.

"Get up," Eahstann hissed. "We leave soon."

Cold pecking rain stung his skin and Holdric mumbled without words. He threw aside the damp weight of his blanket and shivered as the chill washed over him. He groaned and scratched the mist from his hair, his shoulders taut and sore from a night on cold stone. He stretched and reached for his waterskin, took a quick swig to clear his mouth, and spat the water upon the ground.

A sliver of rain ran down his neck and he shivered, then cursed. He looked out into the gloom of the trees and met the eye of a raven looking back. The dark bird watched him from the branches of a long-dead pine, black against slow-rising grey. It croaked once, but it did not move.

"Good morning to you too," mumbled Holdric. Eahstann looked over as he spoke, and Holdric gave him a grim smile. "You let me sleep."

Eahstann shrugged. "Your watch ran long."

Holdric waved the words off. He brushed the rain from his blanket and bent to fold it away. Footsteps crunched wet on stone behind them—Hwaetearn's steps. The thaneling's walk had the firm air of a man carrying word.

They'd decided then.

Holdric swallowed a curse. At least his Ollda could have cast him back himself. He looked up into the spitting rain and waited. Hwaetearn's steps came nearer. Then they stopped.

"Eahstann, Holdric, the old man says make yourselves a fire before we leave. Keep it short and hot, warm yourselves and wash. We move at daybreak, ready or not."

He turned to leave. Holdric puzzled. Was that all?

Then Hwaetearn paused. He turned and looked back. "Oh, Holdric… Huntslaed says mind your watch tonight."

Holdric watched him go, stunned to silence for a moment, then he almost laughed. Of course the old ranger knew, had heard him in the dry grass. Holdric shook his head and wiped the rain from his brow.

"Move!" hissed Eahstann. "Sun's coming. You dig, I'll get wood."

Holdric nodded and Eahstann was gone. Holdric cleared a space and hurried to dig out a narrow fire hole. Soon Eahstann soon returned with a small load of dry deadwood, and Holdric took up his charbox and coaxed a small hot flame to life.

Their breakfast was hurried. A palmful of waybread crumb and a scant dollop of goosefat was all they spared themselves. Still the food sat in his belly like a stone. He brooded as he ate and looked out into the dawning grey.

The high dead pine was bare now, the raven had flown. Holdric stared into the empty branches and mulled on something he could not name.

Eahstann shoved his knee and signed for his cup. Holdric dug out the little wooden noggin and handed it over, and together they washed down their little meal with a hot tea. After the long cold of the night Holdric lost himself in the steam. He wished almost he could climb inside his little wooden cup and bask in the heat of it.

"You good?" asked Eahstann.

Holdric looked out over the morning mist. "I'm good," he answered.

Eahstann eyed him but said nothing.

Too soon daybreak came. Holdric tossed back the last of the tea and kicked earth over their fire. Eahstann brushed out their sign, and together they looked over the site of their little den. All, or nearly all, was again as it had been before. Holdric gave a last glance to the scratched marks on the rock, then looked away and hefted his pack.

They were on their way before the first true rays of sunlight broke from the trees. They moved into the morning, grey-cloaked shadows melting through grey mist and pecking rain. Eahstann raised his hood and grumbled, "Mornings are always wet up here."

Down from the rocks they crept, down again into the trees. There they searched for any sign that ghaestling had come near during the night. Finding none, they moved on into the morning gloom. Mist clung to Holdric's cloak, and he pushed at his straps to give his shoulders rest from the damp wool. He grumbled, but knew the walk would dry his skin soon enough.

He breathed deep, drinking in the cool air. Smell of mist and earth and faint clinging woodsmoke filled his nose. Soon the sun cut through the mist with great rays of gold, and some small brightness came again into his spirit.

He remembered long-ago morning walks like this one. The early ones with Ollda, when he was made to name every track, rock, and tree. The later ones alone, when he made every step a stalk and searched each shadow for fancied foes. Now here he was at last a ranger, and he wished for nothing but a morning amble in the sunlight.

He looked up the ridge. Far above he saw a high yew clinging to life in the stones, the branches worn and twisted by the high weather. His memory showed him another yew tree, branches broken and splashed with red. That memory he pushed away. He stared deep into the mist and bent his ears to the sound of the dripping trees. Slowly woldgast took hold, and on he walked in quiet.

The sun rose high over the wooded ridge and in time the last of the wet burned away. Nooning passed and the day grew sharp and cool, the air thick with the smell of coming fall. In time the ground beneath his feet grew sharp with stone and the sounds of the living wood began to fall away.

At last even the high pines began to thin. Only a few scraggled fir half-heartedly covered the heights, and wind whistled over the high stones above. Kenndric kept well short of the rocky crest, leading them through the thin cover of the last trees. Then they rounded a turn of rock and Holdric was brought short.

Far past the valley below, far past the rolling headlands beyond, a vast wall of mountain crossed all the world—the Himlgartn! Finally he lay eyes upon them! From sky to sky they stretched, a great wall of sharp-peaked crags. Holdric was struck dumb. For many breaths he could not bring himself to move.

Snow gleamed white on the slopes under the late summer sun. They were far away past telling, yet still they reached high into the sky. The whisper of cloud he'd once seen from his far climbing tree was nothing to this. Already he ached to walk in their shadow… and already he knew that he never would.

Few men had ever sought those slopes, and none had come again home. There it was said ghaestling made their home, and there ancient King Beorhtfel had taken his men, never to return. Still Holdric lost himself in the sight. He looked over every fold of stone, dreaming of earth he would never see.

Eahstann gave him a wordless shove. They moved on, but still the mountains did not loose their hold on Holdric's mind.

The way grew steeper yet. In time their pace slowed, too slow for the roughness of the way or the weariness of their bones. The Huntslaed led them now with wary care. Holdric craned his neck and tried to see ahead. At last the sign was passed back from Hwae-tearn: *Halt.*

For too long they waited in silence.

"What's wrong?" breathed Holdric.

"We should have met their guard by now," answered Eahstann.

Ahead Kenndric changed his path, working now back towards them and higher up the side of the ridge. Eahstann cursed, and Holdric looked to him in question.

"We take the eagle's road," Eahstann said.

Walking gave way climbing, and soon the two of them were taking turns heaving each other up onto broad sloped tables of stone. Their breath came short, but they did not stop. There were no ladders here as at Greatwatch, no handholds carved into the stone. In places they could follow a narrow goat path, but for most of the trek they clambered up bare rock.

They left the last of the sheltering trees behind them, and one by one worked their way up a narrow crack through the stone. At last they came out again onto open ground. Beyond was only sky, and below an endless wood that rolled out of sight towards the feet of the far snowy crags. The wind cut sharp and cold over the empty stones.

Kenndric moved low out onto the far ledge. He paused but a moment, then let himself over and dropped out of sight. Hwaetearn followed, and then Aschbroc. Holdric came warily to his own turn. He crawled out onto the ledge and looked down.

Below a narrow bridge of rope-bound wood ran across the cliff face some feet down, and beyond that was only empty air. His stomach swimming in his body, Holdric turned and slid off the ledge before he could think overmuch on what he was doing.

He dropped hard and the bridge swayed wildly under his weight. He cursed and bent low, scrabbling for any handhold as trees and sky and stone swam beneath his feet. His pack shifted on his back, pulling him to one side.

He held tight to the ropes at his feet and slowly the swaying eased. He looked up—a thin tarred guide rope was bound to the stone with iron pins. Warily he eased his grip on the timbers at his feet and took hold of the rope, then slowly rose to his feet.

Ahead Aschbroc knelt on a stone ledge not far away, easing the swaying timbers of the bridge with his hand. He grinned at Holdric, and Holdric cursed. Aschbroc grinned wider at that, but raised a hand to quiet him and signed for him to come near. Cursing under his breath, Holdric crossed the timbers and made it to a broad stretch of stone.

From here he could see the ridge beyond fell away into a steep tumble of rock, then far below broke into the wide saddle of an open pass, just too far across to reach with a clouted arrow. Beyond that the rock rose sharp again into a jagged spine of stone that stretched far to the north.

The ledge where they stood was shadowed by a high peak above. Further back, a rough wall of stacked stone and timber had been built against the living rock. In that wall was an open doorway, and there Hwaetearn stood, his face grave.

"They're gone," he said.

Kenndric looked grim. The thaneling waited as the rest came near, then stood aside so all might pass within. Holdric ducked through the narrow doorway and into Earnsclyff Watch.

The place was no mouse hole, but it was small. The single room looked to have begun as a natural hollow under the peak, then later picked bite by bite into the living stone of the mountain itself. It was smaller even than the Hyssestead, barely the space of Uncle Eikhram's hall. Perhaps a bit smaller yet.

Aschbroc opened the broad oaken shutters of the watch window and sunlight filled the room. They looked over what remained in silence.

The place was in good order. Narrow bunks fashioned of wild timber were built into a hollow on the far wall, just enough to sleep four men at a time. A pair of tattered blankets lay folded on one bunk, the rest held only bare sleeping ticks almost as flat and sleep-worn as Holdric's own. One empty pack hung alone on the pegs at the back wall. No arms hung ready, save a few dust-covered arrow sheaves laid by for the worst.

The narrow cooking hollow in one corner was fire-blackened and long cold. The iron kettle within was well-scrubbed, greased, and put away. The larder jars were nearly full.

Under the broad window was set a high narrow table. Two long benches sat beneath, the better to take meals while watching out over the wide valley below.

Everything in the room told of countless days and nights of boredom. The benches had been worn smooth, the mantle had been scrubbed and scrubbed again. Some fair hand had whiled away the time working at every scrap of wood with his knife. Carvings of hound and gyre graced the timbers of the great window, their paths wound through with twisting branches of flowering aelfsthorn.

The table also was covered over with branching spirals of bird and beast. The ribbon of the great river ran over the board, and with it was twined the twisting great wyrm of the north wind. Home-loving beavers were worked into the crooks of the winding water, each family sheltering in their nests of knotted bramble. Wrens and sparrows flitted through the empty places between the knots, and mice nibbled at fallen acorn-mast. All was worked in so fine a hand the high king himself would envy the board.

Kenndric traced the winding figure of the wyrm. His finger stopped on a game board carved into the timber of the table. There lay a few small polished stones, set down in the ranger's stone-sign: *Will Return.*

Wymud let out a gruff snort when his eyes fell upon the pieces. "But they didn't, did they?"

Aschbroc looked out into the mountains beyond, his face cold.

For a time all were silent, then Kenndric spoke. "Words."

Wymud spoke first. "The watchman left his post, that bodes ill."

"Nothing here speaks of bloodshed," offered Aschbroc. "Perhaps he only fetches game."

Hwaetearn scowled. "To leave the place alone, before his brothers return? No, after the blood of Eomud's man, I back Wymud. Something foul works here."

Holdric looked again about the room. "Most left with gear," he offered. "One—the watchman I wager—left with only his arms."

"They could be spare," said Aschbroc.

"Those are Forric's things," answered Wymud. "He would have taken them had he meant to be long."

"Perhaps he heard someone near then," said Eahstann. "We may find him broken on the rocks below, like the men of Greatwatch."

Kenndric shook his head. "I will not believe Wulfhert's grudge-ghaest walked all the way here from the great mountain. Even if it knew where this place lay."

Wymud grunted. "It wasn't ghaestling. If they'd found this place, they would have wrecked it."

Kenndric scowled. "Killings in the near country, a ghaestling band in the valley, and now all of Earnsclyff missing. We're past blaming chance."

"Fire the beacon, then?" asked Aschbroc. "It's not far."

Kenndric mulled the thought, but shook his head. "The Eorl would be displeased to march half the men of the folksteads from their harvest work only to find a dozen ghaestling and one mad knifeman. We need to know more, that is our work."

He looked to each of them. "These are my words: We go after the Earnsclyff men, find them if we can. If they have found trouble, we aid them. If we find them not, we raise Eomud's men and scour the valley clean." Then he looked to Aschbroc. "And yah, at the worst, we break, fire the watchmen's beacon, and raise the Eorl. After we join with Stalmaht at the Torr and harry the enemy until the fyrd may come."

He looked to each of them in turn.

"This looks to be a longer ranging than we had thought. I need you each to stay sharp. Watch your brothers, watch the shadows. You see sign, call halt and we hunt it together. Yah?"

"Yah, Huntslaed!" came the answer.

"The day is old!" said Wymud. "Make ready. If you lack anything, fill it here, fill it now. We may be out many days."

Each hurried to his work, and soon all were well ready. Wymud led the way out from the little hall, and each made to work their way back down the rocks. Kenndric caught Holdric's arm as he passed by and pulled him to one side.

"Come" he said quietly.

Kenndric moved out onto the stone ledge, and Holdric followed. As they neared the brink, Kenndric lowered himself to his belly and crawled low until he looked out over empty air. Holdric crawled after him. A sharp wind pulled at his hair, cold on the sweat of his brow. They lay side by side in silence. Far off, a falcon circled high in the air.

Kenndric spoke. "Tell me what you see."

Holdric's eyes went first to the saddle pass below them, then to the broken stone that rose up again on the far side. Few trees dotted the pass, only a handful of hardy yew and short scrabbled fir. "Which side of the pass do we take?"

"That's the first question," Kenndric answered. "Chance is our lads are up there"—he pointed farther north, deep into the headlands of the western valley. "That is where we most find sign of ghaestling."

"The Bonemounds lie there?" asked Holdric.

Kenndric did not move his gaze from the valley, but his eyes tightened at the question. "Yah."

Holdric looked over the thick trees of the valley. The green was shot through with the grey of low cliffs and broken stone.

"What else?" asked Kenndric.

"Once we're in that, the ground will be close. Too close to see or shoot far. It will be a thorny hunt."

"It will. And?"

"It will be a hard climb back. Past that saddle, we're pinned against the ridge."

"So you have it."

Holdric looked doubtful. "The Earnsclyff men have not another way up?"

"There are few ways over the rock, all near this pass," Kenndric said. "Further on, none. Not unless you're half goat."

Holdric looked over the ground again, more closely this time. He pointed. "That break in the trees there, is that headwater of the Greenflood?"

"One of them. Under those trees the ground is riven with brook and spring. Some drain into the Greenflood, most don't. Go much south of here and all that valley is a rat's nest of tree and pool all the way to the fens." The Huntslaed turned, looking over his shoulder to see if any were near. He learned close to Holdric. "It we're broken, you make down this ridge for the south. Keep high as you can, stop for *nothing*. Run day and night until you reach the Hyssestead, hear me?"

Holdric bristled, and Kenndric sighed.

"I've asked that of everyone, Holdric. Our eyes are fruitless if none hear our tongues."

Holdric gritted his teeth and nodded. "Yah, Huntslaed."

"Questions?"

Holdric looked long over the ground, working each fold of earth into his mind. "No, I have it," he said at last.

Kenndric smiled. "So you do."

Holdric looked then to his Ollda. "Thank you for not sending me back."

At first Kenndric did not answer. Only the briefest shadow crossed his face. "Don't thank me, Feorson," he said at last. "I did not think you would see so much so soon. I should have."

Holdric's eyes did not leave the far valley. "I knew this was coming."

Kenndric smiled, a sad old smile. "I suppose you did," he said. "I suppose I did…" He sighed and gently hammered at the stone with his fist as he thought.

"I'll vouch your Oath to Eomud."

Holdric did not answer.

Kenndric's brow furrowed. "What?"

"Eomud told me about Da."

Kenndric cursed. "He's wrong."

"What happened then?"

"I don't know. But I knew your Da. He would not have betrayed us. Not for anything."

"Why would Eomud say he did?"

Kenndric made at first no answer, then looked to the sky and sighed. "I wish I knew. I told you there was bad blood that last year."

"The thievings?"

"Not only the thievings."

"The girl?"

Kenndric looked back toward the others, then spoke low. "We'll talk old wounds when we return. Until then, stay close to Eahstann. Do as he says. He's young, but he has a good mind." Then he turned back to the wood below. "That's all."

"Yah, Huntslaed."

Holdric worked his way back from the ledge and rose to his feet, then paused to look back. His Ollda still lay on the stone, staring out over the valley below. Almost Holdric said more. But only almost.

He turned and made his way down after the others. As he climbed, he saw faint traces of coming and going there on the rocks, though which were left by the watchmen and which by his own brothers he could not be sure. The way grew harder yet as he drew near Eahstann, and soon they climbed together, working in silence down open stone into the first scrubby green.

Holdric turned and looked over the valley one last time, drinking in the folds of land below as one takes a last breath before the deep.

CHAPTER TWELVE
A Broken Chase

The sun was still high when they reached the trees, the clouds high and sparse. Wind came chill over the rocks. Just beyond lay the wide saddle of the pass, they could just see open ground through the trees below. There they watched over the ground below and waited.

Nothing stirred.

Soon Kenndric joined them, and wordless each man spread over the saddle of the pass to look for sign. It was Aschbroc who found it first, a crushed flower of seolfrenblos, almost buried in rock and bruised grass. There he found the mark of a too-long foot, the push of a broad hunting stride. Ghaestling had passed this way.

Aschbroc waved the Huntslaed near, and together they looked over the bruised earth.

"How long?" asked Wymud.

"Days," Kenndric murmured. "Not today… but not long past."

Soon they found the first sign of the Earnsclyff men. A sulking yew shaded a damp patch of earth, and there a man had knelt, searching with eye and hand for sign of ghaestling. Sign he had found, but sign he had left. Kenndric followed with his eyes the way both had gone—west, down into the valley headlands. He shared a grim look with Holdric.

They passed down into the valley, and soon they gained again the first cover of trees. The way grew steep as they worked their way down the rocky slope. Soon the forest closed deep and thick over their heads, and all beneath fell into deep shadow. Holdric had guessed sight would be short here, but still the close dark ground gnawed at him.

Soil clung to cold broken rock, chill water spilled from unnumbered springs. Ancient twisted oak shrouded all, their boughs wide and dark and their trunks scarred from long-ago fire. The few young trees stretched thin and sun-starved, and bracken grew thick and close. There was no sound save the all-surrounding trickle of water.

They moved slow and wary. Holdric passed beside a great stone bank, near covered in moss. Something under the green drew his eye and he looked close. Strange-carved spirals covered what open stone remained, winding over the stone as something from a dream. They were time-worn almost smooth, and long ago had been covered over with mocking scratches.

The scratchings were cut in a familiar crude hand. They showed strange gentle creatures hung from trees, and worse things still below. Holdric tore his eyes from the stone and turned again to his work.

Their Huntslaed moved slow. The sign he followed was sparse, and at last he lost the way where a great rushing spring tumbled over open rock. They searched long, and only Kenndric's knowing of the watchmen's ways led them to find the path again.

In time they came to a game-worn trail that wound over the stones, an easy passing up the valley. On the near heights above, a narrow hollow held good sight of the path, just in sure arrow-reach. Kenndric brought his band up the slope and they searched the earth nearby.

Bracken hung bruised, a few fronds pale and limp from being long crushed. The Earnsclyff men had waited here. Small crumbs of waybread lay under scattered leaves, not yet carried away by the creatures of the wood. A scuffed root and an over-broad stride told the last of the tale—the watchmen had left in haste.

Kenndric led his band after them, signing each man to his place. Twice Holdric's way took him again over the signs. The watchmen had been careful, but Holdric could still just find sign of their passing. They had been on the hunt, searching after a lone ghaestling. The creature had run unheeding, and the watchman had stalked after. Never did the creature pause to look behind, never did it move to hide its trail.

Holdric whispered low to Eahstann, "Is this common? One alone?"

Eahstann shrugged. "We've seen it before. Not often."

Holdric looked up into the high dark valley above. Eerie quiet held the wood.

Kenndric stopped. Wymud stood over him, his face grim. With a silent wave, the Second called them in. Holdric followed their eyes as he joined them. He swallowed as he came near, for he could see already what had caught his Ollda's eyes.

The mark of a ranger's footfall lay in the soft earth, a gentle spray of earth just within… and sign of a long and narrow foot nearby. That second sign showed a heavy leaning toe, the ghost of a too-long heel. Swells of earth to either side of the feet told of a rocking crouch, and crushed leaves and scattered earth showed where the thing had left at a run.

The sign was plain. Ghaestling had found the sign of the Earns-clyff men, and the hunters were now themselves hunted. The men of Holdric's band looked to each other, faces grim. Wymud scowled and signed them to their places. Kenndric led them after the hunt, Wymud guarding his shoulder.

Holdric tried not to watch them from his place on the wing. He ached to see more of the tale the Huntslaed followed, but his own watch was work enough. The way was hard, thick with ancient tree and thick scrubby thorn. Often he edged over rock or around and under branch to keep his way.

Nor was the Huntslaed's task easy. Time and again the old ranger stopped to find the next sign, time and again he fell back, moving again to Wymud's side to start the search again. The watchmen had hidden their trail well.

Kenndric paused. He looked up, weighing the shape of the earth in his mind. Then he signed to Holdric and pointed to a shaded telling-place under a great broken oak. Holdric went where he was bid, and soon after came to sign of man.

Found, he signed back. *One.*

Holdric moved down the trail as Eahstann shadowed him behind. Some paces later Holdric was sure, the man was alone. *One, only*, he signed again.

He looked further down the valley to see Aschbroc on the far wing, his nose to the dirt. Then Aschbroc signed his own find, *Found. One only*. The watchmen had opened their march.

Holdric turned again to his stalk of the lone watchman. The man had a long stride, he would be tall. His gait was smooth, and he moved with care. This was a ranger who knew his craft. Only once did Holdric find clear mark from the ranger's foot, and that where the man had ducked under overhanging thorn and stumbled onto damp shaded earth… his next step was not to be found.

Holdric cursed, then backed up and tried again. Eahstann said nothing. Far to one side Aschbroc waved, then pointed. The man Aschbroc stalked had turned to move down the valley. Holdric leaned over the earth, looking for the best way his own man might follow, and there found the next sign. He sighed and took up again the hunt. It was slow, numbing work.

Eahstann tapped his shoulder, then pointed. A scrape of bark not far above his path showed another trail. Holdric cursed himself for missing it, he'd minded too much the tread before him. He ducked under Eahstann's guard to look close. Then he cursed again.

There was more sign of ghaestling here. Holdric tried to guess their number, but found sure tell of only one. He held up the count to Kenndric, and Kenndric signed his answer. The Huntslaed's face did not change.

Aschbroc passed up another sign, *Ghaestling. Three.*

Eahstann cursed under his breath.

Their pace was slow, and their search was hard. Twice the watchmen had cut from their trail, and twice Kenndric found them again. At last the Huntslaed paused, then pointed up a low stony outcrop. It was a small rise, scarce the size of an oxcart. Still the place was sheltered in stone, and the sighting there would be good. Kenndric might have chosen the place himself.

Holdric kept watch up the valley with Eahstann while the Huntslaed climbed the rise. Still Holdric could not help but eye the ground as they waited… the path his ghaestling had taken was just in sight. He tried to follow the trail best he could with his eyes alone. He could not be sure, but it looked the creature moved away, further up the valley. He strained his eyes looking past the last sure sign—

Eahstann cursed, and Holdric turned to look. Wymud stood atop the rise. He held aloft a wooden cup.

Fight, he signed. *Fled.*

Below Aschbroc waved in answer. He raised high a dark ranger's arrow, the shaft broken. Even from where he stood, Holdric could see the feathers crusted with blood.

"They took one at least," Eahstann muttered.

Kenndric came down again from the hide, and Wymud pointed each man to his place. The Huntslaed took up a trail Holdric could not see.

He turned his mind to his own watch. Nearby a broken birch held a smear of dried blood, hand-height. He leaned in to look close. The smear was not left by man. Crushed bracken showed where something had been dragged away. He pointed Eahstann to the sight, and Eahstann passed down the sign while Holdric looked over the ground.

Eahstann leaned close and asked in a half-whisper, "How many? In all, I mean."

Holdric shook his head as he felt at the earth beneath the bruised bracken.

"I haven't seen all. From what the others say… six? eight? Probably not more than eight."

"Probably not more than eight," echoed Eahstann with a curse. He looked again up into the tree-shrouded stones of the valley above them.

Below, the Huntslaed came to a tiny spring. His face was grim. He knelt, then backed away from the spring. A knowing smile came to his lips. He looked up and pointed to Holdric, then to a low gully further on, higher up the valley. Holdric signed his knowing, and crept with Eahstann up to the place they'd been pointed.

The way was hard, the thorns thick and the rocks steep, but there it was—the Huntslaed had judged right. Not far ahead the brush was broken, a way had been pushed through in haste. Holdric came close, looking over the sign… here again was the tread of the tall man he'd stalked before. Another was with him.

He signed down, *Found. Two.* Then he pointed up the valley after them.

Soon after, Aschbroc passed up his own find, *One. Wounded.* He pointed further down the valley, away to the south.

Kenndric waved them in. As they drew near, he spoke low, "Words."

Wymud shook his head. "One south, two north. Nothing north of here but more ghaestling."

"Drawing ghaestling from their wounded?" Hwaetearn asked.

"That holds sense," Holdric said. "I saw no ghaestling upon them, but the men were moving hard."

"And your man makes south for the Torr?" asked Eahstann. "Brings aid?"

Aschbroc shook his head. "So I think he meant his sign to tell, but I doubt he could go so far. I guess his wounds dire. He will be close, if he lives."

"Which way then?" asked Wymud.

Kenndric looked up the valley, then down. "No stag runs forever. Let us hope our wounded man has put off the meeting long enough to tell what he has seen."

So south they went. Soon after Holdric saw the third man's sign. Aschbroc had told the truth of it. The watchman's way pointed ever to the Torr, his sign-story told of measured flight. More than once he had left sopping-trails that came to nothing. But still his footfalls had been too heavy, and still his toes had dragged. He left too much broken green behind him. The man was fading.

The trail grew clearer as they followed it. Time and again the watchman had paused, time and again he had wavered on stumbling feet to look behind. Panic had begun to chew at the man's mind. Soon he would turn for a last fight, soon he… no. No, this man was worn to nothing. He would hide, Holdric knew it in his bones.

It was Wymud who first spotted the place, a shallow hollow dug hasty under the weight of a great fallen pine. Holdric thought he would have missed it, had he been the hunter.

The ghaestling had not missed it. Nor was there any missing it now. Deep ruts scarred the earth where the man had been dragged from beneath the fallen tree. Here his feet had dug deep in panic, here his hands had clawed at the bark…

Near to the hide the leaves of a low briar bore still a dried splash of blood. Below, kicked and scattered leaves told of a fight. Had the man gotten loose?

Holdric looked to where Kenndric followed the man's trail. He hoped for the Huntslaed's path to change, he hoped for even a short halt that might mean the hunted had slipped the chase, but Kenndric moved on without pause.

Holdric's eyes turned again to the earth. Brush was broken, leaves were scattered wide. Many ghaestling footfalls had torn at the ground, each crisscrossing and pounding away the ones below. One track caught his eye. It was deep, it came down hard and slid before pushing off again. He glanced back along its path, knowing already the half-leaping, half skipping gait he would see. How many times had he seen that same joyous skipping, leaping run from children at their games? These things loved the chase. He looked about—the trees had been hacked with great running blows. It would not be long now.

Eahstann stopped. Holdric looked up, and his mind broke.

Before him was a gnarled ancient oak. Something pale and ruined stretched in tatters between the branches. At first he could not make sense of what he saw… then he knew. Eahstann cursed at the sight. Wymud pointed to them, then to the trees at their back. Holdric could just hear Kenndric's order as he turned to his watch.

"Bury what you can."

Holdric forced his mind onto the chill wood before him. He let his vision soften, watching only for moving things. Then he looked sharp again, peering hard into each cold shadow for some sign of the foe. All was still.

Footsteps sounded behind him… Aschbroc's step. Holdric's gaze did not leave the wood. His cousin drew near and spoke in a low half-whisper, "Ollda wants you."

Holdric took up his spear and turned again to the tree.

Kenndric and Wymud knelt over a place in the earth not far from the twisting branches. The two leaned close, muttering over something Holdric could not see. Holdric drew near, but as he came close Kenndric held up a hand to stop him.

"Holdric, close your eyes."

He bristled. The tree was gruesome, but to be sheltered as a babe rankled. Still he did as he was bid. Kenndric spoke again, "Tell me again of the bear track you found at Old Acramm's."

The question startled him, but he answered, "I still do not think it bear, Huntslaed. It was broad, but not so broad as the beast. Man-sized. I only found one track, maybe two. But it looked the mark favored his left."

"Open your eyes and come here."

He did so. His Ollda knelt over a track in the earth.

"Is this it?"

Holdric could only stare at the sign in silence.

He had almost believed them. He had almost thought they'd been right all along. But here he saw the same loping pace as in the mud at Old Acramm's spring. The same broad foot, the same tall, side-heavy limp. But what before had been worn almost smooth, here showed itself clear and sharp.

"Well?" asked Wymud. "Is it or is it not?"

Holdric met his eyes. "It is."

Wymud held his gaze, hard doubt still on his face. "You think so."

Holdric held his ground. "I am sure."

Wymud cursed. "I'll get the men."

Kenndric watched Wymud leave, then rose weary to his feet. He looked first to Holdric, then to the others as they gathered close. He gestured to the sign at his feet.

"Holdric may have found our grudgeghaest."

Aschbroc cursed as he knelt to look. "A man walks with ghaestling? It cannot be so. It must be another of the watchmen."

"No," said Holdric. "I've seen the others. This is not from them."

"Another, then. He could have come later," answered Hwaetearn. "Or sooner."

"Sooner and we'd see sign of the ghaestling hunting him," Kenndric said. "Later perhaps, but the same man at the site of two deaths? That seems strange chance."

Hwaetearn grumbled. "Ghaestling don't keep pets."

Eahstann agreed. "Not in any tale I have heard." His eyes went again to the sign. "Still, there it lies."

Wymud cursed. "A man walks with ghaestling. Or he does not. What changes?"

Kenndric thought. "Little," he answered at last. "Save this, we dare not trust any man unknown to us in these woods." He looked then to the others. "Let's get our brothers."

They made again for where the ranger's band had broken. All moved fast in the cool of the wood, working well clear of their last passing. As they came near again to the place of the watchmen's fight, Kenndric stopped still. Holdric could just see the Huntslaed ahead through the trees. He could not see what caught the Huntslaed's eye, but he knew his Ollda's mind. Holdric cursed under his breath.

Eahstann looked to him just as Wymud sent back the sign.

Danger! We are found!

Eahstann echoed Holdric's curse. Kenndric waved them in, and Holdric looked upon the ground as he came near. Aschbroc's sign was at his Ollda's feet, and Hwaetearn's heavy heel beside it. And between both was the long narrow mark of ghaestling.

A small rise of earth before one narrow footfall told of a sudden stop. A soft divot in the fallen needles showed where knee had kissed earth. Holdric knew his Ollda's words before even the old ranger spoke: "They have our trail."

Each man looked into the shadowed trees, every dark hollow seemed filled now with unseen eyes. Cold dread seeped over the wood.

"How many?" Hwaetearn asked at last.

Kenndric was still a moment, jaw set as he pondered the ground he'd searched.

"At least eight. Moving fast."

Wymud's face was cold. "Given the first blow, we can take that many,"

"About time they took the edge end of the knife," echoed Hwaetearn.

Kenndric pondered but a moment, then rose and set arrow to string. His voice came sure and swift. "The bracken patch by the fallen oak. Just past the last creek. You remember the place?"

All knew.

"That then is our gatherplace. Make your way there, each man with his brother. Leave sign, but make them work for it. Put fear in your steps. Let them think they've shaken our hearts." He looked to each man, his eyes steady. "We meet them, we end them. Yah?"

"Yah!" they answered with low fury.

"Hauwyr guard you. Make haste."

The words had scarce passed his lips before all were running.

Holdric's legs all but shook as he ran. He stumbled over stones, tore branches as he raced down the rocks. He could not pledge the fear in his tracks was fully feigned.

They ran long. He cast about for the place Kenndric had spoken of, surely it must be near. He almost thought the way lost when he heard a low whistle—not far ahead Aschbroc waved his hand. Once sure Holdric had seen, Aschbroc ducked again behind a bank of earth and stone.

Holdric and Eahstann did not break pace, they ran past the hide without stop. Then Holdric's foot hit stone, and he broke to one side. Eahstann followed, and together they picked their way over tumbled rock to reach again their brothers.

As they neared the earthen bank, Hwaetearn broke cover and signed them up the line to Kenndric. As Holdric passed, Hwaetearn leaned close. He spoke in a half-breathed whisper, "You can meet this."

The thaneling meant it as comfort, but Holdric almost cursed, his jaw set. Kenndric glanced up, then nodded to an empty spot behind the bank. Holdric crept into his place, a low hollow in the lee of a twisting oak. He kept himself low, all but biting the roots of the great tree. He smelled at the air… good, the wind was at their nose, what scent they had would be borne away. Still he kept low to the earth.

He unslung his shield and pulled the guard from his spear. He made ready… and then he waited.

And waited.

Sweat cooled on his forehead.

Still they waited.

He looked to the sky. How long had it been?

The ghaestling must know. The things must have caught some false step, they must have read his way. Or their hide had been seen. Even now the ghaestling were creeping to their rear, he was sure it must be so. He ached to turn, to look behind. He knew Hwaetearn watched that way, he knew to trust. Still he ached to look, he ached to move. He cursed himself and wrenched his mind to the woods that were his own to watch.

The forest air hung quiet. Nothing moved.

Sweat prickled on his skin. A stray earwig crawled across his hand. He did not move.

His legs began to ache beneath him. He needed to piss.

He lay still, until there was nothing in the world but the space of woods he watched. Nothing but the late afternoon sun, the haze in the trees, the thick smell of leaves and earth…

His mind was far gone when he felt a soft nudge in his ribs. Eahstann nodded across the valley, back the way they had come. Far off in the trees, where all the leaves were still, a single branch waved alone. Holdric's spine went cold. He remembered edging around the same branch himself. Something moved along his trail… and then all was still again.

Many silent breaths passed. Every footfall Holdric had made to this place haunted his mind.

They must know. They had to know.

Another flash of brush. Then another.

Again all was still.

More far branches moved. Not many, not often, but enough for his wary eye to catch the passing. A wave passed through the green before them, as high grass blown in a slow summer wind. Then came the sound of quiet stalking steps.

Then he saw it.

A man-like creature slinked under a fallen tree, eyes upon the earth. The tales were true.

Ghaestling do look like the dead.

The thing's skin was pallored grey, its limbs long and gangled. Old bones hung upon the rotting harness of hide it wore, scars and burns wove a crazed pattern over its flesh. Worst were the thing's eyes, eyes empty and black as the ragged raven feathers knotted into its greasy black hair.

A flash of moving green on the far left caught Holdric's eye—another stalked them on the wing. He nudged Eahstann. Eahstann followed his gaze and readied his arrow on the string. The things were almost upon them.

Holdric's limbs ached from holding them still. His muscles clenched hard, his legs cramped beneath him. Wymud looked to each of them, a handsign passed down the line.

Almost…

Almost…

Two more of the things passed into sight, creeping behind the thing in front.

Holdric's heart pounded, his limbs twitched with the need to move, a snarling yell smothered in his chest. His fingers flexed on the wood of his spear…

The lead ghaestling stopped short.

It looked up. Its empty black eyes glinted cold, a wave of hate passed over its face—it knew. Somehow it knew. But its knowing came too late.

Kenndric was already up. His bowstring sang, and with a flash of dark feathers his arrow flew. The heavy shaft streaked fast and hard through the trees, cut clean through the lead ghaestling, and went skittering into the leaf litter beyond.

For a breath, all was still.

The ghaestling's blank gaze dropped to the earth. It stared dumbly at the blood pooling around its feet. It looked up—then it buckled and crumpled to the dirt.

Aschbroc's arrow found the second ghaestling just as the first hit the earth. A shriek caught Holdric's ear, and he looked over just as the flank guard fell. The creature kicked at the earth, howling as it pulled at Eahstann's arrow lodged in its flesh.

Time moved slow as pitch. Eahstann reached for another arrow, every scratch and hammer mark of the point sharp in Holdric's eye. His thoughts moved slow. He pondered the broken bark before him, the heedless earwig crawling over rotten wood. He wondered why the bracken before him still swayed, he wondered why Eahstann moved behind him…

A kick from Eahstann brought his mind back to the fight.

He looked to where the ghaestling had first broken from the green. One still lay sprawled on the earth, the last life leaving its body. The rest were gone. Gone as if they had never been, not even a shaking fern to tell of their passing.

Not more than a breath could have passed. It felt as if it had been an age.

A swift dark shadow streaked in the air, and Holdric ducked without thought. He felt more than heard the deep *thunk* of iron on wood, he tasted bark as a spear dug deep into the tree just over his head. A thin wooden shaft, tar-black, quivered on a long point of rough-forged iron.

A shout came from down the line, sunlight flashed—Holdric turned to see a ghaestling fall like cleaved meat before Hwaetearn. Then all were caught in a screaming, howling storm.

Something shoved hard against him, a bow limb cracked hard against his head. Eahstann cursed as his arrow went wild. All the world fell into a clatter of bone and wood and the snarl of angry beasts. Holdric stabbed out with his spear, anything to keep the crazed things off his little hill. His blade pierced hide and sank deep into muscle and bone. Some distant part of his mind reeled... it seemed the killing should have come harder.

In the next breath he was jerked forward as the creature fell back, a wet heavy weight on the end of his spear. The creature was too heavy, Holdric's spear began to slide from his grasp. He dropped his shield and took hold of his weapon with both hands, leaning back and heaving for all he was worth.

"There! *There!*"

Hwaetearn's shout took a note of panic—Holdric looked where the thaneling pointed. Another flank guard stood far off to one side, staring dumb at the sudden fight. It froze for half a breath, then tore off back the way it had come.

Hwaetearn's shouts came frantic. *"Get it! Get it now! Get it now!"*

Eahstann reached for another arrow and angled for a clear shot, without thought Holdric ducked clear of his heavy bow. Wymud leapt down from the bank, running after the thing. Holdric watched him as—

"Get your shield up! Holdric! Shield!"

It was too late.

Holdric reeled as his spear was almost jerked from his hands. The kick from his ghaestling came strong and fast, the blow landed hard against his jaw. Holdric staggered back, then lunged again with his spear, wrenching the point free and furiously stabbing again and again. The thing fell back, and Holdric kicked it with a snarl. The body rolled bonelessly away.

Holdric looked up just as Wymud emerged from the brush. A fresh spray of blood was smeared over his beard and cloak.

Done, he signed. *Danger past.*

All was still.

Holdric looked around… it was over. Each man looked to the others.

"Are any hurt?" asked Kenndric.

Holdric worked his jaw, and shook his head to clear it.

Hwaetearn was blooded, but well. Wymud hobbled a bit as he approached. He waved away the question. Holdric rubbed at his head and felt at his teeth with his tongue… a tooth felt loose, maybe two. He decided not to speak of it.

He looked to the others, surprised they looked so calm. Wymud drew near, then looked him up and down.

"You look like pig shit."

Holdric looked down. He was caked in a smear of blood and dripping mud… then he looked to the ghaestling dying at his feet. His mind worked slowly, trying to make sense of what he saw.

"I did it," he breathed.

The others moved off, looking over the fallen ghaestling. Still Holdric looked on the creature he had speared, trying to decide what it was. Not exactly man, but not beast either, some twisted thing in between. Even dead, it felt somehow *wrong*.

Holdric shivered and drew his foot away from the carcass. Bile rose in his throat.

"How many?" Kenndric's voice was clipped.

Hwaetearn stood on the bank, looking over the bloodied ground. "Five."

"No, six," said Eahstann. "Holdric took one also."

"Six then."

Wymud looked to Kenndric. "I thought you counted eight."

"At least eight."

A long silence followed, each man alone with his thoughts.

Then Aschbroc's voice came flat and dead: "Ollda." It was no question. No call.

They came to where Aschbroc stood and looked at the fallen ghaestling at his feet. No one needed Aschbroc to point it out. Every ghaestling harness had bones stitched upon it, this one was no different. But some of these bones were fresh, bits of flesh still clinging to bone.

They weren't boar.

"From our watchman?" asked Eahstann.

Wymud shrugged. "Can't say. We didn't find all the pieces."

Kenndric cursed. "Aschbroc, find a place to bury those. Hwaetearn, keep watch. Holdric, Eahstann, search for sign—anything you can find. Wymud, with me." He looked to each of them. "Make haste."

Holdric came to where Eahstann knelt, quietly filling his quiver again from the sheaf Holdric had carried. The harper's eyes never left the wood. Silently he rose, and together they began their search. They passed first by the ghaestling that Wymud had run to ground. What was left of the thing stared unseeing up into the trees. Holdric turned his gaze away.

The fight still had not left his blood. His legs felt weak, he grasped his spear tight to keep his hands from shaking. He glanced to Eahstann, then to each of the others. They worked as if nothing had happened. He cursed and forced his eyes again to the earth.

Sign of badger he saw, and small lighting thrush, and… ghaestling. The sign was plain, the shape of a stretched hand pressed fresh into the earth. Here it had crouched low, here it had all but thrown itself into the dirt.

Holdric looked up to the place he had been during the fight, then once again over the ground. He was sure. He had not seen this one in the fight.

Crushed leaf litter showed where it had turned, a kicked spray of dirt on leaves where it pushed its way back into the trees. Holdric looked up along the way it had fled. He had just made to follow farther when a low quiet whistle caught his ear—Wymud waved them in.

Holdric cursed as they left the search behind. He and Eahstann came near just as Hwaetearn and Aschbroc dumped the last of the ghaestling bodies into a low ditch. There was not time to clean the whole of the place, but the worst could be hidden from a careless eye.

Kenndric signed them close. To his unspoken question, Holdric answered, "At least one lives, running west so far as I can see. There may have been others, with time I can be sure."

Wymud looked to Kenndric, waiting his word.

Kenndric looked over the site. "No, we keep to our aim," he said. "Best we be gone before it—or they—can return with aid."

He looked then to the slow-sinking sun. The day's light was already wearing thin. "I would be far from this place before night comes."

Wymud waved them to marching order, and soon the bloodied patch of forest was well behind them. Kenndric led them hard and fast. They circled wide from the places of their passing, making with care their way back to the trail of the watchmen.

The wood was quiet. Holdric flexed his fingers on his spear as he walked. His eyes went again to the fresh-cleaned point. He felt strange.

He'd done it, he'd killed one of them. He had killed. Was he truly a ranger now? A man? It seemed to him that he should feel different somehow, and yet he did not think that he did. That was what felt strangest of all. He lost himself in his mind. His tongue went again to his loosened tooth and he winced. He hoped it would heal.

Eahstann shoved him. Holdric looked, and Eahstann pointed to the place he should be watching. Holdric signed for pardon and looked again to his watch.

They moved long in quiet step. The trail of the watchmen was sparse, but Kenndric did not fail in his seeking. Ever north they went, ever further from Earnsclyff Watch. Holdric wondered on their aim. Those times he came across the watchmen's sign, the traces seemed to speak of panic. He did not think them feigned.

The way grew steep as the men had moved north. At times they had climbed no less than they walked. More than once Holdric's band found sign again of ghaestling, single runners like those before. None of the sign looked old. With each step further up the valley, the gloom about them deepened. Holdric searched each shadow, he paused at each step to listen for a skulking foe. Nothing stirred. The way beneath the trees grew dim, and a damp evening chill sank into the air.

Eahstann cursed. Holdric looked up and followed his eyes. Through the trees ahead he could just see the gentle slope of a wide mound. The shape was strange through the far trees, a low hill broad and even. Even from where he stood he could see the mound did not fit the land. The thing had been raised by hands.

Holdric shivered in the cold damp of the wood, he wished to go no closer. Still their path wound ever closer to the thing. As they came near, he could see shapes upon the top, thin and broken as long-dead trees.

They paused at the foot of the mound. Above all was covered over with broken gorse and thick-thorned briar. Kenndric led them in a winding path up through the thorns. The earth felt strange underfoot, the soil uneven and crumbled. Holdric felt more than heard a soft crack as ancient bone crumbled beneath his foot.

He froze. Eahstann looked to him. "There used to be more," he whispered. "Or so the songs say."

Holdric would not hear it. "Tell me when we get home. Not now."

They edged around another bramble, the earth worn bare beneath their feet. Holdric knelt to look close—fresh ghaestling sign covered the narrow trail. They reached at last the crest of the mound, and there Holdric's stomach turned.

What he had thought were bare trees were tall stakes. The were hacked and fire-blackened, one bearing still the rotting carcass of a poor half-starved fox.

The mound was littered with the reeking castoffs of sloppy butcher work and the charred timber of careless fires. Brush had been slashed and bound into rude shelters, brush that bore still green needles—brush that had been cut not long past. The ground was covered in the sign of many passings. The grass was trampled, in places trodden to bare dirt.

Wymud cursed. "This was no hunting party."

Holdric looked over the ground. How many passed this way? Dozens? Hundreds? Somewhere in the distant valley echoed a ghaestling shriek. He winced at the spine-scraping sound.

Aschbroc looked into the far dark wood. "This is too big for us."

Kenndric looked grave. He cast his eyes once more over the ground, then he looked to his men.

"I have my will, but I would have your words."

"You know mine," said Aschbroc. "I do not wish to leave our brothers more than the rest of you, but the Torr must know. If we are overcome they are blind to this."

"No," said Hwaetearn, "they are near, and we know not their fate. I would not leave our brothers to torment, not when we are so close."

Aschbroc looked grim as he set his jaw.

"Do others have words?" asked Kenndric. None spoke.

Kenndric looked to each man in turn.

Wymud moved to Hwaetearn's side. He did not speak.

Aschbroc remained set and silent. He liked not where he stood, but still he stood. Eahstann wavered, then looked to Aschbroc. He moved to stand beside him.

Two and two.

Kenndric looked last on Holdric. Holdric swallowed. He looked to his cousin, then he looked to Hwaetearn.

"I would go on," Holdric said at last.

Kenndric's face showed no feeling, but his nod was sure. It was done. The Huntslaed gave his words, and they made their way down again into the trees.

Far up the valley, an owl's cry hung lonely in the night.

CHAPTER THIRTEEN
Fire in the Dark

Dimly he felt their path begin to turn. The Huntslaed led them up a steep scramble of rocks and up onto a low rise. Near the hill's crest was the hollow of a long-fallen tree, and above it a gnarled ancient oak, black with the shadow of coming night.

In the last gloom of day they took their places. Kenndric passed to each man, pointing to each their lines of watch and whispering where to meet should they be overcome in the night. Then dark came, and each man was alone with his thoughts.

Holdric reached for his water and half drained what was left to him. He left his pack where it lay, he had no taste for food. Then he made ready his arms and crept out onto the edge of the hollow to watch the ground below.

Eahstann heard him move. His voice came low and quiet. "I'll take firstwatch. It's my turn."

Holdric shrugged in the dark. "I have it. Sleep."

Eahstann grunted weary thanks, and soon the soft sound of his breathing rose from the cold earth.

No stars shone through the thick cloud above. All was quiet. The moon rose slow, a faint silver haze behind a black blowing shroud.

Now and again the clouds would thin, and moonlight would shine weakly under the leaves.

Holdric would sometimes turn from his watch, if only to know that none had been taken in the night. Aschbroc stared ever into the dark valley above. Hwaetearn slept near, scabbarded Fyalclef in his hand. Wymud slept also. Above all watched the Huntslaed, quiet and still as stone.

Holdric looked over each sleeping man, their faces grey in the moonlight. Sometimes another watcher would see his eye and give a quiet nod. It was strange, this kinship of the waking-ones. Always Holdric would feel his mind pulled back into the work, always he would turn and look again into the long quiet.

Once he heard the crack of breaking wood. He listened long… no sound followed. He looked to Kenndric, but the Huntslaed had not moved. Both watched the place of the sound, ears open and sight broad. At last Holdric counted the noise as only sound of the wood.

A long time more he watched in silence, and in time he heard the shuffle of quiet stirring from those behind. He raised his hand to the sky, guessing best he could the place of the moon. The silvery blur shone strongest about three hands high. It was midwatch then, or near enough.

There was just enough moonlight to see Eahstann asleep beside him. The harper did not dream, his face was as near to peace as it had been in days. Holdric did not wish to wake him. Still he knew he would need the sleep himself no less.

Holdric reached down and gave Eahstann's shoulder a gentle squeeze. Eahstann groaned once, then rose without words. The watch was passed, and Holdric moved down to rest against the side of the hollow. He rolled himself in blanket and cloak and lay against the cold hard earth. He was asleep almost before he could close his eyes.

But even in sleep he found no rest.

Mist drifted over the forest floor.

The earth was cold and wet beneath his feet, but any earth was better than those hills of bones. Bones small and strange mouldered there, small almost as those still half child…but those broken old bones were not all the dead, nor were they the worst. Above, things once men hung broken in dark shadowed trees. They had not been hanging long.

The night was wet and cold, the sky black and empty. He ached for light, for light of sun or moon or star. Even the searing light of the stag was better than this unending dark. Still the night hung close about him, heavy as a sodden blanket.

In the far distance, a shriek echoed in the dark.

Then another, not so far ahead.

A great rush fell over him, loud as storm-blowing wind. The night was filled with the press of marching men. Shadow pressed and shoved in the dark. He heard the beat of feet upon the earth, felt the push of sweat and iron, heard the rattle of arms. He found himself moving with them, stepping as one as they pushed through the trees.

He was hunting for something—they were all hunting for something. He felt his spear in his hand, sharp and strangely lean. He felt his shield, heavy and over-broad. The howls from the dark grew louder.

The rattle of metal and wood met his ears, and shadowed words came floating down the line. The words were strange, but their meaning plain—*There are here! They have come!*

Shouts and yells of command rose up, then screams. There was a rush of moving muscle. He tumbled to earth and rolled heel over head as though in a mighty river. The howling shrieks grew loud above his head…

He was running. He did not wish to run, but his legs moved without his will. Thorns pulled at his clothes, thorns scratched at his scalp. He raised his arms to ward his face and found his hands raw and bloody and burned, he found his hands empty. Where was his spear? Where was his great shield?

"Help me!"

The scream echoed through the dark. He looked wildly around, trying to find the voice in the night. The scream came again. First a cry of fear, then of splintering agony, and with it a harsh mocking laugh. The dark night filled with howls of cruel joy.

His brother was in torment! Sickened rage filled his heart. He ached for the fight, ached for battle, but he could do nothing, he *was* nothing. He was only shadow, alone in the night. Cold earth closed over his limbs.

The scream came again, and this time a second voice joined the first.

Holdric jerked awake. His mind howled a warning, but he could not tell why. He searched the night, hunting for he knew not what. Then it came to him… the screams hadn't stopped.

He heard them still, echoes of pain and terror hanging in the far black trees. The cries were joined by the rustle of his brothers rising to arms. Holdric rushed to join them, taking up his arms by feel. All were moving before the last sick shreds of dream left his mind.

Kenndric led them quiet up into the night. Holdric held the edge of Aschbroc's cloak in hand, and behind he felt Eahstann's grasp on his own. Stone by stone, tree by tree, they groped their way through the dark.

"Ditch," whispered Aschbroc.

Holdric passed back the word and felt for footing on the broken ground ahead. Sometimes a wisp of moonlight would slip from heavy cloud, and Holdric would drink in all in sight, fixing into his mind each thorny tangling hedge and every tripping crack of rock. Then cloud and shadow would close once more over the sky, and again he fumbled over ground unknown.

On they climbed, knowing their way only by the sound of torment in the darkness ahead. At every step the cries grew weaker. Just as he feared they would lose even this terrible guide, they crested a low rise and saw far ahead, far up the valley, the dull orange glow of firelight.

They crept closer. A bonfire blazed in a great clearing not far away. Black shapes moved before the flames. Another scream came, weaker now. Then a choking sob, followed by a desperate plea… it had been too long already.

A cruel laughing hoot echoed from the fire. Rage rose up in Holdric and his fingers clenched tight upon his spear. Kenndric's arm rose in shadow against the firelight, calling all to him. His whisper came hard. "We move quickly. Hwaetearn, Wymud, Holdric, move with me. Aschbroc, Eahstann, clean our backs as best you can. When it's done find your brother and flee. This night's oak is our gatherplace. Ready?"

Each man answered hard.

"Then we go."

They moved fast through the trees. Dozens of ghaestling moved in the crazed firelight beyond, howling with a mad glee. Two broken men slumped against scorched trees, their faces slick with burns and blood. Torn charred clothes hung ragged from their torn charred limbs.

One of the ghaestling stood by the fire, drinking in the howls of the others. It laughed and made a show of picking a new brand from the coals, then turned to the bound men. One ranger looked up through blooded eyes, but no sound passed his lips.

Kenndric fit arrow to string. For a last quick breath, he looked back and caught Holdric's eye. Then they were in the light.

Holdric ran. Spear in hand, he ran. A ghaestling was in his path—a streak of feathers rushed past his head, then came the solid *smack* of iron on meat and the thing was down. Holdric leapt over the gurgling body without breaking stride.

The lead ghaestling had just turned their way when more arrows struck home. The creature fell back hard, scrabbling at its throat. Another just past it staggered back, a heavy shaft caught in its harness. It had no time to pull the arrow free before Hwaetearn was on him. Fyalclef sang, and the ghaestling fell to earth in pieces.

The firelight blazed crazily as Wymud kicked at the logs of the fire, cursing at the heat of the coals. The last clear thing Holdric saw were the two men slumped against their bindings on the broken trees, then all was mad dancing shadow from the scattered brands.

Holdric took the last few steps from memory, sliding to earth as he neared where he knew the first man would be. He grimaced as his knee landed in hot coals. With a quick curse he squatted up on his heels and found the tree by touch. He felt about the trunk for the bindings, the bark hot and blistered under his fingers, the smell of meat and scorched wood thick in his nose.

He cursed and scrambled in the dark… finally his hands found the bonds of tight hide and rough twisted bark. He pulled free his knife and began to cut. Somewhere above he heard a low moan.

The first of the bonds came free.

Above the thrum of Kenndric's bow sounded again and again, arrow after arrow hurtled into the blazing dark about them. A shriek carried across the clearing as ash and iron found their mark in ghaestling flesh. Then came a clatter much closer, the rattle of iron on shield-boards just over his head. Hwaetearn cursed, then grunted. His heavy shield hit the earth, the long iron point of a ghaestling throwing spear jutting clean through the wood.

"Give me your shield!" Hwaetearn called.

Holdric freed his shield strap, he struggled to pass his own shield up. Hwaetearn snatched it from his hand and turned back to the fight.

"How much longer Holdric?" Kenndric's voice came tight.

Holdric sawed furiously, another twist of hide came loose.

"Almost…"

The last binding burst, the wrists of the first man came free, and he slumped forward into Wymud's arms.

"Can you walk?" shouted Wymud.

The man babbled, his voice faint. "I…ah… I can…"

Holdric had already moved to the ankles of the second man. Pain streaked up his arm as his wrist brushed hot coals. He bit down a howl of pain, shook his hand free of the heat, and set again to work. The boots were charred, and he struggled finding where boot ended and bonds began. He sawed fierce and desperate, and the rough bonds fell one by one to the earth. But not yet enough.

Holdric closed his mind to the ghaestling howls, pushed away all thoughts of how near they came. Dim came the clatter of another thrown spear. Beside him came another a wretched howl, this one different. Holdric looked back to the first man—in the crazed firelight he saw the slick glistening white of bone as the man's leg pulled free of the charred flesh in his boot.

"He can't walk!" Holdric screamed. *"He can't walk!!"*

Wymud looked down, cursed, and heaved the man up onto his shoulders. A cry, a wet slick sound, and they were gone.

Holdric cut the last bond and the second man collapsed onto him. Holdric struggled to get underneath his shoulder and rise. The man was near half again his size, and barely alive. With a groan of effort Holdric pulled him from the earth.

"I have him." Eahstann hurried to his side, taking the man's other shoulder. Holdric snatched his spear from the dirt.

"*Go!*" shouted Kenndric. He let fly another arrow, then pulled forth his blade. His sword gleamed hungry in the last light of the fire. Side by side he stood with Hwaetearn as more ghaestling drew near. *"Go now!"*

Holdric and Eahstann needed no more. With the last of the watchmen between them they fled into the night. Their man was heavy. He stumbled broken between them, panting and grunting as he tried to walk.

They found by feel a narrow rocky draw and passed down into the shadows. A shrieking howl came from above, too close behind them. Holdric turned. One of the creatures stood black against the last of the firelight. It shrieked again in dark glee.

Holdric crumpled as the full weight of the watchman fell onto his shoulders. Eahstann had wrenched himself out from under their burden, raised his bow, and let fly an arrow. Iron cut meat and the ghaestling fell back into the shadows. The sounds of its dying fell away as they hurried stumbling down into the rocks. Still more howls followed them into the night.

"Here! Here!" Eahstann whispered. They climbed from the draw and sheltered under a great fallen tree, pulling and shoving the great man in beside them.

The sounds of the chase came closer and Holdric laid hand to Brukthorn. Memories of torn earth under a sheltering log crowded into his mind, but he pushed them away. He vowed to himself that he would not beg. No matter what, he would not beg.

The man beside him began to tremble. Holdric laid a hand on his shoulder, and for a moment the man stilled. The howling things came close, then passed them by and carried further down the draw. Holdric listened as their calls faded into the valley below.

The watchman's body shook again, harder now. He began to babble, "So many… so many…"

Eahstann cut him off with a whisper, "We need to go. Can you walk with us?"

"Walk? Walk…yah. I can walk."

They helped him to his feet and began again their trek through the night. There was no light beneath the trees, their way was broken with stone. Each step they found with seeking feet, and time and again thick brush blocked their way. More than once they only just missed tumbling down steep broken rock.

How long they moved Holdric no longer knew. They had just pulled free of another bramble when Eahstann asked, "Which way?"

Holdric looked to the sky, but could see nothing through the thick shroud of cloud. Even the moon's light was hidden.

He thought. "Down."

Down was all they had, and so down they went. When that failed, they felt for whispers of wind and followed the cold air of night sinking into the valley below.

The wood grew cold. The tall watchman's steps came slower, then he began to stumble. Time and again he tripped over the leaves, his weight pulling heavy on their shoulders. At last they stopped to rest in the shelter of a great broken stone. There was a ditch at its foot, and in the ditch a cold spring.

Water seeped cold and black from the earth at their feet. For a long time they sat in quiet, sheltering under their cloaks and rubbing their hands for warmth. Their charge was panting now, whispered words spilling from his mouth. Holdric pulled free his waterskin and placed it in his hand.

"What's your name, Huntsman?" he whispered.

With shaking hands, the man took it.

"Aem—Aem—Aemud… Where is he? Where is Barsti?!"

"Our brothers have him," Eahstann said in a calming whisper. "We're going to meet them."

A branch cracked in the night above. Holdric froze.

Soon came the soft rustle of feet creeping on earth. Many feet, all about them, there was no telling how many. A hiss came from the black above. More steps… and then the creeping things passed them over and faded into the night below.

For long moments they sat in taut silence. They strained their ears, listening for any left behind, but no sound came. All was still. How long they waited Holdric was not sure. Moonlight rose dim through a break in the clouds. They huddled closer under the stone's shadow.

Aemud broke the silence, his voice rough and broken. "I can't see."

The ranger's face was slick, black with blood in the moonlight. His eyes were burned shut. Eahstann and Holdric shared a silent look.

"There's nothing to see," answered Eahstann. "It's dark. Shhhh."

Aemud trembled but nodded quietly.

At the edge of hearing, a branch cracked. Leaves rustled. A fast flurry of movement, and something was in the shadows with them, screeching and flailing. Sharp iron flashed in the moonlight. Eahstann let out a choked yell of surprise. Branches cracked, and his grunts of effort came hot as he struggled in the black.

Aemud staggered to his feet. He began to shout, "Give me a blade! Give me a blade!"

"*Shh!*" hissed Holdric, scrambling to reach the sounds of struggle. A wild, heavy kick across his head pushed him back. He shook his head to clear it and tried again.

"No! Not… Back…" Eahstann's voice came fast—then rose in panicked breaths as the thing fell scrambling upon him.

"*HELP!*"

Holdric couldn't see. He reached out into the black. He found a bare arm and held tight for all he could. He kicked at Aemud—"Here! Aemud! Get the arm! Get the arm!"

The sound of the fight grew desperate. Eahstann's breath came in panicked pants, then came Aemud's heavy grunt. The arm Holdric held tensed—they had the thing! It jerked in their arms, kicking as Eahstann pulled free.

Then came the slick crunch of axe on bone. Another followed, and another and another as Eahstann hacked wildly into dying ghaestling.

"*Get it! Get it!*" howled Aemud.

The arm Holdric held jerked, it pulled hard, then with a guttering wheeze all its strength melted away. It was finished. Eahstann fell back, panting hard. Aemud still howled in rage, punching at what was left of the creature as it died.

"Shhh! Shhh! It's done! It's done!" hissed Holdric.

Finally Aemud fell quiet and crumpled into the ditch. His breath came in hoarse ragged sobs, his cries faded to quiet weeping and then to silence. For many long breaths all was quiet. Then came a mortal scream, far down the valley. Howls and cruel laughing shrieks followed.

The cry had sounded like Hwaetearn.

Holdric sat in silence and stared dully into the shadow. In the dark, Eahstann cursed under his breath. "We have to go."

Holdric echoed his curse. "Yah."

He pulled himself up from the ditch… then saw the little fires. Torchlight danced not far up the valley, dim through the trees. Panic clawed hungry for his mind.

"Let's go… Let's go, let's go, let's go!" Eahstann hissed. Holdric got again under Aemud's arm and they hurried down the rocks. Aemud swayed on his feet, heedless words spilling from his mouth.

"Where are we? Where are we?"

"Shh! They're close!" Eahstann hissed.

Aemud paid no heed. His voice grew louder, more desperate. "Where's Barsti? Where… did you get Barsti?"

"Shhh!" Holdric shook him. "Barsti is safe. We have to go!"

Shadows passed before the torches. Some of the nearer lights snuffed out.

"Quiet now!" hissed Holdric in Aemud's ear.

Holdric was not sure if Aemud understood, or even if he heard, but soon the words became mumbles, and the mumbles fell to silence. The great man's feet slowed, and before long Holdric was all but carrying him. Still they moved, moved fast as they could manage. Clouds swallowed up the moon and all fell into darkness.

Every step seemed an age. He wasn't certain how long it had been when Aemud tripped on the rough stones. The big man went down hard, taking Holdric with him. Holdric groaned as he hit hard earth, then caught himself and listened… nothing. Only Aemud writhing slowly in the leaves beside him, and a faint rustle of leaves as Eahstann came to their side.

Eahstann helped them up and knelt again under Aemud's far shoulder. Together they groped their way through the wood. Aemud managed to match their stride, but all his weight they bore between them. At least his words had stopped.

Little by little they left the searching fires behind. By passing moon and smell and slow groping they found at last again the great oak. Aemud they let gently to earth, and Holdric collapsed like a bag of meat.

There came no howls behind, no sound of rustled brush. They were alone.

"What now?" breathed Holdric.

"We wait," answered Eahstann.

Aemud groaned softly once, then fell silent. He seemed to sleep, but his breath came in ragged gasps.

"Will he live?" asked Holdric.

"I don't know." Eahstann's voice was tired, flat.

"We can't leave him."

"I know."

Holdric looked up. Through shreds of cloud, he saw the bright stars of the Waelstan. The night was wearing late. He looked deep into the shadowed wood, straining his ears for friendly steps. None came. "They said they'd be here."

Eahstann was silent a long time. His words when they came were heavy with weary grief. "We wait for greylight. If our brothers come, we make what plans we may with whoever is left. If not, one of us finds a place to hide with Aemud, the other makes for the Hyssestead and brings aid."

Holdric sat with the thought. "Done."

They turned then to their watch. Each waited in silence, alone with his thoughts. Slowly the light rose under the trees. Far off an owl called, low and chill, and then all again was still.

Greylight came, and still they were alone.

"No one's here," breathed Holdric.

"No one…." echoed Eahstann.

Holdric looked back over his shoulder. Aemud was dead. Eahstann answered the unspoken question, "Not long."

Holdric could only nod.

Silently they hollowed out a space for the man under a fallen tree, and there they laid his body to rest.

The branch is broken and cannot be mended.
The leaves are flown and cannot be gathered again…

The words came too easy now. Eahstann took Aemud's brooch, and ran his fingers over the metal as he stared at it unseeing. Then he breathed a silent verse and tucked it into his pouch. Each looked to the other, mulling on the death in silence.

Holdric broke the quiet first. "Our trail will be easy to follow. We need to go."

Eahstann looked back over his shoulder, back towards the Bonemounds and the trees beyond. His voice came flat, as if he were speaking from far away. "They'll be hunting us from yesterday's sign as well, down in the valley."

Holdric shifted in his place. "They will."

He looked over the broken earth, thinking on the high valley, the broken tumble of ground below, the high ridge above, the high ridge with no pass in a day's walk. No pass unless…

"… Like a goat." Holdric breathed the words to himself.

Eahstann looked to him, not understanding.

Holdric stood and took up again his spear. "We don't go down the valley. We go east, scale the rocks, then make for the Hyssestead along the far side. If we can make it as far as the rocks, our sign up will be hard to follow. Once over the top, we have the ridge between them and us. We can move quickly."

Eahstann was still. He turned to look down the valley before them, weighing the paths in his heart. "That… holds sense," he said at last. "Yah."

Holdric took one last look about the little rise, hiding the worst signs of their staying. Eahstann laid in tumbled stone a last message:

Two. Moving Home.

CHAPTER FOURTEEN
Rock and Sky

Greylight came cold. The leaves were wet and dripping. The air was thick and close. Holdric peered through the dim green ahead, half expecting to see his Ollda there, Ollda who had always led the way. Now his place was empty.

They crept forward over wet stone and soft wet earth, and the gloom did not lift with the morning. Heavy cloud shrouded the sun. Beneath the trees all was dull and grey. Only once was the quiet broken. An owl called, low and far away. Then all fell again to silence.

They moved on, grim and quiet… Holdric's eyes landed on sign. He froze still. Even from where he stood, he could see the long strides of ghaestling. He moved to look closer. Eahstann stood quiet watch as he knelt over the earth.

Passing water had smoothed over the footfalls, and some were all but gone. Still he could tell the creature had run north, further up the valley. Holdric craned his head to look up along the way of its passing. Not far on he saw other, older sign in scuffed moss, and the long-healed scrape over a knotted root. They had found a common trail.

He followed it a short way—then he saw the man's tread. The sign was too clear to miss, sharp and fresh in the soft earth. The man had moved with care. He had taken gentle stalking steps, he had kept his weight heavy in the toe… but his pace had been uneven, and he had walked heavy to one side.

Holdric cursed under his breath. He tugged at Eahstann's cloak and Eahstann knelt beside him, his eyes still on the far trees. Holdric leaned close and spoke in a half-breathed whisper, "The man from Old Acramm's spring was here, the man from the tree, where we found…" Holdric would not finish the words. Instead he pointed—"He went south, back down the valley."

Eahstann's face did not change, it showed no feeling. Still Holdric could tell he was shaken. Eahstann glanced down at the sign, then looked again out into the wood. "How long?"

"Not long," answered Holdric. "Last night maybe." He looked at the dripping trees overhead, then again to the sharp-edged track in the rain-soaked ground. "Surely no older."

Eahstann looked over the path the man had taken, and then back along their own trail. Holdric followed his eyes… just in sight was the twisting oak of their camp, far back through the green. The man had passed within sight of their hide.

A crack of breaking deadfall shot through the woods. They hunched low at the sound, searching the gloom for where it had come, and saw nothing but rain and mist. The sound did not come again.

Eahstann began again to move, and Holdric moved with him. Their every step seemed loud in his ears, and dread hung heavy over his spirit. He shut his eyes to listen to the drip of water and the rustle of leaf. He smelled deep of the wood. He looked deep and sharp into each shadow, and he softened his sight to watch for moving things.

Slowly he fell into woldgast. Fear and time fell away. Only sight and sound, smell and touch, filled his being. He might have known a grim solace, had he still the mind to feel it.

The sun rose high and cold behind the clouds, and still the valley stretched on. Water dripped from the leaves, water burbled over stone. His eyes fell on the empty woods to his left and a pang of emptiness pushed into his mind. Aschbroc should walk there, and Hwaetearn too, the two of them ever in the corner of his eye. Now their place also was empty. Holdric tried to push the thoughts away.

The shadows changed slow, the sun still high somewhere beyond the cloud. The wood was dim and cold, all the world held still. In time Holdric saw rocks stretch high overhead through the trees— they neared the edge of the valley. The ground began at last to rise beneath them and the earth grew rockier beneath their feet. Oak and holly gave way again to thick pine, then to birch and scrubby thorn. They passed old ghaestling sign, faint traces of long-past comings and goings. They pushed on.

Soon they were truly climbing, clambering up and over great rocks. The trees thinned and the light grew not so dim. Still the sun above shone only as a cold light, high beyond the clouds. At last they came out from beneath the leaves and rain pecked upon their hoods.

Grass and bramble grew thin. They came up a last tumble of rock and scree to a great broken wall of stone. Rainwater ran in sheets and swift thin flows down the rock. Holdric and Eahstann looked up the cliff, then far to either side. The rock wall here was rough, the footing sure. There would be no better place to climb than where they stood. Still the ridge stretched high above them, and the heights were lost in mist. It would be a hard climb.

The distant shriek of ghaestling carried across the rainy wood behind, and soon another answered. The hunt had started.

Eahstann pointed to a broken course of rock high overhead. "We go up that path, then up to that ledge?"

Holdric thought on the way and shook his head. "No, see the rock above? There? We will not be able to cross that, not in this. What of… that way?" He pointed further across the face. "Then break north at that crack. It gets us high as I can see."

Eahstann pondered the way. "You have it." he said at last. He bent to bind his bow upon his back. Holdric took a last look upward and swallowed his worry. Then he slung his spear and started up.

The going was easy at first. The stone felt sturdy beneath his hands, the footholds sure. He looked down—Eahstann fared well on the stone below. Holdric heaved himself up another stone, and then another. He wiped his hands upon his tunic to dry them as he went. His muscles began to warm. The climb felt good. They carried on and soon were well over the trees.

He turned to look out over the valley. All was covered in wet mist, but he could just see the place of last night's fight. Somewhere under those trees were the rest of his brothers. Alive or dead, he could not know.

He turned back to his work, but echoes of the night before still pulled at his memory. He pushed them from his mind and worked his anger against the rock. Stone by stone he climbed in a cold rage. His fingers grew chill and his legs began to ache. His forearms burned. Still he climbed.

The treetops were small now, far below. He looked up—they were not yet halfway to the top. On another day he might have rued this climb. Now he could not care. He cursed and pushed himself faster still. The wind came sharp as they moved higher, and the rain grew hard.

The wind carried a ghaestling's shriek. Holdric looked down but could no longer see the earth. Eahstann was braced on a rock below, sheltering as best he could from the blowing rain as he too looked out over the valley. All below was lost in mist and cloud. The shriek came again, and not long after the wracked sound of a ghaestling horn.

Holdric and Eahstann looked to each other. Every dire fear passed through their minds, but here on the stones they could do nothing, and so they turned again to their climb. Rain ran down Holdric's arms. The stone was sharp and cold under his fingers. He pushed until his breath came fast and his hands cramped with pain.

He leaned against the stone, taking what rest he could on the high rock. The heights above were still lost in mist. He could not know how much was yet to go, and doubt began to creep into his heart… but the choice was long since made.

He pushed up another step, and another. His foot slipped upon the stone and he caught himself with a curse. He paused again to catch his breath, to warm his hands. The rain grew stronger, wind-blown spray from the stone filled his face and he spat against the driving water.

High above, empty grey sky stretched over empty grey rock. Still he thought he could just see the top. He pushed on. His fingers were burning now, his legs soft and shaking. He held himself against the cold wet rock and his breath came hard.

Not far overhead water poured down a cut in the stone. Cold spray splashed over his hands. They were almost at the top now, but he saw no way up but to cross through the falling water. He cursed and pushed himself up, clinging hard to the rocks as he passed beneath the flood. Water filled his face and water ran cold over his fingers.

Just as he passed the worst of it, his foot slipped. He held on with hands and elbows, searching for a hold with his flailing feet. Eahstann came quick to his side, full in the flowing water as he reached for Holdric's leg. Snarling with cold he guided Holdric's foot to stone.

"Now!" Eahstann yelled over the falling water. *"Go!"*

Holdric kicked, he heaved himself up, and he was on solid rock again. Eahstann came behind him, sputtering hard with water and cold. Holdric looked up—the last crest was just above. He pulled himself up and over the last swell of rock, kicking as he wriggled onto the empty crest. Behind he heard Eahstann struggling, grunting with work as he pulled his way up behind. Holdric moved aside and reached back, just as Eahstann flopped hard beside him onto the rock.

The harper was soaked and gasping. Both rolled onto their backs and looked up into the rain. Eahstann shouted a curse against the cold. Holdric laughed at the curse, and Eahstann could not help but laugh with him. Together they howled, mad and giddy as they looked up into the soaking sky. Cold rain danced on Holdric's face, washing away tears of sick relief.

At last he coughed and rolled to his knees. The crest was a narrow table of stone, slick and sloping to empty air on the far side.

"Hold my ankles," Holdric said.

"Go rot," groaned Eahstann.

Still Eahstann rolled up, braced his feet as best he could, and took hold of Holdric.

Holdric crept down the wet rock until he could see over the far edge. The slope fell steep away from their perch, the slick mountain stone streaked with broken scree. All below was shrouded in cloud and rain.

"It's too steep here," he called back. "We have to keep to the top before we can get back down."

Eahstann looked into the rain and cursed, "I am never following you again!"

Holdric laughed as he backed away from the edge.

Together they picked their way along the far face of the crest, testing each uneasy step lest they slide into the empty air below. Holdric caught a firm handhold and paused to look out into the rain. He was perched on a small stony island, lost in a sea of cloud.

The wind grew loud and rain gave way to hail. As he picked his way around an outcrop, his numb fingers slipped from the stone. He stumbled on scree and grabbed at the rock in a panic. Cold slush poured down over him and he kicked at the stone in rage. Snarling, he pulled himself back up and pushed on. He felt out another step, and then another. His foot slid again, sending scree skittering down the slope.

He was tired. He was tired, and he was getting clumsy. Some dim part of his mind began to worry. Still they worked their way along the crest, hunting for some way down. At last Holdric saw it—far ahead, far through wind and hail, he could just make out a goat path along the face of the ridge. It was still far off, and looked scarce wide enough for a single footfall, but it would be enough.

He yelled over the wind to Eahstann, "A path! I see a path!"

Eahstann did not answer.

Holdric looked back. Eahstann lagged behind, hunched over the spine of stone. He did not move. When Holdric reached him, Eahstann was barely hanging onto to his place, shaking with cold. The wool of his cloak was soaked through and stiff with clinging ice. His breath came in low ragged grunts.

Holdric looked ahead—the path was still too far. "Come on brother."

Holdric pulled Eahstann from the stone and got under his arm. Wet hail pelted hard and slush hung cold to their cloaks. Holdric jammed his spear into the scree, working it deep. Stones skittered down the steep slope before him, but the spear held. With spear and heel he worked his way down the scree to rest against a crop of stone, and there he braced his spear against the rock.

He pulled off Eahstann's cloak, and his own as well. With cord and brooch he bound them together, stretching both over spear and bow into a rude shelter. He weighted the edge with scree and held Eahstann close under the wool. Hail still pelted through gaps, water still seeped down the earth beneath them, but the stretched cloaks kept off the worst of the wet.

Slowly the air within began to warm. Slowly Eahstann's shivering stopped. For a long time they sat in silence, waiting for the weather to pass.

Finally Eahstann shifted with a curse. "*Rotting fil…* Holdric, you reek!"

Holdric laughed. "Not half so much as you."

The wind howled around them, and they took hold of the sheltering wool lest it be pulled away. It was long before the wind fell away and long before the hail fell silent, but at last all grew still and the grey of the sky seemed less dim. Holdric pulled at the cloak bindings with cold and stinging fingers. The wool fell open, and again they could see the wide valley beyond. A low mist hung over the trees far below, thick and heavy.

No. Not mist.

The wooded valley was shrouded in smoke. Countless fires burned wet beneath the trees. Dozens of fires… hundreds. A ghaestling host lay beneath them, thick as locusts.

Holdric sat stunned. "I didn't know so many even lived."

Eahstann did not speak at first. Then he cursed. "They're making for the folksteads."

Holdric looked to him, trying to catch his meaning.

Eahstann went on, "This is why they drew out the watchmen, made us blind to the east. While we were fighting in the far valley, their host was here, making to cross the Mearcwater where none would see."

Holdric looked on the fires below. "What now?"

Eahstann looked south. "They're less than two days from the Whitefork. And it will take a day at least for the fyrd to rise, once they get the word." The harper looked out over the valley below, mulling on what would be. Soon he decided.

He rose and pinned his cloak again about his shoulders. "We make first for Earnsclyff's beacon, raise the Torr. Torrlaed Stalmaht will pass the fire to Greatwatch. He'll send out riders to scout while the Eorl gathers the fyrd."

"And we?" asked Holdric.

"After we raise the beacon fire, we make for the Torr, meet up with Stalmaht's riders if we can. We tell all we've seen. Stalmaht will send word of these ghaestling to the Eorl and guide him in."

"What of the Hyssestead men?" asked Holdric. "They're in the path of that."

"They'll have to make do. With luck, one of their men will see our beacon from the valley, or the Torr's answer. If not…" Eahstann sighed. "They're good men. They'll stay ahead best they can. They'll get the word out along the Whitefork."

Holdric looked down over the ridge, back the way they had come only a day before. He had not Eahstann's hope. Finally he grunted. "I like it not, but I see no better road. Lead on."

Eahstann took up his bow and stood back to make way for Holdric. "Lead the way, sign-follower." With a grim smile Holdric took his place. They clambered up onto the ridge and made their way to the narrow path, then began slowly to wind their way down the face of the ridge. Long they walked in shrouding mist, and the sun sank from its height as the afternoon wore on. The fires below died away, the smoke over the valley thinned. In time it looked as if the ghaestling had never been.

Still the sight of so many fires hung in Holdric's mind. The things must number far more than all the folk of Heortlea, far more than any mustering he had ever seen. The Eorl himself may not have so many men.

A ghaestling horn echoed across the valley. For a moment Holdric feared they had been seen, no matter the thin cover of cloud, no matter the grey of their cloaks against the grey of the stone. Faint on the wind came shrieks and answering horns, but no ghaestling band broke from the trees far below.

They hurried on lest they be seen on open stone. The goat path grew narrower still, scarce the width of Holdric's palm. He slipped, and with a curse he righted himself. Scree tumbled down the slope towards the valley below.

They moved he knew not how long. The day grew bright and the last of the shrouding mist burned away. At last a large broken boulder rose before them, a great crack across its face and the scorch of long-dead fire at its foot. Eahstann brightened at the sight. He looked again along the crest, then signed, *Not far.*

As they neared the stone another narrow path joined their own.

Holdric cursed, a curse Eahstann echoed—ghaestling sign was thick here. Holdric knelt to look close. The tracks were thickly crossed, rain-washed and wind-softened. Still the footfalls were sharp in the small sheltered places.

He searched until he was sure, then passed up the sign. *Ghaestling, twelve-about. Days, one-about.*

Eahstann glanced down from his guard. *Man also?*

Holdric shook his head. *No.*

Eahstann looked down the path ahead, then back up the crest from where the things had come. Holdric followed his eyes… Ollda had spoken of other trails near the pass, the ghaestling must know them also. They could not tarry here.

Eahstann pushed them fast, angling now down the slope towards cover. They came first to scrub, then thin trees. Soon the green was thick enough to shroud their passing. They moved careful just inside the trees, Eahstann watching the heights above, Holdric the woods below. Ever they moved in silence. Ever they dreaded the sound of another horn.

The slope grew rough again and Eahstann guided them down into a nest of piled stone. Holdric joined him—and saw that he knew this place. They looked again over the wide saddle of the pass, now from the northern side. Far off he could just see their old way down from Earnsclyff Watch. He searched for the watchmen's hide, but could not find it.

Horns sounded again from the valley below, now dim and far away. Holdric looked to Eahstann. Eahstann looked grim, but unshaken. He leaned close to Holdric and spoke in a low whisper. "Look to the peak, then down and east until the first patch of tree, yah?"

Holdric followed his words, then nodded as he found the place.

"Look straight below that, just shy of the top."

"I have it," Holdric answered. Though the stacked stone wall of Earnsclyff Watch was lost in shadow, he could just see the watchmen's ledge.

"Now," whispered Eahstann, "from that peak, the beacon is about half a league on, just down the west side. Look for two yews near a great rock, one splintered. The beacon is hidden beneath a bramble of highthorn. If we're broken—"

"We won't be brok—" began Holdric.

"Don't be careless," Eahstann scolded. "Tell me how to get to the beacon."

Holdric spoke back again the words.

Eahstann gave a grim smile. "Good."

They looked over the ground below. The way down was rough with tumbled stone. Most of the way was shrouded in high brush, but the pass itself was broad and open. They would have no cover for their crossing.

Sure at least they had their way, they carried down the slope into the trees. It was not long before they came to the first sign of ghaestling flank walkers, and the sign was not old. They dared go down no farther.

Eahstann brought them to a narrow hump in the slope, as good a place of crossing as he could find. The little dip in the earth would hide them well from below, and well enough from above—there would be no better. Still they were wary.

Eahstann signed, *I go. You watch. You follow.*

Holdric nodded.

Eahstann paused for a last breath, then darted quick across the open. Soon he was in the cover of the far side. Nothing moved. All was still.

Eahstann signed for Holdric. Holdric rose, but just as he was about to break cover Eahstann held up a hand.

STOP.

Holdric froze.

Wait…

Eahstann's eyes were locked high on the rocks ahead.

Wait…

Wait…

NOW.

Holdric rushed across open ground.

He landed in the brush beside Eahstann, and hasty they burrowed deeper into cover. When they were safe from watching eyes, Holdric looked back. If any had seen his crossing, they made no sign. Eahstann still moved ahead, and Holdric hurried to follow.

They pushed their way further up the slope, until finally Eahstann came to a stop in a thick knot of young birch, and there they rested. Holdric took water and passed his skin to Eahstann. Eahstann nodded his thanks. "Not much farther," he whispered. "Then up and over."

Holdric looked back the way they had come. He could just see the high ridge behind. "What did you see?" he asked. "Back there, I mean."

Eahstann shook his head. "Nothing, I think. A shadow high in the rocks."

"But you're not sure?"

"No."

Holdric cursed. He stoppered the skin and slung it back over his shoulder "Best not stop long then."

Eahstann grinned. "You'll make it home yet."

Together they moved along the ridge. As they walked, Holdric looked up to the crest and found again the place of the beacon. He was sure he had it now, or near enough. Eahstann led them to an ancient goat path that climbed higher up the slope. The rain on the heights had long since burned off, but still the wind came sharp and cold through a break in the trees.

Holdric looked behind. The ground below rolled in waves down into the eastern valley. The woods were deep there, countless trees stretching dark and green until they met the far clouds. The last sign of the ghaestling host was gone, their horns now quiet. Still a dread air seemed to hang over the trees.

Eahstann nudged Holdric and they moved on. The trees grew thin as they neared the crest, and the way grew rough with sliding rock. They were not far. Just as they were to take the last rise, a flash of pale wood in the grass caught Holdric's eye.

He knelt, then whispered a curse. Eahstann looked on as Holdric knelt over the find—the wood was axe-split and stained with black tar. They both looked to the stones above.

"It could have been weather-blown," Holdric said… he wished to believe it so.

Eahstann echoed his curse. "We've come this far. We must try."

Holdric rose and took hold of his spear. He looked for sign of ghaestling on the earth and saw none. Then he peered up into the last stretch of green before the top. Ollda would scout alone now, test the way. Holdric knew he should do the same, knew he was better far in the wild than Eahstann.

He made to say the words… he almost said the words. But something froze his tongue. Perhaps it was the memory of Aemud's empty eyes in the moonlight, or the watchman left to hang in the tree, or the mess of Eomud's wayrunner in the mud. Cold fear held him and he said nothing, and in a heartbeat the moment passed. Eahstann moved on, and Holdric hurried to keep his place.

They came up the last of the slope. Just beyond a few thin trees lay the beacon, or what was left of it. The shrouding briar was pulled down, the great timbers heaved from the beacon stones. Split wood was tossed wild over the rocks.

They came out into the open, dread growing upon them. Holdric looked out over the far ridge. Far off across the western valley he could see the Torr, sharp and proud against the distant hills. Men watched there unknowing, waited there for warning—warning they could no longer send.

Eahstann snatched up a piece of kindling. He turned it over in his hands as he looked over the wreck of the beacon. "This makes two." He cursed as he let the kindling fall from his fingers. "Ghaestling have never used wiles like this. This is not like them."

He walked around the beacon stones, looking over the wreck. Holdric's gaze fell to the earth at his feet. The crush of trodden ground caught his eye, and he knelt to better see the sign. The foot-fall was rounded over, soft and crumbled… but only just. On this high wind-blown ridge it could not be old, days at most. The ball of the foot had been round, the stride broad and even. It was not a stride he knew.

"A man was here," Holdric said.

"I know," answered Eahstann. His voice came glum and empty.

Holdric looked up. Eahstann was on the far side of the bea-con mound. He looked at something on the earth, his face ashen. Holdric made to rise, but Eahstann held out his hand. "Later," he sighed. He looked to the sky. The sun was halfway to its rest, the afternoon already growing thin.

"We have time," Eahstann said. "We can lay the fire again, have light by nightfall. Holdric…"

But Holdric was no longer listening. The hair on his neck prick-led. Something was wrong. Something was wrong, and he was not seeing it. He looked careful over the green and broken wood be-low… past tree, under broken rock, over a low bramble, beneath…

Two empty black eyes met his own.

Holdric hurled his spear with a shout—*"Foe!"*

It was too late. Holdric's spear clattered against empty branches. Eahstann turned just as Holdric bounded down the slope.

"Holdric, *wait!*"

But Holdric was already running. He crashed through the brush, he caught up again his spear. Eahstann's arrow streaked past his shoulder and was lost in the trees below. For but a breath, Holdric glanced back and saw Eahstann running behind him, another arrow already on the string. He turned again to the fleeing creature, raised his spear—

And the ghaestling was gone.

CHAPTER FIFTEEN
Word on the Wind

The crash of brush echoed up the slope, and with it a shrieking call of warning. Grey skin flashed through the green, and Eahstann sent another arrow—too late. The arrow cut empty air and punched through the leaves beyond.

The ghaestling never broke stride. It tore down the slope, then cut to one side and leapt through a thick knot of brush. Holdric and Eahstann pushed after and broke from the trees onto a steep slide of scree. Holdric rushed down the open rock, sliding and struggling to stay upright as the stones tumbled before him. Finally he slid to a stop onto solid ground. Under Eahstann's guard he desperately looked over the earth, hunting for the next piece of trail—

There!

A broken patch of tall grass told where the ghaestling had dived again into the trees. It was still close. They raced after, farther and farther down the slope. They passed over sign of flank walkers, then followed a deep-scored trail down a muddy bank and into the valley.

The slope before them grew shallow. The air grew close under thick trees. Again they caught a glimpse of the ghaestling just ahead, panting against a gnarled oak. Before Eahstann could raise his bow, it howled and ducked again into the green.

The trees grew thick as they followed after. The still air began to reek of dying things, the ground was torn and muddy from the passing of many feet. The sign of the running ghaestling was clear now, long strides chasing after the great host of its fellows. Another shrieking cry echoed through the wood before them.

A narrow sapling still swayed where the ghaestling had raced through the trees. Holdric started after, but Eahstann did not follow.

"Holdric, stop." Eahstann's voice was low.

Holdric began to argue—then held his tongue. He looked deep into the shadows before them. Again the ghaestling shrieked. This time there came an answer.

The second cry hung long in the air.

Holdric cursed. They began to back away… then turned and ran. Behind them came the call of a ghaestling horn, the sound harsh and sour over the valley. It was soon answered by another, and then another. Howls rose up from the woods behind.

Holdric felt the ground bend soft beneath his feet, he felt brambles pull and scratch at his cloak. They sprinted back up the hill, struggling again up the muddy slope. Holdric winced at each great tear he left in the soft earth, but there was no time for craft.

They passed again through the high wet grass, scrambled up tumbling scree. The horns sounded louder, shrieks of alarm not far behind. Finally they neared the top of the rocks, stones clattering down the slope behind them. Still they climbed, and as the woods began to thin Holdric could again see the crest of the ridge far above. His side began to clench from the hurt of running, his breath came ragged in his chest. Still the horns sounded behind.

Eahstann stopped. From farther up on the ridge came the crash of falling water—he brightened at the sound. "I know where we are. Come!"

Their path did not bend at first. Then Eahstann took them up along an old deer path, ducking through brush and under tree. Holdric followed, hot and panting despite the cold of the day. The crash of water grew loud and the shade of trees thick. They came to a narrow spring and turned their way up the streambed, running until at last they came to a steep wall of rock.

A great flood of water spilled from the heights. The air was thick with spray, and sunlight shot through the crashing mist. Cold clean air poured down with the water from above. Eahstann moved to the wet stones.

"Up?" asked Holdric.

"Up," said Eahstann.

Holdric slung his spear and shook out his hands.

"Lead on."

They pulled themselves up great sloping shelves of broken stone, slick with spray. The water crashed loud around them, and Holdric shivered as spray prickled his neck. He pushed himself hard, scrabbling from handhold to handhold fast as he could, aching at every breath. He reached a patch of lichen and worked carefully around lest he scrape away sign for a sharp-eyed hunter.

He strained his ears listening for the chasing horns, but heard nothing over the crash of water. One last hard push and he made the top. Eahstann held out a hand and pulled him over the edge. Holdric came over with a heave and fell panting on the high stone.

He looked back the way they had come. The valley fell far away past seeing, the rolling ground lost in the press of thick trees. Behind those trees the ghaestling came. Already the horns sounded again sharp and loud, already he could just hear the howls over the crash of water.

The two turned and fled. They kept to the water, wading up the mountain creek that fed the falls below. The current was swift, the waters cold, the stones of the bottom covered in thick river slime, but the water hid their passing.

Holdric's feet grew numb, his legs ached with cold fire. Still they pushed on. He searched the banks for sign and found none. The horns sounded fainter now, lost somewhere in the woods below. He stumbled, and Eahstann caught him.

"Just a little further."

Eahstann pushed them hard, until at last they splashed from the creek out onto a broad stony bank, then up into the cover of a thick knot of hazel. There Holdric collapsed upon the earth, and Eahstann sank beside him. For a long time they could not speak, both struggling to gather again their breath. Eahstann's fingers brushed over his quiver and he breathed a quiet curse. He had but six shafts left.

Holdric pulled himself up and moved to the creek to fill again his waterskin. He held out a hand to Eahstann and took his as well. As he knelt on the stone, he sighted back down the creek… they were still alone.

He whispered low to Eahstann, "Where now?"

Eahstann looked up through the hazels into the fading sky. Already the sun was low.

"Straight for the Torr," he said at last. "Take them word ourselves." He studied the sky, thinking. "We'll have dark before moonrise. We cross the heights by dark, then take the west valley with the moon. If we push hard all night, we can make the Torr by dawn."

Holdric looked up the ridge. The heights above were lost in trees. "Ollda said that valley is deathly ground."

Eahstann's face was grave. "It is."

Holdric looked back down the way they had come. Ghaestling horns still sounded in the valley behind. He rose, then stoppered

Eahstann's waterskin and passed it back. Eahstann caught Holdric's eye as he took the skin. "Just keep going. You'll make it."

The faint echo of a shout carried up the waters from not far behind.

Both men froze.

Holdric began, "That didn't sound like—"

Eahstann was already on his feet, arrow on the string. "Doesn't matter, we keep going. Hurry!"

Holdric slung his skin and hurried after. They raced up from the creek past the trees, then broke through thick bracken and into trees again. Up the ridge they ran, and still the calls and horns sounded too close behind. Time and again Holdric thought they must be near the crest, time and again they crested a shallow rise to see the way still leading up before them.

Another horn sounded. This one came from the north, down the ridge and back the way they had come. Another horn answered from high on the slope above—then other calls echoed up and down the ridge. Eahstann stopped and peered through the brush. He set his jaw as he looked back through the trees behind, then up to the heights above.

He mouthed the words, "They're driving us."

Holdric's stomach dropped. Eahstann was right, he had to be. But if the horns sounded the place of the hammer, where was the anvil?

More horns sounded, closer now as the driving line drew across the ridge towards them. The ghaestling were moving fast.

"Up!" Eahstann hissed. "Fast as we can, up! Cross their line!"

Holdric did not need to be told. They darted up a shaded deer path, then broke over a tumble of stone and into a dry gully that ran down from the heights. The gully was choked with brush, but still they kept low beneath its banks. Sometimes they could run at a low crouch, others they had to scramble over the thorns.

Slowly they gained the heights. The trees began to thin, the ground grew rough and rocky. The horns sounded again… soon the first of the ghaestling would burst from the trees. Holdric's legs burned, his back ached from the strain. The crest of the ridge could not be much further.

Soon they were under the last of the trees. Before them lay only coarse mountain grass, and beyond that the naked stone of the crest. Ahead the open grass waved thick under a sky of fading gold. Behind, shrieks sounded from the trees.

The ghaestling cries were near, scarce a stone's throw down the slope. Others sounded farther along the ridge, hidden somewhere in the trees. Holdric and Eahstann shared a last silent look. Each hurried to make ready. Holdric shrugged off his pack and took his spear by the bindings, as Eahstann uncaught his bow.

They flattened themselves against the earth. Dragging their gear behind them, they crept out into open grass. The last of the trees fell behind, only open sky stretched above. Pulling with fingers, pushing with toes, they gained each span of ground. They moved in time with the wind, they pulled grass straight again with finger and toe, they forced their bodies low.

The calls sounded clearer now. The ghaestling had cleared the trees behind.

Holdric froze. His legs ached to rise, to run. He ached even to show himself against the sky, if only he could move. Still he kept his place. Dry summer grass scratched at his face, deep mountain earth filled his nose. He dared not rise even to turn his gaze.

He cast his eyes up the ridge—it was so close. They were a scarce twenty paces from the sheltering stones of the crest, twenty paces that may as well have been a league. He could just see Eahstann in the grass ahead. Eahstann looked back, his face blank.

The shrieks below fell to quiet. Holdric's eyes fixed on small white blooms of seolfrenblos just before his face. Silent whispers of prayer passed his lips. Then came the crash of brush below, and speech, harsh ghaestling speech—the things were in the grass now. How many they were, Holdric could not hear.

The wind came strong again, and the high grass moved over them as a sea. Eahstann moved with the wind, and Holdric followed. Breath by breath, finger by finger they climbed.

Fifteen paces still to go.

The great golden light of evening fell away, greylight loomed near.

Ten paces.

High above the sky deepened to a dizzying deep blue.

Five paces.

The voices came louder, strange and harsh. The stones loomed high over his head, seeming huge from where he lay.

Two paces.

Eahstann slipped through a low spot in the earth ahead, the wind slackened and Holdric stilled. A lone shout cut the air below.

Through a break in the rock, Holdric could just see Eahstann on his back, readying again his bow. The wind gusted again and Holdric was over the rocks.

Careful he found again his feet. Eahstann knelt beside him, arrow to string. Holdric peered through a gap in the rock behind. At least a dozen ghaestling milled over the grass below. In the greying light they seemed almost as things coughed up from the barrow. They called to each other in their fierce tongue, and one pointed back down the ridge.

Holdric looked back along his path up to the rocks. To the un-wary eye, all was as it had been. Still every bruised blade of grass, every flattened spot of earth seemed to scream of their passing. One creature walked across their trail, shouting at the others. Eahstann whispered a curse and ducked lower behind the stones.

For a moment, it seemed almost that the things would leave. Most roamed along the treeline, looking out over the grass as they moved away south along the ridge. Then one paused, a strange limping one near the last, a tattered hood of old wool about its shoulders. It stopped as it came near their trail, and it lowered itself to the earth. Holdric felt a pull on his cloak, Eahstann whispered words past hearing.

The thing looked up through the grass, head low.

Eahstann's hand fell away.

The creature looked up along their path. It looked over every scrape, every crushed blade of grass until—

Their eyes met. It had eyes blue as a faded winter sky…the eyes of a man.

It—no, *he*—stood. The man pulled back his woolen hood. What remained of his hair was crusted and torn, his face was pocked and scarred in strange patterns, the marks old and healed… but still he was man. He stared at Holdric, and his eyes narrowed. A ghaestling standing near looked up, then followed the man's gaze to the stones where Holdric and Eahstann hid.

It raised a blowing horn to its lips.

Eahstann's arrow streaked across the open air. The ghaestling staggered back, its horn fell to the grass.

Eahstann's voice hung in the air. *"Run, Holdric!"*

Behind them the foe fought through the thick grass. Eahstann pushed Holdric on, he stopped just long enough to send another arrow. Ghaestling screeched behind.

Together they ran down the draw ahead. They moved low, their heads ducked behind the stone. The open edge was near, Holdric strained to pick out the place for each footfall in the fading light lest he tumble into the gathering dark. Eahstann grunted hard behind him.

"Come *on*," Holdric hissed… but Eahstann's steps were stilled.

Holdric turned.

His mind locked. He would not believe what truth his eyes told.

Eahstann was on his knees in the graveled stone. A long, fire-black spear swayed crazily from his side. His feet kicked at the earth. He drove his shoulder deep into the stone of the draw, pushing as if some animal piece of his mind meant to crawl away from the point. Eahstann grunted again, one hand scrabbling for the spear in his flesh.

Something flashed on the ridge overhead. For but the space of a breath, Holdric saw the hooded shadow, eager and gloating. With a cry of rage Holdric hurled hard his spear—not fast enough. The man had already vanished into the rocks. Holdric's spear hit only stone, then clattered down the high ridge and out into open air.

Holdric ran back up the rocks. Eahstann had gained his feet again, the wooden shaft of the ghaestling spear broken beneath him. Dumbly, he scratched at the earth for his bow. Holdric ducked under Eahstann's arm, snatched the bow from the earth, and half-walked, half-carried his friend down the draw. An eerie quiet whistle dogged their steps.

The draw led out onto the face of the ridge. The earth fell away before them into empty gloom, only a thin goat path wound down the far side. Ghaestling shrieks and the sound of crashing brush came from the rocks above.

Down they hurried, down under the shelter of a narrow ledge where the path turned round a fold of rock. There Holdric heaved

Eahstann against a large stone. Eahstann grabbed hold and pulled at the stone as he tried to stand.

From up the ridge above they heard ghaestling pushing through brush, hunting for a way down. Rocks crunched on the path behind. Holdric snatched up Eahstann's bow and arrow, he put arrow to string and stepped around the stone into the path.

Two ghaestling stood there, just paces away. Holdric brought up the bow—for a breath the thing in front froze. Holdric heaved back on the string… but Eahstann's greatbow was beyond his strength. Even in panic, he scarce pulled the string a hand's breath.

The ghaestling's eyes narrowed, an evil smile spread across its face. It charged, and the thing was on him. Holdric held the arrowpoint beneath its throat and let loose the string. The arrow clattered off the bow, still with strength enough to lodge deep in the ghaestling's neck. The ghaestling staggered back in shock, eyes wild as it scrabbled at its throat.

Holdric stepped forward in a rage and took the wildly swaying arrowshaft in hand. With a shout he yanked, and pulled hard as he levered the scrabbling ghaestling by the throat off the ledge. It tumbled into the open air below. The second was just behind.

A spear thrust at his face and Holdric staggered back. He swung wild with the bow, fighting to keep away the ghaestling's fast-licking iron. He tripped on the rough ground and landed hard. His head cracked against stone, and through watering eyes he could just see the iron point flash against the darkening sky.

In a panic he kicked at the thing's knees, and it tumbled snarling to the earth beside him. Then the ghaestling was on him, one hand grasping for Holdric's throat as the other scrabbled at its harness for a rough iron knife. Holdric bucked, desperately grabbing at the thing's hands.

The ghaestling rammed a knee into him and Holdric buckled, pain ripping through his guts. Still he held on. The knee came again, and his hands slipped from ghaestling wrists as he choked for air. The ghaestling pulled back its fist and punched Holdric hard in the face, again and again. Through tear-dimmed eyes Holdric saw it take hold again of its knife—

Just as Eahstann's hatchet ended the fight.

Blood flowed over Holdric's face as the dying ghaestling shivered on top of him. Holdric spat and groaned, heaving at the heavy weight of the body. Quiet it tumbled off the ledge and out into the dying light. Somewhere far below it struck rock, then crashed through distant trees.

Holdric coughed and rubbed at his face, trying to see through the pain. Above Eahstann fell back upon the stone, huffing for air.

Holdric looked up. He could just make out Eahstann in the gloom.

"We won?"

Eahstann nodded as he lay back against the stone, eyes closed.

"We won." His voice was a weak croak.

Holdric climbed groaning to his feet. Eahstann struggled to do the same, but staggered and fell again to his knees, coughing. Blood flecked the stone. He tried to raise himself again, but could not.

"Just…" Eahstann was breathing heavy now, taking in deep gulps of air. A dread whistling wheeze followed each breath. Holdric rose, and again got under Eahstann to take his weight.

"Come, brother. I have you."

Eahstann could make no words, but though he staggered he matched Holdric step for step. To one side was rock, to the other only empty air and the treetops far below. The way was rough and narrow, and Eahstann's strength faded with each step.

Holdric hurried, the sign they left be drowned. There was no hiding the trail of Eahstann's dragging feet, and the sheltering cloak of night drew close. Already the first summer stars broke the gloom above. Holdric felt his way down, wary of a stumble that could send them both tumbling into the dark.

"Which way?" Holdric hissed.

Eahstann's voice came weak, "Soon… switch… switchback. Then… what? Down. Cave. Down."

Eahstann's breath was heavy now, the grim whistle chasing each word. Holdric moved deeper under his arm and took his weight. Eahstann gasped, but said nothing.

From high above came the seeking cries of ghaestling.

Holdric hastened their pace, pushing deep into shadow. At last he found the break in the path, more by feel than sight. There the way just widened, and a narrow path fell sharp off to one side.

He felt the way down with his feet. As they moved Eahstann's head sagged. He breathed something Holdric couldn't hear and stumbled towards the dirt. Holdric just caught his fall and pulled him back sharp against the narrow ledge.

"Come, we're almost there…"

Another shriek sounded from the heights above.

Words poured from Eahstann in a frantic whisper, "Go back… Go…"

"*Shhhh,*" hissed Holdric. "We're going!"

Holdric hauled him around a spur of stone. In the last light he found it, a place less cave than a shallow hollow in the face of the rock. Still it was wide enough to hold them, and it would shelter them from sight. It would do.

Holdric all but carried Eahstann the last few paces in and lowered him gently to the earth, then he collapsed hard beside his friend.

Ghaestling shrieks echoed on the ridge high above, but for now the two were safe.

Holdric sought Eahstann in the dark. The sound of his whistling breath made it too easy. "I have you… I have you…"

Eahstann's side was wet. Desperate, Holdric pulled at buckle and cord, jerkin and jack, searching for the wound. Something hard and slick caught at the folds of Eahstann's tunic. Holdric found the edges of the tear and pulled.

There he felt the splintered stump of a ghaestling spear. The thin wood of the shaft splintered off, the iron of the point was buried deep in Eahstann's side, quivering with each breath.

"It's still there? You couldn't get it out?"

"Hurts." Eahstann's voice came in a weak ragged croak. Froth seeped from the wound, burbling at each breath. Eahstann spoke more, words in a soft mumble just past hearing.

Holdric's mind raced. He couldn't think. "What do you want me to do?"

Eahstann's voice came weak and bleary. "She… you…" His mind had gone. He began to shiver. "… wing… little… tell…"

"Shhh…" hissed Holdric. He took the blood-slicked shaft in his hand and gave it a gentle testing pull. Eahstann hissed, but he held in his cry.

Every story Holdric had heard from the old men passed through his head. Some men had walked leagues with an arrow in them, only to bleed dry when it was pulled free. Others tried to bear the point to safety and to the leechmen, only to fall on the march as ghaestling iron worked with each step ever deeper into their flesh. He didn't know what to do.

Holdric's mind raced, he felt again at the broken point. The wooden shaft was slick, the barbs driven deep past bone. The sinew binding point to shaft grew soft and sloppy in Eahstann's frothing blood. Soon the iron would be lost behind his ribs.

Holdric cursed. "I have to get it out brother."

Eahstann gave no answer.

Holdric gave the shaft another gentle, twisting pull. It moved just a hair, and through the wood Holdric could feel the barbs of the point scrape against the inside of Eahstann's ribs. Eahstann cursed and punched at the stone, and Holdric froze. Wet froth seeped over his hand.

Eahstann's words came pained and hollow, "It won't… it won't help…"

"We can get you to the Torr, they can heal you there. Eofoc. Remember Eofoc? His wound was no better. He lives."

"Can't," Eahstann gasped. "Too far."

His voice was weak, wheezing now.

The sinew felt slick and snotty under Holdric's fingers, the point worked in deeper as Eahstann's chest heaved. There would not be another chance. Holdric screwed up his face and caught the point in a firm grip. He gave no warning—he braced against Eahstann's chest and heaved on the wooden shaft with all his might, twisting to clear the wicked barbs from Eahstann's ribs.

It came free with a sick ripping scrape. Eahstann howled in shock and pain.

Holdric dropped the cursed thing, iron clattered on stone. He grabbed for his cloak and held it hard against Eahstann's side as he dug for a better binding. Eahstann choked back another whimpering howl, and Holdric tried to close his ears against the sound.

He worked swiftly. He forced himself not to hear the gasping pain, he lost himself in the finding of staunching herb and binding linens, in the wrapping of Eahstann's side. Still the blood seeped hot, and Holdric felt the sleeves of his tunic wet and clammy against his hands. But at last the task was done.

Eahstann was quiet. His breath was labored still, but it came less wracked with pain. A long time they lay unmoving against the stone, Eahstann's wheezing gasps the only sound in the dark stone hollow.

Together they looked out into the growing night.

After a great long silence Eahstann spoke again. His voice held an eerie calm. "You should go."

Holdric did not turn to face him. "I should."

"You're not."

"No."

They sat side by side. They watched in quiet as stars kindled in far-off night. The starfroth stretched bright across black sky.

Eahstann's words came weak from the dark:

> *Breath… to breath… my words meet wind*
> *Washed… as wounds in water…*

"Eahstann, no…"

Still Eahstann spoke, his voice weak and shallow.

> *Breath to blood, and breath again…*

Holdric sat silent watch. He looked on as the stars carried on their silent march across a cold sky. Eahstann's voice fell to a whisper, words now out of Holdric's hearing. His voice bore the meter of song, verse spilled soft into the empty night. Then his words faded, and his breath came fast and shallow. And then it came not at all.

Eahstann was gone.

Holdric sat in broken silence. He stared without seeing into the starry black. Hifosidth wheeled high, and below her Aeringif holding Ruhnliht, bright jewel of song. Holdric's spirit shrank from the sight, his heart still too raw to touch. In the great empty night there was no rage, no grief, only a numb void vast as all the dark sky.

Dim came a single thought… Eahstann could not be left to the ravens. That would not be right.

Holdric moved as one lost in sleep. He dragged Eahstann's empty body back against the stone, he found stones by feel and piled each over what remained of his friend. As he came to the waist, Holdric's hand brushed the leather strap of Houlen, calling horn of Heortlea. Holdric winced. He did not wish to bear the memory.

Still he took the worn strap of the horn and bound it over his own shoulder. He reached also for Eahstann's brooch, but as he reached for his pouch found he could not bear to bury the thing away. Numb, he pinned the blackened silver to Houlen's shroud. That seemed right.

He turned again to the rocks. One after another he fetched, one after another he placed. The words came unbidden as he worked,

The branch is broken and cannot be mended.
The leaves are flown and cannot be gathered again…

By the time the first moonlight shone into the little stone hollow, only the head and shoulders remained open to the sky. Eahstann's face looked strange in the grey light, empty and hollow. Had Holdric still his mind, he might have felt shame that it came so easy to lay the last stone in place, but Holdric's mind had flown. He lay the last stone without thought.

His hands moved without his will. He took up Eahstann's bow and quiver, the arrows nearly gone. The quiver he wore, the bow he held in his lap. Holdric ran his fingers over the wood. His knife worked without him, scraping wood from the belly in long steady strokes.

He pulled at the string—it was still too heavy. Again he scraped at the wood, again he pulled at the string. With a stab of black guilt, he remembered how once he'd coveted this thing. A simple stick, and he had held envy against his friend for it. He cursed himself.

Finding a wound, the guilt bit deep. What if Holdric had not pushed their path to these high rocks? What if they had run straight for Eomud? What if he had gone ahead alone at the ruined beacon, if he had seen the ghaestling sooner?

That last stung.

He could have gone first. He *should* have gone first. Ollda would have done it. Shame turned to anger in his belly. The anger swirled within him, aching to find some other place to lodge, any other place to burn. Kenndric should have brought more men. Eomud should have warned them. Eahstann should have…

He swallowed a curse.

Eahstann should have lived.

In a rage, Holdric felt in the dusty earth for the iron point that had claimed Eahstann's life. He took it hard in hand. The barbs bit his fingers, and he squeezed it the harder in his rage. With a cry, he hurled the blooded thing out into the black.

He sat long in silence. The moonlight grew bright, the trees below were wreathed in misted silver. It was time to go… it was long past time to go. He pulled once more at the bow. It was still stiff, but it would serve.

Ghaestling shrieked again, not far away in the night. Holdric could not bring himself to care. He looked once more to where the Torr lay in the black. He could just see the shape of the great tower, a shadow of moonlight on stone. He found his marks by the stars, he came to the edge.

And then he climbed over.

CHAPTER SIXTEEN
Shadow and Pool

He felt his way down the rock. His hands moved without his thought.

The moon was shrouded in cloud. All was quiet. All was still. He floated in dark void, alone against a great wall of stone. The shadow of the cave above was black against the stars. Eahstann could not be gone.

But Eahstann was gone.

Holdric locked his jaw, he set his head against the stone. He swallowed salt, fingers tight on unmoving rock as he choked down a rising howl. There was no time for hurt now. He held himself against the rock and fought to calm his breath.

Light swam in his wet eyes. He turned, and his mind could not at first make sense of what he saw. Far to the north flickered a cluster of small orange stars… but stars would not be so far below, and stars would not move so. He wiped his face, peering through wet eyes into the night… then the knowing came to him.

Torches! Torches of searching ghaestling! The little fires moved along the ridge, down from where the pass lay, not far to the north. He watched as they came closer and knew they would be below him before long.

His wrath rose hot. He ached to leap upon them, to cut and tear and howl as they did. He wanted it, but some part of him knew that they were too far too many. He breathed deep, he forced his mind to heel. He needed his mind.

What now? He looked to the heights above and the dark void below, he weighed the far dancing torchlight against the climb. He did not know how high he was, but already he was low enough to be seen. Climb back? He might just be able to reach… no, if they were searching below, surely they would be searching above. And he would not go back, not back there. Down it was.

He scrambled down the rock, fast as he could. Sometimes there was moonlight enough to guide him, most times he moved in darkness, hands fumbling in the black. He looked again up the valley— the torches were close enough he could count them now. A dozen at least, likely more.

He was still high above the trees. The ghaestling came faster than he had guessed. He raced down the rock, he chanced doubtful handholds, his foot kicked free a stone and it clattered down the cliff below. He could not tell if the torches came faster now. Perhaps they did.

The smell of pine grew thick, the shadow of trees heavy against the night. He was still too high. The fires were close, and nearing fast. Soon they would be on him. He felt for his next foothold and found nothing but smooth open rock.

He braced his hands on a narrow ledge at his waist, he dropped and let himself dangle from it with both hands, he reached with his toes for anything to bear his weight… still nothing, the stone was too smooth. Still the torches came.

He looked out into the dark shadow of the trees against the night. He should not be too high, he hoped he was not too high.

He leaned against the rock, he held his weight against the steep slope—and he let go.

He tried to take his weight on the stone, tried to slow his fall. It helped only little. He landed hard on a rocky mound of turf and muddy scree and tumbled back over the earth. He just managed to shelter Eahstann's bow with a turn of his shoulder, though he landed the harder for it.

Shakily he got to his feet. He looked up towards the coming torches. Were they running now? It seemed so, and he thought he heard a call. He turned and hobbled deeper into the trees. The wood swallowed up what little moonlight escaped the clouds, and soon he was in deep shadow.

He could see the ghaestling now, grim grey faces under torches of spitting pine. They held their fires high as they searched the rock above and out into the shadows. Holdric slunk further back into the trees.

Too soon they came to the place where he had fallen. One paused there, lifting its torch high against the rock as it looked up the cliff. Perhaps it spoke, Holdric could not be sure.

For a moment all was still… and then they moved on. Their fires faded into the night as they passed him by. Holdric fell back against the wet earth, the after-shadow of torchlight dancing green in his eyes. Slowly his breath came back to him.

He felt over his hurts. His leg was sound, the pain would fade. He had been lucky. Already the dancing torches were out of sight. He strung again his bow and set arrow to string, he felt the set of Brukthorn at his waist. Then he pushed deeper into the valley.

All was dark beneath the trees. He moved by feel. The earth grew soft and wet beneath his feet, the whisper of dripping water filled the night. His foot came down in a cold pool, and he cursed beneath his breath and felt his way back to the soft earth.

Far ahead, a patch of night sky showed through thick branches, a hint of moonlight kissed the leaves below. He came near and paused under the stars. The night air cool was on his face. Through branch and cloud he saw high overhead the stars of Hifosidth… it was but midwatch then, he had time. He rested there a long moment, drinking in the starlight.

The crack of deadwood shot through the dark. His heart leapt, he sank to his knees and moved deeper into shadow. It had been foolish to rest in the light. He told himself it was dark under the trees, he told himself he could not have been more than a shadow. Still he cursed his foolishness.

He moved deeper into the valley. The sound of slow-burbling streams grew thick as he felt his way through mud and stone. Then from not far up the valley came the soft crack of mouldered wood. He froze and listened for the sound of another step, but no sound came. Still he felt uneasy. All the wood seemed filled with a cold hungry grudge.

He felt his way forward, feeling for each foothold. A splash of water echoed under the trees… his sureness grew. He was not alone. His neck prickled, his thoughts raced. The ghaestling must have seen his sign at the rocks, must have circled back into the wood. Again he cursed himself.

He walked a ragged pace, he listened for their steps and tried to guess their places. Was that a step, just above? A shadow passed in a flash of moonlight, so swift he almost missed it. Still it was enough. He was sure now. He sank to his knees, arrow on the string. He brought himself low to the earth and hunted for shadows against the black sky.

Another step… they were coming closer. The string was taut under his fingers.

Shadow crossed shadow, nearer still.

Almost…

The shadow moved again—his arrow streaked fast and quiet into the night. The shaft was swallowed up by the dark, lost in a faint rustle of leaves. Already he had another on the string, already he had moved from where he had let fly.

Nothing followed. All was still.

For a moment he cursed himself, sure he had guessed wrong, sure he had cast away his arrow at a ghost of worry. Then he heard the soft *thunk* of iron on wood, the rustle of a spear in the leaves… and a whispered curse.

Panic rose in his chest, his breath came fast and he forced it down. He moved slowly back, feeling with his feet for each quiet step. He backed against the twisting trunk of a tree and something moved not far behind. He worked around the tree, ears hot and arrow ready. He held himself low, he searched black shadow against black night. Nothing… then a faint rustle in the brush. He started to turn—and was struck!

A sharp slick punch of iron caught him under his arm. The air flew from his lungs, hot pain streaked up his side. He gasped and staggered back, his arrow flew wild, wood clattered on wood in the night. He fell hard against the earth.

Pain flooded his body. Panic tore at his mind. He scrabbled back from the tree, his feet kicking at the leaves as he tried to get away.

A soft laugh followed him through the dark.

Somehow he was up again, somehow he caught up his bow and staggered down into the night. He stumbled and fell, he gained his feet and fell again. Down the hill he staggered, shaking and broken. His feet no longer minded him, they stumbled on without his will, falling into the dark as he choked on hot pain.

Brush rustled above. He froze, hunched over shaking knees. Something moved there, high up the hill. Quiet steps trod over sodden leaves.

"Hollldi…."

A soft, mocking call drifted through the night.

Holdric forced himself to the earth. His side was slick under his arm. He swallowed the howling pain and held himself flat. The steps came closer.

Ice grew over his side. Sweat was slick on his face. He forced his breath to come quiet. The step was near now, just above him in the trees.

He huddled against a rotted trunk of pine, smell of crumbling punk heavy in his nose, needles thick beneath him. He heard water far away. All else was still. He looked up for the stars, and saw nothing but night.

"Hollldi…"

The voice came again, a strange voice out of nightmare. Fear rose up in him, and with it rage. His hand went shaking to Brukthorn. He would not be put down like some hunted beast.

But nothing came near.

Pain burned against his mind. He scratched at the dirt with his fingers, he forced his legs to hold still. Blood pooled beneath him, hot and wet. He swallowed his pain and choked down the screaming hurt. He forced his mind to hold, he bound his will tight.

Above all was silent. All was still. For so long, all was still. For a mad moment, Holdric almost thought himself safe. Then he knew… the shadow waited for him to bleed dry.

He measured another half-held breath and searched the night above.

Was he bleeding dry? The thought hung bleary in his mind. His hand went trembling to his side. A broad cut pierced jack and jerkin both, wet warmth flowed slick over his fingers. The leaves were sticky with his blood. He bit down on a curse. He would not die like this.

He kept his hand tight on Brukthorn. He raised himself up on one elbow and willed the shadow to come, he willed the thing to try. But the shadow did not come. For a single breath he saw it, or thought he saw it. The hooded man stood on the hill above, black against a breath of moonlight. Waiting.

Then the moon was gone, and all was dark again.

From far up the valley came the low call of an owl. Silence followed, and in time the call came again, low and distant. Then again. A huffed curse floated in the air. Leaves rustled, then from just above came an answering call. And then for a long time no other sound came. No shadow moved in the night.

Holdric waited. Blood soaked his tunic, hot against his skin. He held his hand against his side, he leaned against his arm trying best he could to staunch the flow. His fingers grew hot and sticky. His head began to swim.

He could not stay here. If death were to come, he would meet it on his feet. He shrugged out from under the fallen tree, he rolled to hands and knees. Bloody leaves stuck to his fingers and he wiped his hand on his chest. He rose shakily to his feet, bent over with his elbows on his knees. Pain rolled over him.

He reached for his bow… his fingers slipped numb over the wood. He tried again, and then again. On the third pass he caught it in hand. He reached back to his quiver and hot pain poured down his side. Still he pulled forth an arrow. His last arrow.

He stood straight as he could manage and he pushed on. Through the night, through the dark, he stumbled further down the slope. Somewhere down there was water, and past it the Torr.

He hurt. He held his elbow tight against his side, and still he hurt. He stumbled, he cursed and gathered his feet again, and still he hurt. The sound of burbling water grew louder. Through the trees ahead he saw a streak of lighter shadow, the deep grey on black of shrouded moonlight. He stumbled downward, and soon the clouds closed again.

He knew not how long he walked. He felt the way with his bow, prodding at the ground. The pain filled all his mind now, he stumbled and cursed—then his bow struck air. He came nearer and felt with his foot… the earth fell away from a rocky ledge. There was a cold wet breeze on his cheek, the smell of water in his nose.

He knelt and reached down with his hand. Cold water flowed over his fingers, swift and silent. He felt for a few small stones at the riverbank, listened once more for following steps, then tossed a pebble out into the night. There was a quiet *plonk* as the stone fell beneath the water.

He tossed another stone, a bit further out... another burble as it met water and sank to the bottom. Another, farther yet. This time he heard the clatter of stone on rock and smiled a grim smile. A few more stones and he had sense of what lay before him. The water was not over-wide, by light of day he would not have given the crossing a thought. But now he was wounded, weighed down, and blind.

He looked up into the black night, wrestling with his fear. He scolded himself a coward. He rolled his cloak and bagged his bow, binding both tight against his quiver. He felt for Brukthorn and knotted the blade tight to his waist, he hooked tight his pack upon his shoulder.

He took a last breath, then heaved himself into the rushing current. The sudden cold tore the air from his lungs in great gasping grunts. He kicked hard for the far side, and in only a few strokes he'd made it across. For a single breath he felt the smooth rock of the far bank—then the rock passed beneath his fingers and the heaving water bore him hard away.

He kicked for the bank, he scrambled for anything he could grasp. His fingers brushed against a branch hanging in the water and he held fast. The branch swayed under his grip, then bowed sharply as the current pulled him away. Something cracked and gave way. Holdric kicked again, he grabbed hold with both hands. A great snag broke loose and came tumbling into the water after him.

He tried to kick away, but too late. The broken tree rolled over in the current, then bore him down beneath the water. His feet hit bottom, his boots scraped over loose stone. Panic seized him as he pushed against the rocky riverbed. He came up in a rushing tangle of wet branches and rushing water. He jerked away, but was caught tight in the snarl. The great bulk of the tree rolled again in the water as he pulled, and rushing water filled his ears.

With a heaving lurch they went together over a drop in the river. Holdric's leg hit hard on stone, and he grunted in pain. With a wet wrenching heave he came out again into the air. He jerked and pulled away from the rolling tangle, but the more he fought, the more it tumbled. Again the great thing bore him down, his caught straps would not let him go. He scrabbled for Brukthorn's hilt, but his bindings held fast.

He ripped his little belt knife free and cursing he cut at the tangle of straps. The snag rolled again, but this time he kicked free. As the river carried all from his reach, he just caught hold of his bow. Kicking he pulled it from the snarl, and with it his quiver and bound cloak. All the rest he lost to the river.

He swam hard against the current and heaved himself up onto a steep mud bank, then collapsed on the muddy grass. He coughed out water and closed his eyes.

For a sweet moment he knew rest. Then the pain flowed over him in a wave. He rolled choking with hurt to his knees, then sat back upon the bank. His woolens hung heavy on his shoulders. His side was eerily chill. Dully he opened jack and jerkin.

His gorge rose as his fingers explored the wound. Jack and leather had stopped the worst, but still the ghaestling spear had torn open a handsbreadth gash across his ribs, a wound that grew deeper as it went. Slick bone passed beneath his finger, then he came to where the point just cleaved beneath a rib. Fate or fortune had kept the iron from piercing deeper. Still the feel of his open flesh left him feeling a half-skinned beast at harvest time.

He cursed and forced the thought from his head. He would need to stitch the wound closed, at least so much it would not gape open as he dragged himself through the wild… and the wound would never be cleaner than it was at this moment. He looked about into the night. All was still. He had time.

He unbound his cloak from his quiver and spread it open on the mud. On the sodden wool he laid what was left to him in blind-order. He pulled off jack and jerkin, then belt, tunic, and linen shirt. He felt in the dark for his belt and pouch, and from that took his mending-bag and small wooden salve box. If Maethbry's wound-stuff served for a scrape, it should serve well enough for this. So he hoped, at least.

He dipped his finger in the sweet-smelling grease and felt about the rent in his flesh, grinding his teeth as his fingers met again slick living bone. He hurried to finish and wiped his skin clean. He took next a small needle of polished iron, wrapped round with deer sinew and slick with wool-grease. He unwound the needle and drew out the sinew behind it.

He touched the needle to his flesh, near the middle part of his hurt. He made to pierce the skin… and faltered. His hand would not move. He almost laughed. He was a ranger now. He'd crossed the Mearcwater, he'd killed ghaestling. He could bear something so piddling as a needle in his skin. Wymud would be laughing. Still his hand would not budge.

He screwed his eyes shut and forced himself to push the needle through. The bite was cold and sharp, but no worse than an angry bee. Still he cursed against the pain. Another sharp stab, and he pulled the needle out the far side, taking by feel a large bite of skin. He grimaced at the slick slide of sinew through his flesh, but soon he finished. He drew the stitch tight and knotted it off. Before he could lose his nerve he did it again, and again. His eyes were wet and stinging.

He paused in his work, he wiped his brow and looked out into the empty night… and again he cursed. Through a pinched, wet gaze he saw again the far dancing lights of ghaestling torches. They were far up the valley still, but slowly they came his way. He hurried to gather his things.

The stitches in his side strained as he started to rise. He had not yet done enough, and he knew his flesh would pull open again the first time he worked his arm. He gritted his teeth and made another stitch. He watched the far lights as he worked, watched as they came nearer. He tied off the stitch and made another, he fumbled as the sinew grew short and slick. Still he made two more knots through his skin, and… done. Or done enough.

More fires flickered through the far trees. They made a great beating line, driving slowly towards him. He smeared the last of his salve over his work. All his binding linens were gone, he bound his wound fast with his midgescarf. That would have to do.

He shrugged into his clothes with a grimace of pain, then buck-led on jack and jerkin and belted blades. He shrugged on the empty quiver and took up his bow and his last arrow, then rose on shaking legs and made again into the night. He turned downriver, trudging up away from the water.

The ground was rough, the way thick with tangling brush. Behind the valley was full of scattered torchlight. He looked up, trying to make out the sky through the stretching branches. The moon was risen high in the sky, a smear of dim light behind thick cloud. He tried to think… the moon had risen not long after dusk. It was well past midnight then, far into deepwatch. He was losing time.

He pushed farther on. Clinging brush gave way to mud and sucking water, countless black pools under thick black trees. Midge clouds gathered about him as he moved, whining as they nipped at his flesh.

He splashed again into water. He cursed and tracked back his steps, seeking earth by feel. He could just see the ghaestling faces now behind, scarred and hungry in the spitting torchlight. His legs tangled in broken deadfall and he stumbled to the earth in a clatter of breaking wood.

He froze.

Not far ahead he heard a stumble, then the splash of a foot in water. For a breath, all was quiet. A coarse whisper passed in the night, and then another. From far ahead came the glow of an ember blown to life, then the bright light of a catching torch.

The ghaestling raised its torch high as it peered back towards where Holdric lay. He sank against a broad tree and cursed himself. He should have guessed they would have walkers beyond their torch line, he had seen it already. Another light sparked to one side, then another. Their lights shone crazily on countless black pools under the trees. They called to each other in low harsh whispers as they stalked over the broken muddy ground.

A call floated past from the torch line behind. The shadows of walking ghaestling passed before the torchlight. Some of the torchbearers broke off and made their way towards him. Pitch spit and popped from their high torches, bright flecks of fire fell hissing into wet mud as they drew near. He flattened himself against the seeping earth, clinging close to his sheltering tree. It would not hide him for long.

In the torchlight he just saw the black face of another pool, not far from where he lay. He crept to it on his belly, the stink of swamp heavy on the earth. He gave one look back—then pushed into the water. The cold struck him as a blow. Bottom-filth clouded up about him. His feet sank into deep silt, then his legs. He felt no bottom as he fell back into the water.

Torchlight danced crazily over the face of the pool, they were almost upon him! He let out the last of his air and let himself fall back into the depths. His head filled with stinking water, twisting fronds twined around his wrists. Through burning eyes he saw dancing light above.

His lungs were bursting, his head full of polluted fire. Water roared in his ears as a prodding spear splashed about the pool. He clung to the mud, fighting to stay down and away from the licking iron. His last breath burned in his lungs… and then the spears were gone.

The bright flame passed from his sight and all was still. Lungs screaming, he waited until he could wait no more. He clawed at tendrilled roots hanging in the black, he pulled his face above the water for a desperate breath of stinking air. He held himself there, low under the dead root of a long-drowned elm.

Dim through slitted eyes he watched the floating torchlight. His eyes teared and stung from the black water. He could see no more than a blur of fire, scarce paces away. Beneath the water he felt for his blade and held himself still.

The midge cloud found his face again, stinging and whining about his ears. He did not move. Something in the mouldered wood stung at his neck, he made no sound. The torchlight wavered in his blurred sight… and then as soon as it had come, the fire was gone. Soft steps faded into the night, and fire hissed on water. All was still again.

Holdric was alone in the cold dark. He strained to hear ghaestling steps but heard none. He looked up into the night and saw only black. He waited longer still, listening for sounds that did not come. At last he could wait no longer. The Torr was far, and the night was wearing old.

He pulled himself from the water. His side burned with pain. Not far away, torches moved through the night, passing west up out of the valley. But between himself and the far Torr all was dark. Weary he rose to his elbows and began to crawl. All his body hurt.

He crept low over the sodden ground, around pools and over stone. Mist rose up under the trees, and in time he left the torches behind. The trees grew thin, and still he kept to the cold mud. Before him the fens stretched out under shrouded moonlight, dark earth and silver pools. He could not see the stars, but the moon was near now to its very height. Greywatch loomed.

The mist grew thick, and at last he climbed to his feet and began again to walk. The mud was cold beneath his boots. The ground was sopping wet. A chill ache took his feet, then blessed numbness. The midge clouds were ever thick and biting. He cursed his scarf, bound tight now against his hurt. He pulled up his hood and tried not to hear the biting whine.

On he pushed, alone in the mist. He looked into the far darkness, looked to where the Torr must be. He felt for Eahstann's horn at his side… no. Not yet. The torches were still too close behind, there was nothing but night ahead. He was still too far from the Torr. They would not yet hear him.

He quickened his step, he pushed deeper into the fen. His foot sank deep in wet and sucking mud. He pulled his leg free with an angry growl and barely kept his boot. He cursed and pushed farther on. It was already late. Too late.

He stumbled and picked himself up from the mud. He tried to run, and his feet sank again into seeping earth. He snarled and rose again. He sought firm ground where he could, but there was none to find, only grass and water and mud.

Through the mist, through the biting clouds, through the clinging earth, he pushed. He lifted his eyes from the mud and saw a bright star low in the sky before him. He paused… the star was in the wrong place. It was too low, too bright. Then the light grew brighter, and slowly his mind grasped the truth.

He looked on a beacon—the beacon of the Torr! An unbelieving smile began to grow on his face. They knew! Somehow someone had brought them word! Someone else had lived! Had it been Kenndric and Wymud? Aschbroc and Hwaetearn? All of them?

Half laughing, half crying, he stumbled forward through the mud. He gave no thought for the tale he would tell, be it the tale of a hero or a coward. He pushed forward only to see them again. The fire grew brighter as he walked… and then it grew brighter yet.

His step slowed. The fire was too big, too bright for a beacon. He stopped. The chill sank heavy as knowing came, but still he would not believe.

He walked, and his walk turned to a run. He stumbled in the sucking mud, he rose and fell again. He cursed the muck, and still he ran. The fire grew brighter, he knew not how long he struggled in the mud. As he came nearer, he heard a horn, just at the edge of hearing—a ghaestling horn.

He came nearer yet and heard the distant shouts of men. Still he pushed on. He no longer knew what word to bring, all he knew was that he must reach them. The fire cut bright through the mist, he could hear them clearly now. He heard the shouts of battle, the cries of the dying, the mocking shrieks of ghaestling.

Holdric's steps began to slow... then they stopped. He stood in stunned quiet as the last cries died away. Slowly the light of the Torr fell to night, and he was at last alone in silent dark and drizzling rain.

It was over. Ealdwyrc Torr had fallen. He had failed.

CHAPTER SEVENTEEN
Morning's Light

He trudged on under the moonlight. The mud was cold on his feet, the mist clung wet to his hair. His path did not change… he knew not where else to go. He did not watch the sky as he walked. His eyes did not leave the mud. In time his feet did not sink so far, and only then did he look up. Far before him was a line of trees, thick and black, and above them was the shadow of the Torr.

He took a deep breath and made for the trees. From the far branches ahead, the song of merry wrens greeted the coming morning. Behind the night chatter of the fens fell away. Greylight was on him now, and the stars above faded as he walked.

Holdric dragged himself from the mud and up into the cover of a broken willow. He looked up the last broken rise to the rocky slope. The moon was high now, the silver light faded and empty. Here they had all picked their way down in the morning gloom only five nights before. Only five nights, but so much had changed.

He looked to the Torr, stark against the fading stars. It was scorched and black. Smoke drifted lazily off the stones. He looked for his little perch, the sky-watching place shown him by the young shieldling boy… what was his name? Wydthoc? Holdric could not find the place.

Beneath the paling-wall the fire still smoldered. Most of the timbers still stood, now charred and black against the sky. Here and there the wall had failed, broken as an old man's teeth. All was washed in smoke and steam.

In the moonlight he could just see broken shapes on the rocks below. Nothing there stirred.

He came near. The hillside was littered with the wreck of war. The air was thick, a glutted sickness hung heavy over the stones. Movement flashed—the shadow of a gloating raven winging its way up into the gloom. Something dropped from its beak. Holdric's stomach turned.

Soon he came to the first of the dead, this one a ghaestling. It had been arrow-struck and tumbled almost to the bottom of the slope. He remembered being dazed when first he looked on fallen ghaestling. He'd felt sick to see it, but still he had wondered at the thing. Now he felt nothing. The scars along the thing's arms and face were in a pattern he had not seen, different sigils were hacked into the bone harness it wore. Holdric could not care. Not far away lay a blackened spear, the iron point long and barbed. Holdric looked away, up to the last of the fading stars.

He came next to a group of fallen men. They had been a dozen, more or less. It did not take a ranger's eye to read their fate. The men had rallied at the walls and made a last desperate push out from the killing ground above. Each man lay where he had fallen. One was face down, clothes shredded from his back and soaked black in the greylight. Further down lay another, one lacking shield and weapon both. He must have dropped all when the panic took him. None had made it far.

Above was where they had fled the Torr, out through a break in the palings of the wall. The break had been narrow, but it had been enough. Timbers there were burned and hacked, the earth and stone clawed away.

Holdric came to the wall and squeezed through, then climbed over broken timbers and fallen men and looked over the grounds within. The air inside was still, the earth covered with the dead. The Torr men had sold themselves dearly. Many more ghaestling than men littered the ground, but that had not been enough. Not a soul of the Torr remained.

Holdric walked among them, boots sopping in the gore-stained mud. The air stank of blood and bile and sour woodsmoke. He looked down to one of the fallen… the man had been roused from sleep. He had dressed in haste, his hair was wild, his coat of mail thrown on over only his shirt. But for his linen, he was bare from the waist down. Holdric knew his face.

He remembered this man from the hall, from when the songboard had passed, and Eahstann had… Holdric pushed the memory away and moved on. There were others he knew also. There was the large one who had pushed past him at meat, there the bent horse groom from a table over. Something stirred inside Holdric as he walked among these men.

There was something different here, something not like the fallen rangers in the dark valley he had left behind. It seemed strange to him at first, but then the knowing came. Eomud's waylaid messenger under the yew, poor blinded Aemud of Earnsclyff… though rangers like himself, he had only ever known them as dead men, or men near enough to dead. A distance had lain already upon them.

But here, these fallen he had known as living men, however short had been the meeting. Holdric had broken bread with them. He remembered the sound of their voices, the roar of their songs. And now they were silent. Numb he roamed the tower yard, dazed and mute.

He looked for Aschbroc's friends among the Torr men, and soon he found them. The two had fallen near the stables halfway to their horses. Holdric glanced to the stalls, hoping without hope, but nothing lived. He looked also for the great hound Wyrling, but found him not. He hoped the creature's end had been swift.

The ground was covered in sign. Holdric feared to look too closely, he did not wish to know more. But he could not help but see, and the story of each man's end pushed its way into his mind.

He came to the Torr itself and found all a wreck. The timbers of the upper floors had burned, falling one onto another until the cellar was filled with ash and broken timber. The air reeked of woodsmoke, of scorched wool and burned meat.

Not far from the tumbled stone lay the old cook… Caltbruk, Aschbroc had called him. Holdric sat beside what was left of the old man. He took up the butcher's blade that lay by the old cook's hand. The edge was deeply nicked, the grip stained. Holdric turned it over in his hands as he thought.

Could he have changed this had he not failed them? Would it have been different had he reached them in time? Perhaps. He could not know, but they might have had a chance. He ran his thumb along the edge of the knife… it was dull. A grim smile crossed Holdric's face. Wymud would be cursing.

He looked up. In the far southern sky he saw the light of Greatwatch, its beacon still burning bright against the grey. The Greatwatch men had seen the fires here at the Torr, and they had passed warning to the folksteads beyond. That much had been done.

He let his eyes rest on the far dancing light. At first he found it lovely, a glowing comfort in the grim morning. Then the dread closed upon him. By that beacon, riders were already racing for the Eorl. The Eorl would gather the fyrd. Soon most every fighting man of the folksteads would be massed, and the Eorl would lead them here. All the fyrd he could muster he would march straight through the wood. Somewhere this side of the Mearcwater, fyrd-men would meet ghaestling.

Perhaps they would win. Perhaps they would not. But while they fought here, the ghaestling of the far valley, the ghaestling he had left behind—they would cross to the folksteads.

Holdric cursed.

What could he do? Chase after this ghaestling host, work around them somehow, find the Eorl? No, they had half a night on him already, and they moved with speed. Trying to find the fyrd in all the wood of the Mearcholt would take time, there was no way he could reach them before they fought.

Rally with the fyrd after the fight then? Meet with whoever was left, tell them? He looked over the dead men of the Torr. Tell them what?

His gaze fell to the bloody dirt.

He thought of meeting the fyrd, of how he would shout for the Eorl… and of what they would say in answer to he Holdric, Holthund's son. He knew already what the fyrdmen would think were he to come upon them alone. Holdric son of the coward, come alone from the great wood claiming all his brothers lost and a great unseen army at his back. He'd be lucky not to be hanged a coward on the spot.

And would they even be wrong?

He hurled the knife into the dirt with a curse and buried his head in his hands. Tears threatened and he swallowed them in a rage. He looked up and let his eyes swim in that far sky where the beacon of Greatwatch still burned.

He lost himself in that far light. The fire sparkled bright and gold in the morning gloom, shining as some small part of the sun come to earth… something kindled in his mind. From the Torr he could see the mountain of Greatwatch, and from that far mountain he once had seen…

He scrambled to his feet. He climbed onto the hot low stones of the Torr and looked back the way he had come—not enough, the broken palings blocked too much of his sight. He needed a better sighting to be sure.

He reached to climb further up the wreck of the Torr, but the stones were still too hot to touch. He wrapped his hands in the wool of his cloak and tried again. He climbed higher, the wool hot under his hands. The northerly stones were cooler from the valley winds, and he circled the Torr as he climbed.

Soon he hung in the open air over the broad valley below. There he saw the swamp he had crossed in the night, and the wooded valley upriver, and the far ridge beyond. Past that ridge, past rolling hills and the valleys beyond, far to the east and south, there lay Heahfeldt. And there the ghaestling army would pass. There, or near enough.

Yes.

He could raise Heahfeldt's beacon again, make it shine for Old Aesculf and the Greatwatch men. Let the Eorl know another foe marched, let the folksteads know to be ready—or at least give them time to flee.

It could work. It *would* work… if he could get there. He looked again over the earth below. It was a long way, a very long way. He'd been all the night crossing only the drowned valley below, and Heahfeldt lay at the very edge of his sight, far off where land met sky. He would never make it, not in a single day.

Unless…

He worked his way back around the Torr, back until he had clear sight of the Whitefork. The little river passed east below the tower, the water a dull mist-shrouded silver in the early morning gloom. From here he could trace as it ran east… east and south.

East and south.

Eomud had said there was a way by water from Heahfeldt to the Whitefork, he had said they had floated the wounded down a brook to the river… Holdric shook his hands cool and climbed higher still. He still could not see all the course of the river, but as his eyes moved over the land below, he became more sure. Yes, the Whitefork must come near to Heahfeldt. By water he could reach the place tonight.

Shoot the board.

So Aschbroc had said. It would work!

Eager now, Holdric looked over the ground, fixing his course to memory. Past the ford below the Whitefork narrowed, then flowed swift towards the warming eastern sky. Somewhere past the ford it would be joined by the Greenflood as that great water poured down off the fens. Holdric could not see the meeting, but he saw the swollen Whitefork beyond. Past that he could see the river only in places, the rolling hills of the great wood hiding most from his sight.

Far off he could see a high sighting-place, a great bare bald of stone that rose over the southern bank. There he could take his next sighting. There he would find the rest of his way.

Holdric smiled at old memory. The shape of the bald put him in mind of their old hound Hunling, a great lump as she dozed by the morning fire. It was a well-fated sighting-place. "Hunling's Hearth" he would call it.

He looked again over the river below, weighing the distance… yes, he could be at that high sighting-place by midday. Hunling's Hearth then by noon, and Heahfeldt by nightfall.

Settled, he looked again over course, binding each roll of land into verse.

From ford I fall, fain I seek my sister.
Sister stream seeks south, south seeks east again…

At each bend of the waters, Holdric named the place in verse, knotting each turn to his mind, until…

… High Hunling's Hearth holds home.

The words were doggerel, that he knew. He was no bard. But each line would hold fast the way-knot in his mind, and that would be enough. He closed his eyes and went over his verse again. At each line, he bound the words to the roll of land and flow of water.

From ford I fall…
Sister stream seeks south…

Yes, he had it. He knew his way. He worked back down the hot stone, taking the journey over and over again in his mind.

From ford I fall…

He thought on the fisherman he had seen at the ford. The old man had rested near a boat of timber. Yes, and nearby had been a currock, too. Holdric had a way down the water.

As he reached again the tower yard, he looked to his next task. He would not be in a place of men again for long days. A day to Heahfeldt by river, then… five days back to Heortlea? Four?

He paused, thinking over his Ollda's tales. The Whitefork did in time meet the Mearcwater, but that was well past any country he knew. Call it five days at least, possibly a week. Did he have all he would need?

He had still Brukthorn, he had Eahstann's bow and quiver—all but empty now. He had lost his pack and all his comforts, but for a time at least he could do without them. And his cloak would serve well enough, though he'd not begrudge a blanket if he could find one.

But all of his food was lost. He would need more, and once he was free again of ghaestling eyes, something to cook it in. Would that be enough? He paused to think… he'd lived on less, it would do. He worked his way down the outcrop, shaking the heat from his hands, holding his verse in mind as he climbed.

From ford I fall…

There was nothing to be gained in the Torr itself, its treasure-house of stores buried now under smoldering timber. He turned to the ruined tower yard. He roamed among the dead, looking for what he would need. Much war gear had been taken by the ghaestling, but much still remained. The creatures had not tarried long.

Some arrows he found, though fletched in the bright white feathers of the Torr-guard rather than the dark grey of Heortlea. That worried him. But the arrows were heavy, and their points were keen. They would serve. He pulled the weather-wool of his quiver over the bright fletching and called himself content.

From ford I fall…

He found also a man who had once carried a warknife near the size of Brukthorn. The blade was gone, but the sheath the dead man wore still. A bit of cutting and it fit Brukthorn well enough. Holdric bound it well with pelt and cord, then fixed it to his knifebelt. His blade wore easy now. Good.

Food then.

He came to a fallen fyrdman, of Stanbruk by the look of his cloak. The man looked old, surely on his last fyrding season. His passing had at least been swift. Holdric swallowed his unease, then heaved at the man's wet weight and felt for the bread bag fyrdmen carried on the march. He found it, but it was too far gone to use.

Holdric tried the next man, and the next. He scavenged the burned-out remains of the blacksmith's shed, he searched the wrecked stables. He started to enter the goat hovel and quickly left again with rising gorge.

The tower yard seemed far smaller now, fouled as it was with wreck of man and beast. When all was counted, Holdric had found a fyrdsman's small marching-bag and filled it with just short of a dozen cakes of hard waybread. He added to that the stub of a small tallow candle, an earthen cup, and two handfuls of horses' oatcorn that had not been trodden into the mud. Best of all he scrounged a few bits of hard sausage and broken cheese, and some of Caltbruk's goosefat still in its little box. He found also another waterskin, if old and slightly sour.

It was a small enough hoard, but would hold him for the better part of a week. More if he held himself tight. He tucked the marching-bag of food over his belt fyrd-fashion and stood. He took up his bow and placed his last dark arrow upon it… then paused. He had been careless.

He had missed before, shooting blind in the dark wood. He would need to do better. He drew forth one of the Torr arrows and looked upon the two together. Both were war arrows, heavy and thick-shafted. He'd loosed heavy war arrows from his stripling bow for years and was long used to their wild flight. But he did not know *this* bow yet.

He found a low earth bank and loosed a few arrows into the dirt. The Torr arrows flew wider than his darker one, though neither favored what he'd done to Eahstann's greatbow. Still he learned their flight, though his wound howled at the work. He cursed as he worked his arm again. Well enough. He was ready.

No, he was almost ready. He looked again over the unburied dead. The duty undone pained him. *"… when we may,"* Aschbroc had said. How many of Holdric's kin had lain like this over the years, food for raven and wolf? Holdric spoke the death words, but he took no time for song, no time to raise up pyres. He had duty still, and the morning was already growing bright.

He made for the earthen bank of the tower yard. The paling-wall was scorched and black, the broken bodies of spearmen lay in a heap where ghaestling had come over the wall. Holdric came near and peered out through a break in the smouldering timbers. There he could see over the dike mound, down the Torr-road and beyond that to the ford.

Nothing moved below, nothing but a single hopping sparrow. The little bird turned to look up to the rising smoke of the Torr. It chirped once and flew away. Holdric's face was grim. Even from where he stood, he could see the earth of the road torn by the passing of many feet. And where the road met the water, what was left of the sheds stood in shambles. Worry gnawed at him.

If the little boat he'd seen was still whole, he'd be soon on his way. If not… the river still flowed. He would find something.

From ford I fall…

He squeezed through the hot timbers and out onto the dike, then carefully made his way down the earthen wall. As he moved over the road he better saw the sign of the ghaestling host. Even the cart-ruts were gone, worn smooth by the passing of many feet. How many he could not guess. Hundreds, easily. Shreds of cloth and leather and worse littered the way. Soon he neared the ford, and the broad muddy clearing before it. All beyond was open ground.

He stayed low and eyed the far bank for watchers over the water… nothing. On the near side the sheds and little cot had been torn open, the little gardens trampled. The fisherman's heavy boat was still where it had lain, broken up by the blows of countless axes. Holdric groaned, but he had expected no less.

He came out into the open and looked on what was left. The ground before the ford was covered in the marks of many feet. Hordes of ghaestling had milled here, pushing for their turn to cross the water. Now all was still.

Holdric made for the fisherman's cot. He drew Brukthorn and paused at the broken door… nothing sounded within. He ducked quick inside.

He thought he had been ready for what he would see. He held his sleeve to his mouth to hold his gorge. What was left of the old fisherman lay tangled in his shredded bedding. The old man had been caught in sleep, likely he was the first the ghaestling had found. He had had little warning and less chance. Still he had given a good reckoning for his long years, caught in the night and one against many. But the man had died a hard death, an ugly death. Holdric could not long bear to look upon what remained. The hero deserved a cairn, but there was no time to raise one. Holdric ducked back out of the cot.

The timber-built boat had been wrecked, but the currock he had yet to find. His worry grew. He had little time for withy-work, less still for searching the stables above for a hide left whole enough to use. For once luck was with him. The little currock was here, thrown not far behind the cot. It looked to have been tossed about in the frenzy of the passing horde, then left forgotten as they charged across the water.

He pulled it from the mud and looked it over. It was still in fair shape, only a single rent had been torn through the hide. More, only a few still-supple withies of the willow frame had been cracked. Good enough.

He carried the thing into the cot and cast about what was left of the fisherman's things to make it whole again. An awl of iron, needles of bone, coarse-spun cord of nettle and a small fire-blackened pot of tar… the old man's tools were crude, poor against even those of Heortlea. Still they would serve.

Holdric looked over the broken little boat. He'd never sat one before in his life, but wood was wood and hide was hide, and Uncle Eikhram had not let him reach manhood without the use of his hands. He could make the thing whole again. He thanked his uncle for that much, and he set to work.

The ashes of the old fisherman's fire were still warm. Holdric stirred a little flame to life and sat the tar pot in the coals. With cord and awl and needle he stitched up the rent in the boat's side and tried not to think of his own hide as needle pierced skin and knot followed knot. Still his work was swift and his knots were clean, and he was sure all would hold.

From ford I fall…

He then took more of the cord and bound over the cracks in the willow-withies as best he could. He knew the patching would not hold long, but a day was all he would need. He looked to the old man's bed and to his shredded sheets.

"I'm sorry, Elder."

He reached over the old man and tore free a stained scrap of cloth from the sheet. This he patched over the stitched rent in the hide. He worked hot tar under and over the patch until all the skin looked smooth, then he moved the tar pot to the edge of the little fire to cool. He had one last task.

Near the cot Holdric had spied a wild patch of oxfoot. The closer leaves were trampled near to shreds, but further from the bank much of the green was untouched. Holdric was no leechman, but even he knew this leaf. He gathered up what he could quickly carry and went again into the cot.

He loosened his wound bindings and gingerly pulled them away from his hurt. Next he chewed up a great handful of the leaf. Some he swallowed against fever, the rest he worked into his wound. Over this he spread the tar, then knotted the binding of his midgescarf tight again.

He filled his empty little wooden salve box as full with tar as he could manage. Even Maethbry used tar at times on little hurts, so he guessed it would work well enough. That and the oxfoot would—he hoped—see him home.

He was done.

Holdric ran his hand over the currock. The patch was good, what had not fully set should cure well enough in the cold of the water. He held the thing in both hands and smiled an uneasy smile.

"I name you *Hobblefish*," he said. "Please bear me well."

He looked to the flowing Whitefork. The water ran clean and bright in the growing light of morning. Lingering doubt crept into his heart. He had not the sheltering mist in which they'd crossed the Mearcwater, and Ollda had long warned of taking to the waters by day. The rivers were too open, the passing too easily seen from shore and from high places over the water.

For a moment he wondered if he should wait for dark—then he cursed his fear. It was still early morning. Waiting until night would give the ghaestling the whole of a day on him, and the fyrd needed that day. More, he did not know the Whitefork, not truly. Finding his way would be hard enough under the sun, and he did not want to pass his tall sighting stone in the night. He had taken all the care he could. For the rest he must trust the rest to fate.

He found the fisherman's short oar. The carved sigils of fish and bear upon its haft were long worn, but the wood was sturdy. He lay the oar nearby. Then he unstrung his bow, cased it, and bound both quiver and bow to the currock to free his hands.

He looked once more to the river, then to Hobblefish in his hands and again to the swift waters. He had not done enough. He drew out the last bit of cord and bound the haft of Brukthorn to his body, then his other gear besides. At the little dock he found a short length of rope, and with it bound Hobblefish to his ankle lest he spill off the little craft and lose all. He had let the waters part him from too much already.

He gathered currock in one hand, oar in the other, and made for the water's edge. Then before he could lose his spirit he waded out into the water, set Hobblefish in the current, and tried to step within. The little flat-bottomed craft bobbled out from under him, spurning him time and again as he worked to keep it planted long enough to mount the narrow seat.

Finally with an irked growl he jammed his oar into the river bottom, heaved himself up upon it, and with both his feet guided the shifting thing beneath his rear. Warily he let the currock take his weight, heeling the flat little boat as he sought his balance. Twice he almost toppled, and twice he saved himself on the oar. He grinned now to think of Wymud's scolds.

At last he found his seat, and he lifted the little oar from the river bottom.

He was on his way.

CHAPTER EIGHTEEN

A Once Remembered Way

Holdric eased his way to the middle course of the river, balancing warily on his seat as he worked through the current. The Torr was almost lost to his sight now, the black and ruined stone showing in glimpses above the high trees.

Twice was my riving, and twice my rising…

A grim shadow passed over his face. *Thrice my riving*, now. Sight of the ruin came more scarce as the water bore him on, and then not at all. To either side a deep wall of forest rose above the riverbank. In places he saw the beaten dirt of the Old Trace to his left, all but swallowed by the deep spilling green beyond.

It seemed for a moment something moved there, a streak of brown and grey in deep shadow. Then it was lost. Holdric bent in his seat, he tried to find it again, but the water bore him on. Soon all was only shadow and green and the ever-rarer sight of beaten earth.

Seeing the broken road brought the little shieldling of the Torr to his mind, and the look on the boy's face when he talked of ghaestling on the water. Holdric pushed those thoughts away. Guilt and grief must wait to haunt him later. Too much now remained to do.

The water rose up again beneath his little craft. He took the swell in his hips and shifted fast, stabbing his oar into the current. Quick he righted himself in a spray of water and let out a breath. He was learning the way of the river. That felt well, at least. He eased back in his seat and let the water bear him on.

From ford I fall…

The morning sun soaked into his bones, the water spray on his face chill and sweet. He breathed deep and took in the smell of the river. Sunlight flashed bright on the water and he raised his hand to shield his eyes.

The sun rose with the morning and burned the thick wet away, and a cool breeze played at his hair. It would be a striking fall day, strangely bright after all the grinding horror of the night and day before. He pushed the night from his memory, but still it wore at him.

He could not help but swallow a yawn. Sleep gnawed at his bones. He shook his head and fished in the soldier's marching-bag for a round of waybread, then broke off a chunk and let it soften in his mouth. High above a hawk followed the river, ducking in the morning breeze. Holdric closed his eyes for but a moment, listening to the water and feeling the sun on his face. Without meaning it, he dozed.

Then came a sick heave as the water lurched beneath him, almost tumbling him from the bobbling little craft. He righted himself in a panic and scrambled with his oar, heaving the boat over another pillow of water. Light glimmered on the river ahead, and the heavy crash of roaring water reached his ears. There was another lurch as water billowed up beneath him, and he bit back a curse as he pad-dled frantic for land.

The water surged ahead, pushing him fast to a roaring crest of froth and foam against blue sky. His breath came tight—he would not reach the riverbank in time. He gripped the edges of the currock as the river bore him over hidden rocks and out into empty air.

For an eyeblink he seemed to hang in open sky… then his back and teeth crunched as the little boat smacked hard onto a broad table of spilling water. Hobblefish spun wild about, the crashing roar came louder and the river heaved beneath. Holdric struggled to right himself… through the trees he could see a piling mass of water as a second river struggled into the bed of the first. He had met again the Greenflood.

Sister stream seeks south…

The currock spun about in the current, bobbing through the spray. He scrambled to oar himself over another lurching mountain of water. Dark shadows of stone stood in the path of the crashing foam. He paddled hard against the river, but there was no fighting it. He was going to hit.

With a sick crunch he slammed hard against the rock. The blow punched the air from his lungs, water boiled over his face, the river filled his nose. The currock lurched up and bore over him as the river piled hard against the bottom.

He struggled against the stone. He ached to cry out, but all his breath was gone. He arched his back against the rock and felt the currock ripped from his hands. He kicked hard at the open water, struggling against the rock—and then he was lost in the roiling dark.

There was a flash of sky and roar of water, then all again was dark. His ankle seared with pain, pulled by the rope he had knotted to the currock. Desperate he clawed for his leg, scrabbling to reach the knot… the rope jerked again, pulling him along beneath the river.

He thrashed, he struggled to find his way to the sky, but he knew not which way the sky was. Another jerk and he struck the bottom.

Water ground him over the grit and stones. Something hard struck his legs, and he barely managed to keep from choking in water from the shock of it. He pushed hard against the rock, fighting, pushing, struggling to reach air. For a moment his face was back in foam and roaring froth, then he was under again.

He reached out in a panic, scrabbling for the sky… then as fast as he'd been pulled under he was clear, out of the roiling kettle and once more in the calm flow of the river. The water stretched broad now, swift and calm, the roar behind him.

Somewhere under the water ahead the wreck of his currock still pulled him along. At first all he could do was gasp for breath, pushing against the water just to keep his head in the air.

When he had his strength again, he took a deep breath and pulled up his ankle to work at the knotted rope that bound him to the currock…the knot was swollen tight. The knife it was, then. He pulled free his little belt knife and cut himself loose. Rope in one hand, blade in the other, he kicked for land.

Finally he reached the muddy bank. He crawled on hands and knees to rest under an overhanging bramble, then pulled the wreck of the currock up after. He lay back against the earth and stared panting into the sky.

He laughed. Stupidly, madly he laughed. Eahstann would be cursing him now, and somehow that made it all the funnier. With a mad grin and a laughing curse he stared into the high blue sky until sense came again. Then he smiled, wiped his face, and sat up. He bent to the knot still on his leg. Again he cursed his dull wits, this time without the smile. He should have guessed the danger.

He cut the last piece of rope loose from his boot and tossed it into the currock, then rubbed at his ankle. He rested his head on his knees but a moment more and set to work. The sun was high in the sky—he had time, but still a very long way to go.

He pulled Hobblefish close. His quiver and bow were still bound in place. Careful he loosened them from the little boat and looked them over. The bow had a few new dents from river stone, but it was still sound. The quiver also was in fine shape, though the arrows were soaked through and the fletchings gummy at their bindings. He cursed under his breath and pulled the arrows free, then set them to dry on a sun-warmed rock while he worked. Brukthorn he lay by, easy to hand. Now for the currock itself.

He looked the little craft over with a careful eye. It was not so badly broken as he had feared. More of the older withies had cracked, and the skin had ripped free from its bindings on one edge, but the rest of the boat was still sound. Better still, his stitching of the ghaestling tear had held. He smiled at that. All would not be hard to put to rights.

The fisherman's short oar was gone, lost in the rushing water. He'd need another of some sort. He'd not have time to carve out a proper new one, not and come anywhere close to his sighting stone by evening. What then? A forked branch, a scrap of hide or bark… yes, that he would be able to fashion quickly. He sighed. The sooner started, the sooner finished.

He took the scrap of the rope he'd pulled from his leg and picked it apart into twine, and with this he set to binding the cracked frame of the currock. A few of the broken withies he had to brace with greenwood cut from brambles, but most were sound. Then he moved to pull the skin into place—hot pain shot down his side as he heaved.

He cursed and worked his arm, the pain fierce and sharp. Not now. He would tend to it later. He pulled again at the currock hide, and stitch by stitch sewed up again the lacing… done. Next he set to the oar.

He would not risk more noise. Working his way back from the bank, he found a well-sheltered sapling with a proper fork. First he whittled off the high wood, lowering each piece softly to earth. Then he cut free the shaft of his oar. A plate of bark he cut from the foot of a nearby birch. Some more trimming and binding, and all was ready. He'd left far more sign than he might have wished, but he should be far away long before it was found. Perhaps the ghaestling would think him some poor sod fleeing the Torr?

He looked out onto the water and thought… yes, a man broken by the Torr would do just as he had done so far—flee downriver. The Whitefork would in time meet the Mearcwater, and from there a fleeing soul would come in time to another place of men. More to the point, that broken man would not make for Heahfeldt.

Holdric had his sign-story then. Still it was better to leave as little trace as he could. Hasty he hid the mess of his work, and before long he was ready. He bound quiver and bow tight again onto the currock, then checked his blades. A quick strop of his belt knife and all was in order.

What else?

He looked at the last of the rope trailing from the currock and cursed. He tossed it loose back into the boat. One teaching was enough for that lesson.

He sighted out over the water, peering into the trees of the far bank. He saw nothing under the branches but shadow, heard nothing but birdsong, smelled nothing but the river. So far as he could tell he was alone.

He walked the currock into the water and eased himself onto the seat. The sun was high in the sky, just past noon. There was no time to tarry. He took up his makeshift oar and pushed off into the current.

… High Hunling's Hearth holds home.

The river was smooth and swift, a cool breeze came off the crashing water behind. The sun was high and bright in a clear blue sky. Holdric eyed the river as he thought… the ghaestling host behind had been moving half a day now since the Torr burned. That made them less than two days from Greatwatch, and less than four from Heortlea.

And the ghaestling of the eastern valley? He did not know the land there, but if ghaestling moved as men, and if they rested over the night, they would now be a bit north of the Fellstones camp… but if they marched through the night, they may already be nearing the Whitefork.

He gave the north bank of the river a wary look and pushed on the harder. As he leaned against his oar, he felt the skin of the currock press cold against his knee. He reached down and felt the skin of the craft ripple as the mended withies sagged in place. It would hold long enough, he would not need it much longer.

He could only see trees to either side of the river, low-hanging alder below and high ash above. The ground rose up in rolling hills from the water. He guessed he'd come three leagues from the Torr, perhaps four. He went over again his verses, holding the knotted memory of the rolling land in his mind as he tried to place how far he had come. Halfway, almost? That seemed right.

The water heaved again beneath him. He kneed his way into a smooth flow of current, and he smiled as he righted himself. He was learning already to move the broken little craft as his own body, and he was learning already to feel the flow of the water. Some small pride warmed his heart. The water heaved again, and his body moved with it. For a long quiet time he moved with simple joy over the sun-bright water.

He had lost himself in the sparkling light when the current quickened again—he rose up on his knees to see ahead. A great island rose downriver, dark trees hanging over the water. Whether it was the swift narrow waters that it made of the river or the shadow of its looming trees, he liked it not. He would go by land a time.

Gentle he edged his way towards the bank. He found a sheltered spot well upriver of the island, and there took hold of an overhanging branch to stop his course. He eased himself out of the currock and crept into the trees. There he found a wandering deer trail and paused to look over the ground… there was no sign save that of bird and beast.

He lifted Hobblefish from the water and pushed into the brush. The trail followed the river, and on it he could keep the rushing waters just in sight. The currock was no small burden to carry over the narrow path, but he soon learned the knack of ducking through the green with the little boat upon his back. He was surprised to find himself growing almost fond of the thing.

The trail rose to cross over a small rise. There he found a thick leaning tree, and at its foot a small hollow in the rock. The hollow sheltered him from the loud crash of water below, and the tree roots made good thick cover. Here he could better hear the wood around him, and here he had good sight both down the trail and over the river to the far island. It was a good spot.

As he bent to shed his burdens a streak of pain shot up his side. Cursing, he held his arm against his chest and lowered himself to the ground. He sighed…this next task he had put off enough. One last look about the wood, then he stripped to his bare chest and looked to his wound bindings. The linen of his midgescarf was slick and stained over his hurt, flecks of sloughed-off tar clinging to his skin.

Grimacing, he picked at the knots and worked the bindings open. The cloth slid free and he lifted his arm to look—and winced at what he saw.

The skin about his wound was pink and swollen, the tar flaked and wet. A loose knot stood proud of ripped skin. One of his stitches had pulled through his flesh in the tumble of the river, and another was half torn open. He grit his teeth and cut the useless thread free, swallowing a curse from the pain. He splashed the wound with water from his skin and looked over the hurt, weighing whether to sew it up again.

No. No, he could not bear it, not now. The skin was too swollen, another stitch would only tear out anyhow. So he told himself… it was probably even true. He splashed his side again with water and fished in the marching-bag for more of the oxfoot leaf. He chewed the wyrt into a thick, sweet-bitter paste. Some he swallowed, the rest he worked into his wound.

Flecks of the tar came loose as he pressed the healing herb into his flesh. He set his jaw against the pain as he worked it well into the hurt. He closed his eyes for a moment to breathe, then took up his stained midgescarf. He rinsed the blood and wound-sweat from the cloth, found a fresh spot to place against his skin, and bound the hurt up again. Finally all was done.

He groaned as he pulled his clothes back on and lay back against the tree. He drank from his waterskin and pulled out a cake of soldier's waybread. He brushed away the river filth that his dunking had left, then broke what was left into pieces and began to eat. Already the hard-baked bread was soft from the river. He grumbled. Soon he would be down again to crumb.

He gazed through half-open eyes to the far side of the water. He'd not seen sign of the Old Trace for some time now. If the road ran this far downriver at all, it was well overgrown. Trees rose thick from the bank, and all was wooded rolling hills beyond… but it was the island that called his eye.

Grim rocks loomed there over the swift-flowing water, broken trees hulked over tangled brush and deep shadow. The isle held good watch over the river. Holdric looked long for sign of watching eyes under the trees. He saw none, but felt not the better for it.

Memory haunted him as he stared into that dark green. Memory of a black shape under black trees, of a hooded man and a clattering spear. A hooded man who had called his name, a hooded man who had…

He cursed and looked into the bright sky. He felt warm sunlight on his bones and ate his meal. Haunted river isles and a whispering grudgeghaest were tales for children. Still the chill of memory would not leave him.

He could make no sense of what he had seen. Ghaestling did not leave men alive—and yet a man walked with them. Ghaestling hosts moved never as a fyrd of men—and yet now they did, and broke all before them that might give word.

He spat a curse and rose to his feet. This brooding burned away his time. His way had not changed, and he had lost too much day already. He quickly sought the green about him for watching eyes, brushed his traces clean, and lifted again little Hobblefish. He moved through the trees until he left the dark island far behind. The water still crashed below, and on he walked until the river ran calm. Then he came again to the bank.

He paused just short of the water to check the knots on oar and currock. He watched a while more for spying eyes, then he eased himself and the currock again out into the river

The cool of the day held as the sun followed in its course. Twice more the river grew loud, and twice more Holdric took to the bank to walk in safety. After a time the water grew wide. Holdric let his fingers trail in the river and dreamed of midsummer fires, of lights on the water and the wet smoke of summer fish. Of sweet Frithi's summer kiss, of his sister's clumsy fawning over a young Eahstann…

Those memories hurt, and he hurried to bury them away. He would look on them again another day. The light had just begun to soften into a long-lingering afternoon when the river rounded another bend. Rising before him a tall rocky crest came into sight…

… High Hunling's Hearth holds home.

The shape of it looked different from low on the water, but he was sure. There was the same stony bald he had seen from the Torr, there the same patch of trees on the southern side. He'd come to his sighting stone! His spirit stirred—soon he would look again upon Heahfeldt!

As the high hill grew taller in his sight his wariness grew. Walking between high rock and water he would be easily penned, he must take care. He eyed the trees of the ridge above as he floated close and peered deep into each shadow.

The ghaestling had not likely reached this part of the river, not moving over land… still his eyes drifted to the far northern bank, to trees standing dark and silent. On the open water he felt as a high thistle amongst the corn, and he found himself shrinking low in the little currock.

He shook the shadows from his mind and edged closer to the near bank, searching for a sheltered place to stop. The broken trunk of a river-washed tree was not far ahead, that would do. He pushed his way towards shore, then took up his oar and let the river carry him into the shelter of the trunk.

He closed his eyes, listening to the sounds of the shore. Cheerful came the song of a sparrow high in the woods above, soft came the splash of the water about him. The river breeze tickled at his hair and a quiet smile came to his face. He would miss the water.

Enough. It was time to go. He rose from the currock and eased himself onto the bank. He slipped free the knots binding bow and quiver, then set his arms to one side and tipped the little boat until it took on water. As it sank into the river, he guided it beneath the drowned branches of the fallen tree.

He felt for stones on the river bottom, and stone after stone he placed into the boat until it was well weighed down. He wedged his oar in beneath and stepped back to look on his work… not quite done. He moved branches of the broken tree to cover the place until all was well hidden from sight. Then he brushed away the signs of his passing and was content.

He looked to the far bank and took his marks until he was sure he could find this place again, then he pulled on his quiver with a quiet grunt of pain and strung again his bow. He felt the set of Brukthorn on his belt and pulled forth his last dark arrow. He was ready, as ready as he could be. He set arrow to string and started up the hillside.

Trees overhead, bow in his hand and blade at his side, he felt again a ranger. His gaze pierced every shadow, his step came careful, deftly he passed each easy limbway as he looked for sign. From far off came the frenzied scold of an angry wren. Holdric closed his eyes and listened… there came the answering chatter. Good, only two birds squabbling between themselves. He opened his eyes again and slowly he slipped into woldgast.

A faint breeze rattled in the leaves of distant birch. Somewhere a woodmouse scuttled through fallen leaves. Step by step Holdric moved, slow and careful. The slope rose steep beneath his feet, but soon his way was broken. Broken leaf clutter on the hillside above whispered of striding feet—the long-footed strides of ghaestling. He swallowed a curse and drew close.

At a glance he could see more than two had passed here, though far less than a dozen. He knelt to see more. A fallen leaf lay pressed against the earth, the sign softened with time yet still untouched by rain. Further on, a footfall was crossed over by the amble of a woodmouse.

He guessed the sign a day old then, perhaps two. He gnawed on what he saw, trying to guess the tale. He looked up along their way, then back to the river from where he had come. He could just see the far bank through the trees, dark and quiet. Perhaps these ghaestling were only a wild band, hunting on their own. But on this side of the Mearcwater, and only days ahead of a coming host? That seemed a far chance.

Scouts, then? Ghaestling or no, it held sense. The host over the river had been careful to hide their coming. He had to guess then that these creatures hunted ahead for any who might give warning… that they hunted here for men like himself. It was a simple tale, but it smelled of truth. Dread settled over his shoulders and he cursed under his breath. He had still work to do, and little time in which to do it.

He rose, and soon he was climbing again. Still the nameless dread did not leave him. Too often he paused to catch his breath, too often he wiped sweat from his brow. The climb should not be so hard. The way was steep, but it was not *so* steep… he paused to catch again his breath. He rested but little, then pushed higher up. In time his ears caught the gentle burble of a hillside spring.

He felt the waterskin at his side. It was not empty yet, but better to take fresh water when he could. The spring was not hard to find. When he was sure it was not watched, he came to the water and knelt to the earth. What sign he found was only fur and feather, and so he filled his skin, washed the sweat from his face and neck, and hurried on.

As he stepped over the creek he slipped, his foot tearing a deep gouge into the soft earth. He stopped long enough to mend sign of his passing as best he could, then turned again to his long climb. He hoped to be well clear of this place before ghaestling passed this way again, but he could not trust to such good fortune.

At last the trees ahead began to thin. Soon after he caught first sight of the hulking stone above.

High Hunling's Hearth holds home.

He pressed further, and before long felt the clear breeze off the high ridge. A few thin trees remained before him, and beyond was only open rock and the deep blue of open sky. There was no sound but the gentle wind, no flash of iron or bone. The great stone's bare top gave no room to hide. He was alone. Still he was wary as he made his way to the edge of the green and crept out into the open. There the sight took him.

For a long time he could only stare. High over his head birds danced in the blue, and beneath his feet strange spiral-carved stones held their ancient quiet. He paid them all no mind. His eyes were locked on Heahfeldt.

It looked as something from a dream, a rising hill covered over in sun-bathed grass. He could almost feel the soft waving green of his memory, almost hear the gentle bleat of lambs, smell the spring flowers. Peace took hold of his spirit. The afternoon sun warmed his shoulders and the clear breeze cooled his brow. He found he wanted nothing more than to simply sit and watch, to see the sun move over the far fields.

Had his father known of this place? It seemed that he must have. This rock was too proud, too sure a place not to watch for sign of friend and foe alike. Holdric smiled at the thought. Whatever else was to come, the two of them now shared this lonesome far-away sight. He looked long on the far high grass, and he dreamed.

His eyes fell at last from the grassy heights to the wooded hills below, and then to the dark wood running far to the north out of sight. He shook the few happy memories from his mind. From somewhere under that thick green would come the ghaestling host. He had no time to bask in memory.

He sank to his belly and crept to the edge of the rock. A sharp wind pulled at his hair, a grim smile came to his lips. From where he lay the rise of Heahfeldt could not be missed. Still he knew too well how sight of even the highest places could be lost when down in the trees.

Soon he would be in that dark ground below the heights, somewhere in those woods that lay between the high green fields and the silver Whitefork. Where then was this brook Eomud had spoken of? There was a thin break in the trees on the far side of Heahfeldt's mound, was that it? Holdric could not tell all from where he lay, but if branch it was, it looked to meet with the Whitefork downriver, just past a bend he could not yet see.

That was no promise, but the sight fit the story. Well enough. He would go back to the Whitefork then, and look for a branch spilling into the river to his left not far after the river bent south. If that water were tame, he might be able to push little Hobblefish up almost to the foot of the great rise. If not…

He looked again to the broken line in the trees, trying to guess what lay hidden beyond. Rising from the river, it seemed the branch broke east then northerly again, then bent out of sight behind a sharp rise. If his eyes told true, the way kept its course north from there, and would lead in time not far east of the heights.

He sought again for words to bind his way, but his mind would not heel. Too many memories floated just past his grasp, too thick a fog seemed to hang over his speaking mind.

> *Up… wounded water… east a league,*
> *'till tall…tree? two leagues… north…,*
> *Stones… west… hill… high… beyond…*

No. He shook his head and tried again, and again and again until at last the words came.

> *West from water… wend east a league,*
> *'till turning two leagues north.*
> *Sunward stones speak halfway home…*

He wrestled with the lines, forcing each fold of the far earth into memory. Again he whispered the words as he followed the way in his mind, eyes open and then eyes closed, over and over until the meaning held. Sure at last, or sure as he could be, he looked to the sinking sun. The afternoon was wearing. Already he would be scaling those heights in the coming gloom of night.

He gave himself one last longing look on the far grass of Heahfeldt, on the gentle roll of earth that soothed his spirit. For a moment he let himself dream of making it home again. Perhaps one day… but today he had no time to dream. He crept back from the ledge and took again to his feet. Then he passed into the trees and began again his way down.

> *West from water, wend east a league,*
> *'till turning two leagues north…*

CHAPTER NINETEEN
The Crossing

Holdric's step was gentle as he entered the trees.

He made first for a thick knot of bramble. He had been on open ground and might have been seen. There he waited, watching long enough to be sure none followed… none did. As he moved down the ridge the trees grew thick again, and soon he lost sight of the far bank. The way was steep and the going hard, but soon he thought almost he could smell the water.

His neck prickled. Something was wrong.

He lowered himself to his knees, straining his ears. Up the ridge was birdsong, merry and untroubled… all below was empty and still. He fingered his arrow on the string and crept further down.

Soon he heard them. Ghaestling speech sounded in the trees below, how many he could not say. He pressed on, edging carefully through the trees… the speech grew louder as he neared the river. A second voice answered the first. Through thick leaves came a flash of grey and bone, then the sound of splashing water.

Holdric cursed under his breath—they had found Hobblefish! One of the ghaestling pulled the little currock from its hiding place, and a rustle in the far brush told where another hunted the near ground for sign.

Two then… no, there was a third, that one looked out over the river. Only three? He could not see more. The fight would be a hard one, he wasn't sure he could win it. But he would not have a better chance. He felt his arrow on the string and he set his mark, square on the neck of the largest. He began to rise…

The third ghaestling called across the water. From the far side came an answer, then the blast of a horn. Again Holdric cursed under his breath. More would come. Worse, the water was watched. Hobblefish would be of no more help, even if he won this fight. He lowered his bow with another swallowed curse. He would need to find another way.

Careful he backed away from the water. The ghaestling below shouted again, then the little band began to move up the ridge, searching the ground as they went. Holdric's hand tightened on his bow as he watched. They would make first for the tall sighting-stone, of that he was sure. That rock was an eye-sop like no other.

The memory of his every stumble and scrape up the steep slope hung in his mind… they would find his trail, it was sure. He had little time. Grudging he waited for their steps to fade and then hurried downriver.

He thought as he moved. His sign-story was still sound. A Torr man fleeing by water, his craft found… what would such a man do? He might well follow the Whitefork still, but now he would know the river watched. More, he would know the hunters smelled prey. That man would run. But run where?

His gaze followed the bank as he thought, then went up to the ridge above. Yes, a fleeing man might well go up over the ridge and flee south. That way was likely still free of ghaestling, and in a few days' time would meet the Mearcwater. If the ghaestling trusted his sign, their hunt would take them far away from the Whitefork—and farther still from Heahfeldt. Holdric smiled. The tale was good.

He quickened his pace to a steady jog, and as he ran he counted the cost. If the ghaestling called for help from across the water, he might have to work through a driving line on his way back. That though he might have to face that no matter the course he took. What else? Laying a sopping-trail would take time, time he sorely needed. Already the sun was sinking into late afternoon.

He weighed the cost but a moment—it was worth it. He turned up the ridge, sure to leave just enough sign. Too much and the ghaestling would be on him too soon. Not enough and they would cut ahead, and perhaps catch him on the way back. He must bait the hook.

He steadied himself against the trunk of a young alder, then pulled himself up by a too-thin branch. The wood cracked away from the trunk under his weight—good, the leaves would be drooping before the day was done. He might as well have hung a banner. For good measure he made sure to slip in the wet earth just up the ridge, gouging moss from earth and crushing a mouldering log as he clambered up the slope. A lone Torr man had stumbled in hurried flight, that the ghaestling would trust. Up the ridge he ran, fast as he could manage.

He stopped a moment for air. The ridge had been a hard climb taken at a walk, taking it again at a run was sore work. Still he pushed through sweat and pain and cursed as he stumbled over another mouldering deadfall. He could not limp, they needed to think him hale. If they thought him hurt they might hunt too near. He wanted them looking far ahead—far from the water, and far from Heahfeldt.

Finally he was once again over the ridge. He paused only a moment, and leaned on his knees as he caught his breath. Where were they? He looked back the way he had come. The woods were quiet, still full of fading sunlight. The ghaestling would hunt a long time yet. He needed more room.

He shook the sweat from his hair and took off again at a jog. He jagged one way then the other as the land guided him, but always he aimed south. South to the Mearcwater, south away from Heahfeldt. And always he left just enough sign to keep an eager hunter snared.

After the better part of a league, he paused again in a shallow creek, resting on his haunches as he let the running water cool his feet. He looked back, judging how far he had come… yes, it was enough. He ducked carefully past an overhanging branch, then crept his way back up the spring. He kept well clear of his old path as he made his way back to the Whitefork, keeping always the sinking sun to his left.

The sweat on his brow grew chill in the fading afternoon, and his bones began to long for warm kettles and dry blankets. He cursed himself and bound tight his thoughts. There would be rest enough at home, he needed now his mind. He raised his hood again and ducked low as he neared the last rise before the river.

He moved up through still woods, a deep silence hanging in the trees. He hated the ghaestling horns and their curdling shrieks, but he hated their stalking quiet more. Wary he neared the thin trees at the heights of the ridge.

Nothing moved. He readied his arrow and crept low to the crest. No sound rose from the ground ahead… he hurried into the thick trees on the far side and paused to watch for sign that he'd been seen.

Far off a sparrow sang, nearer a woodmouse explored a mouldering branch of deadwood. There was no glint of bone, no running feet or hunter's howl. The quiet gnawed at him. He ached to make for the river now, but dared not be pinned against the water by daylight. And he dared not hold still, not with ghaestling on his trail. And so he followed the ridge, low in the trees just shy of the crest.

As he walked he sought the trees below for the sight of the Whitefork, but ever saw only trees and earth. And so he kept his way east as the shadows grew long, praying for the light to fade.

Had he been at the Torr only this morning? It seemed already an age. The fyrd would have gathered by now. Likely the Eorl would not march them by moonlight, likely Holdric had still until morning to reach the beacon. But only likely—he could not be sure. He looked again to where Heahfeldt lay, somewhere far beyond hill and tree. The road would be hard, but if he pushed hard enough he could just manage it.

A ghaestling howl echoed from far over the ridge behind him.

Holdric cursed. By the sound they'd come already to the end of his sopping-trail. The sun was low in the sky, but not yet low enough. If they moved with skill, they would have light enough yet to find his path here… and already they had followed him farther and faster than he had guessed. With a snarl he began again to run.

In the fading light he looked back across the ridge behind. He'd lost sight already of his high sighting stone. Every step now took him farther from the marks he'd taken over the water, and already he worried he would not see them again. But he could not stay where he stood, and it was not yet safe to cross the water. And so on he ran.

He had only to keep ahead of them until dark, so he told himself. Then he could cross the river unseen. He ran until his sides ached, then farther still, and on until he could run no more. He leaned on his knees and peered into the wood behind. There was no sound of running, no crash of brush. If ghaestling followed, they came slow. Holdric took a deep breath and pressed on again.

Gloom began at last to gather under the leaves… it would not be much longer. Tonight the moon would not rise until long after dusk, Holdric would be swimming in the true black of night. Never had he taken water so wide, not even in daylight. He pushed away the gnawing worry. He had no better way, and a worse death than the river stalked not far behind.

The shadows grew deeper, the ground beneath his feet dark and hard to see. It was time. If Holdric could not see sign, neither then could his hunters. He turned sharp and felt his way down the ridge. He raced now against the fading light, aiming to reach the water with light enough still to sight the far bank.

A ghaestling howl echoed behind him—they were on his side of the ridge now. He cursed and pushed on, faster than before. The ridge fell ever away before his feet. Each time it seemed there could be no more earth ahead, that he must be almost upon the water, another long hill stretched down into the gloom. He ground his teeth and kept moving.

The hunters had gone quiet again.

Down and down Holdric worked, and still with each step he saw only more earth and tree below. He looked to where the last of the dying sunlight lit the sky, still to his left. He had not turned from his course… but he should have already seen the river.

He had just decided he must have somehow turned his step, somehow turned into a blind broken gully, when finally through the trees he caught the flash of fading sun on water. Relief poured through him and he quickened his step. He came to a break in the trees with just light enough to see over the river.

He was too low now to see the rise of Heahfeldt. His marks were long lost, far now up the Whitefork. He cursed under his breath, turning the shape of the ground over in his memory and trying to fix where he might now be. He could make no answer.

A ghaestling cry pieced the gloom, far up the hill behind him. There was nowhere else now to go. He picked his way down to the riverbank and paused just short of open water. There he sheltered beneath a broken tangle of birch and looked over the far shore.

Somewhere across the water ghaestling eyes looked back towards him. They searched the wood where he sheltered, watching for men on the river. Holdric waited.

The sun sank at last behind the western hills. The first bright stars peeked through the deep above. Still there was too much light on the open water.

From far up the ridge came the crack of broken wood, and Holdric cursed under his breath. Shadow would not be enough to hide him here. Below a great snagged tree had washed onto the bank, tangled in a thick nest of broken alder… it would be enough.

Holdric broke cover and crept lower down the riverbank. The earth grew soft as he came near, the smell of the river thick in his nose. He eased himself under the alder tangle and squirmed into thick cold mud under the mouldering tree. A shiver went through him, but he made no sound.

He rolled onto his back and looked deep into the shadowed trees above, holding his breath, listening… something rustled in the leaves above, then fell still.

All was grim quiet. Holdric waited as the light died. He counted his breaths as he watched the trees above, as he willed night to fall over the water. All fell into gloom.

A ghaestling cry pierced the shadows above. An answering call echoed over the water, not far upriver. Still the open water glowed dim in the dying light.

Holdric searched the shadows of the far bank one last time, hunting for any fold of the ground he had sighted… there! Was that the rise he had seen behind Eomud's brook? He wished to tell himself so, perhaps it was. And high over that spot, dim in the still-fading sky, there hung the stars of the Lady. That at least boded well. Well enough, he would follow her stars then.

He looked again to the water. The river looked still, but he knew already its strength. He would be swept far down river in his crossing. For a moment his spirit quailed. Last night's swim had near ended him, and that had been a mere branch. Again he doubted the wisdom of his way, but that milk had been kicked. The way back up was watched, the woods behind deathly quiet. He was sure ghaestling lingered there, waiting for sound of his moving.

The stars grew many in the sky above. True dark settled under the trees below. At last he could not see even his hand before his face. It was time.

His hands moved fast, working quiet, working by feel. He unstrung his bow and tucked the string carefully away. His cloak and quiver he pulled off, then jerkin and jack. He started to pull off his tunic, then paused. He wanted not the weight on his arms as it seeped full of water, but the river would be cold. He kept it on, and hoped he chose well. He bound the rest into a bundle about his quiver, and strapped that tight across his body. Only Brukthorn he kept free, bound fast to his waist.

Something rustled in the woods above. Had he been heard? He pressed close under the fallen tree, his hand on his blade… all was still again.

More stars birthed in the night above. Little Wulfling caught his eye, glimmering near Wegliht the homecoming star. He smiled at that. The stars at least were with him.

Far over the water drifted the sound of a ghaestling laugh, cruel and mocking. Fires grew there, glowing pockets of light in the dark of night. Holdric searched the far shore and looked for a place to make land. His eyes landed on an empty spot far downriver, far away from the burning fires. Empty of ghaestling, he hoped. Empty of tangling snags, he hoped.

He half-whispered a curse. He was dawdling now. He could delay the moment no longer. He crawled deeper into the water, away from his pocket of body-warmed mud. The cold wash of the river swept over him and stole the breath from his lungs. He held himself still a moment, holding against the current as he grew used to the cold. Then he took a deep breath, felt himself lighten in the water… and he let go.

The river took him. The bottom fell away from his feet, and for a moment panic threatened. He knotted tight his mind, he let the fear wash away. He had only to act. He kicked further into the water.

Rushing void washed over him, deep void flowed beneath him. All was dark and ever-moving water. His legs tired, and still he swam. His arms weakened, and still he swam. Water splashed over his face, water filled his nose and eyes with stinging pain. He choked, for a moment only he buckled, but that moment was enough. The river bore him over and he was driven into the black roiling depths.

He tumbled blind in the deep. Angry he kicked out, and came again to splashing water and rushing air. He forced his head above the river and he gulped another breath. All was night and rushing water, the stars above smeared pricks of light in his stinging eyes. The river pushed him around again and he kicked to stay in place.

He'd lost his marks, he knew not which way he faced. Panic rose up within him and he bound it down hard. The current was to his left, that was direction enough. He righted himself and swam again unstopping. Through river-filled eyes he saw at last the black of land against the far stars.

He thought on the snag in the Greenflood, he thought on the press of water against the stone in the rushing froth upriver. His mind screamed that soon he would be pushed into the dead fingers of a hanging tree or broken on a stone. Still he swam on.

Black shadow rose high above. He felt rather than saw the coming shore, he pushed on against rising dread… then he felt the sweep of his arm brush mud. He let his feet fall in the water, and gently slid to a stop against the river bank… it was done. He was across.

Water rushed over his back with a quiet burble. He listened through water-filled ears and searched the deep black above though stinging eyes. All was quiet. Then from far upriver came another ghaestling shriek, and after it a hooting laugh.

A tinge of sour smoke was on the air. The memory of other ghaestling fires pulled at his mind, ghaestling fires and desperate screams of men. Anger rose up within him, and fear with it, but he had no time for either. He bound the feelings tight and pulled himself up from the mud.

By touch he picked apart the knots of his things. His bow he freed first. He strung it again and laid it aside. Then he unbound his quiver and drew free an arrow. This he laid across the bow, keeping both near to hand. The arrows were soaked again, but there was nothing he could do for that now. With every sound, with every rustle in the darkness, he stopped to listen… still all was quiet. Still he was alone.

He worked on. His pouch swam with river water. He drained it and felt for his tinder bag within… the little store of tow and char was only kissed with damp, that much was good. Next he pulled off his clothes and wrung them dry. He donned them again, and soon the wool warmed against his body. Jack and jerkin next, then hard-wrung cloak and quiver. He had all. He was ready.

He felt for Brukthorn at his waist, set arrow to string, and looked up to the sky. He searched for the Lady but she was not to be seen, the sweet curve of her stars far behind the high shadow of the trees.

Still by the stretch of the starfroth above he knew her place. He took a last look up into the night, took his marks, and set off.

The bank was steep, muddy and overgrown. He clambered through the tangled green up from the water's edge. The slope soon eased, and he came once more to open ground. He followed the earth up again until the trees grew thick.

The sky was black beneath the branches. Now and again there came a pool of starlight in the shadow above, and there he sought for bright Ruhnliht in the highest part of the sky. From there he found the starry throat of Hifosidth, and the sweep of the star-froth behind thin high cloud. Each glimpse of night straightened his northerly road.

The ground rose and fell as he made his way by sky and star. The night wore on and high cloud blew across the stars. The guiding pools of light came more seldom, and then came hardly at all. Winds high in the sky drove the dark clouds before them, always to the north. And so with the first glimmer of far-off moonlight, Holdric followed the clouds, making ever deeper into the forest.

Woodsmoke floated on the air. Thin and far off it seemed, but it had not the sour moulder of long-dead char. The smell came fresh as crackling kindling, the smell of fire still burning. Lights danced in the far dark, campfires small and distant. Shadows moved black before them, and a ghaestling laugh haunted the wind.

Holdric seemed to float in the night. All the world was tree and earth and distant fire. Memories of flame and torment ground always at the knots of his mind, and always he pushed the memories away. Sometimes his side burned sharp with pain. Other times he felt only a dull sick ache, a thing that always had been and always would be. His hair was wet with sweat in the chill air. His feet moved slow and heavy.

Ever on he walked.

Fog rose in the trees, chill on his skin. He shivered. Slowly the smell of smoke faded in his nose, and slowly the fires fell behind. He looked back only once to the dancing lights, blurry in his eyes as they flickered small and far behind him. Another laughing howl echoed through the valley. Nothing else moved.

He turned back again onto his way and the firelight behind fell into memory. The earth beneath his feet grew soft, the air grew thick with pine. For a long time he moved in peace. Pine gave way to bramble, then to prickled holly and gnarled oak. Time and again Holdric would stumble face-first into thorns and pick his way out, feeling his way through grasping tangle until again he came to open wood. Time and again dry cracking branches blocked his way, and time and again fallen deadwood tripped his searching feet. He gathered scratches and bumps, and his mind drifted.

He made his way now by the dim glow of moonlight, shining low in far-away clouds. *Follow the Lady* echoed in his mind. He trudged on to where by moon and earth he guessed she must lie. The chill grew sharp, the night far now into deepwatch. He shook his head, he tried to clear his mind from sleep. His limbs were heavy, his head hung low to his chest. Down he made his way, down and up again. Was he near? How could he know? He had walked he knew not how long when at last he stood high on a clear ridge and searched the sky.

Far to the north the blowing cloud had not yet gathered. There he looked for the Lady, and dumbly stared to where she should be, but was not. Slaugnwint had risen to take her place, grim and hungry. Holdric looked higher… there she was, he could just see the stars of her long throat.

She does look like a duck.

His smile came soft. He tried to keep her in sight as he walked down the hill, the shape of her stars a gentle comfort in his heart.

He shivered again. The cold was deeper now, a sharp biting wind over the hilltop. He pulled his cloak tight about his shoulders. Step by step he trudged down the hill, feet heavy on the earth. He shook again his head, he bit at his cheek and squeezed tight his hands.

Down he walked.

The air smelled wet. The air smelled foul. He looked up and searched again for the stars of the Lady, but saw only empty night, only the cold fingers of a dead branch stretched over the muddy cloud above. His head swam. He swayed on his feet.

He did not feel himself strike earth.

CHAPTER TWENTY

Mist Under the Leaves

The sky was empty.

Cold drew close, deep cold. But not cold enough to mask the stench… the night hung heavy with death. The air was thick and sweet-sour. Water oozed black and reeking from the mud.

He felt something heave in the spinning earth below. His hands clenched in the mud, his fingers closed tight on crooked elder roots. Wind blew over the forest floor. Cold dead leaves rustled in answer. Above him stretched the dying elder tree, branches scratching at the night.

Mocking words came with the wind, chill and silent, oily and mocking.

Look.

The cruel whisper hung in the cold air, everywhere and nowhere. Meaning slithered through his spirit.

Look. Look and see what you have made.

Cold held him, the cold of deathless grudge. He willed it not, but still his eyes rose to the branches above. Too-familiar shadows hung there.

Look.

He looked into the scorched empty eyes of Aemud. What was left of the fallen ranger gazed back at him unseeing. Not far away hung another, Eomud's young messenger dug from his grave on the ridge. The boy's pale flesh was mottled now, grey and broken. Holdric tried to look away, but he could not.

Other shadows hung higher in the tree, shreds and bones…and worse. The deep and ancient cold hung gloating in the wreck.

Look.
LOOK.

Hwaetearn hung there, cold and pale. Hwaetearn, his jaw cloven and hanging. And…

No.

… and Eahstann. Eahstann's empty eyes looked upon him. Eahstann's eyes looked *through* him. The grudging chill spoke now, mocking words hanging in empty night.

They hated you before the end.

It could not be so, and yet he knew it was. The voice spoke true.

They know what you took from them.

The night filled with seeping grudge. Darkness closed over the sodden mud, and the last of his warmth drained away. He stared into the night, empty and alone. Yes, this was the end as it should be. This was the end he had earned.

Ache fell over him, the ache for all he might have done and now would never do. Ache for the weight of his own shaming fear, and ache for all those he had failed, all now dead and cold. Ache for the light he once had seen and now would see no more.

His breath came ragged… and then his breath came not at all. Shadows seeped up from the earth, cold malice closed over his still heart.

Then in the void above, all collapsed into a single dim star. In a breath or in an age, another shone beside it. A third, impossibly far away. He heard their song, sweet and distant. Silver light grew, dim on the low wet earth. The glow grew bright, and brighter still until the mist burned with starlight. Silver light reached across the cloud-streaked sky, and with it the grudging shadow burned away. Mist rose up from the earth, bright and chill.

His spirit fell quiet. He listened as soft silent steps drew close in the night.

He was here.

It would not do to lay before him. He drew a ragged breath, he pulled himself from the earth. The great stag watched as he rose. No words passed between them. The still night was thick and heavy. At last Holdric's words fell upon the earth, empty and drained of all will.

"I will come."

The great stag did not move. His eyes were soft and tender. And he stepped close.

Holdric jerked awake.

His body burned with fire. His head tore with pain. His clothes were soaked in sweat and his breath came fast. Gorge rose in his throat. He rolled to his belly and heaved until his guts were empty.

Dully he looked on his retchings, black in the moonlight. His mind swam, and he fell back onto the dirt. Silver light flooded through the dying branches, the moon cold and white behind high thin cloud. Chill gnawed at his limbs.

Slowly the stink of his retch filled his nose, foul in his hair. The thick smell of elder rose from the muck. His belly heaved again, but nothing came. Nothing was left. Slowly his mind tried to gather itself… he had dreamed. Meaning floated at the edge of his mind. Words slowly formed on his tongue…

"I slept."

His voice came in a croak, he heard the words spill as if from an-other… then their meaning took him. He had slept! Time was lost! He tried to rise, his wound screamed hot as his arm took his weight and almost he fell into the mud again. His belly heaved, but in vain.

He groaned a curse and wearily pulled himself up from the earth. He swayed as he rose and caught hold of a twisting yew to steady his feet. His mind swam slow in his skull, his throat stung with retch. He spat and reached for water.

He looked up to the sky. The moon was high now, shrouded in wind-blown cloud. Blinking he stared into the moonlight… he had lost the night. Already greywatch was near.

He squeezed his eyes shut and tried to shake the pain from his head. He knew not what else to do. He walked. By moon and shrouded star he found his way, step by step he staggered on. Mist thickened as the smear of moonlight moved across the sky. In time cloud swallowed up even the moon, and then he felt his way from tree to tree.

The way grew rough with root and bramble. He blundered past tangled roots and tripped with a curse, saving himself only to land his foot deep in a rushing creek. He righted himself and trudged through the wet. Up he moved and down again, feeling his way past stone and broken tree.

Dry branches caught at his cloak and he pushed past them. Ground fell away before his feet and he felt his way with his bow. Step blurred into step and his mind swam in a fevered doze. He was working down a slick leaf-covered slope when he heard the first high call of an early ruddock. Holdric turned towards the sound, searching the far black of night.

"Save your songs, bird."

For but a moment he glimpsed the wing of Slaugnwint, high and faint through moving cloud. Dread closed over his heart—but only for a breath. Then the moment passed, and Holdric saw again only black night. Dreary he pushed on.

Slowly the clouds grew a brighter grey. Dawn was near. Holdric groaned and quickened his step. Bleary his walking rhyme danced in his mind as he stumbled through fading night.

West from water… wend… east…
'til… turning… two…

Grey light gathered under the trees, the wood heavy with a chill wet. Trees rose stark and grim from grey shadow. The song of a morning thrush drifted over the far branches. A pair of wrens awoke. Holdric walked as one in dream, the early morning mist soft on his cheeks.

In the first dim light of true morning he sought new marks, but all was shrouded in deep wet mist. Above the sky was empty grey. It came to him that he knew not where he was, nor how far he had come. For a moment panic threatened, but only a moment. Habit took him.

Habit carried his feet to where his sluggish mind could not. Habit found him a sheltered spot to watch over the way he had come, and habit bade him sit and cover himself over with his cloak. He shook his head and tried to steady his swimming mind, to gather up the shreds of his thought.

Water. Food.

He reached for bread, but found only damp broken crumb. He pulled out a larger piece and held it to his nose—it stank of the river. Still he ate, and it stayed down. He drank from his waterskin. His mind swam still in pain and weariness, but as he sat the panic fell away.

He needed to know his way.

He craned his neck to peer through the leaves above, eyeing the shape of the eldest branching limbs. He sought the earth for places dark with seeping water, and he looked over tree and stone for where moss and rime grew thick.

Water told of shadow, and shadow told of sun. Sunwards then was… the way he had come, more or less. He had managed a mostly northerly course, that was good. He tried to fix the land he'd travelled in his mind. He remembered the moving clouds, the pools of faded moonlight under the trees.

When had sleep taken him? His mind held the sight of a low moon, of thin fingers of elder against the clouds. Chill touched him at the thought, but he pushed the dread aside. The moon had been low when he had fallen, low and waning, that meant…

He could not think. He shook his head again and rested his eyes. He had crossed the water in moonless night, the rising moon had been… what, a hand high? Two? It had been late into deepwatch then when sleep had overtaken him. He had walked for the better part of two watches of the night.

In daylight on good ground, he could easily cover four leagues in that time. He'd moved at night, so… a league he guessed, or not much more. Less than two. And all he thought—he hoped—north and east from the river. After waking, he'd moved at best half a league in the greying night, still to the north and east as best he could manage.

He thought then on the land as he'd seen it from the sighting stone over the river, he thought on where he had seen the rise of Heahfeldt and how far he had walked along the ridge, high over the water. His sought his mind for his verse…

> *West from water… wend east a league,*
> *'til turning two leagues north…*

The shape formed in his mind as he spoke the words, and he chewed on where he must be. He was still west of Eomud's brook he thought. He doubted he had come so far north as Heahfeldt. So… he would go east until he met running water, then he would follow that running water north. If he held the ground right in his mind, that would take him to Heahfeldt.

It was done, then. He knew his next steps.

He rummaged for another handful of crumb and choked it down. The greying light slowly rose under the high trees. Mist held him close, and already he was chill and weary. He looked again over the way he must go, fixing it in his mind as he tended his feet and tried not to think on what must come next.

Soon he could delay no longer. He took a deep breath, then pulled off quiver and cloak. Dread rose within him as he lay them aside. Perhaps the wound was not so bad as he remembered… he dared hope. He unfastened jerkin and jack, then pulled off tunic and sticking shirt.

The smell hit him first, sick and sour-sweet. Yellow ooze seeped from angry red flesh. He closed his eyes and groaned, he forced his bile to stay inside his throat. He poured a handful of water and after a flinch splashed it on his wound. Pain came as he knew it would, sharp and hot.

He stopped to breathe, then washed his wound again. Wet seeped down his side. His flesh was hot under his hand. The fever would grow, he knew it would. He sought in his marching-bag for more of the oxfoot, but all was long gone.

What then, burn it shut? Even if he could risk a fire, even if he could bear the pain… no. Not and burn the rot inside, that much he knew from Kenndric's tales. He washed the hurt a last time, grinding his teeth against the hurt. He kept his eyes shut hard and waited for the pain to dull. He measured his breath and strained to gather again his mind.

He looked about for any healing wyrt he might know by sight. He saw none, nothing but moss upon a low stone. That might serve, he'd seen leechmen use moss. At least he hoped it would do no harm.

Careful he pulled some up from the rock. He took up again the midgescarf he'd used for bindings, now crusted and foul. His gorge rose again, and he let it fall from his hand… his eyes went to the hem of his linen shirt. Maethbry had spent a full winter at the weaving of it, she would howl to see her work torn to rags. He looked again at his side, and a grim knowing smile crossed his face.

Let her try.

He took up the shirt, and with a snarl tore free a fresh wound-binding from the hem. With that he bound the soft green moss against his open skin. He pulled the knot tight and swallowed his grunt of pain. All was done.

He pulled on his clothes again and reached for his jack. The thing was foul, heavy still with river water, and stinking of blood and worse. He thought… then let the armor fall from his hand. Jack and jerkin he kicked beneath a fallen log, and covered both over with leaves and cruft. He had no more need of them. He had not the strength to wear them.

Far off, far to the south, he heard the distant blare of a ghaestling horn. He looked back and he cursed what he saw. He had thought he'd moved with care, but so far back as he could see his trail looked as one left by a drunken beast. Every kicked leaf, every flattened spray of green—all screamed his passing. Once they found his trail, he would not have long. He needed to move, and quickly.

He raised his waterskin for a last sip, but all was gone. He let the skin fall to his side with a whispered curse. He looked to his way, and began again.

… 'til turning two leagues north…

Cold mist hung heavy in the shrouded wood. His marks were short, but he kept them as best he could in the cold grey. He moved half in fevered fog. Cold sweat mingled with cold mist on his brow. Still he stumbled on, tree by tree. He tried to make sure his way by the sun, but all he could see above was a bright haze in the clouds.

The day did not grow warm. The mist hung stubborn in the trees. He shivered, but still he pushed one foot past another. After a long time walking—he could no longer say how long—he reached the crest of a low wooded hill and looked back the way he had come.

Oak and ash and rolling blackthorn fell back into the mist out of sight. It seemed he had come far, far enough he should have seen some sign of Heahfeldt, but still the ground did not rise before him. He should have come at least to Eomud's brook, but had not seen so much as a narrow creek.

Swaying on his feet, he looked again over earth and tree, made sure his marks were true, and walked on. Ache followed him up deer-worn trails, and weariness trailed him through the water-damp shallows. His feet dragged over the leaves, his eyes heavy.

His gaze dropped to his feet, and soon he saw only the earth as he trudged ahead. Dull worry gnawed at his mind… he still had not found the brook. He sought for sign of water in the dim grey but found nothing. Then at last the ground began to rise beneath his feet, and from not far above a brighter light promised thinning trees. Perhaps he had found a bald or other broken place. From that height he might at least see the ground ahead.

His breath came heavy as he pushed himself up the slope. From somewhere in the mist far behind came the broken wail of a ghaestling horn. Far behind, but not so far as before. He looked back, down into the quiet trees below. He had no strength left even to curse.

He groaned and turned again to the climb. The way grew steep, his thirst burned. He reached for his waterskin and again found it empty. He let the skin fall again to his side and pushed on. The trees thinned, just above lay a tumble of open ground. He grunted bleary and aching against the bare stone, working until at last he heaved himself onto the heights above the endless green. His side throbbed as he swayed on the rocks. One last push, and then he rose to look into the mist.

He could not believe what he saw.

Heahfeldt he could see, but it rose far behind him, leagues back to the north and west. Somehow he had lost his way. Somehow he had turned to the east and left his aim far behind.

Rage boiled up in him and he choked down a shout. Hissing he sank to his haunches, hands in his hair. How had he gone wrong? He tried to think, he tried to force his mind to trace again his steps, but he could make no sense of where he was. He must have passed the water in the night, but how he knew not. He looked again over the mist-shrouded ground, searching for some sign of the running brook he had somehow missed.

He cursed when his eyes landed on the place. What he had taken for a wide creek from his high sighting place across the river had been only a draw of stone through the trees. He must have passed over it unknowing in the night.

Still… still it would help him. The draw lay again across his path, to what he took for north and west. He had only to find again that draw, to follow it rightwards and up, and climb until he reached a high stony ridge. From there he would turn west again. The mist on those heights was thin, and he thought he could see breaks in those distant trees. Once there he would see again the great rise, he was sure.

A ghaestling horn sounded dread and cold in the depths behind. Holdric whispered a curse. He looked once more to Heahfeldt, a great looming shadow in the far mist. He had seen enough. Quickly he looked over the ground below, making fast his marks… there, two gnarled oaks pointed his way to the draw.

Down the hill he stumbled, mumbling his way to himself. He struggled to keep straight the words as he shivered against the wet chill. His feet were heavy, he licked his lips against his thirst. He grasped a branch to steady himself and it lurched in his hand with a crack.

He swayed on his feet as he looked dully up to the broken branch. Then he let it go, and he moved on. At last he reached the foot of the hill. He peered through the grey, trying to find again the marks he'd set for himself from the heights behind.

He found the first gnarled oak, and from that he found the second. He began again to walk, sure at least now of his way. Mark to mark he moved, shivering against the wet as his mind swam numb in a mist of its own.

His weariness grew. Too soon he stopped again and rested his hands on his thighs. He worked his arm, pain ran through him hot and sticky and he closed his eyes against the hurt. From far off sounded again the horns. He cursed and tried to run, stumbling through the endless grey. The wood was unchanging, one rolling ridge after another, all covered in twisted oak and thick-thorned bramble.

He licked again at his lips. There was misting wet enough to chill his bones, but not enough to slake his thirst. He reached again for his waterskin—still empty. He held it to his mouth more in hope than sense, but nothing came. He lapped at leaves and sodden wood, but gave it up. He had no time. He had to push on.

Sometimes he ran, sometimes he walked. He knew not how far, but at last he heard water. He stopped to listen, peering through the grey. It could not be far. He looked once more to his marks before and behind… yes, he was sure he could find them again.

He broke from his way and jogged for the sound of water. At last he crested a low hill, and saw a thin brook just beyond. He pulled at his waterskin as he came close, following the brook up to where the water seeped clear from the earth onto rain-spattered rock. He fell to his knees in the soft bank, and he scooped up the cold water to drink from his hand. Some little life came back to him.

As he drank, his eyes fell on the leaves across the spring… there was sign there. Ghaestling sign, but not ghaestling sign only. Holdric let fall his hand and stared stunned at the faint mark of a man.

The footfall was broad in the ball and gentle on the earth, left by one who had moved with a careful stalker's step. His tread had been gentle, his stride light and measured. Any other might have missed it. But Holdric had known this tread all his life.

At first he thought himself mad with fever. He came closer, he ran his finger over the faint marks in the earth. He could not believe that his eyes spoke true… but they did, the sign was real. A mad smile crossed Holdric's face.

Ollda was here. And he was near.

CHAPTER TWENTY-ONE
Of Thorn and Blood

Holdric hurried to stop up his waterskin and look over the sign at the brook. Ghaestling had passed here, easily a dozen. And with his Ollda there had been others, all rangers by their careful stalking steps. Holdric's heart leapt to see sign of Aschbroc, and even the mark of Wymud's squat foot brought a grin to his face. There were other men here also, three whose strides he did not know.

Eomud's men from the Hyssestead? Holdric tried to see in his mind the length of one-eyed Ulfraeg's stride, the shape of his distant kinsman Byrcstod's foot. He could not be sure, but it might be so. But of Eomud he found no sign. That man's broad foot Holdric would know, and it was not here.

Nor was there sign of Hwaetearn. Holdric told himself the thaneling scouted some other way, or that Ollda had sent him alone for aid, but he could not make himself believe it. He looked into the mist, over the broken deadfall and scattered leaves, and cold knowing held his heart. He breathed a quiet curse.

Holdric's bones were chilled. His mind churned slow and heavy. But he knew not else what else to do, and so he began again his work. The earth held sign. The sign told a tale. That was enough.

Ollda would have seen the fire at the Torr, of that Holdric was sure. And Eomud had pledged to send his men scouting for ragfolk along the Whitefork. It held sense then that Ollda would come downriver to hunt up what aid he could find, to search for Eomud along the water.

But what would have brought them all so far down the Whitefork? And leagues now north of the river? And why hunt these ghaestling south again? Holdric stood, turning in place as he looked over the sign. He swayed on his feet, and steadied himself on a tree.

His head swam. He willed himself to think. The sign at his feet was fresh, not yet scarred by the misting rain. Surely it had been made since morning. His brothers could not be far. Longing filled his heart. He looked back the way he'd come, back to the marks he had taken behind. His last mark, a broken pine, hung in the mist through the trees, still just in sight.

Somewhere far beyond that tree lay Heahfeldt, far to the north and west. And somewhere beyond Heahfeldt was the coming ghaestling host… but the others tracked ghaestling south. If he followed them, every step he took would take him further from the beacon, and further from his duty.

Misting rain clung to him as he sat upon his haunches, weighing the choice. His eyes softened as he watched the forest… and he saw sign. Chill took his heart.

It was only a spray of fallen leaves that looked not quite as they should. But that spray was too far from the other sign, too out of step. Holdric came close, some dread part of him knowing already what he would see. There, where a passing foot just brushed the soft leaf-shaded ground, was a man's track. The right foot was heavy along the outside of the pace, it left a dragging scrape where toes left earth. The next pace he found just where he knew it would lie. This step was too heavy in the heel, the mark filled with crumbs of dirt where toes smeared earth. Holdric knew this loping run.

He crept forward, straining as he traced the loping stride for dozens of paces. The work was hard, but Holdric was sure. Not once did another track pass over these, not ghaestling and not man. This one had come last of all. Then the loping stride shortened, the weight came heavy at the front of the foot as the hunter had slowed his loping run.

Holdric's fingers traced the dim press of a crouching knee. Faintly lighter patches on the earth showed where leaves had been moved, where the drizzle had not yet sunk so deep. Holdric moved the leaves… and saw his Huntslaed's footfall. Dread fell over him.

Ollda is hunted.

Holdric shivered and pulled his cloak tight against the chill. There was no choosing, not now. He rose with a curse and stalked after.

Whoever the hooded man was, he knew the ranger's craft. In places he left easy sign in haste, but he had a gift for leaving little trace even at a lope. Here the man betrayed himself by the faintest scrape of lichen on log, there by a crease under shifted stone. But that was all. Only by knowing his Ollda's familiar stride could Holdric keep the trail, and still time and again he had to work back to search for where he'd lost the path… then the trail fell out of all sight.

Holdric cursed. He brushed the chilled sweat from his brow and started again. He cast back over sign of ranger and ghaestling both, and found nothing for his long work. At last the next mark came, far off Ollda's path. The hunter had left the chase and bolted west at a run. Holdric looked up after the hopeless track and sighed. He had not even the strength left to curse. He slumped against a tree and rested his head on his knees.

What was he doing? He was broken, he was hopeless. Even Heahfeldt was lost to him now, his marks far behind in shrouding mist. Cold sweat mingled with the mist on his face, and his weary head swam as he tried to think.

Water dripped on fallen leaves. The distant sound of running feet whispered through the mist. Holdric stared dumbly into the dripping wood. The sound came closer. His mind worked slowly against the sound, meaning just past his...

Ghaestling!

He had no time, he threw himself to the earth. There he lay flat in the wet leaves, hiding his face in his hood. In the far grey he could just see the shadow of a running ghaestling. The sound grew louder as the creature came close. It crossed over a low rise scarce a stone's throw away—and then it passed by.

The mist swallowed the thing up again, and the sound of running feet fell away out of hearing. Soon all the wood was still, as still as if the creature had never been. Holdric lay where he was, waiting for more. None came.

Think.

He struggled to weigh what he had seen. The ghaestling was not a bested foe, of that Holdric was sure. The creature had not the feel of panic about it. And it had come from the place Ollda's tracks pointed, that surely wasn't chance. A messenger then? Holdric's mind felt thick and heavy, he shook his head and tried to force his thoughts to flow.

Gentle rain misted the quiet earth. All was still. The horns were quiet. Slowly something kindled within him… the ghaestling had sent a runner! They had sounded no horn, they had howled no cries into the wood. They worked in quiet—which meant they feared being heard.

At that a true smile came to Holdric's face, and he breathed in quiet thanks. Some of the rangers then must live, and some must still be near! He rose from the earth and made for the runner's trail. The ghaestling had paid no heed to its steps, the way was easy to follow.

Holdric looked back the way it had come. That way, he hoped, lay his brothers… and those who meant to kill them.

That way Holdric went. Sometimes he shivered, sometimes he stumbled, sometimes he ground his teeth hard against the seeping pain, but always he walked on. The trail fell ever away from him, every step shrouded in mist. Then he was struck still.

Dim through the mist, far up the ridge ahead, he could just see the shadows of ghaestling. A hushed voice came in whispers down through the mist… the voice of the hooded man. A chill ran down Holdric's back.

The man pointed over the ridge ahead as he spoke, and the ghaestling followed his rough speech. Holdric eased himself slowly to earth. If any had seen him, they gave no sign. None looked his way. He clung close to a thick root, and sidewise he watched them. They spoke low and quiet, their words clipped and their voices faint through the mist. One of the ghaestling craned its head to look over the next ridge.

A trap was brewing, Holdric was sure. Was Ollda close? The ghaestling took care to hold their silence, he must be. Holdric shifted to gain better sight. His hand brushed Houlen's woolen shroud, and the faint scratch of root on horn lingered in the air.

Did the hooded man look his way?

Holdric froze. The moment was over in an eyeblink, he could not be sure. The man stood no differently, he spoke no differently, Holdric could not see the ghaestling eyes through the mist. And yet… they knew.

Somehow Holdric was sure, he'd been seen. Slowly he backed away. None looked up. He stayed low to the earth, trying again to make his way up the ridge, far wide of his first path. After long work, he looked through a break in the green to where the ghaestling band had been—all were gone. A lone sapling swayed in windless air on the crest beyond.

Holdric held still, straining his ears. A faint rustle sounded through the trees behind. He looked back and saw nothing, but he knew the sound… ghaestling were searching for him. He swallowed his curse.

The wood was still, full of eerie quiet. Shadows moved on the ridge above. He heard the soft stalking steps of ghaestling moving further down the ridge, seeking the place he had been not long before. Behind sounded the soft crack of mouldered wood.

Dim in the mist behind he saw their shadows. How many they were Holdric could not yet tell, but two had found his trail. Panic haunted the edges of his mind. He crawled low, fast as he dared over the wet leaves. After too long he reached the top and looked down the far side…

There were so many.

Shadows moved thick on the hillside below, shadows bristling with bone and lean wicked spears. Somewhere past that line— somewhere close he hoped—Ollda and his men must be. But Holdric could get no closer.

The sound of quiet stalking steps behind came nearer. Holdric could see his hunters clearly now. Two ghaestling climbed through the mist behind him, poking at the brush with their spears as they went. He had no more time, he would have no better chance… his fingers brushed the grey feathers of Eahstann's last arrow, ready on the string.

Careful he set bow and arrow to the earth. He reached under his muddied cloak and pulled forth the great horn Houlen. He paused a single heartbeat, tracing a finger over a bloodstained crack in the horn. He looked on the blackened brooch pinned to the shroud, dark in the shadows of the wood.

"One last song, brother," he whispered.

Then he held the horn to his lips, and he blew. The valley filled with the clear blare of the danger call:

BAWP BAWP BAWP!
BAWP BAWP BAWP!
BAWP BAWP BAWP!

Howls rose up from all around him, screams of shock and rage filled the trees. He let fall the horn and took up his bow and heavy dark arrow.

Low and right…

Dim and far away he heard the shouts of men. They had heard him, they knew their foe was near. His task was done.

Low and right…

The two ghaestling below came running to the echoes of the great horn. As Holdric brought up his bow, one sighted him.

Low and right…

The ghaestling shrieked and raised its long spear, but Holdric's arrow had already left the string. The heavy shaft lofted slow down the hillside, grey feathers cut lazy through the air. The ghaestling saw the arrow as it fell, it tried to dodge—but too late. The heavy point hit home.

The ghaestling tumbled down the hill, howling as it pulled at the shaft buried in its body. The other shrieked and hurled a black spear up the rise in answer. Holdric ducked fast, his next arrow flying wild into the trees. He reached for another, but the thing below was gone.

All the ridge behind was howls and cracking limbs, the ghaestling host hot behind him. Holdric ran. He ducked under branches, he leapt over fallen deadwood. The slope fell steeply away before his feet. His running steps became leaps, his leaps became great bounds. His course turned more fall than run, and barely could he keep his feet beneath him. Fear took him as he sought some way to end his fall.

A flash of movement below—a lone ghaestling burst from the brush, it turned at the sound of his coming. For a single breath it froze at the sight of him. Holdric lurched towards the thing. Hate filled its eyes. It dropped its horn, it lifted its spear, but already it was too late.

Holdric was in the air, his feet tucked close. The tail limb of his great yew bow he aimed square for the thing's chest. They came together in a howling crash and tumbled down the ridge in a flurry of rolling muscle and crashing limbs and pain. Through closed eyes Holdric heard a splintering *crack*, he hoped it wasn't his own body… and then he was alone.

He slid down the leaf-covered slope, he put out his limbs to stop his slide. Pain clotted at the edges of his mind, then sank over him in a great wave. His side was the worst, he was sure he'd pulled himself open again. One knee screamed with pain, hot and sharp. He didn't want to look at that yet. His head was bleary with the hurt.

Straining he got to his feet. Dimly he tested his leg… he could stand. His knee was hot with pain, trouser leg blown open and blood-spattered, but his leg bore his weight. The hurt was ugly, but it was shallow.

Further down the hill lay the crumpled remains of the ghaestling, unmoving on broken rock. It was very, very dead, a splintered shard of Holdric's broken bow clean through its throat. It lay in a misshapen heap, its broken limbs twisted freakishly around its body. Holdric stared stunned at the sight of the wrecked creature. Fever and cold fell over him as he watched the last of life leave the thing.

Bleary he rested his hands on his knees. Sweat was cold on his neck. He ached to rest, to close his eyes for just a moment. But horns and shouts echoed through the woods above, and again he ran. With each hobbling step his knee howled.

The wood was alive with shouts and horns and the crack of iron on living wood. They were near! They were near, and they would find him. He needed shelter, he needed to hide. All the world was howls and screams and… the faint splash of water on stone.

That was direction enough. He stumbled on, his fevered steps dragging at the earth. Somewhere far behind came the harsh cry of a man, and with it the shriek of a ghaestling. Who had ended who, Holdric could not say.

He ran stumbling across the face of the ridge. The sound of water grew louder, and before him stretched a brush-covered creek. He vaulted over a mass of bracken, then sank low in the shallow spring. The cold water shocked his mind awake.

Fronds of high green bracken stretched over him, already scarred brown by coming fall. The cover was thin, it would not hide him long. Above him shadows tore howling through the mist. He ducked low, molding himself into the chill mud of the creek bed. Ghaestling calls and horns echoed through the cold wood all about.

Where now?

Above the running spring grew shallow. The thick bracken there dwindled to nothing, and beyond was only open wood. He turned, rising up on an elbow to look down over his shoulder. There the cover thinned in places, but still the water cut deep enough through the earth to hide his passing. Further down the slope the creek ran into a small hollow, and there it flowed under a thick blackthorn hedge.

There.

He crept down the creek bed. Chill water ran down his legs and up over his arms. The shock of the cold was long past, now all was numb. He took what care he could against sign, but still he swept slime from rock, still he pressed stone into mud. He could do no better.

As he neared the hedge he startled a little wren and she flew off with a chattering scold. He froze, but the horns were close now. He hurried down the draw. The thorny mass rose over him, thick and tangled. Another horn sounded somewhere over the ridge.

He pulled up his hood and tucked his hands into his sleeves, he wormed his way under the thick cover. Thorns scratched his knuckles through the wool of his clothes. Thorns pulled at his hood, dragging the cloth from his head and ripping at his scalp. Deeper still he wriggled, until he could scarcely see daylight back the way he had come.

He was covered in shallow cuts, he was pressed between the thick hedge and the running stream, but he was hidden. He shifted onto cold muck, mostly out of the running water. And then he settled in to wait.

The sound of ghaestling horns were far too close now, only paces away. Soon running feet and harsh mocking snarls filled the clearing. In the narrow band of sunlight between hedge and earth passed the shadows of many feet, and ghaestling howled and called to one another in their harsh tongue.

Holdric thought he saw a flash of grey as faces poked beneath the hedge, but none lingered. If they saw him deep in the shadow, they gave no sign. He willed himself to keep still, he forced each breath to come deep and smooth and silent. The call of voices echoed above him and his heart raced, sure any moment the hedge would be filled with their searching spears.

None came.

Soon they would go. Soon they *must* go. But time passed, and still they hung near.

A shadow hovered near the hedge. Feet moved to the edge of his hide. Not far off another ghaestling called, and the shadow called back. Holdric's hand closed on Brukthorn. Then came the sound of piss on water. The smell hit soon after as the ghaestling's water joined the creek. Shouts and harsh laughter followed. Soon after came the sound of axes and breaking wood.

Holdric's mind filled with thoughts of flame and thorn, of writhing in a burning snare. He looked to all sides of the hedge, a cornered jackrabbit searching for a path to scramble when all above him turned to fire, but no fire came. He smelled woodsmoke, but no heat reached him, no crackle of burning thorns filled his ears. Then the knowing came—the ghaestling were making camp. They called to each other as they rose up shelters and built their fires.

He tried to count them by ear… a dozen? Two? He gave up as voices moved in and out of the little clearing. Too many too fight, too many to flee. He was pinned here.

The mist-shrouded sun moved across the sky, and what bright of the day there was began to wane. Holdric's fear turned to restlessness, then to rage. At last even rage burned away to mind-killing, listless boredom. Still he waited, alone in mud and thorn. The ache of laying still burned into his bones. His mind began to unknot.

He thought of far-away places, he chewed on old verses, he thought on anything to turn his mind from the misery of his flesh.

> *I've living green beneath my feet,*
> *the gyre-road blue above…*

The deep thorn scratches stung, the rough open meat of his knee throbbed, his torn side crawled with itching heat. The scent of blood and worse hung over him. He ached to move, to at least grunt for the pain of it, but he dared not. The day burned on.

> *I rest in walls of ash and yew,*
> *my roofboard's rived of stars…*

Holdric thought over every half-remembered verse he held. Sometimes forward, sometimes backward, anything to keep his mind working.

> *Wing, wing my little wren, dancing in the dew…*

Not that one. He couldn't dwell on that one, not now. He let his wandering thoughts touch on his work, on his herd, on his promised labor for old Hegwyn. He thought on how he might trade for another ewe, how once he grew his herd, he might again ask…

No. Not there either. He should not dwell on thoughts of home, there lay despair and sorrow. Verses were better. Verses were safer.

> *Hifosidth do I know her, she-swan, singer of…*

Memories too sweet to bear pushed on his flesh, and he rushed to force them from his mind. Still the sorrow flooded in.

Beneath him the water grew foul. The ghaestling had made the creek their midden, and the mud under the hedge grew rank with their filth. Holdric moved as much as he dared, and he strained to keep his open wounds from the foul stew growing under the hedge.

Ghaestling called to each other in their harsh tongue, and Holdric listened. More than once shouts turned to blows, then great cackling howls as the others cheered the fighters on. The fight would flare, ghaestling would laugh and jeer, then all would be still again.

From the clamour of shouting voices, at length some sense came. One word came often. Holdric could not quite shape his mouth to the word, but it seemed something like a dog's bark, part greeting and part threat. Another came more often yet, that he was sure was a curse.

How long might he have to hide to learn ghaestling speech? More time than he had, of that he was sure. Still he tried to force his mind to follow their words, to make some use of them should he live. But weary pain washed through him, and he could not make himself hold the sound.

His mind faltered. Verse came again, the oldest words he had.

> *Mouse on the… mealchest,*
> *calf… in the… in the corn…*

The light was fading. Some part of him thought that odd, it did not seem so late. And yet the long stillness dragged on. His body began to fail. Every muscle ached, every bone hurt. His wounds itched hot in the filth, every scrape and cut tingled with sharp fire. His own bladder had long ago begun to nudge him, and now he could think of little else. Through it all he dared not move.

He cast his mind about for anything to think on besides his pain. He tried to think, tried to listen, tried to knot his mind on anything but the hurt, but over and again his own stubborn flesh kept dragging his mind back to misery.

Rain came. A light sprinkling rain at first, then with a rush of wind it became a drenching pour. Shouted ghaestling curses filled the clearing. The thicket over his head slowed the flood, but still the water found him. An icy stream found its way under his torn and ragged hood, the cold rain traced a chill down his back. Holdric shivered.

The world outside grew dim, water soaked through his clothes. Without his meaning it, his bladder give way at last. Dully he felt the rain wash the warmth away. For a moment it felt almost good. That did not last.

Dusk followed fast on the heels of the downpour, and with the rain the last of his heat left him. Ghaestling fires licked bright through mud and haze and thorn. The flickering light taunted him, the sweet smell of smoke and the hiss of steam wormed deep into his mind. He ached for fire.

His clothes were sodden, his cloak heavy on his back, his trousers soaked through. Cold water welled in the mud under the hedge, and soon he was in a great broad puddle. His toes were numb and his fingers cramped. All the world was wet, and all the world was cold. Another shiver ran down his back. The deep chill of coming night gripped him hard. He clenched his fists, he shut tight his eyes, he tried to make himself feel anything but the cold. He was lost in his own misery when he heard a scream.

It was not the mocking screech of ghaestling. It was the raw scream of a wounded man, and it was a voice he knew. Holdric lifted his head and tried to see through the thorns. Another pained howl filled the clearing, followed by a shouted curse and harsh mocking laughter. The clamour grew louder. Mocking howls and loud hoots filled the draw around the hedge. Then another shouted curse, and more jeers after... almost it could have been his uncle's shout. But it was not his uncle.

Ghaestling dragged Byrcstod swearing into the clearing. The old ranger must have joined Eomud's search along the Whitefork. His bow and blade were gone, his jack hung ragged and bloody. He had surely given the ghaestling good fight. But now he was caught, and alone. Holdric's heart fell. He knew at that moment he would never see the beacon of Heahfeldt, never finish his duty.

It was the laughter that had done it. He knew he had not the heart to hide while torment came to his kinsman, and he knew he had not the strength to best the numbers they faced. And so here he would fall. Greatwatch would be overrun before the next sun was high. There would be no more chances. He had failed Eahstann, he had failed his brothers, and now he had failed Byrcstod. All was done.

But at least his kinsman would not die alone. In that would be some measure of honor, no matter how quickly it would be snuffed out. Holdric moved with the rain. With each blowing gust of wind he dragged himself a handsbreadth through the hedge. When the air stilled, he plucked himself free of thorns and waited until finally he neared open air. He clasped Brukthorn tight and licked his lips.

He watched the band above, weighing his chance to strike. Ghaestling crowded around the clearing, eager and jeering. The hooded man of the ghaestling stood among them, burning brand in hand. The ghaestling pulled Byrcstod before him, beaten and broken. His cheek was scorched, his arm hung strangely to one side. But still he stood, tall and proud.

His face changed when he saw the hooded man. He looked confused—then heartbroken.

"Brocca?"

At first the hooded man only looked on him. His face was cold. Then he laughed a croaking laugh. Byrcstod seemed to search for words, hurt warring with rage-soaked sorrow.

Holdric gathered his feet beneath him, making to leap. Somehow Byrcstod saw Holdric in that last breath. For only a moment their eyes met, but that moment was enough. Shock passed through Byrcstod's eyes. Knowing followed, and then sorrow. Last of all a plea, the faintest shake of his head—

No.

Byrcstod looked quick to where the man of the ghaestling stood, then he spat, he kicked, he strained at his bonds, he howled. Blows landed hard upon him. Then fire. Byrcstod screamed, and worse followed.

The air grew thick with the smell of pain, thick with the sound of torment. Holdric wanted to bury his face in his hands, to stop up his ears, to burrow into the mud, anything to shut out the sound. Still he forced himself to watch. Coward or no, he owed his kinsman that much.

It did not end quickly. In time the screams stopped, and much later the tears. Blood mingled with filth and mud and rain.

Long after, the ghaestling howled and tore at what was left. Long after, they sang and shrieked. Still the rain droned on, and finally the last light of day died. Howls faded to noisy chatter, and chatter fell to quiet. Fires burnt to ashes, and then nothing was left.

Holdric lay alone. The pall of death hung over him, taunted him. Hope was a distant memory, cold as ashes. All was gone. All but Heahfeldt—that remained. That he could still do.

The sun had long since set. Soon the moon would be above the trees, soon silver light would shine over the leaves. But for now, all was dark save the dim glow of dying embers. A deep shiver took him. He braced his body against the mud, he forced his limbs to still. The cold seeped deep into his bones. He bit the flesh of his wrist lest his teeth chatter. He could wait no longer.

He sheathed his blade, and with a final scrape he worked his arm, then his face, free of the thicket. He dragged himself out into the full cold weight of the rain, and missed at once the shelter of the thorns. Still he dragged himself across the open mud.

The fires of the camp were low. In the light of dim embers lay sleeping ghaestling, and over them crude shelters of brush and skin. Nothing moved. Holdric ached to rise, to run, but he dared not. A breath at a time, he wormed his way over the forest floor. Chills racked his body. His eyes fell on the nearest fire as he passed, dread and longing both at war within him. Rain pelted his back. On he crawled, handsbreadth by handsbreadth.

He came to where Byrcstod had fallen. The smell of blood was heavy on the wet leaves. Holdric paused there but a moment. His eyes screwed tight, verses passed quietly over his lips. Then he pushed on, and slowly the ground rose beneath him. The earth grew firm and slick beneath the rain-covered leaves. He was almost through the camp.

He felt a hump of land beneath his belly, then the ground began to fall away again in a shallow slope. He risked a look behind—only a few fires still burned in the pelting rain, and those low and dull. Nothing stirred, no shadow moved before the light.

Rain still fell heavy on his back and his shoulders began to shake from cold. He cursed beneath his breath, he strained his limbs, he forced his hands against the earth to keep them still. On he went. The shallow slope grew steep, and soon he left the last feeble light behind.

Down he crawled, down over the soaking leaves. Ten paces he crawled, then twenty. Finally he rose to his feet. No… he tried to rise to his feet. He tried again, he willed his body to move. Still it would not. He looked back unseeing at his stubborn legs.

He drove his head against the earth, he half-pulled one knee under his chest, then the other. With a swallowed grunt of effort he rose to a hunched kneel. His hands trembled in the falling rain.

He spat a curse and hugged himself tight. He strained every muscle, he willed himself simply to straighten and his body would not answer. But he had at least his feet. Down he staggered, feet shaking and dragging over the earth… and fell again onto the wet leaves. A cramped leg kicked out against brush and rain. He clenched his teeth and squeezed tight his hands and the shivers would not stop.

He willed his hands back to his middle. He clenched tight, he curled into a ball. A grunt of deep aching cold rose deep inside his chest, and he forced it back down to quiet. He tried again. Groaning, he reached his feet. He made one stumbling step, and then another. He moved. He was half blind and broken, but he moved. He minded not which way his feet took him. Down was all the direction he needed, down was away. He went down.

His will unknotted, his mind wandered free.

Down down little mouse…

It seemed almost he could hear his mother singing, sweet and without care as she did so very long ago.

…m-mouse in the… in the mealchest…
… cock on the… corn…

Twice—thrice—he fell as he stumbled in the cold black wet. Each time he rose, and each time was harder. He felt a growing warmth inside. Old stories sang in the corners of his mind, songs of the birds of winter, songs of their warming draught of mercy-mead. Some distant part of mind felt that to be ill-omen. The warmth changed shape within him.

He knew this embrace. The last time he felt this warmth, Ollda had taken him from the dark wood. But now Ollda was gone. Holdric had failed him, and so Ollda was gone. Some part of Holdric's spirit knew he should not drink of the warm mercy-mead, and yet still he ached for it. Still the birds called him to their honeyed rest. Had he not earned it? Had he not done all his folk had asked, and more besides? He had done enough.

He knew it was not right, and yet he could not make himself care. The golden cup danced behind his eyes. He staggered towards it, further down the slope until he collapsed into a dead soaking oak. There he waited to find again his breath. Rain fell over him, and he did not care. He smiled.

Yes… yes. He would drink, and he would sleep. Just for a moment…

No. Not yet.

He shook his head, he slapped at his face with numb fingers. He rose, he swayed on his feet, he staggered on. Farther, and farther still. Sweet mercy grew in his chest, warm and easy. His pain began to fall away. Down he moved, one stumbling step after another—

Then his foot found only air.

He pitched headlong down a short bank, down into a deep cut in the earth. At its bottom a torrent of rainwater rushed, only a handsbreadth deep but burning with cold. The cold ripped at his chest. This time he couldn't stop a gasping croak.

He staggered up out of the water, he bit down hard on his arm to stop the heaving grunts of cold. Strange tears were hot on his face, and all thoughts of tempting ease fell away. He needed warmth. All his body shook.

He choked down huffing grunts of cold, he trudged foot by foot up the cut until he found a large tree against the bank, and there a shallow muddy ledge still above the rushing rainwater.

He grasped for his cloak pin, then grasped again. He pulled at the heavy sodden wool of his cloak, and reaching into the stretching branch above, he fumbled with shaking fingers until he managed a makeshift cover. Beneath it the rain fell no more.

Told you it would work…

The words echoed in a numb sing-song in his head.

Told you… told you…

He fumbled again for Brukthorn. Twice his trembling fingers slipped from the hilt, and twice he grasped again, and at last he pulled the blade free. With hands and sharp iron he hollowed out a little hole in the mud between his knees, a place to lay his ranger's fire. Water seeped from the soaked soil into the hole, and soon it was full. His fingers met only a new puddle in a sea of soaking puddles.

Dumbly, angrily, he tossed the great knife down in frustration, holding his face in his hands. He wanted to scream with rage, but his lungs only hacked in the cold night.

Thought came, dim and far away. He scrambled at his waist, fumbling for the soldier's marching-bag. He rummaged through the little sack, his hand closed on the earthen cup. He placed the cup in the muddy hole and bent his body low to shield it from the rain.

Next he reached for his pouch, and from that his precious store of tinder. Praying with each breath, he unfastened the tie and un-rolled the grease-soaked bag. He felt inside—the tinder was still dry. He took only a small measure of the dried tow and grass and placed it into the cup. He could make a proper fire later, a taste of warmth now would be enough.

Working blind he felt for the candle stub, then his charbox. He took the little iron box and set it on the cup. Taking the lid in his teeth, he forced his hands to close on stone and iron. His hands were shaking, his fingers numb. Tools slipped from his trembling grasp.

Tired tears welled in his eyes. He held his hands under his arm-pits, rocking back and forth, willing even a spark of life into his unfeeling hands.

He tried again. His fingers dumbly held the sharp flint and little iron… but they held. Dull orange sparks streaked like flaming stars in his little sodden world. Finally a hunk of charred punk caught. Quick he fished out the dry little nest and cradled it around the ember.

The ember faded before he could catch it.

He was too broken now for anger. Or for hope. His hands worked without thought.

He struck again. Nothing.

Again…

Again…

Again…

At last another ember caught, a bright snake of light that glowed its way across the char. That one hair of orange-gold became the center of all his world, his one treasure in all the earth below and all the sky above. As gently as if he were teasing sweet Frithi, he took up the little orange glow in the nest of scraggly tow.

Gently he blew the little ember alive. Gently, so gently…

The little pile of tinder came alive. Holdric dropped it into the cup and let the tiny flame burn for a few sweet breaths. Before the tow burned all away, he caught the flame on a sliver of greasewood, then passed the living fire to his grubby little candle stub.

He had light.

He had warmth.

As the candle came to life, Holdric flushed with the first hope he'd had in all his memory. For many breaths, he held the flame close to his face, eyes closed and drinking in warmth like a long-drowned man.

Sure the candle was well lit, he doused the taper of greasewood and gently eased the little candle into the cup. Fire he would need still, but for now the candle made his wet woolen world come alive. His trembling eased, then it stopped. He rubbed his fingers in the rising warmth over the cup. Slowly the space inside the cloak began to dry and warm.

He prayed his thanks and lost himself in the little flame. Holdric let himself become drunk on the tiny glow, he stared into the light, he burned the colors into his eyes.

His mind swam, his fingers moved without thought… he hungered. Little enough was left to him, but still he had the precious little box from Caltbruk, some of the honeyed goosefat still clinging to the sides. He licked the little box clean, all but breathing in the fat. He scraped next the last handful of sodden crumb from his marching-bag, sucking the last smear of paste from cloth while he thought.

What now?

He was still far from Heahfeldt, but it could not be yet deepwatch.

He tucked away his charbox. He weighed if he could weather the rain again so soon, he wondered if he were far enough from ghaestling to risk a proper fire. He stowed his tinder and shut his pouch.

Best to let the candle burn a bit more, then he could pick up and…

CHAPTER TWENTY-TWO
Among the Graves

He was in the Night Forest. All was shadow and thorn.

All but Ealdorholt.

The white stag walked before him, and Holdric followed his silvered steps. Together they walked through dark night. Holdric tried to frame his question, but found no mouth to make the words. The question hung in his spirit:

"Where are we going?"

From the stag came no answer. In silence they moved over wooded hills and through broad thorn-choked draws. They moved for time past counting. The way came gentle at first, so gentle that the man who had been Holdric did not notice. He felt it in his skin, the distant itching tingle of far-away thunder, the rushing lurch of a coming storm.

Stronger it grew, an unseen cloud on silent winds. A rushing flowed through him, flooding down his back, a searing on his skin like Frithi's teasing touch, a lightning clap drawn out across all time… something was coming.

Something was coming, and he was not ready. He tried to cry out, to beg for time, to ready himself…

"I can't."

Why not? He needed a reason…

"I'm dirty."

Ealdorholt's voice without a voice was unmoved.

"You will be clean, child."

"I'm scared."

"I know."

He looked at his fear, and he found it far away. It no longer mattered. Behind it came sorrow.

"Will I… miss… back there?"

Already the memories were fading.

Ealdorholt turned, and for an instant their eyes met.

The cold was gone. The night seemed far away now, distant as rain outside a tight warm hall. A sweet gentle breeze filled Holdric's heart like the first breath of spring, growing until all the green smells of summer filled his spirit.

In the space of a whisper, all the ages of the world fell into one. He felt friends near, too close to see. And in the far summer haze, there he could just see the walking shadow of a man. The man was far distant, and yet Holdric could clearly see his face, a face from long-forgotten memory…

"Da?"

It was.

Holthund's mouth moved in speech, but Holdric had not yet ears to hear the words. Beyond him others walked. Holdric could not see their faces, and yet kin they felt. Farther on walked those of ancient time, their spirits hazy and distant… there walked the Mountain King, only Dunstugh now, and Aranmaede his consort.

Hearoch shining bright and golden, and his swan-maiden with him, in peace at last.

That would mean…

Holdric turned. Behind upon the trace came Hleolea his mother, and Maethbry far behind her. Maethbry's face was worn, her hair thin and grey. She brightened to see him. A gentle smile crossed her face, and then happy tears. She turned, she waved back to someone beyond his sight. Others came too, farther yet behind. He craned to look…

A footstep sounded in the dark wood. Shadows flooded close and cold, the wind filled with wild screaming howls.

Maethbry stood now beside him. Young she looked, fresh as yesterday. Tears cut paths through blood upon her face. She stared at him, pale and empty-eyed.

And then all was night.

The sound of breath was close. Holdric looked wildly about, searching for he knew not what—

Ealdorholt's gaze caught his flailing spirit and held him where he stood. Holdric froze, and still the gaze bore into him. A new voice floated on the air, a whisper from far away.

"Go back…"

Ealdorholt heard it also. His eyes were gentle, his eyes were knowing. Choice hung in the air.

"Go…"

The man who had been Holdric chose, and Ealdorholt nodded his great head.

Holdric started awake. The air under the cloak was cold. The candle had burned itself out, now a smear of tallow and wax clinging to the bottom of his cup. His cloak was wet. The rain was silent.

He was still chilled through to his bones, but the dreadful shivers had stopped. How long had he slept?

Gingerly he lifted the edge of his cloak and peered out. The moon was just above the trees, clear silver light broke through heavy shreds of dark cloud. He stared dazedly up into the sky, straining to remember he knew not what.

A footstep sounded and he came full awake, the chill tight around his throat. Then came another step, a gentle secret tread over last year's sodden leaves… *ghaestling*.

Holdric reached to his waist for Brukthorn—not there! In a near-panic he felt blindly for the blade, his hand closed tight on the haft. The sound of steps on the earth above drew nearer…a soft press of leaves sounded just above his little shelter.

Could they see within? The moon was low, but the clouds had opened and silver light brushed the earth at his feet. Holdric sidled from his little tent, still sheltered by the lip of earth above. He held Brukthorn low, hiding the watery blade from moonlight.

Two dark shadows loomed black against the night. The shape of their thin spears was sharp against the cloud, their voices were low whispers. Holdric tensed. He pressed himself against the earth, his fingers clung tight to Brukthorn, his heart beat loud… they were just above him now. For a single too-short moment, it seemed they would pass by.

Then the steps fell quiet.

Hushed voices floated in the moonlight. A stretching shadow loomed out over the trench… iron gleamed in the moonlight as a spear point pressed against Holdric's tented cloak.

Holdric didn't stop to think. He snatched out with a hand, took hold of the shaft and heaved down with all his weight. The ghaestling tumbled after, rolling over to land hard in the cold water. Holdric followed it down with Brukthorn and drove his blade deep through gristly ribs into the thing's heart. It shrieked like a cornered boar and kicked blindly out into the black.

The kick took him hard, he fell back against the mud, Brukthorn lost somewhere in the night. Water splashed as the second ghaestling leapt down into the ditch. Holdric scrambled for iron, for his little belt knife, his fingers closing on the haft just as the ghaestling bore past him in the dark and drove him down into mud and water.

Holdric reached out from the mud—he grabbed the thing's ankle and heaved. The ghaestling toppled into the water away from him, but Holdric was already stabbing. First he struck at the shin he still had hold of, then climbed up the ghaestling's body, frantically punching his little blade into anything he could reach.

The thing kicked and howled and bucked, but Holdric held tight. Somehow he managed to get his weight across the thing's spear, pinning the weapon and the arm that held it. The other arm was somewhere out of reach, somewhere free in the dark. Holdric kicked out blindly towards it, hoping to ward it off as he kept punching with his little knife. The next thing he knew he was bucked into the air.

He landed hard in the water—before he could move the thing was on him. One hard hand seized his knife arm, another ground his head hard against a river stone. The ghaestling pulled his head back off the stone by the hair and made to dash him onto the rock. Holdric lurched in the mud. He missed the rock as he came down again, but water flooded over his face and he coughed and sputtered for air.

The weight above shifted as the iron hand drove his face deep into the mud.

Holdric clawed at the sinewy arm, but it only pushed back harder. Pebbles ground against his cheek, water filled his nose. He kicked and bucked, flailing to rise above the muck. He managed a single breath before the thing rose up, shifted its weight, and firmly planted Holdric's head under the flowing water, grinding his face against the stones.

But that shift was enough.

Holdric wrenched his arm free, and he buried the sharp little knife deep into the side of the ghaestling's leg. As the last of his air faded away, Holdric raked the blade up the thing's thigh. He felt the keen edge tear deep through flesh, the tip of the blade nick bone.

The weight was gone. The thing fell off him off howling, clutching unthinking at the gaping wound. Holdric rolled with it, stabbing deep into its neck. The ghaestling snatched wildly at Holdric's arm. The clawing scratches came first fast and strong… then slowly their strength faded. The last batting blow came slow, then fell limp from Holdric's arm. The ghaestling lay still.

It was done.

Holdric rolled off the thing, panting. From somewhere in the black came a rasping lung-rattle as the other ghaestling neared its end. Then all was quiet.

Holdric stared dazedly up into the sky, into little seas of stars hazy and broken between high dark clouds. Slowly his mind came again awake. He felt in the dark for Brukthorn, he gathered up his things and he pulled himself out onto the forest floor.

Moonlight bathed the wood in dull silver. Long pits of shadow stretched under the trees, the rolling earth cut through with deep stream-worn scars. Grey mist hung cold over the broken ground.

A shiver ran down his back and he pulled tight his cloak. He crouched close to a tree, hand on his blade, waiting for the sound of ghaestling. No sound came, no sound but the drip of water from rain-soaked trees.

Where was he?

The moon was a haze behind the night cloud, it seemed now about three hands high. The moon had risen late, so… about halfway through deepwatch then. Yes, his belly told the same. He rose, and holding his arms wide he stared at the sky. He wheeled slowly in place as he pieced together the path of the moon and the few patches of sky he could see. High in the sky he saw a part of the Lady… and there through that thin cloud, that would be bright Aeforliht of the Waelstan. Holdric traced the arc of the starfroth overhead with his hand, seeing in his mind the place of shrouded stars.

There.

The northern gyre was behind thick cloud, but he trusted where it lay. Holdric looked over the roll of the land under the moonlight, trying again to remember how he had moved the long day before, how he had found the thorns in which he hid, and the way of his stumbling path through the rain after. He sought his mind for the shape of the land as he had seen it from his high misty hill.

He had seen a stony ridge, long and leading the way to Heahfeldt. That ridge was north and east of the draw, of that he was sure. And he was now—he thought—not far east of the draw. So… north then, and a touch east. Find the high ridge. From there he would find what he could. He'd done all he knew.

He lined up his marks in the moonlight and made again for Heahfeldt. The moon passed slowly through the sky as he climbed. Sometimes he could see the wood around him, dim and silver-grey. Other times cloud so covered the moon he was lost in the night. He moved as he could.

An icy breeze cut through the trees, and still he stumbled on. Far ahead silver moonlight danced on wind-shaken leaves. Dream crept into the edges of his mind. He pushed back the fevered sleep. He could sleep when all was done. Still his mind softened.

A flash of silver passed through the trees far up the hill. He stopped, staring into the trees. Again came the light, a flash between deep branches.

No…

Far ahead, the silver stag stood in the deep trees of night.

Holdric's mind broke. He tried to guess if he still walked in waking lands, he tried to guess if he still lived. He did not know, he could not know, and yet…Ealdorholt had not moved.

The great stag stood still, waiting. Waiting for him.

It could not be. And yet it was. Holdric closed his eyes hard. He could not make himself believe, he would not believe. And then the stag turned and began to walk, and Holdric found himself following after. Without his will he followed, step after quiet step.

Brush blocked his path, thorns caught at his sleeves. He pushed the bramble away, but became more tangled. Darkness pressed in, darkness and thorns. The silver light began to fade as the stag moved on before him.

"Don't leave me!"

He ripped, he pulled at the thorny tangle, he pushed himself free. A branch smacked hard against his side. He placed his hand to his hurt, felt his body slick and wet… and felt no pain.

Silver light pulled at his spirit. Ealdorholt walked on, and Holdric followed. The air grew thick. Far off he heard the ghaestling screams, dim as something from a distant dream. Here was only the moonlight, only the leaves below his feet, shaded in silver.

Ever the stag walked, ever just ahead. Ever Holdric followed. Together they walked in quiet. The trees thinned before them, and a great shadow loomed against the sky. Over those shadowed heights, hanging in the far sky, there shone the trailing lights of the Seolfrenblos.

Holdric paused to look on the stars, small and cold and distant. He could not see the great Hound of the northern sky, but it seemed he could almost hear him, a cold wailing howl over the dim echoes of ghaestling. But Ealdorholt did not stop, and so Holdric followed. Ever on they walked, up and ever up.

The earth grew soft beneath his feet. The scent of pine needles grew thick, and all the air was still… his feet were wet. He looked down to see his foot in a small seeping creek.

He knew this place.

He faltered. The great stag turned to watch him from the rise above.

"We're here, aren't we?" Holdric asked.

Ealdorholt only looked on him in silence, eyes gentle and sad. The stag did not need to answer. Cold fear sank over Holdric's shoulders. His voice came small—

"I don't want to go there again."

Ealdorholt waited but a moment, then the great stag turned and passed from sight over the rise. Holdric stood alone in the darkness. A great heaviness fell over him, and a deep sorrow. He walked up the ridge to follow after the stag. He knew what he would see before he reached the rise. He climbed the soft silent earth, he passed through the shadow-tangled pines… and there it was, just as he knew it would be.

The laughing-pool.

It was real. It had always been real.

Moonlight rippled on the dark water… it seemed so small now. He remembered a great wide water, not this small quiet pool beneath the trees. But here was the faded spiral-carved stone, and here was the wide rock where he sat and splashed. He knew this place.

It should have brought him peace, but something dark ground against his spirit. Echoes filled his mind.

Where is she?

Worry gnawed, and worry grew to panic.

He said she would be here. He said she needed me, he said she was…

Holdric—no, not Holdric. Holdric was a mere babe. *Holthund* cried out into the shadows—*"Hleolea!"*

He thought too late to stop his shout. His voice hung heavy in the quiet wood.

Nothing moved.

He came to edge of the pool, silver-grey in the moonlight. He looked within, and there in the waters he saw the stars, falling away into the depths of time. The air was sweet. Laughter played on the water, a child's laugh. He knew this would be the last time he heard the sound, and he smiled a sad smile.

They're coming.

He didn't know how he knew, but he knew. He would not have long. He stepped into the pool, stepped where he had stepped before. Peace whispered to his spirit, but only for a moment.

An echo of a step sounded in the shadowed woods. Holthund looked up, his breath fast in his chest. He drew Brukthorn, his fingers tight on the haft.

I don't want to do this again Da.

The voice echoed far away in his mind, his own and yet not his own. Knots of shadow moved in the trees.

There.

There across the pool, there in that broken spot in the rocks where Holdi saw his bogey. That was where he had walked, on his last night long ago. And so that was where he would walk again.

He waded deeper into the dark cold water and something in the rocks ahead caught his eye. There on the far shore he saw sign under the moonlight, sign he already knew. Even in the dim silver-grey, Holthund knew this tread, knew it too well already. The stride was long, the foot broad. And yet it seemed still strange to him, as if it should be not quite so straight, not quite so sure. But here it was. Across the water came the crack of breaking deadfall.

They're here.

They had been waiting.

Holthund rose and looked into the night behind. Slowly the story made itself whole… Acramm had spoken false. Eomud had to know! No, not Eomud. The night was too far gone now, and Eomud too far away.

The wall, then. The wall was nearer, and it was home that needed most to know. Cloud covered over the moon. Shrieks of ghaestling echoed strange in the night. Holthund broke onto the twisting deer trail and he ran. He ran with feet not his own, he ran with breath strangely short, but he ran. Distant and unearthly came the great howl of Hauwyr, almost mournful under the shrouded stars.

Behind him came the empty echo of running feet. Holthund hoped, he strove, but as he ran he knew that the way was too great, that it was not enough. He would never reach the wall. He howled his rage, he screamed his thwarted will into the empty night.

"Hleolea! Ghaestling!"

Dark laughter floated around him. He stumbled and rose and ran again. He cursed his stolen horn, and he shouted again for all he was worth. The sound of a thrown spear rattled through the trees. It was almost done. He would die on a summer night.

Yes, that was as it happened.

Still he ran. The ground rose steep before him and he broke through the trees. Above were only rocks and clear sky, only the stars over the great shadow of Heahfeldt high above. He was so close. He was so far. He howled his warning, and the wind carried away his cry.

He leapt to the rocks. He clambered up silver-lit boulders and scree, he pulled himself up by scraggly brush. He hurt and he knew not why. Still he climbed. Behind came the echo of running feet.

Holthund turned. From the night behind came the echoing scrape of iron on rock, and cold laughter echoed with it. Shadows drew near, a roaring mass of shadow all about. He lashed out with Brukthorn and with a howl a shadow fell away. Another took its place. Cold hands locked on Holthund's throat. He kicked, he slashed and screamed his wrath into their face.

For a moment he was free. He turned, he reached to climb away. Distant came the sound of spears on stone. Another spear clattered, another laugh echoed. Something crashed hard against his legs and he felt his bones splinter inside his skin. He felt himself begin to fall, he reached to hold fast to the stone…

…Holdric touched wool.

The echo in his mind fell away.

All was quiet. He was alone.

The air was cold and calm. High above, the Seolfrenblos sparkled bright against the night. He looked down from the sky, the skin of his hand pale in the moonlight, the mouldered wool dark beneath his fingers. Shaking, he drew the cloth aside. Beneath was the worn white of wind-weathered bone.

Holdric moved dumbly, only half in his mind. He pulled aside the stones, he brushed away the piled cruft of many winters. More bones he found, scraps of wool and broken leather…

He stopped.

There, pressed between weathered bones and rotted cloth lay a tarnished brooch. Trembling, Holdric reached out. He pulled the blackened silver free and held it in his hand, he traced the workings upon it with his thumb. A hound was wrought there. A hound and stars, a heron and turning gyre. Holdric fell back upon the stones. He laid his hand on the mouldered bone.

"It's you."

He looked to sky, his eyes wet.

"Da…"

He clenched hard his jaw, his eyes he lost in the stars. He knotted tight his mind, willing it to hold fast. Then he let his eyes fall to where earth met sky. There against the rise of earth above he saw two poles, each stark in the moonlight. The bounds of Heahfeldt.

You were almost there.

Holdric squeezed the brooch tight, the metal biting hard into his hand.

You almost made it.

He pinned the brooch upon his cloak, near to his own.

A ghaestling shriek echoed across the valley below. Holdric looked down, down into the night behind. The sound came again… they would not be long.

He began again to climb. Up he worked, picking his way over stone and scree. The slope rose steep and steeper still, and then at last grew gentle and he clambered up onto open ground.

The high grass of late summer stretched up before him in the moonlight, shot through with stands of gorse and broom. The bounding poles loomed just above, an empty gate on an empty hill. Between them a long-faded path was worn through the waving grass.

Holdric came near and placed a hand on the carved timber. The wood felt strange beneath his fingers. He remembered looking up at these carved poles in awe as they towered high into the sky… now they were but spear-height. He traced the patterns: a ram for the high meadows, trails of sweet meadowyrt twining about his legs, and above all a gyring falcon for the northern guide, his feathers wreathed in a winding breeze.

Holdric passed between the poles. Voices whispered at the edge of his hearing—or the shadows of voices. The long-overgrown road wound up before him, up through the rising field. He stretched his hands out, fingertips lost in the high swaying grass. Chill settled deeper on his shoulders.

Almost there. Almost done.

He crested the last rise. Before him slumped the overgrown wreck of the old burgh wall, and not far before it a single lonesome tree. There he saw without seeing the ghaestling host that had swarmed the wall, saw the choking dead upon the ground. He heard without hearing the echoes of long-ago screams, felt without feeling the burning grass. Chill settled into dread.

Grudge hung cold in the air, grim and thick with spite. For but a moment Holdric knew the tree as it once was, sweet and green and full of white flowers. But now he saw a tree dead and broken in the moonlight, branches cracked and long overgrown with thorns. A band of ravens huddled there, watching him as a cloud of moving shadow.

Holdric drew near. One raven broke from the others, it flew scolding from the tree to the burgh wall ahead. There it raised up on the broken wall, watching him in mocking silence, daring him to come further.

Holdric returned its stare as he came near, his eyes hard as he came close… it seemed almost that something broke in a place he could not see. The raven flew croaking and alone into the night.

Holdric came to the wall. The gate had long ago fallen in, the passing-way was choked with brambles. But the mounded earth of the burgh wall was worn and overgrown, and the timber palings burned and broken. It was an easy climb. He trudged up the steep earth and passed between two broken timbers, and soon he looked out over the infold beyond. Memory held him fast.

Meadow grass rippled in moonlit breeze, tall and swaying in the dying summer. Broom and gorse had grown up thick through the grass, but still the sweet scent of mead-blossom floated over the field. His breath caught in his throat…

He was home.

The high fields rose up before in a gentle slope, then gave way to open sky. Beyond that, far almost past seeing, there he could just see the white line of the Himlgartn. Far-away snow gleamed in the moonlight. Above the starfroth rose clear and deep over the silvered fields… but the stars of Slaugnwint were high, the Waelstan just behind.

At the far end of the field the beacon mound rose dark against the northern stars. Beneath it lay black broken halls, and ruined things too dark to see. For but a breath, Holdric remembered the field in daylight. He saw young trees and halls of high fresh timber, he smelled fruit and fresh grass and the thick greasy wool of grazing sheep. The sun was warm, laughter spilled over the green… then the memory passed, and all was shadow and ruin.

He stumbled down the burgh wall and pushed through the high grass. Thistles pulled at his cloak as he walked, sharp thorns caught at his legs. Fading summer grass waved in smoke he could not see, the night filled with screams he could not hear. Still he walked, still he stumbled, alone beneath the stars.

The fold wall rose before him, a low rise of earth overgrown with a thicket of mouldered berry and small sharp thorn. He pushed up and through the bramble, he pushed aside a wattle fence now burned and broken. Thorns scratched his hands.

He looked at the thin streak of blood on his skin, black in the moonlight.

"Hush Holdi," she had begged.

He looked back the way they once had fled, back the way he had come, back over the infolds. The waning moon shone high in the southern sky, and the stars of Hernweart rose over the black shadow of Greatwatch. He stared long at the deep shadow of the great mountain, the shape strange now from where he stood.

Hello, Ruhnleod.

Holdric turned again to his work. He felt the haft of Brukthorn upon his waist and looked out on the wide grass that stretched out before him. He remembered a boy playing on the highfolds, a wooden knife at his side and a field of sleeping sheep before him. He remembered a boy playing at being… at being here.

Here, on this mounded earth beneath his feet where all had happened. Here had fallen the people of Heahfeldt, here had been the battle that shaped his life and the lives of all his kin ever since. The earth and the stones beneath his feet… they looked the same as those he'd known all his days.

It was just a wall.

It was just a wall, and now the games were done. He climbed from the stones and stepped down onto what had once been the open green. A bone crunched beneath his foot, one of many. Scattered bone shone white under the moon. Iron black with fire and rust mouldered under the open sky.

Graves had been dug here, and graves had been torn open. Stakes had long ago been set into the ground, stained with fire and worse. Binding leathers hung from them still, burned and broken and old. Rags swayed softly in the breeze.

Holdric willed himself not to look closely upon what was still there. He forced his eyes to the beacon and he walked on. Here had been gardens, here had been bees and sweet-smelling herbs and laughter. Here had been birdsong.

A lone ruddock sang in the far dark.

A great hulk of shadow rose before him, broken timbers reaching from the earth like an old man's hand. A memory of the old folkhall danced at the edge of Holdric's memory. He reached out and laid his hand to the weather-soaked char.

The timbers had once been fresh, bright and sweet-smelling. And carvings, the sharp and winding forms of… what had they been? Birds? He thought he remembered sweet-carved wrens, flitting high in carved trees. The floor beams had been new and rough, the hearthstones yet unblackened.

Now all was wreck and ruin.

He let fall his hand. Smaller hulks he passed, shambles once homes now burned and overgrown. More memories came as he walked on, but he pushed them away. Only one thing was left to do.

He looked further up, up to where he knew it would be. Past the sky-stones, fire-blackened and overgrown, past the orchard… there rose the shadow of the beacon mound, the grass waving silver beneath the sky.

It was not the great mountain of his memory, not the fearsome high hill he had climbed when none would see. It was only a mound of grassy earth, scarce two men high and crowned with a jumble of bramble-covered stones. Just a simple mound beneath the starry sky. The stars of Hauwyr shone above, and it seemed he could almost hear the great hound upon the wind. He smiled at that.

Below the beacon was a tangled shadow of an orchard grown wild. The sweet-sour scent of fallen fruit filled his nose as he came near.

I missed appling day…

"Remember me, sweet bird." He smiled as he passed through the trees.

The beacon pyre had burned away with the rest of the old village, but the stone bier still stood. The rocks were black and cracked, the stones overgrown with bramble.

He looked once more to far Greatwatch—the sky was still clear. Above, the stars of the Waelstan were driving already Slaugnwint from the heights. Thrush song floated on the air.

He set to work. A fire high enough to be seen from Greatwatch would take time in the building. He looked around, searching for fuel. A paling-wall stood along one side of Heahfeldt's rise, not far from the beacon mound. Much of it had burned, much had rotted away, but still there was timber enough to raise a high fire. That would do.

He climbed down the mound again, stumbling as he made for the wall. The palings were half again the height of a man, the wood thick and well-set in the ground. He moved down the wall, heaving and pushing against the timbers until he found one loose in its footing. It was heavy, but it and a few of its brothers would be fuel enough for a long high fire. He clambered around the paling, pushing it to and fro with all his weight until it toppled to earth.

He bent to one end, he tried to raise it from the earth but could not. The weight was too much. Hasty he pulled off his fyrd belt, and hasty he pulled Brukthorn free. He stowed the sheathed blade in his quiver, then drew the strap of the belt around the thick paling and made it fast. With all his weight he heaved on the beam, and grudging it moved.

Another heave…

Another…

The great timber moved slowly, but it moved. Holdric heaved and sweat, step by painful step hauling the timber up the mound. He dug his heels in hard, heaving at each step. Then something caught. The timber bit deep into a divot in the earth and would move no more. With a fierce snarl, Holdric gave the belt a savage jerk. The buckle gave way, the strap unfurled, and the timber rolled to the bottom of the mound. With a cry of rage and long-buried frustration, Holdric hurled the useless strap after the fallen log.

He cursed. He trudged again down the hill. Heaving and shoving, pushing and cursing, he finally managed to work the thing to the top of the mound.

One.

He sank to his knees, breathing hard, and he looked again to the sky. Slaugnwint still held the heights, but only just. Already the Waelstan threatened to take his place. If Holdric could move no faster, it would be dawn before he could get a second timber to the pyre.

He cursed. Greylight was coming. What else could he use? Would he find smaller timbers in the broken homes? No, what hadn't burned was surely half rotted by now, and was farther even than the paling-wall.

He looked again on the apple orchard below. It was largely live wood, and small, but if he could get enough of it burning, it would be fire enough. And with that fire, smoke. Smoke that Greatwatch would see even as daylight came. He drew forth Brukthorn and hurried down the mound.

The trees here were young, almost all wild coppice grown up since the fire. Most of the trunks were no thicker than his arm. He took the first large sapling in hand and heaved it over with his weight while he hacked at its trunk like a mad beaver. It didn't take long before he'd chipped his way through and naked wood gleamed in the moonlight. He hauled the tree up the mound and returned for more.

A second tree. A third. He worked fast. A fourth. His fingers blistered, and the blisters opened. He angrily tore another shred from his shirt and wrapped his hands. More. He gathered deadwood too, the largest pieces he could carry. The pyre grew high upon the beacon stones, and the stars above began to fade into the deep blue-black. Greylight was coming. Faint on the air below he heard the ghaestling horns, nearer now.

He looked up at the pyre he had made.

It was not so large as he wished, but there was no more time. It had to be now. Better a fire in the night than trust to far-away smoke in the day. He slashed at the dry summer grass, piling it deep beneath the branches. More he added, enough to be sure even the wettest trees would catch. He was ready.

He climbed onto the bier. High above, bright Aeforliht began to fade into the grey. Holdric pulled forth his charbox, he knelt and took sharp flint and tinder in hand, he readied his striking-iron… and all was gone.

Iron clattered on stone, lost somewhere in the night. He stared dumbly for a moment at the place his charbox had been. Cold pain seeped up his arm. A cold mocking laugh hung on the air. He looked up.

A hooded shadow stood over him in the gloom.

A rush of air, a crash of bone and wood, and Holdric went tumbling off the bier. He thrust out his arms to catch himself. His right hand crumpled against the earth and he screamed from the pain of it.

He struggled to his knees, he tucked his broken hand under his good arm as he backed away.

"Where are you going, Holdi?"

The mocking voice hung in the greying night. Footsteps came around the bier. Holdric reached for Brukthorn, scrambling to grab hold of the haft with fingers numb and bloody. The shadow lashed out, a spear shaft cracked against his head and drove him back into the dirt. His ears rang and he tasted blood. He shook his head, he tried to clear it, but it did no good.

The shadow loomed above him, dark and gloating. Holdric scrambled back, striving to get space to think, space to move. A cold fire spread through his shoulder as iron pricked his flesh. Holdric cursed and spat. Another stab ground against his hip, and Holdric felt iron scrape bone. He choked in pain, a sound more grunt than cry. He kicked out with a rage—his boot scuffed against the man's shin, and met only laughter.

He tried to rise, he struggled to get his feet beneath him, but another blow across his head brought him low. With a moan Holdric crumpled. His feet ground uselessly against the earth. He felt a solid kick and tumbled onto his back. His head lolled, he held his crippled hand above him, trying vainly to ward off the next blow he knew was coming.

A foot pinned his broken hand in the dirt. He howled.

The shadow ground a heavy foot into the hurt, and Holdric shrieked. His feet worked in the dirt, but he could rise no more. He felt the spear point rest against his chest. It pushed against his breastbone, iron taunting flesh. In the first dim grey of the coming sun, the man called Brocca pulled back his hood. His turned his pocked, scarred face to Holdric…. and he smiled.

It was done.

 Holdric looked out on the burned ruin that was Heahfeldt, the ruin that soon would be Heortlea. All that he had ever loved turned to bones and ash, lost for all time.

His heart broke.

Slowly Brocca pushed the spear against his breastbone. The point was dull and cold. Holdric felt his flesh open, his ribs begin to give way. He kicked once more, kicked without strength. Brocca blocked the blow and kicked him hard. Holdric choked. He howled, tears of loss and rage and long sorrow finally finding voice. Brocca raised his spear… and then he too was gone.

The sound of fighting whispered cold through the greylight. Grunts and curses came from across the bier, the sound of blows and strangled breath. Holdric rose, with both hands he scrambled to find his dropped blade. And he heard the cry of death.

Ollda…

No.

Holdric rounded the beacon stones, and there in the dim grey light he saw his Ollda's blooded face, eyes lolling crazily as he worked his mouth, blinking into the open sky. Brocca stood over him, a wicked iron knife in his hand and a spray of blood across his arm.

Brocca staggered on his feet, he turned from Kenndric, he raised his blade—

And Holdric drove Brukthorn into his face.

Brocca staggered back, voiceless, his hand went to his blooded head, his blade fell from his fingers. Holdric slashed again and again, cutting at his arms, striking at his head, driving him back with each biting blow.

Brocca stumbled, he fell back onto the dirt. With a roar, Holdric leapt upon him, blade first. He drove Brukthorn deep through rib, heart, back, and down into the earth beneath. Brocca began to die.

Holdric's hands were numb. He fell back on his haunches and Brukthorn slid from his broken fingers. It was done…

No, not yet done.

He dragged himself to his feet. He stood over Brocca, and with his good hand wrenched Brukthorn free. He went to the bier. There he struck Brukthorn into the earth, and finding flint and char again he struck sparks against the battered blade. The sparks caught, the ember took hold. He took all in a nest of grass and he blew, willing it to life with the last of his strength.

Spark became flame, and flame he set in the cradled kindling. He snatched up Brukthorn and backed away. The fire rose slow at first, then it caught and roared fierce and hot, driving him back. He staggered down to the grass, leaving the mounded stones to the fierce flame.

Now all was done.

From far below he heard the shriek of ghaestling. They had seen his fire, and they would not be long in coming. He staggered across the mound to where Kenndric lay crumpled in the grass. They could die together, then. Holdric dropped to the earth beside his Ollda.

Kenndric turned his head. His eyes were weak, but still they had followed Holdric as he drew near. The elder man stretched out a bloody hand to the younger. Holdric took his hand and they sat together. Ollda had never seemed so frail, so very old. His eyes fell on Holdric's cloak, and he reached out to Holthund's brooch upon it.

"You…" his voice came in a croak. He struggled to make the words. "You found him?"

Holdric nodded.

Ghaestling horns sounded again, not far off.

The old ranger was fading quickly. He gathered his spirit, he struggled to rise. He failed, his arms had not the strength to push himself from the earth. Still he shoved against Holdric's shoulder, still he tried to make words, even though his voice would not answer.

"Go…" he mouthed.

Holdric only shook his head. He let fall one word—

"Can't."

Kenndric's eyes shut hard, he shook his head. The old man struggled to raise himself again, fought to will his body to rise and drag

Holdric from this place. But his body would no longer answer. The old man's face screwed up in voiceless pain.

Holdric squeezed his hand tighter, but he did not look. He could not bear to meet those eyes again. He looked instead to the rolling grass of Heahfeldt, and to the morning sky beyond. A plume of smoke rose into the sky, black and thin from far Greatwatch. Old Aesculf had seen their fire. The word had been given, and the word had been passed on.

Holdric let his head fall back against the earth and closed his eyes in the first real rest he'd known in years. Perhaps the first real rest he'd ever known.

He raised his head and squeezed Kenndric's hand, he pointed to the far beacon.

"We did it Ollda."

The old man looked on the far fire and a light crossed his face. He smiled, for a moment ageless. Then he looked at Holdric, one last time.

He closed his eyes.

And he died.

Holdric fell against him, too beaten even for tears.

Then he saw only night.

In Dream

Holdric did not know how long he slept. From far off in the haze came the sound of voices… voices he knew. He felt a hound's nose in his face, eager sniffs and whines.

"Holdric!"

Was that Aschbroc? Holdric blearily opened his eyes. Faces swam in his sight, faces not quite strange. He felt hands feel him for hurts, his pain dim and far away. Words swam in the light above.

"… get you home, cousin… done."

"… know that!"

"… brook gets us to…"

"… by way of… back. Can he…?"

"… blood, but….

"…hurry…"

Through slitted eyes Holdric saw the first gold rays of sun, the first clear blue of day. Then he slept long, and deep.

CHAPTER TWENTY-THREE
Turn of Season

Holdric opened his eyes. It was day. High above stretched warm timbers, smoke-stained beams bearing up a roof of boards. Where was the sky? And where was he?

He remembered lying on a broad, wet stone, his face against the cool rock. He remembered water sparkling in the sun. Water and stone… but no blood. That didn't seem right somehow. That was not how the verse had gone.

He remembered being borne up on the water, swaying and heaving in splash-dappled sunlight. He remembered cold water, and the low speech of men. He remembered the sweet-sour smell of healing herbs, and smoke in a small room. He remembered nothing else.

Now he was in the fyrdhall, and in old Hauccael's bed. He started to rise, but his hand would not hold his weight. He groaned and raised his arm. It was swathed in linen from knuckles to elbow, and thin boards of ash splinted his bones. He looked on his hand, fingertips pink and whole peeking out through the swaddling.

"He's up! He's up!"

Maethbry's voice rang in his ears, and he turned to look just as she ran out the door. It came to him that he lived still—that seemed strange. Then the memories came.

Ollda… And Eahstann.

He looked again to the high roof and closed his eyes. A whine came from the floor below. Wyrling! The great hound of the Torr nuzzled at his hand, and Holdric scooted to make room. Wyrling leapt up, then came close and nuzzled his good hand.

Holdric hauled himself up on an elbow and grimaced as he tried to move. As he sat up, something tumbled onto his lap. Small gifts spilled about his blankets, whether left in hopes of healing or as grave-gifts, he wasn't sure. Those who left them might not have known themselves.

Brukthorn lay near his side, bound again in its pelt of wolf. That he pulled close. There was also a small carved stag of antler, Aschbroc's gaming piece… yes, Holdric remembered seeing Aschbroc's face above him. Aschbroc lived, then. That was good.

Wyrling whined, and Holdric scratched his head as he looked over the rest. A tattered hound stitched from wool, that from Maethbry's hands no doubt. Two pairs of thick-knotted socks, Widow Blóssig's work by the look of them. Holdric shook his head.

There were other things, but what most caught his eye was a small bowl on a low table near the bed. Hard cheese and sausage were there, and bread also. He snatched a sausage first, and half he swallowed before he could think. Then he gave a big piece to Wyrling and reached for another.

He'd hardly gotten the first bite down when the door opened again and all his family poured inside. His mother and sister, Aunt Claefry and little Segli. With them was Uncle Eikhram, leaning on Aschbroc, and Aschbroc's wife Rinna also.

Uncle Eikhram hobbled now, his hair shorn on one side around the stitch of an angry scar. A long fyrdknife hung upon his waist, and if he hobbled, still it seemed he walked the taller.

Holdric's mother saw his questioning look.

"There was a fight," she said simply.

"HOLDIC!" Segli shouted. She climbed into Holdric's bed and clung to him. He winced as the girl knocked against his aching ribs, but he laid a hand upon her back as she held tight. Wyrling sniffed at her feet, and she laughed and squirmed away.

Holdric looked to Aschbroc. "Who lives?" he asked, his voice a croak.

"Of us—You, me, Wymud…" Aschbroc's voice turned to question, "Eahstann?"

Holdric shook his head.

Maethbry cried out, leaning against her mother. Aschbroc's face lowered, grave. Then he found again his words. "Of the folksteads, most. Eorl Ufthugh rallied the fyrd. Two fights in one day."

Uncle Eikhram's face was glowing. "We stopped the first at the Mearcwater, like ants in the rain!" He shook his head. "It was glory."

Aschbroc's lips grew thin, but he smiled as he clapped his father upon the back.

Eikhram went on without stop, "It will be long years before they've strength enough to—"

"Holdic! Holdic!" cried Segli. She clasped the stitched little hound in her dirt-stained hands. "I help make this! Do you like it?"

Holdric took it from her with his good hand. "I like it," he managed. He held the thing before her face, mock growling as he held the thing to nip at her nose. "Wuff! Wuff! Grrrrrr."

Segli shrieked with laughter and fell back against the covers. Wyrling sniffed at her again, and she kicked in joy. A foot landed against Holdric's ribs, and he grunted in pain.

"That's enough, baby girl." Aunt Claefry leaned in and lifted Segli from the bed. She reached for the stuffed hound and Holdric handed it to her.

Rinna caught his eye. "Aschbroc said the second fire was yours. Is that…"

She fell silent as a shadow crossed the door. All looked up to see Wymud in the doorway. "Steadlaed Eomud comes on the morrow," he said. "I need the boy now." It was not a question. He cast a grim look to Aschbroc, then to Eikhram and the women. "You'll have him soon enough."

His mother would not move, but Wymud's face did not soften. "Tomorrow, Hleolea."

Aunt Claefry touched her shoulder, and grudging she gave way. She bent to smooth Holdric's hair and kiss his brow, and then she was gone. All of them were gone.

The hall was strange and silent without them. Wymud came inside, then fetched a bench and set it before the bed. Holdric rose in his sheets, watching as Wymud moved across the hall.

"Where's Hauccael?" he asked.

Wymud's answer came cold. "He's dead."

The dour man's footsteps sounded heavy on the wide floor as he fetched next a low small table. There he set a heavy crock of strong-smelling ale, and two large mugs beside. He settled onto the bench and stared silently at Holdric. Then he lifted the crock, filled a mug, and set it hard on the table between them. His stare left no room for question.

Holdric took the mug. Wymud watched in silence as Holdric took first a sip, then a deep quaff. He wiped his mouth and set the mug upon the table. Wymud held his eyes.

"Tell me what happened." There was no pity in Wymud's voice, no warmth. "All of it. Leave nothing out."

Holdric paused, searching for where to start, and then he began to speak. He told of their flight from the Bonemounds, and of the long night with Aemud. He told of scaling the high rocks, of the wrecked beacon, of the fight… and of Eahstann. He told Wymud all.

Wymud spoke not a word. He sat still as stone, listening to the tale in quiet. The day burned low and the shadows grew long. When at last Holdric finished, Wymud sat still for long moments. Then he reached across the table for Holdric's empty mug and he filled it again to the top.

Holdric drank.

"Tell me again," Wymud said. "All of it. Leave nothing out."

Again Holdric told the story. Again Wymud listened. Night came deep and dark before the second telling was through. Wymud lit a greaselamp and set it upon the table between them. Again he filled Holdric's cup.

In the low orange light, Wymud began his questions. Why did Holdric tarry before seeking the Torr? Why did he leave his kinsman Byrcstod to his fate? Every choice Wymud questioned. Holdric tried to find answers, but drink and deep weariness tangled his words.

Still the questions came. Every shadow, every crack of creeping doubt in Holdric's spirit, Wymud pried open. At last they sat in silence. Wymud nodded to himself and rose from his bench. He moved to the hearth and poured a mug of honeyed evening tea.

He set the drink before Holdric. "I will see you on the morrow. Hegwyn will look in on you before."

His eyes fell to Holdric's folded cloak at his bedside and to the two brooches upon it. He raised his eyes to Holdric in question. Holdric nodded his leave, and Wymud bent to take Holthund's brooch. Without word he looked it over, then he placed it in his pouch.

"Tomorrow, Holdric son of Holthund."

He turned to go. As Wymud neared the door, Holdric called to him, "Who was Brocca?"

Wymud looked back only a moment. "Acramm's boy. Rotting cast-off never was right."

And then he was gone.

Holdric sat in long silence. He stared into the flickering grease-light. It was too much. He cupped his good hand about the flame and blew it out. A last swig of the tea and he lay back against the bed, staring into the darkness of the hall.

His head swam from the ale. He lay in silence, dwelling on the shadows above. He could just see stars through the high smoke holes. The stars of Aeringif would be high, Ruhnliht would be bright. He closed his eyes and he tried to think on nothing. Wyrling nestled under his hand. Holdric was almost asleep when he heard the door creak upon its hinges.

He elbowed up in the bed. Frithi stood there at the threshold, alone in the moonlight. She clung to the doorway and peered into the hall.

"Holdric?"

They stared at each other a long moment, each too frightened to speak. She trembled at the door, afraid to meet his eyes… and then she did. He could never say who broke first, but she ran for him. He pulled her close, and he grunted with broken pain. He didn't care.

Together they lay long that night, speaking quiet of things both hard and gentle. He felt her whispers upon his cheek, and each said all that need be said. Each did all that need be done.

Hegwyn came and went, and with smothered laughs Frithi hid, only to come again. High above the wooden hall, the stars rose and fell and Holdric did not care. It was near greylight when at last she left him, creeping back to home and kin. He smelled her still upon his sheets.

And he found the peace of sleep.

❧

The morning was crisp and chill, the trees bright with red and gold. Holdric took another step up the path. His steps were still not sure, but he matched his cousin's pace.

Today the Eorl was come. The fyrdhall had for this day been opened to all, and it was there that the Eorl made his court. His men stood in rows outside the doors, their mended cloaks woad-blue, their nicked spears keen and bright.

Above the wide doors stretched the twining beasts of earth and sky, the shapes of Hound and Lady and mighty Stag. Below them, Holdric's eyes fell again upon the graven brambles of the door. He knew those thorns now, as he knew those who had passed before him through the night. Holdric's fingers traced the graven trees, and dark memories held him fast.

He felt Aschbroc's hand upon his shoulder. "It will be well, kinsman."

Holdric swallowed. "Yah."

He forced his eyes from the carvings, took a breath, and passed over the threshold. Today the hall was filled with benches and spread blankets upon the floor. All the families of Heortlea sat within, and many others beside. The fyrdmen of Stonehall and Ettenmede and Dorbruk stood against the walls. The hall was packed tight, the air was hot despite the fall chill. It had never seemed so small.

But it was the head table that claimed Holdric's eyes. There sat Eorl Ufthugh Beartorn, Eorl of all the folksteads. He looked to have earned his name. He was a big man, thick and black haired, his scalp crossed over with old scars. He had not been idle in the fight. Fresh scars cut now across the old, still red and angry. He had claimed Thane Haestearn's seat.

437

Beside the Eorl sat the Thane, and by him his son Hwaetearn's seat, now cold and empty. Next was Wymud, Kenndric's stag brooch upon his breast. Then Eomud, master of the far Hyssestead. The big man scowled to see Holdric came within. Last of all sat Master Uhlseid. The old bard stood, and all within stilled.

Master Uhlseid gave the verses of meeting, and then the great Eorl rose and spoke.

By ring and word of King Eacandeor, I, Ufthugh Eorl of Markstone, do open the time of judging. All who have words for the King, bring them now!

None moved. The Eorl looked to Holdric. Holdric flexed his hands, his breath tight in his chest. He'd been told to wait until…

"Holdric, son of Holthund!" The Eorl's voice was grim and strong. It filled every corner of the timbered halls. "Come."

Holdric stepped forward. Every face followed him as he made his way between the benches to the head of the hall. He forced his eyes straight ahead, he forced himself not to meet their stares.

He knew these families. Too many were missing from the benches, too many of the spread blankets had open places. And of those here, many bore marks of the battle. Heortlea had been badly bled.

As he neared the high table Holdric passed the bench where his own family sat. Uncle Eikhram looked grim, and with no little fear behind his eyes. His mother and sister watched his every step, hope and dread mixed on their faces. Segli waved. Holdric smiled weakly, but did not break his stride.

He stopped before the high table, and the Eorl looked on him. The big man's brow furrowed, only just, as he studied Holdric's face.

His eyes were hard as he spoke, "What has come of my friend Kenndric Farstride, Holdric son of Holthund?"

Holdric looked first to the timbers of the floor, trying to find his words. Then he set his jaw and looked strong into the stern grey eyes of the Eorl.

"Kenndric my Ealdfader was slain. Slain as he defended these folksteads, slain as he defended my life."

"Slain by who?"

"Slain by a man called Brocca, son of Acramm. A man who marked himself as the ghaestling do, and who fought alongside them."

A murmur sounded behind him. The Eorl silenced all with a glance. Then he looked again upon Holdric.

"And what has come of this man?"

Holdric spoke clear. "He also is slain, Eorl. Slain by hand of Kenndric my Ealdfader—" Holdric licked his lips, steeling his heart— "and by mine." Holdric's words came tight, and his words came hard.

The Eorl did not answer at first. His head barely moved, his eyes hard upon Holdric. Finally he spoke. "I cannot take your word, Holdric, would that I could."

Holdric had no answer. He knew the next words the Eorl would speak, and speak them the big man did. "You are son of Holthund Oathbreaker, are you not?"

Holdric was silent.

The Eorl leaned forward. "Answer me."

Holdric held the man's eyes. "I am."

The Eorl looked about the table. "Can any vouch this man's oath?"

Wymud rose in his place, his face grim. "I would speak."

The Eorl looked to Wymud and nodded leave. Wymud looked to those in the hall.

"I have never held Holdric son of Holthund as friend, that I do not hide. But I have never known him to speak untruth." He turned to meet Holdric's gaze. "Until now."

Holdric froze in place. "Seco—" he began, then caught himself. Wymud now wore Ollda's title. "Huntslaed?"

Wymud did not move his gaze. He took a ranger's brooch from his pouch and he raised it high so all could see. No longer tarnished, the silver metal gleamed like a bright star as he held it high. Hound and star, heron and gyre glimmered in the light.

Wymud lowered the brooch and slid it across the table to Holdric with a grunt. "Take it," he demanded.

Holdric took the brooch in hand. Wymud leaned upon the table and caught his eyes.

"You found that below the bounds of Heahfeldt?"

"I do not deny it."

"And you found it amongst the bones of a man?"

Holdric swallowed, his throat tight. "I did."

Wymud leaned closer upon the table. "I know this thing, Holdric. And I knew the man who bore it. And so I know those bones."

Holdric held his gaze. The words came hard and tight. "The bones were Holthund, my father."

Neither did Wymud look away. "They were."

Wymud looked to the Eorl, then rose from the table. He raised his voice so it carried to the corners of the hall.

"I know not what others saw"—he looked to Eomud—"but I looked upon Holthund's bones, my Eorl. I have seen more bones than I would count. His was the grave of one slain in secret, and one buried in secret."

The Eorl looked to the brooch in Holdric's hand, quiet as he pondered. Wymud looked again to Eomud. Then he spoke again, loud.

"I believe and give Oath that Holthund son of Hraed did not flee his watch. I believe that he was slain as he sought his people. I give Oath as Huntslaed that I judge Holthund to have fought for Heahfeldt. I give Oath that I judge he was overcome before ever the first torch was laid."

The Eorl's eyes looked again upon the brooch in Holdric's hand, then they met Holdric's eyes. He pursed his lips, thinking. Then he rose. He looked at the gathered people of Heortlea.

"Do any challenge these words?" He looked about the room. He looked to Eomud. "Speak now, or hold forever your words behind your teeth!"

Holdric turned and watched their faces.

Eomud looked to the floor, his face grim. He then looked up, locked eyes with the Eorl, and waved his hand.

The Eorl turned to Holdric. "Then you are not Holdric, son of Holthund Oathbreaker. You are Holdric, son of Holthund, first to fight. Do you deny this?"

Holdric straightened. "I do not."

The Eorl was quiet. Wymud leaned close and spoke into in his ear. The Eorl's eyes narrowed. "Tell all what happened upon the mound of Heahfeldt, Holdric son of Holthund."

"I came upon Heahfeldt from—"

"Louder!" shouted the Eorl. "To them!"

And so Holdric told again his story, told it loud for all to hear. When at last he finished, the hall was quiet. The Eorl nodded and he laid his hands upon the table. Then he rose and stood before the people.

"All hear me…" His voice filled the hall, strong and loud. "Hear my words, folk of Heortlea, folk of Stonehall, folk of Ettenmede, and all others. Listen to the word-giving of Eorl Ufthugh Beartorn, honor-bound to King Eacandeor!

"In Heortsfell upon the trees, a cairn is to be raised to Hunts-laed Kenndric Farstride, son of Secenwulf. To Hwaetearn son of Haestearn, to Eahstann son of Brythugh."

Thane Haestearn shifted in his seat, his jaw set.

The Eorl continued, "Holthund son of Hraed is known for all days as Holthund First-fought. His name holds great honor."

Quiet murmurs and soft whispers met his words. The Eorl raised his hands. He spoke again. "Holdric son of Holthund, I name now Holdric Wardkindler, Holdric Farstride. His name holds great honor."

"Holdic Scare-the-ram!" shouted Segli in the back. Aunt Claefry moved quickly to hush her.

The Eorl raised an eyebrow and grinned.

"Holdric Scare-the-ram," he chuckled.

He clasped Holdric upon the shoulder and raised his open hand to the people of Heortlea. "These are my words," he bellowed. "Do any challenge them?"

Only cheers sounded under the hall.

Others came and went before the Eorl, but Holdric could not hear the words. When at last the talk was done he stumbled outside. He shook his head, not quite able to make sense of what had passed. The moot seemed over almost before it had begun. Nothing had changed… everything had changed. How did such things happen?

Nearing steps jarred him from his thoughts.

"Greetings Scare-the-Ram," laughed Aschbroc as he drew near. Holdric looked to him and reached to clasp him in greeting. He winced as his cousin took hold of his linen-swathed arm.

"Second Aschbroc," he answered.

Uncle Eikhram came close also, and all the household with him. Holdric's mother clung crying to his shoulder, she held him and would not let go. But she too seemed to stand the taller now.

Many were those who came to speak with Holdric, many were the welcomes and clasping of arms. But all parted when Thane Haestearn came near. The voice of the Thane was still strong, he stood still tall. But his face was haunted now, and for the first time the cloak of age had settled about the man's shoulders.

He spread his arms and took Holdric in embrace. "I am proud of you, kinsman."

His words were firm, and if his voice quavered none would speak of it. Then he backed away and reached out an arm to an elder man alongside him. This man Holdric recognized. Brythugh, father to Eahstann.

"Wardkindler," the man said softly. "May we speak?"

Holdric looked to his family, then back to the grief-stricken father.

"Of course."

Come Morning

"I pulled a greatbow today."

Holdric looked out over the valley. The stones were chill against his back.

"Stronger even than yours, I think."

He turned and looked over the cairn.

"… maybe not stronger."

Wyrling whined and nuzzled at his hand. Holdric reached down and ran his fingers through the thick ruff of fur at the great hound's neck. He smiled weakly and moved to scratch the hound's ears. The bones worked stiff inside his hand.

His hand still pained him, but the pain faded with each passing moon. Maethbry knew well her art. Maethbry, and Frithi too.

He looked again to far Greatwatch, and to the long road that ran down from the orchards below. The slope was thick with the flush new green of spring, the aelfsthorn bright with white flowers. A cool breeze washed over his face. His eyes rested on the far mountain, and he remembered the cold stone of Greatwatch and all that lay beyond. Clear pools and endless forest. High snow-covered mountains and ancient pools. Sweet summer meadows… foul swamp and grasping black hedge. Broken tower and cold-piled stone. He winced at the memory.

He shook his head to clear his mind, and looked down to great Wyrling. The hound whined and turned to lick at his hand. Without thought, Holdric's hand traced the scar at the great hound's shoulder.

Wyrling had not left his side since he had woken in the fyrdhall. Even on the nights when the dreams took him, when all the air was so close and quiet that Holdric made his bed outside upon the grass. Sometimes he would wake to find Frithi curled up against him, wrapped tight in her blankets. Sometimes not. But always Wyrling would be near.

He leaned back and closed his eyes, seeking peace in woldgast. His ears he gave over to the sound the wind, his closed eyes to the warm glow of sun upon his face. Cool air and swaying trees washed over his spirit.

Faint footsteps sounded on the path below. Each step came slow, slow and careful. He barely opened his eyes, cocking his head to look back down the highfold. Through the shreds of morning mist he saw the shape of Frithi, hobbling up the highfold road on her walking stick. Her belly showed now, and she picked her way carefully around the stones of the field.

"You tracked me," he said as she drew near.

She leaned on the walking stick, wiggling a bit as she wrinkled her nose at him. She glowed with the morning sun.

"I knew where you'd be," she answered with a smile.

He smiled too.

She leaned on her walking stick and held his eyes.

"Come home with me, Huntsman?"

Holdric spared a last glance to the great height of Greatwatch, to air and waters and woods that went on past knowing. Then he stood and he turned again to his wedded love.

"Yah. Let's go home."

Upon the Highfolds

"*Wegscaewr, Way-shower, Always I see him…* find him, and know your way."

Holdric followed his Ollda's pointing finger into the sky. The grass was thick beneath them, the soft grunt of drowsing sheep not far away. Holdric leaned to see better, and Kenndric took his hand, pointing it into the sky.

"There, see the point of his left wing? There, that one."

"Yah!"

"That is Haldliht. The gyre wings ever around that star, circling as he looks on us below"

"And I find him by Hauwyr?"

"Now you can. But where will our Hound be come greylight?"

Holdric puzzled, looking on the stars.

"He follows the gyre," helped Kenndric. "A bit further around each night from dusk to dusk. And how long is it from now until the next dusk?

Holdric smiled and pointed. "There. He'll be down there, by those trees."

Kenndric smiled also. "So you have it. What if you're down low, and can't see him for the trees?"

"The Lady!"

"Yah, and where is she?

"Now, down there." Holdric pointed. "So come morning… up there, high, where Ruhnliht is now."

"Not quite, but close. More… there, off the corner of Hifosidh's wing."

Holdric turned his head, holding his hands up to the sky as he mimicked the turning of the stars.

"I see."

Wolfsong sounded in the night, far away. Holdric started up and peered out into the darkness.

Kenndric laid his hand on Holdric's shoulder. "No fear, Feorson. They are over the Timberwater. It is still early summer, and they have much nearer prey to find. They won't come close tonight."

Holdric lay back against his Ollda and together they stared into the sky, and together they shared many stories. Stories of the stars, and of things long ago, and of things perhaps yet to come. And at last Holdric slept.

The Stars of the Northern Wards

Not all folk know the stars so well as Holdric and his Ollda, but all can find the Hound, and with him the turning Gyre of the Northern Star. Winter or Summer, early night or late, some part of the northern wards will be in the sky, and by these all can find their way.

Wegscaewr, the Gyre. The high-circling falcon, watchful eye and faithful guide.

Hauwyr, the Hound. Most ancient guardian of the folk, especially of children.

Seolfrenblos, the noble-drops. Wherever the bloodied paws of wounded Hauwyr met earth, there small white flowers of seolfrenblos bloomed.

Lihtenstil, the Heron, the Lady. Healing-mother, spring of life, font of peace and gentle spirit.

The Stars of Summer, the arc of night

Holdric has learned to keep time and place by which stars hold the very highest part of the sky at each part of the night.

In the late summer and early fall, the night begins with the Swan and the Salmon in the heights. By Midwatch, the Stoat and the Rushes are rising up to take their place. The Heron moves across the heights through Deepwatch, and she is followed by Slaugnwint the Raven over Greywatch. Finally, dawn comes just as the Wellstone rises into the highest part of the sky.

The stars of Firstwatch:

Hifosidth, the She-Swan, mother of young love. She bears *Swosslight,* one of the three jewels of summer.

Aeringif, the Salmon, knower of music and ancient wisdom. He bears *Ruhnliht,* one of the three jewels of summer.

The stars of Midwatch:

Liefcradl, the Rushes, the ancient birthing-place of all mortal life.

Cuiccandt, the Stoat, fierce and clever, he braves the waters of the Starfroth.

The stars of Deepwatch:

Lihtenstil, the Heron, the Lady. Healing-mother, spring of life, font of peace and gentle spirit.

The stars of Greywatch:

Slaugnwint, the Raven, bringer of fall's chill and the death of summer's green.

Waeldeop, the Wellstone, the well of souls yet to come into the world.

Of the Three Jewels of Wolknfel, and the naming of the stars.

The summer night begins with the three bright stars of the summer triangle.

Seahnliht of *Rammlouf,* the he-swan. Jewel of a father's protection, of explorers, of deep-seeing.

Swossliht of *Hifosidth,* the she-swan. Jewel of love, especially maiden-love.

Ruhnliht of *Aeringif,* the Salmon. Jewel of bards and of fishermen, of poetry and song, of flowing water and secrets of the deep.

It is said in ancient times that Rammlouf and Hifosidth were living man and woman, and that they lived alone in high mountains far, far away. Rammlouf knew the high stones of the mountains as no other, and Hifosidth gave names to all the stars in the sky, and she loved them each as her own.

In time the lovers were given a son. Aeringif they named him, and they taught him all the names of the stars and all the stories of the mountains.

At the end of their days on earth Rammlouf and Hifosidth were taken up into the sky. For long after, Aeringif mourned them alone. Seeing his sadness, the two each fashioned bright jewels, so that they might show their love to their son below, and their hopes for his life yet to come.

When Aeringif grew to manhood he came down alone from the mountains. He became a hero, and a wanderer, and a learner and discoverer of many things.

Some say that when his own time came, Aeringif also was taken up into the sky. Others say that he took a wife on earth, and that he chose to stay with her here below, and with their own children, but that he took all that he had learned, and all that he had loved, and with it he fashioned his own jewel.

This he gave to the noble riverfish, who took it for him into the sea, and from the sea to the high stars above, so that some thanks and some part of his journeys would be known forever to those who gave him life.

Whatever the truth may be, to this day young parents will lie in the grass with their children on clear summer nights. They will point to the three bright stars, and they will tell their children the ancient stories of the family that once was, and of the love they shared, a love so bright that it crosses all the years of the earth and all the depths of the sky.

Along the Path

"Feeling better?"

Frithi smiled up into his eyes. Her fingers wrapped about his hand, holding the wet slop of oxfoot tight against his wrist.

"Much."

The angry red string of the nettle bite was fading, but that was not what held his mind. He reached for her, but she held fast to his hand and danced away. He moved again to catch her, but before he held her in his arms a voice carried over the green—the call of Frithi's sister.

Holdric groaned. Frithi smiled with mischief, and her eyes twinkled. "Find me, my huntsman." She winked and ran after her kin.

Holdric grunted and whispered a curse to himself. He looked down to the smear of bruised leaf over his wrist. The sting had faded, his skin now dry and pale where not long past it had been fiery red. The girl did know her art.

She knew too many of her arts.

The common folk of Heortlea spend no less time around the many green things of the earth than their rangers. Some are found in the paths and gardens close to home, others only in the wild places well past the tended fields.

Aelfsthorn, a holy tree, a sharp-thorned warding tree, it is planted by long tradition at the edges of settlements. Aelfsthorn branches are covered in white flowers in the spring, and with deep red berries in fall. These berries are made into a tart sweet jam with honey, and the leaves are used often in a tonic tea. It is one of the most beloved trees of the folk.

Bee-blossom, called also Meadblossom. A tall herb with blue star-shaped flowers. It is often planted at the edges of gardens and orchards to draw in bees, occasionally eaten, and sometimes used in winter tonics or in chest poultices.

Brewyrt, called also Mucwyrt, Goosefoot. A bitter herb with silver-bellied leaves. It is one of a number of herbs used to flavor teas and ales, especially morning brews of steeped roasted barley. Sometimes brewyrt is found wild, more usually it is grown along the edges of gardens. Expecting mothers avoid it.

Briarberry, a thorny briar, the canes bear white flowers, and dark sweet purplish berries in their second year. It is a common planting along south-facing hedgerows, and found not uncommonly in the wild.

Greensweet, a sharp, sweet herb with pointed green leaves, thick smell, and in the late summer stalks of small white flowers. It is used often in evening teas, in fresh cold springwater on hot summer days, and as a rub for strongly flavored meats.

Highberry, a low thick-leaved shrub. It bears small red berries with deep red flesh, very tart. Sometimes planted, it is often found wild in high rocky places.

Highbriar, one of a number of wild flowering thorns. In early summer it bears smallish white flowers, and then in fall small tart fruit, red-skinned with thin pinkish flesh and many bristly seeds.

The fruit is sometimes made into honeyed jams or added to autumn brews, more often it is dried and used in tonics against the long dreary cold of winter.

Knitbone, called also Mother's Friend. A deep-rooted plant with drooping blue flowers and thick-veined, deep green leaves. Planted often near homes and along the edges of gardens, the roots and leaves are used in healing poultices to speed the healing of open wounds.

Nettle, called also Quicksting, Aelfscloak. Nettle grows wild in thick clumps along the edges of fields and woods. The tall stalks are covered in sharp hairs that leave a burning sting, and the leaves and seeds are common in tonics and healing teas. The long stalks are gathered throughout the summer and spun into fiber for cordage, for coarse wildcloth, and more rarely for finer things by those with little linen.

Mayweed, a low sweet-smelling herb, used often in calming evening teas. Sometimes mixed with lungwyrt to ease breathing ailments, or with greensweet and willow bark for mild aches.

Meadowsheaf, called also First-green, Morning-bloom. Welcomed as one of the first eating-greens to grow in spring, meadowsheaf grows wild in any open grasses. Sometimes the young yellow flowers and tender green leaves are taken as a tonic or even added to pale drinking-brews. The puffy white seedheads are popular delights of children, sometimes to the chagrin of their elders.

Oxfoot, once called Aelfsfoot, a low broad-leaved plant found often along roads and paths. Used often as an eating-green, and as a medicine to draw out fevers from wounds or to ease angry skin.

Stauchwyrt, called also Staunchfeather, Fyrdman's Friend. Its leaves are fine feather-like fronds, its flowers are tightly clustered, small and white. The leaves are used often in healing poultices to slow the flow of blood.